Praise for Je...
Take a C...

"Witty repartee, memoral... powerful attraction skillfu... eager for the next in the series."—*Publishers Weekly*

"If this well-written debut novel by Dawson is any indication, she is an author to watch out for."—*RT Book Reviews*, 4 stars

"Jennifer Dawson launches a series with this marvelous tale. The characters own the pages with their vivid personalities, and the scorching love scenes border on erotica in their fiery detail. The small-town charm of the setting will also appeal to many readers."—*Affaire de Coeur*, 5 stars

"Jennifer Dawson is a wonderful author who knows how to pen a well-developed plot with depth . . . characters are mesmerizing, the dialogue is rich, the setting is inviting, and the sex is off-the-chain, which is a testament to her writing skills."—*BlackRaven's Reviews*, 5 stars and a Recommended Read

"I thoroughly enjoyed this book. It was refreshing and funny with characters I adored and some hot alpha males I wanted to know better . . . if you like Jill Shalvis, you'll truly enjoy *Take a Chance on Me*."—*Night Owl Reviews*, 4.5 stars

"*Take a Chance on Me* by Jennifer Dawson is a richly illustrated, character-driven novel that is definitely worth the risk."—*The Romance Reviews*, 4 stars

"The book is full of steamy romance and characters that you will remember long after."—*Examiner.com*, 5-star review

Books by Jennifer Dawson

The Winner Takes It All

Take a Chance on Me

Published by Kensington Publishing Corporation

The Winner
Takes It All

JENNIFER DAWSON

ZEBRA BOOKS
KENSINGTON PUBLISHING CORP.
http://www.kensingtonbooks.com

ZEBRA BOOKS are published by

Kensington Publishing Corp.
119 West 40th Street
New York, NY 10018

All Kensington titles, imprints and distributed lines are available at special quantity discounts for bulk purchases for sales promotion, premiums, fund-raising, educational or institutional use.

Special book excerpts or customized printings can also be created to fit specific needs. For details, write or phone the office of the Kensington Special Sales Manager. Attn.: Special Sales Department. Kensington Publishing Corp., 119 West 40th Street, New York, NY 10018. Phone: 1-800-221-2647.

Zebra and the Z logo Reg. U.S. Pat. & TM Off.

First Printing: December 2014
ISBN-13: 978-1-4201-3427-8
ISBN-10: 1-4201-3427-2

First Electronic Edition: December 2014
eISBN-13: 978-1-4201-3428-5
eISBN-10: 1-4201-3428-0

10 9 8 7 6 5 4 3 2 1

Printed in the United States of America

To Stacy,
who knows all my secrets
and
loves me anyway.

Chapter One

"We got the lead story." Nathaniel Riley's voice sounded over the car speaker.

The news didn't surprise Cecilia. Reporters don't shove a scoop like this to the back page, especially since it gave them another way to trot out the "senator recovering from a blackmail scandal" angle.

Cecilia stabbed the speaker's volume button until it lowered to a reasonable level. "Then everything is going according to plan."

"I trust you're happy." Her father's purring tone made it clear that he, at least, was one satisfied cat.

She clenched the leather steering wheel.

Happy. Now there's a word. When was the last time she'd been happy?

Stop. This was *not* the time to get philosophical. If she wanted a chance in hell at winning the congressional seat come election time, this was what needed to be done.

It was the smart move.

And she needed to win.

She'd get over the distaste curling into a knot in her stomach. She always did.

A green highway sign came into focus. Revival. Fifteen Miles. Where everything was sunshine, laughter, and genuine happiness.

Her skull throbbed.

"Cecilia?" Her father's voice fractured her thoughts. "What did you think of the article?"

She didn't read it. This morning, she'd thrown the unopened paper in the trash and deleted the Google alert links sitting in her e-mail. It was a fluff piece, carefully crafted by the senator's finest. The first of many that would lead to a final press conference where she'd announce her bid for congress. It was all part of a perfectly planned public relations strategy, designed by her.

A fine sheen of sweat spread over her back. She punched down the air-conditioner button in her understated Mercedes sedan and let the cool air wash over her face.

"Paul did an excellent job." After years avoiding the truth, the evasion was smooth as silk.

"Since you were unavailable, Miles and I had final approval," Nathaniel Riley said in his polished politician's voice.

"Of course." While her tone rang with a practiced strength, her stomach rolled. What was wrong with her? She needed to get it together. This was the price her dream demanded. She wasn't losing anything really important. Nothing that mattered.

Life in politics was all she'd ever wanted. When other little girls were pretending to be princesses in faraway lands, she played at being president in the Oval Office. It was the only dream she'd ever known.

She'd been content putting her career aside for her father's aspirations, but that ended when his scandal broke. She'd sat at her kitchen table, reading that dreadful headline, and saw her whole world crumbling under her feet.

The young woman who'd attempted to blackmail the

senator had eventually been caught and her schemes exposed, but not without damage. Cecilia had managed the fallout to perfection, minimizing the whole sordid affair, publicizing how he'd been a victim of greed. It worked, the senator was well on the road to political recovery, but she couldn't shake the worry.

This wasn't the first mess she'd helped him escape. At some point his bad decisions would have to come back and bite him. And where would that leave her?

It had been a slap in the face. A wake-up call delivered by a five-alarm fire truck.

"I'm proud of you, Cecilia," Nathaniel said, and she could practically see him sitting there in his office in Washington, scotch in hand, smug in his oversized leather chair.

Six months ago she would have lapped up his approval like a grateful puppy, but now she recognized the lie. He wasn't proud of her. This latest plan helped *him*. How, she wasn't sure and didn't care, but it had nothing to do with her.

It never did.

The truth only made her more determined.

A speed limit sign whipped past and she checked her speedometer to see the needle creeping past eighty-five. Easing her foot off the pedal, she started to say thank you for his sparse compliment but instead blurted, "Don't you have any reservations?"

"We talked about this," he said in a patient tone that grated on her last nerve. "This is your best shot."

Clammy sweat broke out on her forehead, forcing her to turn the air down to arctic levels. Wasn't thirty-three too young for a hot flash? She swallowed the taste of the bile clinging to the walls of her throat. "It doesn't bother you?"

"Why would it?"

Because I'm your daughter? The truth pained her, causing her voice to crack. That he hadn't even noticed she was upset made the cut that much deeper.

She shook her head. It didn't matter. Nothing mattered except getting out from under his thumb. She squared her shoulders. "Never mind. Is there anything else?"

A momentary silence fell over the car, filled with nothing but dead air. She prayed for a dropped connection (one would expect it in farmland Illinois), but the squeak of Nathaniel's desk chair quelled her hope.

"Are you almost there?"

Her jaw tightened and her ever-present headache beat at her temples. "I'm about fifteen minutes outside town."

"And your mother?" The question was clipped.

Part of Cecilia still wanted to believe that under all his bluster and power trips he genuinely cared for his wife of forty years, but she had no more delusions. "She's already there."

The green mile marker sign came into view. Revival. Twelve Miles.

She hadn't been to the small town since her grandma's funeral.

A sudden, unexpected tightness welled in Cecilia's throat and she swallowed hard.

"I see," he said and another silence descended.

She dreaded spending the next two weeks in a house filled with strangers, watching her brother fawn all over his bride-to-be. Not that she begrudged Mitch his happiness, she didn't, but witnessing it caused a strange yearning she didn't want to contemplate.

She gripped the steering wheel, tight enough her knuckles turned white. "I still think a couple of days before the wedding would have been plenty."

"Cecilia," Nathaniel said, in his patient tone. "Voters love a wedding and we need the family solidarity. This will help your image."

The logic couldn't be refuted, but she tried anyway. "And two or three days doesn't accomplish that?"

"Under normal circumstances, yes, but with Shane Donovan already at his sister's side and that football player on his way, it doesn't look good if we're not there."

An image of Shane snapped through her mind like the lash of a whip. He was one of Chicago's corporate giants, and his sister's impending marriage to the senator's notorious son had been a hot topic on a slow news day. If it wasn't for him, she'd be home where she belonged.

"So you get to stay in Washington but I have to play nice," Cecilia snapped.

"I'm in committee," her father said.

The whole situation annoyed her and she spoke without thinking. "And God forbid the voters find out your wife and son aren't speaking to you."

"That's enough. I'm still your father."

Something tightened in her chest. Was he? He didn't feel like it. She straightened her shoulders and modulated her tone to neutral. "All I'm saying is I'm not sure it's necessary."

"Trust me, it's necessary."

She laughed, a hard, brittle sound. "Trust you? You almost ruined your career."

"But I didn't," he said, his voice cold as ice. "I'm doing what I need to do, and if you want to win, I suggest you do the same."

She fought it—the pull that longed for his approval—but the habit was too old and her anger too new. She took a deep breath. "I understand."

Sometimes it was best to concede the battle to win the war. Or at least that was the political spin she sold herself today.

"Good. Remember the plan."

Ah yes, the plan. She ate, slept, and lived the plan.

Revival. Eight Miles.

Two weeks with Shane. Two weeks with his sharp, disapproving gaze. Two weeks of playing the ice queen he expected, pretending he had no effect on her.

She was exhausted just thinking about it. "I remember."

"And on that note . . ." Nathaniel said, his voice rich and pleased.

Her stomach dropped with dread.

"I spoke with Miles and Paul this morning and we decided right after the wedding we'll announce you're running for office."

She frowned. "What do you mean, 'right after'?"

"At the reception. We'd call in a few reporters to cover the wedding. You could let it slip and have a press conference the next day."

"No," she said, shaking her head. Was *nothing* sacred to him? "It's Mitch's day. Let him have it."

"The timing—"

She cut him off. "No. This is *my* campaign, and I'm putting my foot down."

She might not be close to Mitch, or have the slightest clue what to say to him, but she respected what he'd done and how he'd turned his life around after the senator had gone and fucked it all up. She wasn't about to ruin his wedding to gain a few points in the polls.

"Cecilia, let's be frank. You're a long shot."

Yes, the factors working against her were endless, but she was sick of him pretending he wasn't part of the problem. Venom filled her tone as she spit out, "Thanks to you and that little intern *I* told you not to hire."

He scoffed. "That's easy for you to believe, but we both know your image needs work."

Nausea roiled in her belly. "I didn't get blackmailed, you did."

"The voters forgave me. After all, I didn't do anything wrong."

"Ha! You didn't get caught. There's a difference."

"Perception is reality, my dear. You know that better than anyone."

What did he mean by that? He sounded smug, as though he knew something she didn't. "I'll build my own perception."

As soon as she figured out what she wanted that perception to be.

A long, put-upon sigh. "You can't connect. You're logical and pragmatic, which can be a benefit, but it doesn't win votes. People don't love you. You don't inspire them to act, or empower them to believe that government is within their grasp. You have no voice. No vision."

The truth. It was like a stab to the heart, but she refused, absolutely refused to give in to the tears that pricked the corners of her eyes. She did not cry. Ever. Instead, she steeled her spine and said sweetly, "Awww, you always give the best pep talks."

Never show weakness. Never break.

"It's up to me to tell you the truth."

A cocktail of riotous emotions threatened to bubble to the surface, but she pushed them back down. "I will not let you ruin Mitch's wedding so you can play father of the year in front of a few reporters." Her training had served her well, because there wasn't even a hint of a quaver in her voice. Her hurt was hidden down deep where it belonged.

And since he was so keen on truth, she'd dole out some of her own. "As *your* adviser, let me return the favor. If you want a chance in hell at winning your wife back before the next election, you'd better stop using your son to gain points in the opinion polls. You're losing her. She's starting to loathe you. Maybe because you had sex with an intern younger than your daughter?"

"Watch your mouth." His voice filled with outrage. Unlike her, he'd never been a pro at hiding anything unless he had an audience. "I did not sleep with that woman."

She laughed, the sound filled with rough, bitter edges. "Do you think I'm an idiot? You think I didn't see how you fawned over her? How you preened at her ego-stroking?"

Fifteen seconds must have ticked by before he spoke. "Have you told your mother this?"

She scoffed, shaking her head. This was so like him. All he cared about was covering his ass. Another mile marker sign flew by. "Good-bye, Father."

He hung up without a word.

She exhaled a slow, steady breath.

Well, that was ugly.

She'd held her own and scored her point, but the victory was hollow.

Revival. Next Exit.

She slowed to fifty-five and changed into the right lane. She had to block out this noise—her family crisis, Shane Donovan, the wedding—everything, and concentrate on what was important.

Winning the election.

It was the only dream she'd ever had and she couldn't let it die along with everything else.

Cecilia had been banging on the front door of her brother's farmhouse for five minutes and still no one answered. She glanced around the front yard filled with large oaks and weeping willows from her past, but where her grandma had planted shrubs, her future sister-in-law had lush hydrangea bushes in vibrant pinks, lavenders, and greens.

It was like stepping into an alternate universe where time stopped and reality altered just enough to make the familiar, foreign.

The breeze blew gently, sending the old porch swing swaying, and a burst of nostalgia filled her chest. How many summer nights had she sat there as a little girl, smelling of Off! and the river, curled up to her grandma's side reading *James and the Giant Peach*?

She could still see her grandma sitting there in her house-dress, looking like she was part of the earth. A tightness grew in her chest at the memory.

Would her grandma even like the woman she'd become?

She huffed out an exasperated sigh. Where was all this emotion coming from? She needed to shake it off and get it together. She turned away from the past and rang the bell, then rapped hard against the panes of glass.

Met with nothing but silence, she twisted the handle and found it unlocked. Since they expected her, she took a cautious step inside. Her heels clicked against original hardwood floors that gleamed with a richness that spoke of the care someone had put into restoring the wood.

"Hello?" she called out, peering around the empty foyer. The walls were different. The rose-patterned paper had been replaced with a soft, dark gray paint she'd never have picked because of the dark wood moldings, but it looked exactly right.

She called out again, "Hello?"

A distant male voice yelled back, "In the kitchen."

Why on earth hadn't he answered the door? She tossed her bag on the bench and walked down the narrow hallway leading to the swinging kitchen door that had been in this house since its creation.

The kitchen told another story, thrusting her out of the past and into the future. It gleamed with newness. With gorgeous, industrial stainless steel appliances, distressed white cabinets, and polished granite countertops in various shades of cream, gold, and brown.

Under the extra-deep double sink, a man sprawled across

the floor, his head under the cabinet. "Can you hand me that wrench?"

That voice. It never failed to send an irritating trail of tingles racing down her spine. She ground her back teeth until her temples gave a sharp stab of protest. Of course, Shane Donovan had to be the first person she ran into.

He bent one knee, pulling the worn fabric of his jeans across powerful thighs. Her throat went dry as her pulse sped.

Why him? Out of every man she'd ever encountered—and in her line of work, she encountered plenty—why did it have to be him? For heaven's sake, he even belonged to the wrong political party. She shuddered.

It was all so . . . embarrassing.

But her body didn't care, hadn't cared since the first time she'd met him at Mitch and Maddie's engagement party. The second her palm had slid into Shane's, a disconcerting jolt of electricity traveled through her fingertips and up her arm. She'd had to force herself not to yank away, to keep her face impassive.

It was a good thing he didn't like her. It was the one thing working in her favor. If she stuck to her current strategy of nurturing his disdain, he'd stay away, and her exposure would be minimal.

She walked over to the box of tools and stood over him.

Half hidden under the sink, he fiddled with her brother's plumbing. Annoyed at his pure perfection, she wrinkled her nose.

At six-four, his frame stretched beautifully across the hardwood. His hips were lean. His stomach flat. Shoulders ridiculously broad. Most of the times she'd seen him he'd been dressed in a suit, but today he wore a pair of beat-up construction boots, faded jeans, and a thin white T-shirt. It was a crime against nature that a man who spent most of his time in boardrooms had muscles like his.

She'd analyzed her attraction, and for the life of her, she couldn't come up with a logical explanation. Sure, he was good-looking, but so what? Good-looking men weren't impossible to find. He was nothing like the men she dated. She preferred, well, men like her. Men who were more interested in politics and strategy than carnal pleasures. She enjoyed a relationship where sex was secondary to their intellectual connection. Not that she had a problem with sex—she didn't. Her past encounters were all pleasant and civilized.

But nothing about Shane Donovan was civilized. And somehow she doubted sex with him was *pleasant*.

She shouldn't be attracted to him. Period. End of story. Only her libido didn't agree.

A loud *clang* sounded under the cabinet followed by a grunted curse. He stretched out his hand. "The wrench."

Without a word she reached down, grabbed the tool, and plopped it in his palm with far more force than necessary.

"Easy there, honey." The warm tone of his voice clearly not meant for her.

Who was 'honey'? A moment of panic washed over her. Oh no. Was she going to be tortured by watching him with another woman?

The thought bothered her so much, she blurted, "I'm not your honey."

He stilled for a fraction of a second, before sliding out from under the sink like the teasing reveal in bad porn. His strong jaw tightened as his piercing green eyes met hers. "If it isn't the ice queen herself."

His favorite name for her. He'd never called *her* honey, not even once.

The fine hairs along her neck bristled as something she refused to name sat in the pit of her stomach. It didn't matter. Even if he tried, she'd have to put him in his place on principle alone. Endearments were dismissive, every good feminist knew that.

She slipped into the role he expected, ignoring the jab to ask coolly, "Where's the happy couple?"

He got up from the floor with much more grace than a man weighing at least two hundred pounds should, turned, and flicked on the faucet with the touch of his fingers. "Your brother's out back."

The muscles under his thin T-shirt flexed as he washed his hands.

She squared her shoulders. Good thing broad shoulders, muscular backs, and lean hips didn't affect her. She was a sane, rational woman, not driven by hormones.

Her eyes locked on his ass.

Good thing she was above all that.

When the water ceased she snapped her gaze away and smoothed her expression into her most remote mask.

He turned and gave her an assessing once-over. "I didn't think you'd show until the rehearsal dinner."

A muscle under her eye twitched. "I was invited. Mitch is my brother. Why shouldn't I be here?"

"You Rileys aren't much for family support." He assessed her with a shrewd gaze. "So there must be another motive."

Her spine bristled and she had the sudden urge to smack him across his smug face. Of course she didn't, because that would be revealing and out of character. "I'm sure I don't know to what you're referring."

He scooped up a beer bottle and raised it to his lips, taking a long, slow drink while watching her in that predatory way he had.

How could someone's eyes be that green? So sharp and clear, it felt as though they pierced right through her.

The continued scrutiny gave her the urge to tug at her

navy suit jacket and smooth her knee-length skirt, but she refused to fidget. "Is my mother here?"

"She went to the store with Maddie." He placed the bottle back on the counter and rested his palms on the ledge of the granite that replaced the linoleum she remembered. "We're out of Cheetos and Mountain Dew."

She planted her hands on her hips and returned one of his long, disdainful glances. Her gaze settled meaningfully on his flat-as-a-board stomach. "Ah, that explains it. I've heard after thirty-five things go south rather quickly."

His expression flashed with what looked like amusement. He straightened from the counter and took a step toward her.

The urge to retreat rose in her chest but she didn't dare step back.

Never show weakness. Never break.

His eyes narrowed. "How'd you know I turned thirty-five?"

Damn it. See, this was why she ignored his barbs; she always said something far too telling. She shrugged one shoulder. "Oh, I hear things."

"Investigating my background? How sweet. I didn't know you cared."

Of course they'd investigated all the Donovans when her brother became involved with Maddie. Just like Shane had investigated all of them, when his sister ran away to Revival. That's the way it worked. Everyone knew that. *Maybe* she'd spent a little too much time on the oldest Donovan brother, but only because he was the most dangerous.

So yes, she knew all about Shane. Had a list of stats she could rattle off in her head in her sleep.

Occupation—CEO and owner of The Donovan Corporation.

Last significant relationship—one year ago with some tech genius.

High school grade point average—an abysmal 1.65.

College degree—none.

Arrests—one at sixteen, for underage drinking.

The list went on, and as many times as she went over the facts, the essence of him was missing. How did he beat such impossible odds? Overcome such dire straits?

All by his thirty-fifth birthday.

Which she *should not* know was three months ago.

One week after hers to the day.

At the memory of her own birthday, she frowned. It hadn't been a good day.

She'd spent her birthday in strategy meetings concentrating on repairing her father's tattered image. Other than a small fifteen-minute work break, when the interns shoved a cake under her nose, her mother had been the only person to call.

That night she'd sat alone in her Gold Coast town house eating Chinese takeout by herself. After a bottle of wine, she'd contemplated her accomplishments, trying in vain to pat herself on her back.

Only to realize the things she'd listed had nothing to do with her.

She'd done nothing for her own life.

Not a single damn thing.

Chapter Two

Was that emotion on the ice queen's face?

A frown curved the corners of Cecilia's mouth downward, as she seemed to drift off and forget Shane was there. He'd never seen her look anything but distant and remote and the flicker of feeling transformed her classically beautiful face into something stunning.

He didn't like it.

He preferred her inhuman. It helped cool the stab of irrational lust that kicked him in the gut every time he got within fifty feet of her. A lust he sure as hell didn't understand but couldn't seem to control. She was fast becoming an itch he couldn't quite scratch, annoying as hell and impossible to ignore.

Those mysterious, blue-gray eyes of hers darkened. Her expression was tight, highlighting her high cheekbones and the hollows of her cheeks. Twin lines formed over her normally smooth brow. Wherever she'd gone, her thoughts were distressing enough that her customary mask slipped away.

Why was she unhappy?

He shook his head. It didn't matter. It didn't have anything to do with him.

He didn't even like her. He liked his women smart, soft, and warm. While she was plenty smart, nothing about Cecilia Riley—from her patrician bone structure to her severe suits—spoke of softness or warmth.

Except for her mouth.

That mouth had been designed for a different woman. His gaze dipped to her full, pink lips. Lush and bitable, they looked like sex. Raw, dirty sex. The kind he was positive she didn't have.

The back door banged opened and Cecilia's expression jerked back into focus. She blinked, those stormy eyes of hers shuttering closed before he could decipher the emotions lurking in their depths. And just like that, the mask was back in place, leaving him to wonder if he'd imagined the whole thing.

She raised one elegant brow, crossing her arms and closing herself off.

He wanted to ask what she'd been thinking, but Gracie Roberts called out in a singsong voice, "Oh Shane, where are you?"

Cecilia's porn-star lips tightened.

"In here," he called back, his gaze never leaving her face. That was twice now. When they'd first met he'd tried to rattle her and there hadn't even been a flicker of awareness. But today, he'd seen more emotion on her face in the last ten minutes than in their entire acquaintance.

What was going on in that brain of hers? And why the fuck did he care? She wasn't his business.

Mitch and Maddie's neighbor waltzed into the kitchen, a stark contrast to the woman across from him. Unlike Cecilia's golden-brown hair, cut razor sharp and falling in perfect place at her shoulders, Gracie's curly blond hair was wild and carefree. Just like the woman. With a pretty face, dancing cornflower-blue eyes, and a body out of a teenage boy's wet dream, she was a walking, talking fantasy come to life.

He couldn't work up even the slightest interest.

Why couldn't he be like any sensible red-blooded man and have the hots for Gracie? It was irritating as hell. He tried. Hell, so had she. And while they flirted like mad, there wasn't a lick of heat between them.

Fucking annoying.

When Gracie saw Cecilia, she jumped, sending her *Playboy*-worthy breasts jiggling in a red tank top. "Ce-ce!"

Ce-ce?

Cecilia's chin tilted to a regal angle, but she overplayed her hand when she ran a smoothing palm over her sharply cut navy business suit. A prim, contained nod. "Hello, Gracie, it's been a long time. You're all grown up."

Gracie beamed, and in her normal exuberance, opened her arms and ran to Cecilia. Gracie locked her in a big bear hug and squeezed her tight. "It's so great to see you."

Cecilia's brows furrowed as she patted the other woman awkwardly on the back. "Thank you."

Gracie pulled back, still holding Cecilia by the shoulders, and gave her a thorough inspection. "Well, look at you. You haven't changed one bit. You're still all fancy."

"I came from morning meetings," Cecilia said, stepping out of the other woman's grasp.

Gracie planted her hands on curvy hips encased in skintight white capris. "Every summer, Ce-ce would show up, all neat and proper in her shiny shoes and ironed clothes." She winked at him, laughing. "But we managed to mess her up."

"Did you now?" Shane cocked a brow at Cecilia, who stood with such perfect posture she'd have made a finishing-school teacher proud.

Her lips pressed together but didn't speak.

Gracie nudged Cecilia with her elbow. "By the end she was as wild and dirty as the rest of us."

He couldn't imagine her wild and dirty. "That's hard to believe."

Cecilia tugged at her suit jacket. "I'm sure she's exaggerating."

That, he believed. "Ce-ce?"

"My grandmother used to call me that." Her voice was cool, but something flashed in her eyes, darkening the gray.

The nickname didn't suit the woman, but Shane couldn't help wondering about the girl she'd been before the power suits. Apparently, she'd been wild.

And dirty.

He searched her face but couldn't find any trace of carefree.

She sensed his gaze, turned and stared at him as though to say, *What are you looking at?*

"Well, come on, everyone's out back." Gracie waved an arm in the direction of the backyard.

He didn't glance away. Instead, his gaze drifted to Cecilia's mouth and his mind filled with illicit images.

Christ.

As though she read his mind, her gaze flicked scornfully over his before shifting her attention to Gracie. "I'm afraid I'm not dressed for a picnic."

The other woman laughed and jutted her thumb to the swinging door. "Go change, silly." Then she turned to Shane. "You, I need."

Cecilia gave a sharp tug at her suit jacket, her shoulders squaring.

He slanted a wicked glance at Gracie. "What do you need, honey?"

Cecilia's lips pressed into a firm line. She looked past him, out the window overlooking the backyard.

"Your expert advice. I experimented with a new recipe," Gracie said, before blowing out an exasperated breath. "Maddie's gone, Mitch likes everything, and your stupid brother refuses to eat one." She gave him an adorable little pout. "That leaves you."

A baker, Gracie had made one delicious concoction after another and his health nut younger brother refused to try a single thing. Shane grinned at her. "I told you Jimmy hasn't touched refined sugar since the great Christmas of 2012."

She threw up her hands and let out a scream.

Cecilia's eyes widened.

"He's impossible." Gracie stomped a foot, her righteousness so cute he should have wanted to eat her up with a spoon, but Shane's lust stayed stubbornly focused on the woman across from him.

"He's training for the marathon. You'll never break him, so don't even bother trying." Shane frowned as that ever-present worry for his siblings niggled at him. It wasn't healthy, James's total self-control, but Shane didn't know what to do about it. His brother was thirty-three, old enough to live his life the way he wanted.

"How does someone pass up dark chocolate cupcakes?" Gracie asked, pulling him away from his thoughts. "They're filled with warm caramel and iced with salted chocolate frosting. How do you refuse that?"

Cecilia's smooth brow furrowed.

Gracie placed an open palm on her chest, appealing mournfully to Cecilia. "I mean, can you imagine?"

"How many calories are they?" Cecilia asked, her tone so deadpan she had to be joking. Only, she wasn't the joking type.

She was like his brother that way. All serious. No cupcakes allowed.

"Are you *kidding*?" Gracie's tone indicating Cecilia belonged in a mental institution. "Who *cares*? It's *chocolate*."

Her shoulders slumped, her expression so dejected, Shane took pity on her. He pulled her close and kissed her temple. "Don't worry, honey, I'll eat all the cupcakes you want."

In that split second, he saw what he'd been waiting for. She hid it very quickly, and if he hadn't been paying such close attention he'd have missed it, written in big, bold letters all over her face.

Cecilia Riley was jealous.

And wouldn't he just have to find out what that was about?

She was not jealous. She did not get jealous. Jealousy was a base emotion. Uncivilized.

So what if Gracie Roberts was 'honey.' It made sense; she looked sweet enough.

Good. Great.

This worked to Cecilia's advantage. Two weeks watching Shane and Gracie fawn all over each other was certain to cure her of her fixation. Problem solved.

She forced a smile to her lips. Perfect. It was all going to work out.

She dropped her bags on the floor. The room hadn't been changed since the last night she'd spent there. It was still the frilly girl's room from her youth. Bright and hopeful in pale blue, white, and lavender. She ran her hand over the quilt her grandma had made for her, a soft white cotton with embroidered forget-me-nots that brought a sting to the back of her throat. She traced the flowers, quelling the ache in her chest, before moving to the white dresser.

There was a vase of vibrant pink Gerber daisies with an aged silver frame sitting next to it. She picked up the picture only Maddie could have put there. It was of Mitch and

Cecilia when they'd been young kids. Skin tan from the sun, they wore matching grins. They sat on a thick branch of the tree that hung over the river, dressed in their bathing suits, their gangly limbs dangling. They looked happy. Carefree. Like brother and sister instead of the strangers they were now.

She traced the edge of the pewter frame and put it back on the dresser.

Maybe this trip would help bridge the gap between them. Or at least she could pretend she wasn't an outsider. If even for a brief respite.

A boisterous round of laughter filtered in from outside. She walked over and peeked through the lace curtains. Down below, on a new brick patio, the light from the late afternoon sun streamed down on the group. Her brother was there, his long legs stretched out, lazy and relaxed. Nothing like the man he'd been back in his Chicago days. James, the quiet Donovan brother who didn't eat refined sugar, sat there too, sipping what looked like a glass of iced tea.

She swallowed hard as her gaze drifted to Shane and Gracie. They were sitting next to each other, their blond heads golden halos in the bright sun, knees touching.

They were so . . . together. Comfortable and at ease with each other.

Gracie dangled one of her ten-thousand-calorie cupcakes under his nose, teasing him with her dazzling smile as he laughed and pinched her before grabbing it out of her hand. He took a huge bite, shoving half the treat in his mouth.

Did he devour Gracie the same way?

Cecilia appraised the woman, mouthwatering in her red tank top and white capris. She dripped with sex appeal.

Of course he did.

A dark emotion that was *not* jealousy sat in the pit of her stomach.

Shane draped an arm around Gracie Roberts's chair and

said something that caused her to throw her head back with laughter.

They were perfect for each other.

Cecilia's fingers tightened on the lace curtains. She was happy for them.

Her eye twitched into hyperdrive and she covered it with a fingertip until it stopped.

Now she had no excuses and could focus all her energy on the campaign. She'd use this time to work. To plan. Craft *her* message—away from the advisers, her father, and Miles Fletcher—and find her voice. Because as much as she hated to admit it, her father was right: If she didn't find a way to connect to the voters, it didn't matter what she did. She wouldn't win.

So she'd use this time to figure out how to connect.

The muscle under her eye spasmed again.

Cecilia's gaze drifted back to Shane.

He belonged with a woman like Gracie. Lush and vibrant. And she could cook. Cecilia didn't even know how to boil water.

She remembered her summers with Gracie. How fun she'd been. After all the years Shane spent taking care of his family, he probably needed fun.

As though he sensed her, Shane lifted his head and peered up, his gaze locking on hers. Her heart rate sped, pounding against her ribs and she stepped back, moving away from the window with a jerk. Had he seen her?

She sank down on the bed, put her elbows on her knees, and rested her forehead in her open palm.

No. He couldn't have.

She shrugged off her suit coat and flopped back on the bed to stare at the ceiling. She took a deep breath, slowly exhaled, and vowed to stop thinking about Shane Donovan.

Ten minutes passed. She yawned and her lids grew

heavy. It was so quiet here, still and peaceful. Her muscles uncoiled as though she'd unrolled an invisible carpet. A laziness she never allowed in her Chicago life crept over her and she drifted along in that perfect place between awake and sleep.

Her phone cheeped, signaling an incoming text and startling her from her doze. With a groan she glanced at it, expecting her father, but it was an unassigned number. She swiped her finger over the screen.

Stop hiding.

All traces of sleepiness disappeared as she shot straight up on the bed.

Was it—no, it couldn't be.

She blinked, her cheeks growing warm. It was a Chicago area code—who else? She tapped the keypad. Who is this?

The phone beeped a second later. Now, Ce-ce. Don't make me come get you.

An inappropriate shiver raced down her spine. It *was* Shane. But why?

Wasn't he busy eating Gracie's cupcakes? Alone in the privacy of her room, with nobody watching her, she didn't have to hide her expression and a wide grin spread over her lips. Which was wrong. Schoolgirlish. And she didn't care. There was nobody to see her. She typed, How'd you get this number?

When the phone beeped thirty seconds later her stomach leapt.

The same way you got my birthdate.

She knew it. He'd investigated her.

Another ding. One week after yours.

The room seemed to grow ten degrees hotter as she dropped the phone on the bed and covered her face with her hands. What did that mean? Surely nothing. She tried to suppress the wild rush of excitement, but it was impossible. It was like being fifteen all over again and for the first time getting a call from the boy you liked.

Okay, she needed to stay calm. It didn't mean anything. More so, it *couldn't* mean anything. She took a deep breath and grabbed the phone, determined to respond in the same manner she always did, as though he stood right in front of her. Don't call me Ce-ce.

When the phone beeped she was embarrassed to realize she'd been holding her breath.

You have five minutes.

The comment was completely high-handed and entirely like him. A rush of warm tingles raced through her body and she shuddered. Alone, she didn't have to pretend it didn't thrill her. Not that she planned on letting him get away with it. She typed out, I'm not afraid of you.

A beep. Four.

She grinned, buried her face in her hands, and laughed.

Shane half listened to the conversation swirling around him while keeping one eye on the time and the other on the back door. What exactly was the icy Cecilia going to do now that he'd bossed her around? He didn't think she'd take it lightly, but he was almost positive he wouldn't get the excuse to go get her.

Which was probably a good thing, because he wasn't sure how he'd handle it now that she'd revealed she wasn't as uninterested as she seemed. Her indifference had kept him in check on more than one occasion, but he doubted its effectiveness today.

Not after he'd seen her in the window.

He'd almost convinced himself the jealousy he'd read on her face had been an apparition. Until he'd spotted her in the upstairs window, her slim hand pressed against the glass.

Staring up at her, he knew he wasn't going to let this thing with her go, despite his instincts to the contrary. He'd always been as stubborn as a mule that way.

He'd texted his administrative director and close family friend, Penelope Watkins, for the cell phone number sitting in the file he had on the Rileys. Two minutes later the number sat in his messages.

He didn't know if it was smart or stupid, but he was going to push Cecilia. Ruffle her. And then he was going to do any number of unspeakable things to her.

Things that would probably shock her.

He glanced at the time on his phone. She had one minute left.

He narrowed his gaze on the back door.

Just how far did that propriety go? Was it real? Was she a good girl all the way down to her toes? Or did she have a hidden streak of wicked?

Could he break her? Make her scream? He suspected it would take a lot of torment—

"Shane." Gracie shook his arm, startling him from his thoughts.

"What?" he asked, totally clueless.

His brother-in-law-to-be scratched the scruff on his chin and gave him an assessing look. "Maddie texted to make sure we don't need anything from the store. They're getting ready to check out."

"No," Shane said, and picked up his bottle of beer from the round teak table. He paused, remembering his conversation with Cecilia in the kitchen. "Wait, have her get some Cheetos and Mountain Dew."

Mitch cocked a brow. "Interesting choices."

"How can you eat that stuff?" In obvious disgust, James shook his head.

Shane rolled his eyes. "Do I have to hear a lecture every time I eat junk food?"

How had his brother turned out this way? Where had he gone wrong? Sometimes all the mistakes he'd made while trying to raise his three siblings kept him up at night. Shit, after his dad died he'd just been trying to keep them off welfare. He hadn't thought about their emotional well-being. He'd barely been an adult himself.

Now he had James on one hand, his control so rigid he wouldn't eat a fucking cupcake, and Evan on the other, who lived to take one stupid risk after another. He shook his head thinking of his youngest brother. Off surfing the Cyclops in Australia because he was running out of things that made him feel alive.

Shane shook his head. At least Maddie was back on the right track.

Although he couldn't take credit for that one. His sister had done that all on her own without any help from him.

"You're thirty-five now," James said in that reasonable tone he had before taking a sip of his decaffeinated, antioxidant-rich, black iced tea.

Shane frowned. What was the deal with his age? And why did everyone keep saying that? "Yeah, well you're thirty-three. Live a little before middle age hits and it all goes to hell."

Gracie pushed her plate of sinfully decadent cupcakes

toward his professor brother with an overly sweet smile on her face. "If you're going to live a little, have something actually good."

James shot her a droll look. "Did anyone ever tell you that you're a food pusher?"

Gracie clucked her tongue. "Duh, I'm a freakin' baker."

Mitch chuckled, shaking his head at the lot of them before shifting his attention to his phone.

Shane checked the time: five minutes had come and gone. So she was calling his bluff, was she? Fine by him, not that he had a clue what he planned to do once he found her. But he was sure something would come to him. It always did.

He moved to stand, but the back door opened and out walked Cecilia. Disappointment had him settling back into his seat.

Damn, just when things had been about to get interesting.

Cecilia stepped out onto the patio looking like a magazine ad for Hamptons living. Dressed in what he supposed passed as her version of casual, she wore a pair of tan pants, a white button-down top that showed absolutely nothing, and a pair of ballet flats. Her shoulder-length hair had been twisted into a neat little bun that sat perched on top of her head. Inconveniently, her eyes were hidden behind a pair of dark, tortoiseshell sunglasses.

She looked completely out of place with the rest of them. Hell, even Jimmy looked more relaxed than she did.

Mitch nodded at his sister. "You made it."

"Yes," she said, as though she spoke to a perfect stranger.

"Maddie will be happy," Mitch said, making it clear he didn't give a shit if she was there or not.

Cecilia's lips pursed fractionally before she offered a

courteous smile. "She made it quite clear when she invited me that no wasn't an option."

Mitch grinned and shrugged. "She's small, but mighty."

"Indeed," Cecilia said, not even a hint of amusement lurking in her tone.

Shane didn't understand one thing about the Rileys. They were so goddamn polite all the time. Like they had no connection to each other at all.

It baffled him. He'd lay down his life for his family. Had dedicated the last fourteen years to their survival. Worked his ass off to make sure they wanted for nothing. Even when they were total pains in the ass he couldn't imagine not being close to them.

If you didn't have family, what did you have?

He peered at Cecilia. What *did* she have?

"How is everyone?" Cecilia asked, sliding into the teak lawn chair, offering a polite nod at his brother. "James, it's a pleasure to see you again."

"You too," James said. "How was your drive?"

"Fine, thank you." She folded her hands in her lap and while her eyes were covered, she hadn't looked in his direction once. Chicken.

He, however, watched her unabashedly.

She turned her attention toward James. "Congratulations on your recent publication. I saw the *Times* picked up a piece of it. Your university must be very proud."

Was she letting him know she kept an eye on the other members of his family? That it wasn't exclusive to him?

James's expression turned mildly surprised. "With TV the way it is, forensic anthropology is a trendy topic."

Gracie gave a delicate little snort. "How can looking at a bunch of old bones be trendy?"

James was well respected in his chosen field and did

consulting work with the FBI and law enforcement offices all over the United States. He did a hell of a lot more than just look at bones, although it wasn't clear if Gracie knew that or not.

James's jaw hardened but he just shrugged. "Talk to the *New York Times*."

Shane lost interest in their drama and concentrated on the mystery of Cecilia. He was sure she'd been jealous back in the kitchen, and he was positive something was going on with her. Could he get a reaction from her again?

He put a hand on the back of Gracie's chair.

Cecilia stiffened, so slightly he couldn't be sure it wasn't his imagination.

Testing further, he twined a lock of Gracie's hair around his finger.

Cecilia's lips firmed into a thin line and she crossed her legs.

Of course, she still pretended not to watch him. He wrapped his hand around Gracie's nape, his fingers massaging the curve between her neck and shoulder. Ever helpful, she moaned, tilting her head to the side to allow him better access. "God, that feels good."

This time he was awarded a dark glare from his brother, and Cecilia's foot started to bounce, giving him all the confirmation he needed.

She did not like his hands on Gracie.

Way more pleased than he had any right to be, he said, "Gracie, honey, maybe Cecilia wants a cupcake."

Cecilia scowled. If he had to guess, she was glaring behind those dark, movie-star shades. She also placed a palm over her flat stomach, revealing her hunger.

Was she hungry for the cupcakes, or to throttle him? He was pretty sure he'd enjoy either.

Gracie pushed the plate toward Cecilia with a grin.

"Well, I don't know how many calories they have, but I can tell you it's more than five."

Cecilia's chin lifted and she took one from the plate. "Thank you, I'm sure one indulgence won't hurt me."

Mitch assessed his sister. "I think you can afford more than one. You're too skinny."

"I hardly think so," she said, putting the chocolate confection on a napkin.

"You've lost weight since I've seen you." Mitch's tone indicated this wasn't a compliment.

She picked at the edge of the paper liner but made no room to eat the cupcake. "Not much."

"At least five or ten pounds," Mitch said, the words rubbing Shane the wrong way.

If her brother wanted her to eat, making a big deal about how crappy she looked wasn't the way to go about it. She might be his sister, but it was pretty much Women 101.

"Things have been hectic," Cecilia said, frowning at her cupcake.

Mitch narrowed his gaze. "You're pale, and I bet you look just as tired under those sunglasses."

Cecilia folded her hands in her lap, abandoning the cupcake, an overly polite smile on her face. "A pleasure as always, Mitchell."

"Just calling it as I see it," Mitch said.

Shane felt his blood pressure rise, although he didn't know why. It wasn't any of his business if the Rileys wanted to treat each other like crap. He was just about to open his mouth and insert himself where he didn't belong, but Gracie beat him to it.

"Geez, what's wrong with you?" She slugged Mitch in the arm then shook her head at Cecilia. "Don't listen to him, Ce-ce, you look great."

She didn't actually. She looked pretty much as her brother

described. Too thin, pale, and tired as hell. Which bothered him on some visceral level. She was a beautiful woman, and had the potential to be a complete showstopper, but there was something missing in her. A vitality.

He'd met plenty of women like Cecilia. Powerful, sophisticated women who played everything close to the vest for fear someone would exploit their weaknesses. Women who carefully planned every move they made and let nothing catch them off guard. He saw that in Cecilia. How she worked to cultivate her image, from the cool expression to her well-modulated speaking voice.

But he couldn't get over the feeling it was an act. An act that didn't quite work on him, although he wanted to believe the story she was selling. He'd been telling himself she was nothing but an ice queen, but he kept baiting her, prodding and poking, waiting for her to respond. And today, he'd finally gotten the reaction he'd been waiting for, making him all the more determined to find out what was under Cecilia's smooth, oh-so polished exterior.

Because any woman who worked this hard at her facade was hiding something.

Too bad for her, he'd always been like a dog with a bone. Never give up. Never say die.

"How's dear old dad?" Mitch asked, his voice so nonchalant Shane was sure it was feigned.

Cecilia leaned back in her chair and peered into the sun. It streamed over her pale skin and turned her hair to coppery gold. "Oh, you know, same as always."

"He keeps calling for Mom, but she refuses to talk to him."

She glanced around the table, shifting restlessly in her chair. "This probably isn't the time to discuss it."

Mitch waved a hand over the table. "They're family. They know everything."

Shoulders squaring, she went rigid, as though caught in

a freeze-frame. "They might be your family, but they're strangers to me."

"At least tell me what happened." Mitch continued to push the issue despite Cecilia's protests.

"I don't know." Cecilia crossed her legs and folded her hands neatly on the table.

Shane had spent a lot of time in negotiations, and over the years he'd learned everyone had tells. Even Cecilia. She was controlling a desire to fidget. That much was clear by the white around her knuckles.

"You must know," Mitch insisted.

If possible her spine grew even straighter.

Oh, she knew, but she wasn't going to talk.

"Ask Mom," she said.

"I did."

"And?" Smart of her to turn the conversation back on Mitch. Too bad her brother was a shark of a lawyer.

Mitch's gaze turned hard, and he stared her down for a long, awkward moment that increased the tension around the table tenfold.

Not that Cecilia broke; she just stared right back.

"Funny thing, she told me to ask you," Mitch said.

Gracie shifted in her chair and James looked downright interested behind his wire-rimmed glasses.

Cecilia closed in on herself even more.

The conversation was distressing her, and Shane didn't like it. Watching her was like watching a rubber band being pulled too tight, stretched beyond capacity, about to snap at any moment. "Let the woman eat before you start grilling her and telling her she looks like shit."

Three sets of curious eyes turned in his direction. Mitch cocked a brow.

Cecilia's chin jutted up. "I don't need you to fight my battles. I can manage fine on my own."

This wasn't any of Shane's business, but he'd made his stand and he wasn't one to back down. He narrowed his gaze, pinning her with a look that sent grown men scurrying to carry out his command. "Eat your fucking cupcake."

Cecilia straightened. "Excuse me."

He sat forward, putting his elbows on the table. "You heard me."

"Don't tell me what to do, what to eat, or insert yourself where you don't belong. Understood?" The words heated his blood despite her intended coolness.

Maybe another man would be thwarted, but to him, she'd just thrown down the gauntlet. After a long, slow appraisal, he said, "Somebody needs to, since you're doing a shit job of it on your own."

Her jaw hardened, as though she was grinding her teeth. "I can assure you that you are *not* the man for the job."

His lips quirked. Well, they'd just have to see about that, now wouldn't they? "Eat it."

A small smirk ghosted her lips. "Make me."

Challenge accepted. "You don't think I'll do it, do you?"

She scoffed and waved a dismissive hand. "No, I don't."

"You forget, *Ce-ce*," he said, putting a mocking tone into the nickname. "I'm not like those civilized boys you're used to dealing with."

"And you're forgetting I'm not like those simpering girls you're used to." She studied her pale pink manicure that seemed to be the staple of professional women. "I don't need a big, strong man to make decisions for me."

Goddamn, he was having a good time. He grinned and turned to his brother. "Jimmy, get the rope."

Chapter Three

Cecilia had to force her jaw to remain tightly locked for fear of her mouth flapping open like a fish. Just who in the hell did he think he was? She worked on her righteous indignation, while ignoring that she liked the inappropriate things that came out of his mouth.

She parted her lips to speak, but nothing came out as a rush of illicit images flooded her brain.

Luckily her brother saved her.

"Whoa!" Mitch held up his hands. "Let's not get carried away here."

Shane still watched her, a knowing grin on his lips.

She didn't understand it, but the man made her want to forget everything but the thrill of the battle. But poise had been beaten into her since she was old enough to walk, and with the composure she wore like a second skin, she put her elbows on the table and laced her fingers. "You come near me with a rope and you'll be singing soprano for a month."

Gracie laughed, but Shane didn't even glance in her direction, making her wonder if she'd misread the situation between them. Would he be acting like this if he was sleeping with her? And would Gracie be so amused if her boyfriend had just threatened to tie another woman up? Cecilia didn't think so.

His green eyes lit like he'd won a jackpot, but before he spoke, the back door flew open and Maddie came flying out, that long, red hair of hers streaming.

Much more subdued, her mother followed and all Cecilia's enjoyment disappeared, turning to lead in the pit of her stomach.

For the tiniest moment she'd managed to forget about the mess back home. She sighed and sat back in her chair, all the good-natured fight leaking out of her.

Maddie wore a little jagged-cut jean skirt and a white tank top, as petite and adorable as ever. She beamed at Cecilia. "You came!" She turned to Mitch, planting her hands on her small hips. "See, I told you."

Cecilia's heart gave a little lurch when her brother's expression softened at the sight of his future wife. "Yeah, you did."

No one had ever looked at her like that. Like the world was right because she was in it. It shouldn't bother her. The last thing she wanted was for it to bother her. Not now, when she needed to convince herself those things didn't matter.

But seeing her brother's happiness, it mattered.

Maddie walked around the table toward her. Raised to be polite, she stood in greeting and outstretched her hand, but Maddie ignored it and wrapped her up in a big hug, squeezing tight. "I'm so glad you're here."

Her future sister-in-law was always like this, warm and inviting, somehow able to ignore the awkwardness ever present in their family circle. No wonder her mom loved her. Cecilia was pretty sure Charlotte liked Maddie better than her. And who could blame her? Maddie was everything a woman could want in a daughter.

Cecilia patted her clumsily on the back and tried not to feel uncomfortable as she waited for Maddie to let go. At long last she did, stepping back to assess Cecilia. As her clear green eyes searched her face, her brow furrowed. "How are you?"

"I'm fine, thank you." Cecilia cringed at her overly cordial tone. Needing a distraction, she smiled at Charlotte, standing regal in a yellow blouse and tan walking shorts, her champagne hair in its customary neat bob. "Hello, Mother."

"Cecilia." Their greeting the equivalent of an air kiss.

Maddie plopped down on Mitch's lap and he immediately curled his arm around her, his fingertips slipping under the edge of her shirt. He gave her a private smile. "What took you so long?"

Maddie threw an arm around his neck. "We stopped at that new bookstore in town. The owner saw my work at the library and wants me to do a mural for her."

Mitch kissed her temple. "Good for you, princess."

Cecilia marveled at the easy affection between them. She couldn't even imagine sitting on a man's lap. How did one accomplish it and still remain dignified?

Maybe this farmhouse cast a spell on people. Her grandparents had been like that too.

She peered down at the cupcake and her stomach growled. God, she wanted it—she glared at the offending treat—but now she couldn't eat it, thanks to Shane.

Damn pride, and damn him, for making a big deal about it. It would be in her stomach right now, satiating her hunger if it wasn't for him.

She glanced up and their gazes met. Those green eyes of his practically glowed, like a jungle cat that had its prey in sight. Something had changed, although she wasn't sure what. Over the handful of times they'd interacted, Shane's actions toward her ranged from mildly antagonistic to indifferent.

So why was he changing his game plan?

It wasn't attraction. She was 150 percent positive she wasn't his type, even if Gracie wasn't in the picture.

So what?

All she knew was he'd better stop because she depended on his disdain to control her twisted fascination with him.

"What's going on here?" Maddie asked, breaking Cecilia from her thoughts.

"Oh, nothing," Mitch said mildly. "Your brother is threatening to tie Cecilia up."

Cecilia jerked her head away from Shane and cursed the hot flush she felt crawling up her neck.

"Oh really?" Maddie looked back and forth between them. "How interesting."

"It's not interesting at all." Cecilia crossed her arms over her chest, refusing to sink down in her chair like she wanted to. "Your brother is quite impossible."

Maddie laughed. "Oh, you don't know the half of it."

Cecilia's phone chimed and she pulled it out of her pocket. It was another text message from Shane. She frowned as the tiny thrill of excitement beaded her nipples. She swiped the screen and opened the message. I always make good on a threat.

A smile twitched at her lips. She resisted the compulsion to look at him, irrationally sure everyone would know what was going on if she did. She typed back, My knives are sharpened and ready for use.

After she hit Send, she paid elaborate attention to a conversation Maddie and Gracie were having, appearing to hang on their every word. Not that she had a clue what they said, because all her focus was on the man across the table.

Thirty seconds later she heard him chuckle. She held her breath, waiting, experiencing that desperate, schoolgirl longing for him to respond. She willed all her energy on the phone in her hand, waiting for it to beep.

Someone tapped her on the shoulder, and she about jumped out of her skin. Thankfully, she'd managed to repress the shriek. She twisted around to look into her mother's somber expression. "We need to talk."

The nausea that had plagued Cecilia on the drive, rolled through her stomach.

She slid her phone back into her pocket. The game was over and now she had to get back to work. She nodded. "All right."

Maddie's brow furrowed as she looked at Charlotte with concern. "Is everything okay?"

The older woman nodded, but she fingered the strand of pearls around her neck. "It's fine, dear, I just need to speak with Cecilia."

Bile rose in Cecilia's throat and she pushed it back down as she stood.

She could feel Shane's gaze on her. Watching. Studying.

But she didn't look back. She couldn't, not with her mother reminding her of what the future held, or how she wanted to escape it.

What in the hell was that about? Shane rubbed his jaw as Cecilia and her mother disappeared inside. He shifted his attention to Mitch and cocked a brow.

Mitch shook his head, and rubbed Maddie's back. "Did my mom tell you what was going on while you were out?"

Maddie frowned. "No. I asked, but all she said was that I'd find out soon enough and it wasn't her place."

"What does that mean?" Mitch asked.

"I don't know," Maddie said softly. "But your dad called at least a couple times."

Mitch's shoulders stiffened at the mention of his father. The two had a crap relationship. Not that Shane blamed

Mitch. Senator Riley was a brilliant politician but a horrible father.

The senator had been involved in some risky business deals, but when the finger was pointed at Mitch, he'd kept silent to save his own reputation, even though stepping forward could have saved his son's career. Shane still didn't understand how a father sold out his child.

It was light years away from how Shane had been raised. Patrick Donovan had always put his family first, even when he couldn't afford to. His dad might be dead, but Shane was secure in the knowledge that his father would have done anything in his power to keep them safe.

A lesson Shane never forgot.

Maddie put a palm on Mitch's chest, as though her mere touch would soothe him. "She cried a little but didn't take any of the calls."

Mitch sighed. "I'll talk to her again and see what I can get out of Cecilia."

Maddie's heart-shaped face wrinkled with concern. "Okay, but be nice."

"I'm nice." Mitch squeezed her tight.

He'd better be.

Shane's gut tightened at the unexpected burst of protectiveness. What was he thinking? The ice queen was more than capable of taking care of herself. But he couldn't shake the feeling that something was off.

She was different from the last time he'd seen her.

Shane stared off into the weeping willow trees hiding the river just beyond, trying to puzzle it out. The mild breeze blew softly, ruffling the long branches hanging from the trees, but no answers came to him. But he intended to find out. Sure, it wasn't any of his business, but fuck it, he was making it his business.

Gracie yawned, interrupting his concentration. She stretched, her top riding dangerously low, before she stood and rolled her shoulders. "Break's over, I need to get back to work."

"Don't forget, tomorrow Penelope and Sophie will get here at one," Maddie said, still not moving off Mitch's lap even though Cecilia had vacated a seat. "We have our final fitting at three."

Gracie rolled her eyes. "Geez, I know, you only told me a thousand times."

"I don't want you to forget," Maddie said.

"How can I with you yapping about it constantly?" Gracie said, but affection danced in her blue eyes.

Shane chuckled. "See, Gracie, you missed your chance. You should have been a bridesmaid the first time. Back then she'd run out of the room screaming if anyone mentioned the W word."

"Hey! You know you're not supposed to bring that up." Maddie scowled, puffing out her bottom lip in a full-blown pout that used to get her everything she ever wanted from their father.

Shane suspected it worked equally well on her future husband.

Unconcerned, he shrugged. "If you weren't the bride from hell we wouldn't have to mention these things."

"I am not the bride from hell." Maddie straightened, perching herself on Mitch's knee and gesturing at him. "Come on, tell them."

"Well, yeah, you kind of are," Gracie said, not waiting for Mitch to speak.

Maddie huffed and threw her hands up. "I can't believe this."

James sighed, looking dejected. "I'm going to have to side with Gracie here."

"James!" their baby sister yelled, her notorious red-headed temper getting riled. "How could you?"

He rubbed his jaw, and then adjusted his wire-rimmed glasses. "You handed out to-do lists over breakfast."

Maddie had the decency to blush, but she squared her shoulders. "I just want everything to be perfect."

Mitch tugged her wrist until she relaxed and leaned back against him. He kissed her temple. "We know you do, princess."

Gracie snorted. "That's easy for you to say, you're the only one she's nice to."

Maddie snuggled in under his chin. "That's because he's working on his first big case and I don't want him stressed."

It was still odd for Shane to see his sister be so affectionate toward Mitch. She was always all over him, burrowing close, smiling at him like he hung the moon, pretty much being obnoxious about the whole thing. Shane would have missed the days when she barely tolerated her ex-fiancé's presence if she wasn't so damn happy.

"Lucky bastard," Gracie said, shielding her eyes from the sun, looking off toward the lemon-colored house she shared with her brother, before scowling at James. "You're moving into the apartment over the garage to make room for the wonder twins, right?"

The logistics of everyone coming in and out of the house were starting to get crazy and James was a man who liked order. Since the Robertses had a small garage apartment they'd offered to out-of-town guests, he'd claimed it for his own as soon as he found out Penelope and Sophie were staying in the main house.

He nodded.

She waved a hand in the direction of the garage. "Do you want to check and make sure it's got everything you need?"

James stood. "I'm sure it's fine, but I'll check and let you know."

Shane cringed. Bad move.

"See that you do, your highness." Gracie turned and stomped off.

"I will never understand that woman," James said in his normal, calm tone, shaking his head. "I don't think she likes me."

"Gee, what was your first clue?" Despite the sarcasm, Shane wasn't so sure Gracie didn't like his brother. It hadn't escaped his attention that she flirted good-naturedly with every man she came in contact with—except James.

And there had to be a reason for that.

"It wouldn't hurt for you to try some of her cupcakes," Maddie said, sliding from Mitch's lap and into the chair next to him.

"I'm training for the marathon," James said, as though that answered everything. The guy had been running the Chicago marathon every year for the past three and kept trying to outdo his previous record.

His dedication to fitness was damn annoying.

Shane ran with him yesterday. After seven miles, James had gone on like a machine, leaving him behind hoping his lungs wouldn't explode.

Maddie picked up said cupcake and peeled the wrapper. "I thought you were supposed to carb load for that."

"Not with simple carbs and refined sugar."

Maddie frowned. "I don't think one is going to kill you. Can't you just humor her to keep the peace?"

James stared off at the house next door. "Maybe later. I'll go check the house out."

After their middle brother left, Maddie tsked, speaking around a mouthful of cupcake. "I blame you and Evan."

"What did we do?" Shane grabbed his warm lemonade from the round teak table and wished it was spiked with vodka.

"You guys used to tease him."

"We didn't tease him," Shane said. "We toughened him up."

"Well, he's plenty tough now, isn't he?" Maddie slipped her palm into Mitch's, and their joined hands swung between the side-by-side chairs.

Damn, they were sickening. "Speaking of junk food, where are those Cheetos?"

Maddie jutted her chin toward the back door. "In the kitchen."

"I fixed your leak." Shane stood and started toward the door.

"Thanks," Maddie called after him.

He walked into the kitchen expecting to find it empty, but Charlotte and Cecilia were there, standing on opposite sides of the table, arms crossed, faces tense. The conversation came to an abrupt halt as they both looked at him.

It was the first time he saw the resemblance between them and in that moment, with their gazes narrowed and mouths turned down, they looked like mother and daughter.

Cecilia tapped the toe of her shoe. "Can we help you?"

The question rubbed him the wrong way. He spotted the orange and red bag on the counter and walked over to stand next to it, propping his hip on the counter and ripping open the bag. "Nope."

Chapter Four

Cecilia took a deep breath and tried to figure out if she was thankful for the intrusion or wanted to throttle him. Frowning, she watched as he shoved another handful of Cheetos in his mouth then popped open a can of Mountain Dew.

In a haughty tone, she asked, "Do you mind? We were talking here."

He scratched his head. His blond hair shone like spun gold in the sun streaming from the window, casting him in angelic light that was entirely at odds with his true personality.

Her mother sighed then glanced toward the swinging door. "I need to go change anyway. We'll finish this later."

Cecilia pinched the bridge of her nose. This was not a good day. Hell, this wasn't a good month and the edges of her control were starting to fray. Shane wasn't helping matters.

"What exactly is going on here?" Shane asked, that deep voice sending a tingle down her spine despite her fatigue.

They'd find out soon enough. In fact, she was surprised none of them read the article. She should tell him and end this little game he was playing once and for all. Except she didn't want to. As soon as he discovered the truth he'd go back to looking at her with the contempt he'd always shown her, and selfishly she wanted to enjoy her reprieve a little longer.

She shook her head. "Nothing."

"Bullshit. You're making everyone tense." He popped another cheese curl into his mouth.

It stung, a lot more than she cared to admit.

It shouldn't; she'd always been an outsider, especially with this bunch. But before, when she felt lonely or excluded, she'd relied on the knowledge that she was her dad's favorite. That someone in this world loved her and thought she was special. Now she knew better. The loneliness covered her like a wet blanket, damp and cold and heavy. Not that she'd ever let it show. In a calm tone, she said, "I just got here."

"And you're putting everyone on edge."

"What am I doing?" Temper flashing, she put her hands on her hips. "I showed up because *your* sister wanted me to. I've been polite, cordial, and haven't once mentioned the nation's deficit. So how exactly am I making everyone tense?"

"That's what I want to know." He took a big gulp of his stupid Mountain Dew.

He was infuriating. Plain and simple. "How is this any of your business?"

He put the can back on the counter. "It's not."

She blinked, thrown off guard by the unexpected answer. She steeled her spine. "Then we're in agreement."

"Not really. I'm still going to find out."

"What do you care? You don't even like me." It was the first mention she'd made about the way he treated her, and she didn't even know why she said it. It was probing. Fishing for answers. She knew it and he was smart enough to know it too.

"You're right, I don't like you much." His tone matter-of-fact.

And there it was: the truth.

The little spark that had grown inside her every time he texted flamed out. Disgusted to find she'd harbored some sort of deep-seated hope. For what? She wasn't sure and refused to let herself wonder. Throat tightening, she put on her most impassive expression.

Well, good. She had evidence now. Evidence sure to cool her desire. She squared her shoulders. "Then stay out of my way and I'll stay out of yours."

He put both hands on the counter. "Yeah, that's not going to happen."

She almost took a reflexive step backward but was able to stop at the last moment. Instead she said, "Excuse me?"

Nice comeback. Not.

He pushed off the counter, his green eyes looking distinctly predatory.

She was too damn tired to do battle with him. She wanted to retreat until she felt like herself. But she couldn't do that.

Never show weakness. Never break.

"There's no way," he said, standing mere inches away but thankfully not touching her, "I'm going to be able to ignore you for a whole two weeks."

What did that even mean? "Look, I don't know what your problem is, but we are living in the same house, so for Mitch and Maddie's sake, let's just be civil."

"Here's the problem with that," he said, his voice dropping an octave. "I don't feel civil around you."

Another woman, a more flirty one, interested in capturing his attention, would ask seductively how she did make him feel, but Cecilia wasn't that kind of woman and never would be. Better to keep her distance. Besides, he didn't like her. In her most dignified tone she said, "I don't know what game you're playing, but stop it. It's not welcome."

Liar, liar, pants on fire.

"Is that so?" He curled his hand around the back of her neck, touching her for the first time, and it was like an electric shock. She had to force herself not to wrench in response. His thumb brushed over the pulse hammering in her neck.

So very telling.

"Yes." The word entirely too breathless. Light-headed, she forced her eyelids to remain open as his fingers stroked over her skin. She should pull away, but couldn't find the willpower. Who knew if he'd ever touch her again?

"I don't think your girlfriend would appreciate this." The second the words left her mouth she wanted to kick herself. Why on earth would she say something so revealing?

Her only excuse was that he was so close and she was so tired.

One golden brow, several shades darker than his hair, rose. "Girlfriend?"

She sucked her bottom lip between her teeth.

His eyes darkened to a deep shade of emerald.

The damage was done, she'd shown her hand, and now the only thing left to do was spin control. She tried to pull away, but his fingers remained locked on her neck. "Let me go."

His mouth twitched as though containing a smile. He lowered his head, making her heart beat frantically against her ribs, and whispered, "I knew it."

She sucked in a breath. God, he smelled good: like soap, and spice, and summer. Somehow she managed to say in a calm voice, "What are you talking about?"

"You're jealous of Gracie."

How did he know that? She reared back. "I am not!"

"Even you have tells."

"You're insane. I don't have tells." Did she? How had she given herself away? She'd been so careful. She waved a hand in a failed attempt to bat him away. "Besides, there's nothing to tell."

His fingers played over the cords of her neck as though he had every right to touch her. "I'm not sleeping with Gracie. Or any other woman, for that matter."

Relief, swift and powerful, stole through her. But she managed to say the good, proper Cecilia thing. "Who you do or don't sleep with is none of my concern."

"We'll just see about that, won't we?"

"No, we won't," she said, surprised at the steadiness of her voice.

He smiled, and it was pure carnal sin, transforming his too good-looking face into something dangerously gorgeous. He dropped his hand and stepped away.

To her humiliation, she immediately missed his heat.

"Game on, Ce-ce." Then he turned and walked away.

Game on? What in the hell did that mean?

Cecilia pressed cool fingers to her hot cheeks and tried to figure out what just happened. He said he didn't like her. So why had he touched her? Not only had he touched her, he'd made it clear he had plans. That he considered her some sort of challenge.

She closed her eyes and counted to ten. She was so damn confused.

This day, already fraught with drama, was turning into a roller coaster she wasn't prepared to deal with. For so long she'd been living on the surface, skimming through life and people and events without any attachment. She didn't know how to cope with this sudden, emotional upheaval.

It was exhausting.

All she wanted was a nap, a good solid couple of hours

of rest. Like everything else, she'd been getting by on the bare minimum and it was finally catching up with her. Maybe if she got some good REM sleep she'd be back to normal and able to recapture her previous cool, detached disposition.

She sighed. She couldn't rest until she finished the conversation with her mother. Cecilia had never been able to relax, let alone sleep, when there were important matters to deal with.

Charlotte was not happy about the Miles Fletcher situation and had made it clear before Shane interrupted that she was furious with both Cecilia and her father.

Somehow, she had to find a way to get her mother on her side, despite her protests. Charlotte had always been a constant presence in her life, but one she'd taken for granted. Unlike her dad, Charlotte never made her work for approval, and stupidly, Cecilia had viewed her mother as less valuable because she didn't have to strive for her acceptance.

And now, when she needed Charlotte's support, she refused to give it. Somewhere over the last year her mom had grown a spine of steel and Cecilia hadn't caught up to her yet.

But Mitch had. He was the good one again. The golden boy who could do no wrong. And Maddie, with her easy affection, was a bonus. Like winning the jackpot on a scratch-off lotto ticket.

It just made Cecilia feel that much more alone.

She left the kitchen and her confusing exchange with Shane behind, trekking upstairs to knock on her mother's bedroom door. She needed someone on her side. "Mom, it's Cecilia."

A moment of silence before her mom called, "Come in."

She entered the room—one Maddie hadn't gotten ahold of. Like her own room, it was still in her grandma's old style. The nostalgia of the décor eased some of the tension in her shoulders. "This reminds me of Grandma."

Her mom sat on a faded green brocaded wingback, looking out the window, a book on her lap. "I asked Maddie not to change it."

Cecilia walked over to the bed and her eyes filled with unexpected tears, which she blinked quickly away. "Is this her wedding quilt?"

"Yes, we found it in the attic."

Ivory from age, the cotton quilt was embroidered with intertwining tulips symbolizing the circle of a wedding ring. "When we used to visit I'd spread it out on the floor and roll myself up in it like a cocoon." It was a memory from out of nowhere, one she hadn't thought of in so long it seemed like it belonged to someone else. "Then Grandpa would pick me up, cuddle me on the couch, and tell me the story of how he met Grandma. How he knew he'd marry her from the second he saw her."

The window was open and a breeze blew in, sending Charlotte's expertly highlighted champagne-colored hair flying. "They were very much in love."

Once, Cecilia questioned if that kind of love really existed. She'd convinced herself she'd imagined the way her grandparents looked at each other. Romanticized her childhood summers until they were something magical and beyond her reach. But, like the rest of her illusions, it was wiped away every time she witnessed her brother gaze at his bride. He had that same look her grandpa used to wear.

She ran her hand over the fabric, soft and worn, but the fibers were still strong. "Maybe some people aren't destined for great love. Maybe we're only destined for one thing and we have to make sacrifices along the way."

"I don't believe that," her mother said flatly.

Cecilia took a chair from the secretary's desk and brought it over to sit next to her mom. She stared out the window, overlooking the idyllic yard full of ancient, timeless trees, roses, and plush green grass still new from spring.

She wondered if her mom had loved her dad that way. If once upon a time they'd had a fairy-tale love. She wanted to ask, but didn't dare. The wounds were too fresh and the hurt too deep. Instead, she said, "Won't you please understand?"

There was a long pause. "No, I can't. Everything about this is wrong. I won't pretend you're not making a huge mistake."

"Mom," Cecilia said, her voice a bit pleading, "I have so many factors against me. And this is something I can control."

Charlotte's fingers tightened, turning her knuckles white. "You will regret this, I promise you."

"I'm not losing anything I believe in." She knew what life had in store for her.

"You've always been stubborn. Even as a young girl you never listened to me." Charlotte turned to look at her with sad eyes. "I'm wasting my breath trying to change your mind, aren't I?"

The question filled Cecilia with shame because it was true. She'd only valued one opinion, and even now, with all her disillusioned bitterness toward her father, she believed he was right. Believed his words over her mother's. She had doubts, but she'd never admit them to anyone, least of all Charlotte. She'd take them as a sign of hope. And Cecilia refused to be cruel. She shook her head. "I have to do this."

Charlotte pressed a fingertip briefly to her lips before saying, "When you were a little girl and your dad was around, you'd come home from school and line up all your work on the dining room table. As soon he walked in the door, you'd take him by the hand and make him look at what you'd done in school that day. At first I was proud of how diligent and hardworking you were, but after awhile I became concerned."

Cecilia looked down at her manicured hands. She remembered doing that. Remembered her desperate need for approval. How she'd hang on his every praise and be crushed by every criticism. "I was an overachiever. Isn't that a good thing?"

"You were so obsessed with being perfect," Charlotte said, her voice soft. "If he corrected you, you'd do it over and insist you'd never make the same mistake again. It was too much pressure."

"I don't like mistakes." She tried to make the words light but failed miserably.

"After a month, I told him to stop correcting you. You just wanted his approval so much. And I hated watching you try so hard."

Had his approval always been false? Something to appease her?

Charlotte put her hand over Cecilia's, her fingers cool but surprisingly firm. "Don't do this to please him. To prove to him that you can succeed."

"I'm not. I'm doing this to be free. To have something to call my own. Can't you understand that? Since I was a girl, this is all I ever wanted."

"But why?"

Cecilia blinked at the question. "What do you mean?"

Charlotte gripped her hand harder. "Why do you want to run for office?"

"Because the seat is open and I'm tired of waiting."

"That's not what I'm asking. Why do you want to be a congresswoman?"

Cecilia didn't understand. "You know it's all I ever wanted. This is the first step in achieving my dreams."

"I know that's what you've always said, but I don't understand *why*."

Clueless, Cecilia shook her head. Her answer wasn't satisfying her mother. Instead, it seemed to distress her further. "I need to prove to *myself* I can do it."

"Is that what you'll run on? The need to prove yourself?"

The words stung. She brushed imaginary lint from her skirt. "I don't have my campaign slogan yet, but I will. I just haven't had a chance to think about it." There'd been too many other details to take care of, but now that she had time to think, her message would come. "Please, Mom, I need your support right now."

Charlotte sighed, a great weary sigh that sounded like it came from the tips of her toes. "Cecilia, you're my daughter and I'll support you and help you in whatever way I can, in all things but this."

"Thank you," Cecilia said. She should be relieved. The weight should lift from her chest, but it didn't and she didn't understand why. She'd gotten what she came for and, realistically, begrudging support was all she could expect.

All she could hope for.

But today, sitting in this room that reminded her of her grandma, she wanted more.

Chapter Five

Shane rubbed his gritty eyes in the silent, dark kitchen, illuminated by the screen of his laptop as he sent off another e-mail. Twenty-five more to go.

He glanced at the digital clock on the stainless steel microwave. Five after eleven. He'd been working through his e-mails for the last couple of hours and the list of problems from his battle with the new head of city planning was growing exponentially. He really should be in the office, dealing with the city contract from hell, but he refused to disappoint his sister. It wasn't her fault she had to get married at the worst time.

He opened an e-mail from his VP of Communications. After the first sentence his eyes blurred and his mind drifted to other things . . . namely Cecilia.

Where had she disappeared to?

She'd gone upstairs after their interlude this afternoon and he hadn't seen her since. It seemed unlikely she'd avoided him—Cecilia Riley wasn't the kind of woman who tucked tail and ran at the first sign of a little challenge. So why hadn't she shown up at dinner?

When Mitch asked Charlotte about her daughter's whereabouts, the other woman just got a troubled expression on her face and said she didn't know. Mitch shrugged it off and the conversation moved on.

Shane had wanted to probe but held his tongue. He wasn't ready to explain his interest to anyone. He'd waited, none too patiently, for one of them to go find her, but neither of them moved from the dinner table and Maddie hadn't seemed inclined to track down the missing Riley.

Didn't they see something was going on with Cecilia? It was clear as day. But her family seemed unconcerned with her well-being.

It bothered him on some deep level he didn't quite understand.

When she hadn't shown up by eight thirty he'd lost patience and texted her, but unlike before, she hadn't texted him back with one of her sassy remarks. While his phone cheeped, beeped, and rang at a steady clip all night, it had never once been her.

The sleek, gunmetal-gray Mercedes she drove still sat in the driveway and hadn't moved.

As far as Shane could tell she'd locked herself into her room and hadn't come out.

The question was: Why?

He pinched the bridge of his nose and squinted, wondering if he was going to need fucking reading glasses soon. He kept meaning to make an eye doctor appointment, or at least tell Penelope to make him one, but he conveniently kept forgetting until he stared at a screen for four hours straight.

It wasn't that he cared about getting old; he didn't. But his age reminded him everything else had aged too, and he didn't know quite what to do with himself. It was like he was still going Mach 10 while the rest of the world had gone into slow motion.

Since his dad had died he'd been working his ass off.

From the second he'd received the call about the car crash he'd been in crisis mode, fixing the mountains of problems left behind by two ill-prepared people, taking care of his siblings as his mother focused on Maddie's recovery and struggled with her grief, paying off debt after debt. He'd barely breathed all those years. Barely thought. He'd just put his head down and bulldozed through every obstacle that came into his path.

Then one day he'd finally looked up and realized he'd done it. He'd saved them all. His mom would never have to work a day in her life. His brothers and sister were grown. And, somehow, after all his years of being a slacker, a fuck-up, he'd built a company that employed thousands of people with a bottom line that still staggered him.

Everyone was finally safe. Finally secure. If he died to-morrow they'd be taken care of. He'd made sure what happened before would never happen again.

Only, he couldn't seem to break out of panic mode. That feeling of being one step from disaster still plagued him.

He frowned, not liking the direction of his thoughts.

He had a company to run, a contract to straighten out, and e-mails to answer. This wasn't the time to turn intro-spective. He refocused on the message from his VP, shot off his comments and opened the next e-mail.

Twenty-four to go.

The kitchen door swung open. He expected Mitch or Maddie, but instead it was Cecilia.

She screamed, her hand flying to her chest as she pulled a silky robe tightly around herself. "Are you trying to give me a heart attack?!"

He grinned. Instantly the vague unease troubling him disappeared. "Sugar, I was here first. You walked in on me, not the other way around."

She tied the sash around her waist, cinching it far too tight than he thought necessary. "Don't call me sugar, that's despicable."

He chuckled, wondering what she had on under those clothes. "Where have you been hiding all night?"

Her shoulders squared. "I haven't been hiding, you arrogant ass. If you must know, I fell asleep."

"And woke up on the wrong side of the bed, I see." He stretched his legs and watched her with avid interest, wishing for much better light so he could see more of her.

"What are you doing?" she asked in a haughty tone, taking another couple of steps into the kitchen.

He waved at the computer. "Answering e-mails."

"Oh," she said, tugging the lapels of the robe closer together. "Don't let me disturb you. I just came for some water."

He gestured toward the cabinets. "Third door on the left."

She moved across the floor with the practiced, studied grace of a rich girl.

Coming from a humble background, he'd never thought that was something he'd be attracted to, but she made it work. He'd bet dollars to doughnuts she'd taken years of ballet.

She reached for a glass, her back arching, her calves flexing as she stood on tiptoes to grab what she wanted. The moonlight streamed in from the window, casting her in its glow, and his breath caught. In the pale light her face was still soft from sleep, her hair rumpled, and she lost all that polish.

Goddamn, she was beautiful. His cock stirred. It was more than her face; there was something about her, something that reached inside of him and squeezed.

One day in her presence had rid him of all his delusions that he could keep her at arm's length. She was a mystery that had gotten under his skin and now he had to figure her out.

He wanted her and intended to have her.

She moved to the fridge and filled her water from the automatic dispenser before lifting it to her lips and taking a long drink. The delicate cords of her neck worked and he remembered earlier this afternoon when her pulse had hammered under his thumb, belying her cool nature.

When she was done, she turned and looked at him, one hip cocked. "You're staring."

He'd thought a lot about his strategy with her, and in the end, he'd decided brutal honesty would be most effective. He shrugged. "You're a gorgeous woman, of course I'm staring."

Her brow furrowed, as though the statement perplexed her. "Even though you don't like me?"

He flipped the lid of his laptop down. "Maybe I misspoke earlier. I don't know you well enough to like or not like you. I think you work damn hard to keep yourself at a distance, and until now, it's worked."

She glanced at his computer, then took another sip of her water and placed the glass on the newly installed granite. "Don't you need to get to your e-mail?"

He gave her a slow, easy once-over. Gaze skimming down her body, over the swell of her breasts and curve of her hips covered in powder-blue silk. "What are you wearing under that robe?"

She laughed, shocking him. It was full and throaty, matching that porn-star mouth of hers. The sound vibrated straight to his balls, sending a jolt of powerful lust through him. "As if I'm going to tell you."

He knew a challenge when he heard one. "You don't have to tell me. I can come over there and find out."

She tilted her head to one side, her expression speculative. "What exactly is your game here, Shane?"

He liked the sound of his name on her lips. Liked the way she didn't skirt around the issue even better. "My plan is to take you to bed. It's just a matter of when."

She straightened for a fraction of a second before relaxing back against the counter. "Isn't that a bit presumptuous?"

"Hell, it's a lot presumptuous," he said, meeting her eyes in the eerie moonlit glow. "But it doesn't make it any less true."

"You're very crass," she said, still looking completely unruffled.

It was an act, he was sure of it. He didn't know exactly what lurked under that cool exterior, but he knew she wasn't unaffected. If he touched her, she'd be hot. Ready.

As easy and casual as she, he smiled. "If I was being crass I'd say, 'I'm going to fuck you' and call it a day."

She sucked in her breath, just a quick little intake. "The words don't matter much, but the fact that you act like I don't have a say, does."

He stood.

She straightened.

He took a step around the table.

Her gaze darted to the kitchen door before shifting back to him.

He stopped, giving her a chance to run, not the least bit surprised when she didn't.

They were alike that way, unable to resist a dare.

He advanced. "You have a say. You asked me my plan and I told you. What you do with the information is your choice." When he reached her, he put his hands on either side of the counter, trapping her.

She looked up at him with those storm-blue eyes. "I don't recall giving you permission."

He laughed. "I'm more an ask-for-forgiveness-not-permission type of guy."

She swallowed hard but said nothing.

He was close enough to feel the heat of her body, see the bead of her nipples, the fast rise and fall of her chest. "But I'll respect a no." His gaze dropped to her mouth. Those lush, fuckable lips. "Even if I know it's a lie."

It was very hard to stay calm with Shane Donovan so damn close.

How many times had she thought about this moment? Fantasized? Lain in bed after a night in his presence, addicted to that rush he gave her. But here she was, trapped between his strong, powerful arms.

She knew this was fleeting. A momentary blip that would flame out as fast as it started. Maybe her nap had addled her brain, but while the word "no" hovered on her lips, she found herself unable to say it out loud.

In a calm voice, she said, "Do you try to intimidate a lot of women?"

He frowned, looking vaguely disappointed. "No. And even if I did, you're not intimidated."

Something inside her couldn't give in. Couldn't back down. No, within her, buried so deep she hadn't known it existed, lurked a devil that wanted to play. It's what had pulled at her since she met him, and in this darkened kitchen she gave in to the temptation.

"I'm not." She flicked a dismissive glance over him. "Are you going to back off?"

His lips quirked. "Are you going to say no?"

She pressed her lips together and their gazes locked.

For a very, very long time.

He straightened, and she experienced a keen disappointment, which disappeared the second he put his finger on the knot of her robe. He traced the fabric, over and over, watching her closely.

Her nipples beaded into hard, almost painful points. Between her thighs, her core heated, and wetness slicked her skin. How did he make not touching such a turn-on?

It would have been embarrassing, if it wasn't so erotic.

"Say no," he said, his voice a rasp against her skin as he hooked his finger where the knot was bound.

And let him win? Never. She sucked in a breath and said, "Step back."

Of course he didn't. Not that she expected otherwise.

He worked the knot with those long, strong fingers until it loosened and he pulled it free. Then he gripped the belt where it was tied by one tiny little X. "Are you naked under this robe?"

She wasn't; she had on a matching nightgown with sheer lace cups. Her guilty pleasure: pretty nightgowns nobody saw. "I'll never tell."

He shrugged. "I'd rather find out myself."

"You're waiting for an invitation that's never going to come." The words were a deliberate challenge. She shouldn't be taunting him this way when she knew full well he wouldn't back down.

A hard tug on the belt had her hips tilting with all the invitation he needed. "I'm not waiting, I'm just enjoying the anticipation."

Another pull and her back arched, forcing her to brace her hands on the counter to keep from falling. Her hips brushed his and she had to fight the gasp that rose to her lips.

His gaze met hers, panther green in the glow of the moonlight streaming from the window. "I want you to know how wet I can make you without a single touch."

It called exquisite attention to the heat between her legs, the slipperiness on her thighs.

The belt came free and she relaxed back against the counter, the granite cool through the silk on her overheated skin. He spread his legs, planting his feet on either side of hers, before parting the lapels using only the brush of his fingertips. The fabric fell away, revealing her nightgown. He ran his hands over her stomach, to the curve of her waist. "I knew you were hiding something good under all those business suits."

Jesus, his hands were so big, so hot, sliding over the silky fabric as though he had every right, and she did absolutely nothing to stop him. "There's nothing wrong with dressing professionally."

He stroked over the swell of her hips, pausing as he looked at her. "No, there's not. A guy sure as hell couldn't work if he knew you were wearing this."

Her fingers gripped the edge of the counter. She wanted to touch him back, but couldn't yet. "Maybe the men I work with are more focused than you."

"Or more stupid." He tilted her hips and sucked in a breath as her belly brushed the hard ridge of his cock. "I can see your nipples through the lace."

The reminder of how hard they were, how much she wanted to be touched by him, had her biting her lower lip.

He moaned, brushing the under curve of her breast, which seemed to grow heavy as though descending for his touch. "Don't do that."

"Do what?" He was barely touching her, hadn't even kissed her, and she was worked up into a sexual frenzy. Right now, in this moment, he could bend her over the damn counter and shove inside her and she'd probably come in one stroke.

She was that desperate. That mindless.

For a woman who'd always been in complete control, the abandon was as intoxicating as the man himself.

One hand slipped around her waist, while he raised the other to brush against her lips. "That mouth. It's enough to make a grown man weep."

She parted her lips, sucking air into her lungs, as he rubbed the wet flesh with his thumb. "Do you always talk this much?"

He gripped her neck. "I'm holding back about ninety percent of the filthy things I'm thinking."

She wanted to know, and was bold enough to ask. "Like what?"

His eyes flashed, and he rocked his cock against her belly. She wanted it lower, where it could do more good. "Like how I'm going to suck on your nipples through that lace until you moan."

Her breasts tingled in response, as though he'd touched her. She'd never known talking could be this much of a turn-on. Every word he spoke made her hotter. Made her melt a little more. His gaze dipped to her mouth, but he said nothing more.

And she wanted more.

His voice had always stirred a response, but with him talking like this, it was enough to set her on fire. She could listen to him all night. Shameless, she asked, "And?"

His lips curved into a wicked, sinful smile. "Are you trying to get me to talk dirty to you, Ce-ce?"

Yes! Now, do it! But of course she didn't say that; instead she waved a hand. "Just curious, is all."

"Liar." He leaned in close. "Are you wearing panties?"

"No." Her voice breathless.

He slipped a hand down her waist and gripped her leg, raising it to his hip. "Too bad, I would have liked to rip them off you."

"As if I'd let you." He bent his knees and she shifted, the soft worn denim brushed against her clit and she gasped, gripping the counter.

"Let's not pretend," he said, his gaze darkening as he nudged between her thighs. "If a woman ever needed her panties ripped off, it's you."

Her head fell back against the cabinet. *Oh God, yes.* "You're delusional."

He palmed her ass, lifting her. "I want skin to skin. I want to slide my cock over your clit until we're both dying to come and then I want to bend you over that kitchen table and fuck the hell out of you."

Need and lust curled an iron fist inside her belly and wouldn't let go. She was going to come. He'd barely touched her and the orgasm already coiled tight inside her. She released her grip on the counter and wrapped her hand around his neck, unable to take it a second longer.

It seemed to be what he was waiting for because the second she tugged, he pulled her close and his mouth finally claimed hers.

There was no slow start. No soft exploration.

It started fast and turned furious.

Their mouths fused. Tongues met and tangled. Their breath instantly harsh.

She dug her nails into his neck. Fighting. Needing. Desperate to get closer. She plastered herself against his body.

He growled against her. Slanting his mouth to deepen the contact.

It was like no kiss she'd ever had. There was nothing nice or civilized about it.

It was raw.

Dirty.

Not like her at all.

And she loved every minute of it. Was greedy for more.

All at once she wanted sex like he described, sex that held nothing back. Sex where she felt taken and possessed. Like he couldn't get enough of her.

She wanted it from him. Only him.

His tongue stroked hers, his lips hot and possessive.

She needed more. Needed closer. She rubbed her aching breasts against him.

He heard her plea, cupping her breast to rub his thumb over her nipple.

She cried out, the sound lost and muffled against him.

He tore his mouth away, pushed her up on the counter. Her legs wrapped around his waist as he delivered on his promise and his mouth closed over her lace-covered nipple, sucking it deep.

She shuddered against him, moaning. "Jesus."

He rumbled something unintelligible, and laved at the beaded tip with his tongue, rolling the other between his thumb and forefinger.

It was crazy. Better than any fantasy. A visceral chemical reaction.

She wanted it all.

As hot and dirty as he could make it.

All she wanted was more. Much, much more.

She clutched at his neck, pulling him close. "Harder."

He bit her, his teeth sharp and stinging as he squeezed and tugged the other hard peak.

Her head thunked against wood cabinets. "Oh God!"

He did it again, holding longer and harder until need coiled so tight inside her she thought she might break. She wanted to keep quiet but found she couldn't, it was impossible. "You're so . . . so . . . good at that."

He laughed, moving to the other breast and bathing it

with his tongue until the fabric was wet against her skin. Then he raised his head and captured her lips in a brutal kiss.

It was demanding. Arrogant. Possessive.

And so right. So perfect.

She threw away what little reserve she still maintained and abandoned herself to him.

And it was glorious.

His hand went to her thigh. Squeezed, then moved between her legs. He groaned, breaking the kiss long enough to murmur, "So fucking wet."

Pure sensation had her belly dipping and pulling tight.

He stroked her clit. His rhythm a slow tease that made her want to scream.

She bit his lower lip, scraping her teeth against him as her hips rose to meet his hands.

"Please," she whispered, needing more.

"What do you want?"

"You," she said simply.

He groaned, and his knuckles brushed against her aching flesh as he went for his zipper.

Yes, oh yes. It was wild and crazy. Not like her at all, but she just didn't care. She reached for him, desperate to help, because he couldn't move fast enough.

And then the kitchen door flew open and someone flicked on the light.

Chapter Six

Shane blinked against the brightness, rushing back from all that lust and heat. He zipped his half-open fly and covered Cecilia's spectacular thighs, his blood still a heavy rush in his ears. He whipped around, standing in front of her to shield her from the intruder.

An amused James stood there in a rumpled T-shirt and shorts.

Shane's hands curled into fists. Shane wanted to take him out. Right here. Right now.

Behind him, the sound of silk rustled as she slid off the counter.

Shane wanted to punch someone—namely his brother—but he settled for yelling, "What the fuck do you want?"

Cecilia stepped out from behind him, her long, lean body wrapped in her robe. She clutched the lapels closed at her throat, but it didn't do any good. Her hair framed her face in a wild mess of tangles, her lips were swollen and pink, and her cheeks flushed.

James laughed, ending in a fake cough at Cecilia's fierce glare. "Sorry, I didn't mean to interrupt."

"You didn't," Cecilia said, her tone as cool as ever. As

though she hadn't been burning him up a minute ago. "There's nothing to interrupt."

Shane ran a hand through his hair and glowered at his brother. "Would you get the hell out of here?"

"No, no." She skirted away, pulling her robe tighter around her like a shield. "I'm leaving. I need to go to . . . um . . . sleep."

"Sure, sleep," James said, unable to hide his shit-eating grin.

Shane wanted to grab her by the arm and insist she stay put but thought better of it. The moment was gone and he still didn't know what the hell happened. Had he really been about to bend her over the table? He'd only meant to kiss her, tease her a little bit. He'd thought he'd have to coax a response out of her. Damned if that theory hadn't been blown straight to hell.

Jesus. Fucking. Christ.

She smoothed her hair, refusing to look at his brother. "I was, just . . ." She turned toward the door. "Getting a glass of water."

She bumped into the chair, stumbling.

Shane lunged forward, catching her as she swayed on her feet. "Hey, easy."

She yanked away, flushing ten shades of scarlet. "Oops, silly me."

Then she practically ran from the room.

It was the first time he'd ever seen her flustered and he couldn't deny his amusement, or that he wanted to see her that way a hell of a lot more.

The door swung closed and he crossed his arms and glared at his brother. "You are a dead man."

James grinned, holding up his hands in surrender.

"Look, this is not my fault. I mean, hell, when I left you were deep into e-mail. How could I have anticipated this?"

Disgusted, Shane shook his head.

He'd been so close.

If James hadn't interrupted he'd be inside her right now. Even though it would have been all kinds of wrong, he hadn't been thinking about consequences. Shit, he hadn't been thinking about anything other than how spectacular she was under his hands and the lust pounding fast in his blood.

James leaned against the wall. "So, you and Cecilia? That's . . . different."

"I don't want to talk about it." Shane ran a hand through his hair. Truth be told, he was a little flustered himself.

James laughed. "She didn't look too icy from where I stood."

"Would you just shut the hell up?" Shane walked over to his laptop and scooped it from the table. "I'm going to bed."

His brother grinned. "Good luck with that."

"Not one word." Shane's tone was pure steel. The last thing he needed in this house full of people was everyone talking about him and Cecilia. "Or you'll regret it."

"I'm real scared," James said, clearly not intimidated at all.

Shane figured it was only fair to turn the tables. After all he was going to bed with blue balls because of his brother's not-so-timely interruption.

Although sex on the kitchen counter, where anyone could wander in, hadn't been his brightest move. He was lucky it had been James. Who was discreet and wouldn't tell anyone.

Not that Shane didn't intend to make his point, to be on the safe side. "I know a woman with some cupcakes, who could make your life a living hell."

The amusement died a quick, sudden death as James straightened. "I don't know what you mean."

It was Shane's turn to smile. "It means what you walked into isn't the only interesting thing going on here."

James strolled across the kitchen to the cabinet that held the glasses. "Weren't you off to bed?"

"Yep." Point made, Shane went to his room.

Fifteen minutes later he hadn't done anything but stare at his open e-mail. He flipped the cover of his laptop closed, tossed it on the nightstand, and turned off the light.

He was still hard. Still aching. Unable to get the way she'd responded out of his head. How had Cecilia, the most reserved woman on the planet, ended up as one of the most explosive sexual encounters he'd ever had?

And they hadn't even had sex.

He scrubbed a palm over his face. Jesus, he was going to be up all night. He picked up his cell phone and was surprised to find a text message from Cecilia waiting for him. He swiped his thumb across the screen and grinned.

That was a mistake. Let's not mention it again.

Into the darkness, he smirked. She had to know he wasn't going to agree. Which meant she was so flustered she wasn't thinking it through. The normal Cecilia response would be to ignore him completely until he pushed the issue. He typed out, You're mine. It's merely a question of when.

His cock was like granite. He fisted it, hoping to quell the ache but it only made him hotter.

His phone cheeped. It's not going to happen. It was a MISTAKE.

He remembered how much she'd liked it when he'd

talked dirty to her. That little surprise had been the tipping point that made him lose complete control of the situation. The only mistake was being interrupted before I made you come.

A full minute passed, and just when he'd given up, she responded, Please don't talk like that.

In his mind, he read the text as a plea.

Fuck it. He hit the number at the top of the message bar. It rang a half ring before she picked it up and hissed, "What is wrong with you? I'm right down the hall and you're calling me?"

He chuckled. "Fine, I'll come to your room."

"Don't you dare!" she shrilled. "This needs to stop, right now before it goes any further. I apologize for my behavior, I don't know what came over me, but it won't happen again."

Okay then, she was on the move. Which he'd expected and he liked a good chase. "Are you sure about that?"

"Yes!" She sounded sure enough, but he didn't buy it.

Not when it'd been so damn hot. "Just so I'm clear. You don't want me to kiss you again?"

"No." Her tone lost some of its frantic tension.

"Or touch you?" He lowered his voice into something dark and intimate.

A rustle of fabric over the line. "Yes, that's right."

He imagined her lying in bed, staring at the darkened ceiling a few feet away. It would be so easy to go to her. They were both so on edge, one kiss and they'd be back to where they started. But he decided on patience. "Or bite and lick your nipples."

And teasing.

She squeaked, and another noise he couldn't distinguish came over the line. "Exactly. Because it was a mistake."

There wasn't an ounce of conviction in her tone.

"So I shouldn't think about how you'd taste, how your clit would feel under my tongue?"

"I think that would be best," she said, her voice soft and breathless now. "Please stop."

"Maybe that would be easier if I'd felt you come." He was so hard he hurt.

"Not going to happen. Ever."

He stroked his cock. "Are you going to touch yourself?"

She gasped. "That is not the point."

"You didn't say no," he pointed out, tightening his hold on his shaft. "You know what I think?"

"I don't care," she said, her words strained.

"I think you're a liar." He slowed his pace to leisurely. "I think you're squeezing your thighs together right now. I think you're wet and ready and you're not going to have any fucking choice in the matter."

There was a long, long pause where nothing but the sounds of their shallow, too-fast breathing filled the line.

"You're wrong."

He laughed. "Sure, I am."

"You are."

"All right," he said, knowing not arguing with her would infuriate her all the more.

"Thank you!" she snapped, clearly getting agitated again. "Now can we just agree this is a mistake and move on?"

"No," he said simply.

She let out a strangled scream that had him grinning into the darkness.

"Oh, and for the record," he said, his grasp turning tight and demanding so she'd be damn sure to hear he wasn't lying. "I'm going to lie here, stroke my cock, and think of all the things I'm going to do to you. All the ways I'm going to talk dirty to you until you're out of your mind and willing to do whatever I want."

"Stop this." The words needy instead of forceful, the way he was sure she'd intended.

"Not going to happen, babe," he said, his mind already concocting a thousand scenarios.

"I hate you," she said, her voice all liquid heat.

He laughed. "Goodnight, Cecilia."

Cecilia made her way down the stairs and toward the kitchen with her head held high.

Shane would not know what she'd done last night. He had no proof of anything. He'd never know he'd been right about his little late-night phone call.

She'd tried so hard but had been unable to resist.

It wasn't her fault. It was his.

That voice. The way he talked. All the craziness in the kitchen. Knowing what he was doing down the hall.

She'd had no other choice.

She'd made it a whole twenty minutes. The covers pulled up to her chin, she'd recited the order of the presidents in her head, hoping against hope that picturing George Washington or Andrew Jackson would dull the heat between her legs.

When that failed miserably, the rationalizations began.

The whispers that promised he'd never know. He could suspect, but he couldn't prove anything.

She was an expert at masking her expressions. She'd never give herself away.

In the end, she'd caved. Forced to give herself an orgasm—not because she felt like it, or needed the tension relief—but because she'd been so turned on her skin had felt like it was on fire.

Every move she'd made, every press of her thighs, was excruciating. When she'd broken down, it had taken all of thirty seconds. The climax was so explosive she'd had to bite her lip to keep from crying out. It hadn't been enough. She'd come again, ridiculously fast. Then, embarrassingly, again. In the aftermath, as she'd lain panting for breath, damp with sweat, still filled with an unquenchable wanton heat, her first conscious thought had been that he'd know what she'd done. How crazy she'd been. How abandoned.

Even though that was impossible.

Now, in the light of day, she had to face him and reveal nothing. She took a deep breath.

Easy peasy.

She was bound and determined to get this situation under control and her mind back where it belonged—on her campaign.

She'd dressed carefully in a pair of tan cotton slacks and a white three-quarter-sleeve top. No one would think of sex dressed in white and beige. With her hair pulled back in a sleek ponytail and light makeup she could pass for a librarian. Nothing about her carefully constructed appearance would suggest her lascivious actions.

Now she'd get through seeing Shane and pretend nothing ever happened.

Head held high, she walked into a kitchen filled with chaos. The radio was blaring "Let the Good Times Roll." The air was filled with the smell of butter and syrup as Maddie flipped pancakes at her new industrial stove. Mitch grabbed a stack of plates out of the cabinet while her mom sat at the table sipping coffee, flipping through a magazine and tapping her foot to the beat. James read something on an iPad, seeming oblivious to the commotion.

It was a full house.

And there was no Shane.

Cecilia didn't know if she was relieved or wanted to kick something. She'd been all prepared, worked herself up to face him, but instead everyone else in the house was there but him.

Spatula in hand, Maddie swung around. "Morning. Did you sleep well?"

Everyone in the room turned to look at her, and she put a polite smile on her face, willing her cheeks not to heat. "Great."

Mitch handed her a cup of coffee. "Black, right?"

"Yes, thank you," she yelled over the sound of the music.

Maddie lowered the volume to mere background noise.

Awkward in a room full of people who were all comfortable with each other, she said, "Can I do anything to help?"

Maddie took three pancakes off the griddle and then grabbed a pitcher. "Would you mind running over to Gracie's house and getting some of that homemade blueberry syrup she has? I already called her. I have the worst craving for it."

Mitch squinted at her flat belly. "Craving, huh?"

She slapped him on the arm. "Bite your tongue!"

Charlotte glanced from the magazine, a frown on her face. "Please don't tell me you don't want children."

Cecilia blinked, shocked that her mother would ask such a blunt question.

"Mom," Mitch said. "That's not appropriate."

Charlotte raised one brow, managing to look regal. "And is it appropriate to tease an old woman about grandchildren she may never have?"

Irrationally, Cecilia was irritated Charlotte assumed she

didn't want kids. Unfair, considering Cecilia had never given her mother any indication that she was interested in anything but her career, but it still irked her.

She was used to being the good one. And she begrudgingly admitted she was jealous. Petty, yes, but true.

Maddie laughed and waved a hand in the air. "No, we want kids, but not now. We're not even married yet."

"Soon, I hope," Charlotte said, her tone chastising but her expression amused. "Mitchell is thirty-four now."

"I'll knock her up soon enough," Mitch said.

"Don't be so crude," Charlotte said.

"You started it," Mitch pointed out, his voice filled with an easy affection that made Cecilia's stomach tighten.

They were family now. Comfortable with each other in a way lost to her.

The domestic tranquility wore on her already frazzled nerves and, thankful for the escape, she grabbed the small glass pitcher from Maddie. "I'll be happy to get the syrup."

Maddie beamed, her cheeks flushed from the heat of the stove. "Thanks. What are your plans for the day?"

"I'm not sure yet," Cecilia said, knowing she should work on her campaign plans, but the thought made her stomach turn to lead. The idea of sitting in that bedroom, all by herself, poring over her laptop, sounded like one of Dante's seven circles of hell.

Right now, watching paint dry sounded more appealing. Which was odd. Normally she was a workaholic. She'd been looking forward to the free time so she could work on her plans, so why was she resistant?

Maybe because every time she thought about running, her mind became a blank slate. She knew what she needed to do, she'd done it a thousand times before for her father, but when it came to her own vision—nothing.

She shook her head. All she needed was a break. She'd worked almost nonstop for the past couple of months—maybe she'd finally hit a wall.

Yes, that must be it.

Because she definitely wanted to run for office. She needed to pursue her dream.

It was just that the article had upset her more than she'd anticipated. Once she got over that, made peace with the choice she was making, she'd be fine. Her motivation would come roaring back and her vision would become clear.

Maddie nodded. "Your mom and I are going to the outlet mall if you want to come."

The outlet mall? The shock had her forgetting her campaign worries. When had her mother started shopping at outlet malls? "Sure, that sounds like fun."

"We won't be too long," Maddie said. "We have our final fitting at two."

"We know," James said from his spot at the table. "You've told us all a million times."

Cecilia smiled and risked a peek at James.

Their eyes met, and heat rose to her cheeks. She glanced quickly away.

Maddie's head cocked as though scenting something on the air. She stopped and looked back and forth between James and Cecilia, then shrugged.

Cecilia cleared her throat. "Let me get that syrup."

She grabbed the pitcher and walked out of the chaos and down the hallway, the sounds from the kitchen growing distant. When she passed the office, opened up by glass French doors, she heard a laugh.

Her stomach dropped.

Shane sat in the chair, his feet propped on the desk, tossing a mini basketball in the air over and over again. "What's the projected budget?" he asked, and Cecilia realized he was on a conference call.

The phone was in the middle of the desk and his laptop was open, right next to it.

Someone on the line rattled off a number in the millions.

Shane nodded and tossed the ball in the air again. "And phase one? What's the completion date?"

Cecilia should move. Walk away. But she couldn't, she just stood there frozen.

There were noises over the line as people scrambled to get him what he wanted. A woman's voice answered, "End of first quarter."

Shane's eyes narrowed as though in contemplation then peered at his computer screen. He tapped away on the keyboard. Frowned, his forehead creasing. "That's not going to work. You're going to need to rework the budget. Labor alone is going to eat up sixty percent of those numbers. Let's be realistic here."

He rubbed his eyes and glanced over the screen, his gaze catching Cecilia's.

His lips slowly curved into a wicked smile.

Oh. My. God. He knows.

Cursing, she rang Gracie's doorbell. What had she been thinking, running like that? How could she convince him how unaffected she was if she acted like a prepubescent schoolgirl? She took a deep, cleansing breath. Okay, there was nothing she could do about it now. She'd do better next time.

She was a professional who sold composure for a living. Shane Donovan would not best her.

The door opened but instead of Gracie, a blond-haired, blue-eyed, gorgeous man stood there.

He gave her a slow, lazy smile. "Cecilia, you've finally come home."

She blinked. Wow. Little Sam Roberts? Like his sister, he'd turned into a stunner with high cheekbones and a long lanky frame, completely at odds with Gracie's lushness. He wore a pair of faded jeans and a black T-shirt that said *make yourself useful and get me a beer,* which made Cecilia smile. "Sam, it's been a long time."

He waved an arm, gesturing her into the entryway. "We've been waiting for you."

She frowned. "You have?"

"Yes," he said. "Maddie's happy to have you here. She's looking forward to getting to know you better."

"Oh," she said stupidly, not knowing what else to say. "How have you been all these years?"

"Good, how about yourself?" Sam led them down a hallway almost identical to next door. "Still working for your dad?"

"Yes, I am." For now. The thought made her think of her campaign. Maybe she needed to skip shopping and buckle down. It was the smart thing to do. What she'd always done. Immerse herself in work and forget everything else. Including Shane.

If she got to work, he'd stop distracting her and she'd stop with all these wayward emotions that were getting in the way of her end goal.

She huffed out a breath.

After breakfast she'd explain to Maddie that she couldn't go to the outlet mall, and head straight to her room.

"And how's he doing?" Sam asked, breaking her from her tumbling thoughts.

"Fine, thank you." She cleared her throat. "I was sorry to hear about your mom. She was a lovely woman."

About ten years ago their mom had been stricken with breast cancer and died shortly after. She'd been a single mother, and losing their only parent had to be a blow.

Sam looked back at her, his gaze somehow intent and knowing. "Thanks, we miss her."

They walked into the kitchen. A bright, airy place with white cabinets, buttercup-yellow walls, and an industrial-size stove. Gracie stood at her counter, standing over a commercial-grade mixer and frowning. She looked up, her downturned lips easing into a smile. "Hey, Ce-ce. How'd you sleep?"

Awesome, now that she thought about it. In fact, she was better rested than she'd been in the last year. Not all that surprising considering she'd taken a four-hour nap, had multiple orgasms, and slept later than she had since college. "Great, thank you." She held out the pitcher. "Maddie wanted some syrup."

Sam glanced at the clock. "I need to get to the bar and get some paperwork done."

Cecilia nodded. "I forgot you work with Mitch."

Sam shrugged. "He doesn't work there anymore."

That's right. After a scandal had derailed Mitch's career in Chicago he hadn't practiced for years, but had recently returned to work as a lawyer in the county prosecutor's office.

Cecilia frowned. "I guess I'd forgotten that too."

Suddenly, it felt wrong to be so disconnected from her family. Another thing she could blame on the Donovans. If they weren't so close, she wouldn't notice.

"You girls have yourselves a good day." Sam turned to

leave, pausing with his hand on the back door and turning back. "Don't work too hard."

Cecilia frowned, somehow getting the impression that his words had been meant for her. Which was silly. She handed the pitcher to Gracie.

Gracie wiped her hands on her apron and went to the fridge. "I made it this morning, she just needs to heat it up." She grabbed the glass container and filled it to the brim before handing it back.

The smell wafted up and filled her senses. So heavenly her head swam and her mouth watered. "This smells divine."

Gracie beamed at her. "Oh good. After yesterday and with you being so thin, I thought you might be one of those women who doesn't eat."

Cecilia placed a hand on her stomach, practically concave now, making her realize she hadn't eaten in almost twenty-four hours. "I eat. Things have been a bit hectic lately and sometimes I forget."

Gracie put her hands on her hips, her lip curled in scorn as she shook her head. "I'm so jealous of women like you."

"Of me?" she said, shocked. How could Gracie be jealous of her? "I can assure you there's nothing to be jealous of."

Gracie laughed. "There could be a bomb going off and I'd never forget to eat. As you can tell by the unfortunate size of my hips."

There wasn't one unfortunate thing about Gracie's body.

"We should all be so unlucky," Cecilia said in a wry tone before tilting her head in the direction of her brother's house. "You should come for breakfast."

"I'd love to, but I've got a million things to do, orders to fill, deliveries to make." She grinned. "And let's not forget our fitting at two."

Cecilia laughed, really laughed, and her heart lightened considerably. She glanced at the mixing bowl and an impulse took hold of her. This was work. A couple more hours of avoidance wouldn't hurt. "Do you want some help?"

Gracie's blue eyes widened as though surprised. "Are you serious? Don't you have a bunch of more important things to do?"

She thought of her laptop sitting in its leather case. The phone messages she hadn't checked and e-mails she hadn't returned. "Nope."

"Don't you want to relax?"

She shook her head, not understanding what had come over her, but knowing it was true. "No, I want to bake."

Chapter Seven

After finishing his conference call, Shane walked into the kitchen, his stomach rumbling from the smell of his sister's pancakes cooking on the griddle. The whole lot of them were already at the table.

Including Cecilia. She must have snuck in through the back door, because he'd watched the front like a hawk. She gave him a prim smile before taking a dainty bite of pancake. Well, wasn't she back in control? And wouldn't he have to do something about that.

"Morning," he said, moving to the counter to refill his coffee.

There were two spots open to him—one across from Cecilia and one next to her. He decided on across. There were too many people to do anything interesting sitting next to her, and he wanted to see her face.

He sat down and grabbed a big pile of pancakes. "How'd everyone sleep last night?"

There was a murmur of *good*s.

He locked in on Cecilia. "And how about you?"

Those eyes of hers flashed with hints of gray. "Like a baby."

"Really now?" Shane leaned back in his chair and rubbed

his jaw. "I'd have thought you'd have trouble, being in a strange place and all."

"But this isn't a strange place," she said, her voice oh-so-light and unaffected. He'd have bought it too, if she didn't have a death grip on her fork. "I've been sleeping in that room since I was six. Right, Mitch?"

Mitch put his elbows on the table, peering at his sister like she might sprout another head, before nodding slowly. "Right."

"See," she said, waving her hand. "I'm more at home than you are."

Shane grinned. Well, good for her, diverting attention. He stretched out his legs under the table, and when he hit her foot she jerked back. Of course, she displayed no signs of this to the outside world. "But still, *something* must have happened to make you sleep so soundly."

A faint flush rose to her cheeks and her shoulders squared. "Just fresh air, I'm sure."

Liar.

James started to chuckle. When she scowled, the chuckle faded into a crooked grin. He picked up his orange juice and toasted her. "I know fresh air always helps me sleep too."

Shane laughed, and Cecilia shot him one of those you're-a-dead-man glares that never failed to turn him on.

Maddie looked back and forth between James, Shane, and Cecilia. "What's going on?"

Cecilia straightened and fiddled with her napkin on her lap. "Nothing. Where's Mom?"

"Upstairs," Mitch said, his voice curious. "Yeah, what is going on?"

James shook his head. "I have no idea what you're talking about."

Maddie and Mitch turned to Shane. He shrugged. "I asked the woman how she slept. I was being polite."

"Ha!" Cecilia said, then frowned as though surprised she'd spoken.

When Mitch and Maddie turned their attention on her, she twisted a thin gold chain around her neck. "Sorry, I . . ." She glanced around the table. "I swallowed a bite of pancake wrong."

Mitch's expression was pure speculation as he stabbed a pancake covered in syrup with his fork. "Is that so?"

"Yes," Cecilia said, giving him that direct, level-eyed stare of hers. "What else could it be?"

He chewed slowly then swallowed. "I don't know—but it's something."

Cecilia smiled, bright and cheerful. "Everything is wonderful." Then she turned to Maddie. "I can't believe what you've done to this place. It's gorgeous."

Maddie tilted her head to the side, her green eyes still filled with curiosity. "Thank you."

"You did a great job updating while still maintaining the architecture and charm of the original house."

Yep, complete diversion.

Shane ate and watched as she asked Maddie various questions about the renovations and pretty much pretended he didn't exist.

James stood and grabbed his plate and cup. "If you'll excuse me, I have work to do."

Shane asked, "Off for another run?"

"In a bit," James said, walking over to the sink. "You can come, but I'm doing twelve miles again."

"You're a sick, sick man," Shane said.

Hands now free, James pointed at their sister. "Maybe you should stick with Maddie. She's more your speed."

"Asshole," Shane called after him as he left the room without a backward glance, before turning back to the table. He shook his head at his sister. "He's like a fucking machine."

Maddie nodded, her brow creasing. "I know, it's not healthy."

Shane pondered his brother's iron control. As a child he'd been nothing like that. It wasn't until their father died that he'd changed. "Was I that hard on him growing up?"

The question clearly caught Cecilia's attention because he could practically see her ears perk up as she leaned forward.

Maddie tapped her fingers on the table and let out a big, exasperated sigh. "No, you were great. Would you stop that?"

"Stop what?"

"Stop worrying that you messed us all up," Maddie said, her voice quiet, the corners of her mouth pinched. Mitch slipped a hand under her hair and rubbed her neck as though sensing her distress, making Shane wonder if they'd discussed the topic before.

He stiffened and glanced at Cecilia, who didn't try to pretend she wasn't listening. He changed the subject.

"What's on the agenda, baby sister?" He held up his hands. "Besides the fitting."

Maddie studied him for too long before she finally said, "Charlotte, Cecilia, and I are going shopping."

"On that note." Mitch got up and stroked a hand over Maddie's flame-red hair. "I've got to get to the office."

Maddie smiled that big, gooey smile at him. "What time will you be home?"

He tucked a stray lock around her ear. "By six." He leaned down and brushed a kiss over her lips. "Have fun at your fitting, princess, and try not to drive everyone crazy."

Maddie laughed and curled her hand around his neck to pull him close again. "What fun would that be?"

He kissed her again, just a peck, nothing at all inappropriate, but the look they exchanged was so deeply intimate Shane had to glance away.

Cecilia stared down at her plate of half-eaten pancakes, her shoulders stiff.

"Don't spend too much money," Mitch said, and left.

"Don't hold your breath," Maddie called after him. She turned back to the table and said to Cecilia, "We're going to leave in about thirty minutes. Does that work for you?"

Cecilia shifted in her chair, then smoothed down her sleek ponytail. "Oh, about that. I hope you don't mind if I don't go."

His sister's face fell. "Sure, no problem."

Cecilia shook her head. "No wait, it's not that I don't want to, I do. But I went over to Gracie's and she sounded so swamped." Her perfect mouth curved into a frown. "And, well, I offered to help."

An interesting turn of events Shane hadn't expected.

Maddie's eyes widened, apparently as surprised as he was. "How sweet. I'm sure she'll appreciate it."

Cecilia tilted her head, her blue-gray eyes still clouded. "Can I take a rain check on shopping? Because I *would* like to go."

Maddie patted her hand. "Of course, I'd like that."

Cecilia's tight expression eased. "Me too."

Shane saw an opportunity and took it. "It's settled then."

"What is?" Maddie asked.

"Since you cooked, it's only fair Cecilia and I do the dishes. That way you can go get ready."

Cecilia blinked, opened her mouth then shut it again.

Maddie threw down her napkin and bounded from the chair. "I never turn down a chance to get out of cleaning."

Cecilia's hand clenched on her butter knife, and Shane wondered if she contemplated throwing it.

All innocence, he smiled at her. "I'm sure even a rich girl like you can do the dishes."

* * *

That jerk!

Cecilia gritted her teeth as Maddie left the kitchen like she was on fire.

He'd manipulated the situation. He knew perfectly well she couldn't object without looking like an insolent house-guest. She cataloged all the ways she could maim him with a butter knife—the list longer than she'd have thought.

She glared at him.

He looked so smug.

She threw her napkin down on the table. "You are the most despicable man on the planet."

He laughed. "I'd never have figured you for a drama queen."

"I am not. A drama queen," she hissed, leaning across the table. "You tricked me into being alone with you."

"Of course I did."

She let out a tiny scream. Ugh! She hated this about him. He wasn't supposed to be forthcoming. It was so irritating. "You don't even have the audacity to deny it!"

He shrugged one shoulder, highlighted to perfection in a black T-shirt that stretched over his chest and biceps in a way that should be considered illegal. "Nope."

"Nope?! That's it?" She sliced a hand through the air. "Just nope?"

"What would you like me to say?" he asked, his attitude so mild and calm she wanted to throttle him. He was enjoying himself way too much.

Somewhere in the back of her mind, rational thought still prevailed, urging her to slow down. With a deep inhale she sat back. He wanted to rattle her. He baited her on purpose. If she didn't give him what he wanted, he'd stop.

She steeled her spine and smoothed her expression over.

"Nothing." She stood. "We'd better get to work. Gracie is expecting me."

She grabbed a handful of dishes and carried them over to the sink.

"That reminds me, why are you helping Gracie?" he asked in that amused tone of his.

She forced herself to gently place the plates in the sink instead of throwing them at his head. "That's none of your business." Pleased she sounded like her normal, unruffled self.

She studied the faucet. A new stainless steel number with a high arch that looked sleek and expensive. She frowned. There wasn't a handle.

"So you're going to play it that way, are you?"

How in the hell did you turn this thing on? "I'm not playing it any way. What I do or don't do is none of your concern."

The chair scraped and a second later he was behind her. She could feel the heat of his body. She held her breath as he reached around her, standing way too close. Lungs burning, she sucked in air.

Detached. Cool. All the things she was so good at. She just needed to ignore him until he stopped.

Those long, strong fingers of his brushed over the faucet's arch and the water went on. "It's activated by touch, rich girl."

He didn't move away.

She closed her eyes against the spike of desire, raw and hot, that burned brighter every time they were in the same room together. She clenched the edge of the sink. "You know, you're way richer than I am."

He placed his hands on either side of her and she was once again trapped.

"I know." His voice low and seductive. "But I didn't grow up privileged."

"Does it matter?" Trying to remember to breathe.

"Yes. You have a different way of looking at things."

Needing something to do, she touched the faucet and it changed streams, then she touched it again and it went off. *Do not lean back.* "Another mark against me."

"That just shows what you know." He leaned in close, his breath warm on the shell of her ear. "Did you come for me last night?"

She started like she'd been jolted with electric shocks.

He did not know. He did not know. He did not know. In her best haughty tone, she said, "Don't be so arrogant."

He laughed, and to her extreme disappointment moved away.

A clatter of dishes sounded behind her. She opened the dishwasher and flicked on the faucet, rinsing away the sticky syrup before she put the plates in the machine.

The best thing for her to do was stay silent. Clean the kitchen then go on about her day. But she couldn't, she was too curious about him. Since he had no problem butting into her business she decided that turnabout was fair play. "How'd you do it? Build your company from scratch?"

The noise of the dishes went silent for a moment before the clanging resumed. "I didn't have a choice in the matter. Isn't it all in that file of mine you have?"

She didn't bother denying the file or the extent of the research she'd done. They'd already confirmed that yesterday. "It has the mechanics, but not the how. I know what you did. How you started working for your uncle, then went out on your own before branching out into the commercial side of the business. But I don't know how."

He put the dishes down, turned, and propped his back against the counter so he faced her. "Why do you want to know?"

That was the million-dollar question, now wasn't it? If

she wanted to keep him at arm's length, asking him to tell her his story wouldn't accomplish that. But the truth was, she had wondered about it for months, had thought about it late at night. She'd like to believe she needed to understand because it might help her with her own battle.

But really, she wanted to understand him. How he'd overcome such impossible odds.

Their gazes locked, and she found herself giving him the truth instead of an evasion. "I'm curious about you. It's remarkable. What you've accomplished—that kind of drive and perseverance—it boggles my mind."

He crossed his arms over his wide chest. "You probably have more drive and perseverance than I do."

She thought about her own overachiever tendencies. The constant drive for perfection that had run through her veins for as long as she had memories. But her drive had never been about her. It had been about her need for approval. She had plenty of accomplishments but wasn't accomplished. She'd always worked hard to be the best, but only at the things in which her father wanted her to excel. Her own desires had never factored into the equation.

It struck her then like a slap in the face.

For the first time she was trying to do something for herself. To accomplish a lifelong goal and she was *failing*. Worse, she couldn't even force herself to get started.

What was wrong with her?

Once again she thought of her abandoned laptop and all the research she could be doing to transform into the perfect political candidate. She was so good at it. It was one of her talents. She'd even helped her father's colleagues on more than one occasion.

So what was she so reluctant about?

Maybe she was still recovering from knowledge of what

she had to do to accomplish her dream. And that there was no way around it. She'd been perfectly fine with her decision, and whom she needed to climb into bed with, until she'd shown up in Revival.

Although maybe that was coincidence; after all, the press release happened on the same day.

She frowned. Had it been only yesterday? It felt like a lifetime ago. All this thinking was making her head hurt when all she wanted to do was go bake with Gracie.

It was the only thing that seemed clear to her at the moment, so that's what she was going to do.

She glanced up from the sink, realizing too late that Shane was studying her. What had they been talking about? Oh yes, drive and perseverance, and his belief that she had any. She shook her head. "You don't know anything about me."

He crossed his arms. "I know you graduated with a near perfect grade point average. I know you're well respected in the political community." He gave her a sardonic grin. "Even though you're on the wrong side."

The teasing tone brought surprised laughter to her lips, and she was happy for the diversion from her future. "My side is the only sane, rational one out there."

"Clearly somebody's been watching too much news." He grinned, scooting closer to her. "Don't drink the Kool-Aid, Ce-ce."

She put her hands on her hips. "Um, excuse me, but the only one crazy here is you."

He ran a finger down her arm and goose bumps broke out over her skin. "Before we get into a big political debate, tell me: Did you pick the party because that's what you believe, or because that's what the senator is?"

At the mention of her father some of her enjoyment dimmed. "I'm my own woman."

Those green eyes of his met hers. "Are you?"

The question was a direct hit and she jerked away, turning back to the dishes. "Yes."

He grabbed her wrist and the sponge fell from her grasp. "I'm sorry."

She shrugged. He'd touched a nerve she had no intention of talking about, so she shifted the topic back to him. "You didn't answer my question."

He released his hold and crossed his arms. "Hell, I'm not sure I know."

She flicked off the faucet again and dried her hands on a dish towel. "What do you mean, you don't know?"

He dragged a hand through his hair. "It wasn't a plan. I barely graduated high school. For the most part I was a fuck-up, but when my dad died . . ." His jaw hardened and a muscle jumped in his cheek. "When he died, everything was a mess. My mom was a wreck. Maddie was on the verge of death. My dad had a pile of bills. Maybe those would have been manageable, but the insurance ran out. There was the cost of the funeral. Hospital bills that just kept coming. Catholic school tuition. The list went on and on. James and Evan were school; what could they do? Somebody had to pick up the pieces and make sure we didn't lose the little that we had left." He shrugged as if it was no big deal. "I just did what had to be done."

She closed the dishwasher and looked at him. "I think that's bullshit."

His head jerked. "Excuse me?"

"It's bullshit, although I believe that's what you tell yourself."

"What in the hell do you know about it?" His voice raised several decibels.

The gruffness didn't scare her. "People don't build multimillion-dollar companies by chance. And they sure as hell don't just"—she made air quotes—"happen."

He dragged a hand through his hair again. "It's not bullshit, that's how it started."

"And?"

He peered at her with those intense, catlike eyes of his. "It's not all that exciting, but if you want to know, you have to give me something in return."

"What's that?" Excitement played tug-of-war with trepidation.

He gave her a slow, sinful smile and trepidation won as her belly dropped. "Tell me if you came last night."

A hot flush crawled unbidden up her neck. She turned to the counter and wiped down a water spot. "On that note, I should be getting to Gracie's."

"Chicken."

Absolutely.

Chapter Eight

Two hours later she stood over one of Gracie's industrial-size mixers and frowned. "Are you sure you want me to do this?"

Gracie planted her hands on her apron-covered hips. "Did you or did you not help your grandma make the best oatmeal raisin cookies in the world?"

"I was six!" Cecilia said indignantly. Somehow, over the past several hours, they'd fallen into the pattern established in their youth when they'd been summer best friends: affection mixed with antagonism.

She'd forgotten. How wonderful Gracie was. How fun and real. And now, standing in her kitchen, she missed it and wished she could go back and make sure their friendship didn't drift away.

Gracie dismissed her with a wave. "It's like riding a bike."

"We weren't selling those cookies," Cecilia insisted, holding a recipe card in her hand that seemed more daunting than the Declaration of Independence. "You're making this for a customer. What if I screw it up?"

Gracie threw her hands up in the air. "Well, obviously my whole business will die a miserable death." She clucked her tongue. "Duh, get over yourself. It's pound cake for the school bake sale. I'm not asking you to create a four-tier wedding cake with sculptures made out of modeling chocolate and fondant."

"But—"

Gracie shot up a hand. "You're throwing stuff in a bowl, mixing it up and pouring the batter into loaf pans. It's not rocket science."

Why had Cecilia thought this was a good idea? She could be shopping at an outlet mall! She chewed her bottom lip and glanced nervously at the recipe card again. "Don't you have any more non-baking stuff for me to do?"

"No, you cruised through all that like you were the Energizer Bunny." Gracie scowled at her, but her cornflower-blue eyes sparkled. "Did anyone tell you that you're annoyingly organized and efficient?"

Cecilia huffed. "Yes, but they're normally more appreciative."

The blond woman pointed to the mixer. "The pound cake."

"I'm sure there's something else. Do you need help with your books?"

Gracie laughed. "Maybe tomorrow, but today I need to make pound cakes. If you do that, I can focus on my cupcakes for little Lucy Tompkins's birthday party. You don't want her to go without treats, do you?"

"No. But Gracie, you don't understand, my stove still has the sticker on."

"You'll be fine. I'm sure you're exaggerating."

"No, I'm not. I never cook. Like ever."

"How do you eat?" Gracie asked, momentarily distracted from their argument.

"I live in Chicago. I can get takeout twenty-four hours a day," Cecilia said.

Gracie wrinkled her nose. "That's disgusting. I hate you."

"What did I do now?"

"How can you be so thin and eat takeout all the time? I'd be six hundred pounds."

Okay, that was the third time Gracie had made a comment about her weight. Something was going on here. Gracie was a confident woman and her body was drool-worthy, albeit more voluptuous than today's standards. But still, the other woman had to know men practically fainted at the sight of her. So why was she having an issue? Cecilia said cautiously, "I have a high metabolism. And, well, between you and me, I've been having a rough time lately and it's affected my appetite."

She blinked. Now why had she gone and confessed that? She was notoriously tight-lipped. Back in Chicago she hadn't admitted to anyone she was having a bad time. She didn't trust any of them enough to tell them.

Wasn't that sad? That the only people she called friends she didn't trust? Last week she'd had lunch with Stephanie Williams, a woman she'd known since first grade, and she hadn't hinted at her troubles. Worse, it hadn't even occurred to her.

Shouldn't she have one person in this world to call a true friend? One person she could confess her secrets to?

Her mom knew what she had to do in order to help secure her candidacy, but she didn't approve. It would be nice if she had a girlfriend like Gracie who'd tell her she was crazy.

She squared her shoulders. What was happening to her? Why was she suddenly concerned with things she'd never cared about before? She didn't care about confidants. Or how her mom liked Maddie better than her. Never thought about how she wasn't close to her brother.

So why now?

Gracie tilted her head to the side. "Is that why you're ignoring your phone?"

Her cell had rung numerous times over the course of the morning, and when Gracie asked if she needed to get the call she'd breezily said no and ignored it. There were only three types of calls she received: something needed to be fixed, her father wanted to hound her about her mother, or Miles Fletcher wanted to discuss strategy for their impending arrangement.

All of which she wanted to ignore. She contemplated diverting but instead decided to answer honestly. "Yeah, that's why."

The corners of Gracie's mouth dipped. "Do you want to talk about it?"

Yes! The word screamed through her but Cecilia stuffed it back down. Gracie might have been a dear childhood friend, but she was a virtual stranger now. She couldn't pour out the truth, but she could lighten some of the burden she carried inside. Gracie was safe. "It's just . . . I don't know. Everything is messed up right now. I'm being pulled in a lot of directions and it's like I can't hear myself think."

Gracie nodded. "I'm sorry."

Now that the dam had broken, Cecilia couldn't seem to shut up. She crossed her arms and hugged herself tight. "I got in a fight with my father. Which is silly, because I'm a grown woman, but"—she bit the inside of her cheek—"I care. I don't want to, but I do. And there's . . . other things . . ."

Pure panic zinged through her as she thought about the article that, thankfully, nobody in Revival had read. It was only a matter of time before someone found out.

Before Shane found out. And then there'd be hell to pay. He would hate her. That much was certain. She wasn't ready for him to hate her again.

Even though she knew it was inevitable.

She should tell the truth. She was being selfish. And wrong. But still, she avoided it. If she didn't speak of it she could pretend it wasn't real. She needed to pretend.

She cleared her throat. "Things that would take all day to talk about and we have work to do."

Gracie sighed, walked over to her and gave her a big hug.

The gesture startled her. It had been a long time since anyone had shown her any kind of affection. Well, if she didn't count her entirely uncharacteristic behavior with Shane last night. But that hadn't been affection. That had been sex. Chemistry and heat.

Her eyes teared and she squeezed the other woman back. "Thank you. I must have needed that."

Gracie stood back and smiled. "You're not the hard-ass you pretend to be, are you?"

"Today, I guess I'm not."

Gracie checked the clock. "Are you going to make those pound cakes or not?"

Cecilia skimmed down the recipe card, more complicated than the original version that called for a pound of each ingredient. She'd graduated at the top of her class. She could do this. "Okay."

Gracie beamed. "Fantastic! And tonight, after our fittings with the bride from hell, we're going out."

"We are?"

"Yep, we're going to Big Red's, home of the two-step and drinks the size of your head." Gracie rubbed her palms together in glee. "You and I are going to get drunk."

But she didn't get drunk. She was the designated driver.

As quickly as the rejection materialized, she dismissed it. Why not? Didn't she deserve a break? She grabbed a sack of flour. "Deal."

* * *

Cecilia bounded through the back door, yanking Shane away from his last e-mail.

Wasn't this his lucky day. She was the first one home.

They were alone. And damned if he wasn't going to take full advantage.

Might as well, since he hadn't gotten jack shit done.

He had a serious case of lust that would not quit.

About an hour ago, he'd moved from the office to the kitchen so she'd have less chance to evade him. He wanted another taste of her and wasn't in the mood to be dissuaded.

"What are you doing here?" she asked with her customary demanding tone.

She looked considerably more rumpled than when she'd left. Her top and pants were dusted with flour. Caramel-colored strands had fallen from her neat ponytail to hang haphazardly around her face. Her cheeks were flushed and she'd lost that gaunt, haunted look she'd been sporting.

He scrubbed a hand over his jaw. "I figured you'd try to sneak in through the back way, so I set up shop here."

"I was not sneaking!" She planted her hands on her hips. "Why are you waiting for me?"

One of the things he liked best about her was that he could tell her the flat-out truth. There was no sugarcoating with Cecilia. With most women he'd always been careful to not get too assertive or bossy. He didn't have that problem with Cecilia. He could be as bold as he wanted and she just took it in stride. He gave her a slow once-over. "Because we're in a houseful of people that's getting fuller by the minute, and I have to take my opportunities to get you alone when I can."

Her chin tilted with a hint of defiance, but he could swear he detected the tiniest hint of a smile on that lush mouth of hers. "Being alone is not a good idea."

"I think it's a very good idea."

"Don't you think this is getting a little out of control?"

"Hell yes," he said, standing and eating up the floor to get to her.

Her eyes widened and she sucked in a breath. "Shane."

He curled a hand around her neck. "I'm not in the mood to play."

"Wait," she said, putting her hands on his chest, but instead of pushing him away she curled her fingers into the cotton.

It was all the invitation he needed. He covered her mouth with his before she could say another word.

All the lust that had been pounding through him all day roared to the surface, making him more than a little demanding. More than a little possessive.

But for all Cecilia's reserve, she didn't seem to have any fear, and met the brutal press of his mouth with a fierceness that surprised him.

He gripped the curve of her hips, pulling her close.

She groaned into him, twining her hands around his neck and rising onto tiptoes to plaster herself against his body.

She was tall, at least five-eight to his six-four, and damned if she didn't fit his body like she was made for him.

He slanted his mouth deeper, twining his tongue with hers. A low rumble vibrated in his throat as she pressed her breasts against him.

It was too damn fast.

Too damn much.

But hell if he cared. He just fucking wanted her.

He lifted her leg, hooking it around his waist, then rocked his hard cock between her thighs, sucking in a deep breath when her hips tilted to meet his.

She smelled delicious, like sugar and vanilla, and he wanted to devour her.

The kiss went on and on.

Wetter.

Hotter.

Wild.

Desire stampeded through his blood until he could think of nothing but stripping her naked and pounding into her.

Her nails dug into the back of his neck. Demanding more.

She was like him that way. Greedy.

He tore away and skimmed his lips down her delicate throat, loving how she moaned under his tongue. How her pulse was a furious beat against his mouth.

He had the unbearable urge to mark her. Stake his claim. The need to possess her drove him hard. Like a primal, demanding need. He bit her, sinking his teeth into her soft, pale flesh.

She cried out, tilting and twisting against his erection.

He palmed her breasts, rubbing his thumbs over her peaked nipples. Frustrated, he let out a growl. He wanted skin to skin. He slipped his hands under her T-shirt, skimming over her flat belly up to her satin-covered breasts. He whispered in her ear, "Upstairs. Now."

She lifted her head, her eyes dazed. "Shane. We can't—"

He met her gaze. "Yes, Cecilia."

"But—"

He kissed her again and she melted into him until she practically climbed up him in an effort to get closer.

Breathless, he lifted his head. "I need to see you come. It's all I can think about and it's distracting as hell."

Those big storm-blue eyes peered at him. "I'm distracting?"

"Fuck yes." He gripped her chin. "It's going to happen sooner or later, and it can be later if that's what you need—but I have to make you come. Right now. And I'd prefer to be somewhere we're not interrupted. Like my bed."

She took a deep breath. "Why?"

Because he needed to mark her. Claim her. Make her orgasm so hard, every climax she had without him paled in comparison. A mad rush of illogical, irrational thoughts. He settled on the least confusing of the bunch. "I want to see you lose control. I want to know it was by my hands. I want to see what you look like."

Her brow furrowed. "That's a lot of pressure to perform."

He kissed her. A hard brush of his mouth. "Trust me, you're not going to be doing anything but begging."

Her eyes flashed but he didn't miss the quick intake of breath. "I never beg."

He lowered his gaze to her lips then raised it to meet her direct gaze. "Challenge accepted."

She blinked, the dazed expression clearing as rational thought prevailed.

All he needed to do was take her in his arms and all the raw chemistry between them would take over, but he didn't want that. As much as he wanted her, she had to choose him. He stepped back. "So what's it going to be, Cecilia? You coming with me or not? Yes or no."

Her lips quirked and she tilted her head to the side. "Did anyone ever tell you that you're bossy and arrogant?"

"Yep," he said, tone matter-of-fact. "Your call. Yes or no?"

He waited, honestly not sure what she'd say or do, and he liked that about her too.

She was a surprise.

"I shouldn't," she said, her tongue darting out to wet her lower lip.

"Why? We're adults."

"I have my reasons." Her eyes flashed, like a storm cloud lit with lightning before she shifted her attention. "We should stop this."

Something that resembled vague unease niggled in the

corner of his brain, but he pushed it aside. He wasn't in the mood to analyze. He was in the mood to act. And as far as he was concerned she hadn't said no yet. "Yes or no?"

She assessed him, carefully looking him over. There was no flirt in her gaze, no seduction in her movement, just a slow, steady appraisal.

He never got his answer.

The door swung open and a gaggle of women flew in.

Cecilia straightened, crossing her arms over her chest.

Shane wanted to put his fist through the wall as Maddie, her two best friends, and Charlotte filled the kitchen.

Maddie smiled at them, her hands full of shopping bags she plopped on the kitchen table. "Look who I found outside."

Cecilia stealthily took three steps to her right, distancing them. Other than her swollen mouth, all traces of passion had disappeared like a mirage.

He gritted his teeth. "Soph, Penelope. Good trip?"

"Hey, Shane," Sophie said, waving at him.

Penelope, neat and orderly as ever, with her brown hair pulled into a clip and her serious black-framed glasses perched on her nose, nodded at him. She was a godsend to him and held the key to his business life, but right now he wanted to fire her on general principle. Only, as usual, she'd done nothing wrong, so he didn't have a good excuse. But he gave it a good college try and barked, "Did you get those spreadsheets to the mayor's office before you left?"

She huffed. "Nice greeting. And clearly you haven't been reading your e-mail or you'd have seen I got them off."

Of course she did. Sometimes her efficiency really pissed him off. Especially when he hadn't had sex in three months and Cecilia was giving him a serious case of blue balls.

Maddie glared at him. "Stop that, she's on vacation."

Shane shrugged. "Well, it sucks for her that she's stuck on vacation with her boss, doesn't it?"

Penelope flicked a dismissive glance over him. "Boundaries, Shane, remember your boundaries."

Sophie, a cute little blonde with a wild, rebellious streak that had always gotten his sister into trouble, grinned at him. "We need help with the bags."

Shane ground his teeth.

So. Fucking. Close.

Maddie hung her purse on the hook next to the back door and smiled at Cecilia. "Did you have a good day with Gracie?"

He watched the reserve roll over her—the straightening of her spine, the squaring of her shoulders, the way her expression smoothed out.

"It was quite lovely," Cecilia said, her tone once again polite instead of the husky rasp from minutes ago. She nodded at his sister's friends. "Penelope and Sophie, it's a pleasure to see you again."

Penelope smiled. "You too, and congratulations on your big news."

Cecilia gasped, shock and horror flashing over her face.

Shane's gut tightened.

Charlotte walked over to Cecilia and her arm lifted as though to comfort her, but then she stopped and pressed two fingers over her lips.

Shane recognized the feeling—the suspension when everything hung in the air as he waited for the rug to be pulled from under him. The unmistakable moment of dread when the inevitable couldn't be stopped.

Maddie frowned. "What news?"

Penelope's mouth etched in confusion. "You didn't tell them?"

Cecilia blinked and clenched her hands. "No, not yet."

"Tell us what?" Maddie asked.

Cecilia looked at him. Her eyes seemed pleading for a fraction of a second before shuttering closed. She turned away.

A bone-deep chill.

She tilted her chin, her posture taking on the look of royalty. "I'm getting married."

Chapter Nine

Dread constricted Cecilia's throat as her skin turned cold and clammy. She couldn't even look at Shane. Couldn't stand what she'd see on his face.

All that heat, gone.

She missed it already.

Shell-shocked, all she could do was stand there, frozen and stiff as Maddie squealed and threw her arms around her. "Why didn't you tell us?"

Cecilia patted the smaller woman on the back. "I didn't want to take away any of your thunder."

Over Maddie's head, she glanced at her mother, who was frowning, her amber eyes filled with dark shadows.

Cecilia swallowed the emotions that wanted to rise to the surface.

This house, this place, and Shane, made it so easy to pretend. To hope.

She steeled her spine and pulled away. Time to return to reality. To her real life. Her future.

Maddie still held Cecilia by the arms. "I can't believe this, I didn't even know you were dating anyone."

She hadn't been. It was a modern-day arranged marriage

meant to improve her political position. "We've kept it very quiet." Their standard PR line.

Maddie dropped her hands and searched her face, her brow creased. "But we're your family."

A coldness washed over her skin and she wrapped her arms around herself to ward off the chill. "His name is Miles Fletcher."

"I assume he's coming to the wedding," Maddie said, and Cecilia's heart beat fast from sheer horror.

"Um," Cecilia said, her mind blank. She could feel Shane's gaze on her back. Sense his anger beating at her. More than anything she wanted to turn to him and explain, but she couldn't do that. "I'm not sure that's possible."

Maddie's head tilted to the side. "Invite him for the weekend so we can get to know him."

Cecilia forced a smile to her lips. "Maybe after the wedding when things have calmed down."

Above all else, Shane was a man who appreciated honor. He'd never forgive her. Never understand why she had to do this.

She didn't even like Miles Fletcher. Well, in fairness, she didn't dislike him either. He served a purpose. He was a wealthy businessman with political inroads and the right party connections. With his old money and connections Miles would influence the good old boys who wouldn't support her without a proper husband.

Her father had arranged it and nobody denied his logic. She needed a husband. Miles agreed to the arrangement. The terms had been drawn. Problem solved. That's business.

When she'd agreed, she hadn't believed she was losing anything important. She'd never wanted to get married. Never wanted to risk it. She'd spent too many years watching her mom lose to the senator's true love—his career. As a young child she'd vowed never to love a man like that.

And she'd kept her vow.

Only, since the article had been released and she'd come to Revival, she'd been plagued by doubts. Doubts she couldn't give voice to because to do so would give them even more power.

Maddie's attention shifted to Penelope. "How did you find out?"

Penelope, who possessed a kind of sensibleness Cecilia could appreciate, said, "It was in the paper yesterday. Don't you guys read?"

Maddie shrugged. "I don't get the paper."

"Let me get this straight," Shane said, finally breaking his silence.

She cringed, bracing herself for what was to come. Her stomach felt as if it fell to the floor. She wasn't ready.

He grabbed her elbow and spun her around.

For the first time in her life she was struck with the desire to run, but it was too late.

All four of the other women's faces opened wide in surprise. Someone gasped.

With narrowed eyes, she tilted her head toward the all-too-interested audience. "Shane."

"Forget them." His green eyes were filled with a kind of cold fury that told her in no uncertain terms that he would never, ever forgive her. "You're fucking engaged?"

"Yes." The word like broken glass on her tongue.

His grip tightened. "To Miles Fletcher? That asshole old enough to be your father?"

Not quite, but Cecilia didn't correct him, nor was she surprised Shane knew him. Miles owned an energy company; it made sense their paths had crossed. She nodded. There was no denying the truth now. "Yes."

His jaw hardened and his eyes turned to chips of ice.

It shook her. She'd gotten used to his warmth. The strength of his arms. The way he looked at her.

She'd lost something after all. Already the price felt too high. Which was crazy. How well did she even know him?

Penelope cleared her throat and looked at the other women. "Maybe we should . . . go."

Maddie looked back and forth between Cecilia and Shane. "What's going on here?"

Cecilia stared at the floor, Shane's fingers a vise around her elbow.

"Leave." Shane's tone broached no argument and sounded so deadly Cecilia wanted to scurry along after them.

The younger women filed out of the kitchen, the swinging door flapping behind them, but her mom stayed firmly in place. Full of questions, Charlotte's gaze met hers.

Cecilia nodded, signaling she'd be okay.

Charlotte opened her mouth, then shut it, and left.

When the door swung shut, Shane yanked her elbow. "Explain yourself."

Oh, how she wanted to, but that wasn't possible. "What do you want me to say?"

"Did it ever occur to you, at any point when I touched you, to mention that you were getting married, Cecilia?"

The truth was, no, it hadn't. Miles Fletcher and their arrangement hadn't crossed her mind, because she had no connection or loyalty to him. But that was impossible to explain. It was better this way. She shook her head. "I'm sorry."

"You're sorry!" he yelled, his voice loud enough to shake the rafters. "What kind of woman are you?"

She let her mask slide over her expression and met his gaze, unflinching. "I should have told you."

"That's it?" He dropped her elbow fast, as though she'd burned him. "That's all you have to say for yourself?"

She swallowed hard, blinking as her eyes pricked with tears. Why was it so hard with him? To stay cool and distant when it had been so easy in the past. "I don't know what else I'm supposed to say."

He looked at her for a long, long time and every second that passed his eyes grew colder. A muscle in his jaw worked as he said through gritted teeth, "I should have stuck to my first fucking instinct about you."

She nodded but said nothing.

He turned and walked out of the house, slamming the door behind him.

It was better he hate her. Better in the long run.

He'd continue to believe she was an ice-cold bitch, and she'd go back to being one.

The problem of what to do about Shane Donovan had been solved.

Shane threw his car keys down on the bar and said to Sam Roberts, "Give me a double scotch, neat."

One brow rose up Sam's forehead. "Tough day?"

Shane's gaze narrowed. "Just get me the fucking drink."

"Guess so," Sam drawled lazily, then moved down the bar, grabbing a rocks glass on the way.

Shane dragged a hand through his hair. The bar was dark and nearly deserted, matching his mood and furious thoughts.

He could not believe she was getting married. He wanted to hate her. The anger and rage burned hot inside him, but he couldn't latch on to the hate.

And he needed it.

It was the only way he could get through the next two weeks.

Something in her eyes had reached inside and grabbed ahold of him. They'd been filled with—fuck, he didn't know—despair? Loss? She'd looked hurt. Like she was the wronged party. When he'd watched her struggle to pull herself together he'd had to leave, because instead of the appropriate fury, he'd wanted to gather her up and protect her.

Which made no fucking sense.

He gritted his teeth. She was getting married. There was nothing left to say about the matter. She didn't need his protection. Hell, she didn't need anything from him.

It was over. Period. The end.

Only . . .

Sam returned, thankfully interrupting his thoughts. He set the glass down and free poured a healthy dose of scotch. Shane squinted at the bottle, an eighteen-year-old single malt. Shane pointed to it. "Is there a big demand for hundred-dollar bottles of scotch in Revival?"

Sam set the bottle down on the counter. "It's good to keep on hand for those times you need a little something extra."

Shane grabbed the glass. Yep, this was one of those times. He gulped it down in three swallows, not appreciating it the way he should, but grateful nonetheless. He slid the glass across the bar. "Hit me."

Sam poured another two fingers and Shane downed it. "Again."

Sam swiped up his keys. "If you want another, I'm going to have to take these."

"Fine by me." Shane pushed the glass forward.

The alcohol was already rushing to his head and he hoped like hell it would knock some sense into him.

Sam filled the glass a third of the way. This time Shane didn't gulp but took a measured sip, savoring the taste like he should. "This is damn good."

Sam nodded and tucked Shane's keys into his pocket.

Needing a distraction, he looked around the drab, dingy bar. "You haven't made many changes." The place was still as run-down as the first time he'd come here to claim his runaway sister and found her in the back room doing things he still had nightmares about.

Sam looked around, rubbing a hand over his stubbled jaw. "I'm still trying to figure out what I want to do with it."

"Sell it?" Shane offered. The bar needed a lot of work before it was a place anyone besides alcoholics and manic-depressives would step foot in.

Sam laughed, not insulted in the least. "I like fixing things and I only just bought it from Mitch a couple months ago. Now that it's mine, I can figure it out."

Shane took another drink, letting the alcohol burn down his throat. "Well, when you decide, let me know, I'll send you guys."

Sam grinned. "See, the single malt is paying off already."

Shane laughed. Surprised he could with the anger burning hot in his gut.

And what really pissed him off was he was angry about the wrong goddamn thing. All his anger should be focused on Cecilia, where it belonged, but instead he was furious the women hadn't shown up an hour later.

After he'd had Cecilia.

Because he sure as hell couldn't touch her now that he knew. His fingers tightened on the glass, his grip way too tight.

"Wanna talk about it?" Sam asked. He picked up a rag and ran it under the faucet before wiping at a spot on the bar.

"Nope." Shane downed the rest of the drink.

This time Sam refilled without asking. "You're going to be shit-faced at this rate."

"That's the plan." His head was already fuzzy.

The other lone patron put his bottle of beer on the bar and stood. "Later, Sam."

Sam waved to the guy. "Later, Dave."

A brief beam of sun fell on the open room, blinding Shane for a moment before the door closed. He rubbed his eyes. "You should start with some windows; this place is enough to turn you into a vampire. Besides, it's depressing as hell to sit in the dark all the time."

Sam nodded. "Where would you put them?"

Shane swung around and surveyed the place. The windows were too small and high to let in any real light. "Start by lengthening the existing one and then add windows on the side. He pointed at the empty dead space. "You should put a pool table there. Give people something to do besides drink."

Sam continued to lazily wipe down the bar. "Sounds like a good place to start."

Shane fell silent, shifting his attention to the Cubs game. "God, they suck."

"Yeah, they do."

"Never been a baseball fan," he said, his words getting a bit slurry. "Too boring."

Sam nodded. "Want me to turn on HGTV?"

Shane jerked his head toward Sam, his eyes narrowing. How did Sam know his dirty little secret? So he liked to watch do-it-yourself home shows. Big deal. But how did Sam know? He asked in overly careful, measured tones, "What did you say?"

Sam shrugged. "Just a suggestion."

Shane took another drink and decided to pass it off as a coincidence.

Sam put his hands on the bar. "Wanna talk about it now?"

"What could have changed from a few minutes ago?" Although, he had to admit his tongue felt a lot looser.

"A couple more ounces of scotch," Sam said.

It reminded Shane of his drink. He took another sip. The numbness crept through his body.

Sam moved down the bar, tossing the lone beer bottle in the recycling bin before coming back to stand in front of Shane. He didn't say anything, but expectation hung in the air and finally Shane blurted, "I fucked around with Cecilia."

Shane expected some sort of surprise but other than a grin, Sam's expression didn't change. "And this is a bad thing?"

"She's getting married."

Sam scratched his chin. "I guess that would put a damper on things."

That was an understatement. He frowned into his drink. "Worse, I found out when Penny congratulated her on her engagement. It was in the damn paper."

Sam tossed the towel over his shoulder. "That's odd."

Shane's head was equivalent to a big ball of cotton, his brain too muddled to figure out what Sam meant, so he settled on an astute, "Huh?"

Sam poured more scotch. "What woman gets engaged and doesn't say anything to anyone?"

"Cecilia, that's who." He took another slug he definitely didn't need, but drank anyway. "She's such a tight-ass."

Sam's lips quirked. "Not so tight-assed she couldn't get under your skin."

Shane's mind filled with how she kissed. Like she was starving for him. "I don't want to talk about it."

"All right," Sam said, leaning back against the bar and turning his attention to the Cubs game.

Shane tried to focus on the game too, but now that he started he couldn't seem to shut the hell up. "She's not even wearing an engagement ring."

"Hmmm," Sam said. "Maybe the guy didn't give her one."

Shane grit his teeth. "She's marrying Miles Fletcher. Believe me, he gave her one." Just the thought of that complete asshole made Shane want to punch something.

"I don't know the name."

"Old Chicago money. Slick as hell. I had to play golf with him once. He's the kind of guy who miscounts his strokes." Shane pointed at Sam. "Never trust anyone who cheats at golf."

Sam chuckled. "I don't play golf."

"Well, if you do," Shane said, his words sticking to the roof of his mouth like he'd eaten too much peanut butter, "remember that."

"Who are you going to want me to call, in case you pass out? Mitch or Charlie?"

Shane took another swallow, which went down like water. He couldn't stand the thought of going back to the house. Officially drunk, he didn't trust himself with Cecilia so damn close. And he sure as hell didn't want to explain to all the nosy women why he gave a shit if Cecilia got married or not.

If only he could reverse time and go back twenty-four hours and keep his hands to himself. Then he wouldn't have any idea how good it was between them. How hot. He shook his head, trying to clear away the memories, but it didn't work. How had it been only a day? She felt imprinted on him somehow. Or maybe that was the booze talking? "Can I pass out in the back?"

"Sure," Sam said.

Shane downed the rest of his drink and his vision went blurry. Yep, he was shit-faced. "That last bit wasn't a good idea."

"Probably not."

"You wouldn't know it to look at her, but she's not all that straitlaced."

Sam grinned. "Doesn't surprise me at all."

Shane experienced an unwelcome, and entirely inappropriate, stab of possession. "What do you mean by that?"

Sam held up his hands. "Chill out. I never touched her."

"You better not have." Shane's drunken brain didn't care that he didn't have any right to make the claim.

Sam shook his head and rolled his eyes. "When Mitch and Cecilia used to visit their grandparents in the summer, Cecilia would always show up in this little grown-up dress, hair all neat and tidy, and her shoes polished."

The vision was one Gracie had already painted in his mind. Shane nodded. "Yeah, that sounds like her."

"But as summer wore on, she'd get a tiny bit messier every day. Until one day, her hair was full of tangles, her feet were bare, her knee skinned. By the end of summer there was never any sign of that miniature adult who'd shown up. She was a wild child just like the rest of us."

When Gracie had said something similar he hadn't been able to picture it, but now he found he had no problem. He'd seen it. Those flashes of abandon. Hell, he'd felt the wildness under his mouth and hands. "I wonder who's the real girl."

"Why don't you find out?"

Jesus, he wanted to. "Because she's getting married."

Sam shrugged as if it was no big deal. "I'm sure you

didn't get where you are by letting a little obstacle stand in your way."

No, he hadn't. He bulldozed right over anything that stood in his way. The room swayed as he slid off the stool. "I've got to pass out now."

Sam jerked his thumb toward the hallway. "You know where it is."

He started walking—well, weaving—down the narrow corridor. "It's hardly a little obstacle."

"Time will tell," Sam said.

It was the last thing Shane remembered.

Cecilia lay in bed staring up at the ceiling, unable to sleep.

The rest of the day had been a disaster.

At the notorious fitting, Maddie had been a vision of loveliness in white silk that skimmed over her small frame and somehow managed to make her look tall despite her petite stature. Her best friends had cried, fawning all over her, and Cecilia had stood back, ignoring the pang of jealousy she had no right to feel.

The women had done some not-so-subtle prying about the scene between Shane and her, but she'd been stubbornly tight-lipped and they'd finally given up. When the girls had traipsed over to Gracie's house, full of happiness and joy, Cecilia had made her excuses. Gracie had cajoled, and Maddie had given her that disappointed frown she had, but Cecilia insisted she had work to do.

She wanted to join them but couldn't stand pretending she was one of them.

So, she'd made herself the outsider.

It was this house, these people, casting a spell on her. Making her want things that didn't matter to her in her regular life.

After she'd returned to the house, desperate to be alone, she'd had a run-in with her mother. Charlotte's words had haunted her for the rest of the night.

"You're fooling yourself. In the end, you'll lose more than you can imagine. If you go through with this sham of a marriage, one day you're going to realize what's really important. And I promise you'll regret it. It isn't right."

"How do you know it isn't right?" Cecilia had asked, her throat tight and achy.

Charlotte looked at her with mournful amber eyes. *"Because if it was, you'd be happier."*

When Gracie called about their plans to go to Big Red's, Cecilia had pleaded a headache nobody believed and spent the night in her bedroom.

She glanced at the nightstand where her cell phone lay abandoned. There were fifteen missed calls, seven voice mails and a hundred and twenty-seven unanswered e-mails.

None of them were from Shane.

She'd tried to work. Had even opened a Word document to start the first stages of crafting a message, but instead stared at the blank page for an hour before giving up.

She couldn't think of anything she wanted to say. Everything her father had said to her the other day was correct. She had no vision.

All those years of dreaming and she'd forgotten the most important thing: passion.

She hadn't felt passion for anything in a long time. That was, until Shane had kissed her.

Restless, she shifted in bed, the covers tangled around her legs.

She was exhausted, but sleep wouldn't claim her.

Instead, she waited. Listened for Shane's car pulling into the driveway. The fall of his boots on the stairs.

But he never returned.

Chapter Ten

The next morning Shane's head pounded like a jack-hammer and it was making his brain bleed.

He pressed his thumbs into his eye sockets and prayed for death. He felt every one of his thirty-five years.

Every muscle ached.

He had a kink in his neck.

A pain in his hip.

Someone was doing dropkicks at one-minute intervals in his stomach.

He was officially too damn old to sleep on a Dumpster couch.

And Cecilia was still marrying another man.

He glanced at the kitchen clock. He had a conference call with the mayor's office in fifteen minutes that promised to be hell on earth.

Then he could die a slow death in a halfway decent bed.

A cup of coffee was set down in front of Shane and he peered into his sister's concerned face.

"Rough night?" she asked, brow creased with worry.

"Don't talk so loud." Grateful, he wrapped a hand around the mug.

"If Sam hadn't called and told us you were safe, I would have been worried sick." She slid into the chair across from him looking like sunshine in a yellow halter top, her red hair in a ponytail and her cheeks a pretty pink. Ugh. She was too bright and healthy.

He glared at her. "Okay, Mom."

"So," Maddie said, propping her elbows on the table. "What exactly happened yesterday?"

"Nothing," he said, the word a snarl. "Back. Off."

Mitch walked in, wearing a charcoal-gray suit.

"Control your woman," Shane said with a growl.

Mitch cocked a brow. "Good morning to you, too."

"Fuck off."

Mitch grinned.

That's one thing Shane appreciated about his soon-to-be brother-in-law; they spoke the same language.

Mitch poured himself a cup of coffee and leaned back against the counter, taking a sip before he said, "I should so give you shit right now."

The statement confirmed that everyone in this godfor-saken house knew something was going on between him and Cecilia. Correction: had gone on. She was off-limits now. "What are you complaining about? I took it easy on you." He'd barely given Mitch a hard time about Maddie.

Maddie scoffed.

Shane shot her a menacing glare. "If I remember cor-rectly, he tried to choke me and I didn't even kick his ass."

Mitch shrugged. "Your sister's honor was at stake. I had good reason. What's your excuse?"

Shane shook his head and immediately regretted it as his brain beat at his skull. He didn't have an excuse. He'd wanted her and had intended to have her.

Penelope walked in, followed by Sophie, and Shane wished he had a gun to put him out of his misery.

Penelope took one look at him and clucked her tongue. "Oh dear," she said like she was an eighty-year-old woman. "Maddie, do you have some Advil?"

Maddie jumped up and ran out of the room while Sophie flopped, way too loudly, into the chair next to him. A minute later, Penelope put a glass of orange juice in front of him. "Drink it."

Shane looked up at her. "You're fired."

She patted his cheek. "You couldn't last five minutes without me." She pointed to the glass. "Drink."

Shane did what he was told because when Penelope ordered, people obeyed. He downed the whole glass in three gulps, and felt marginally fresher, but still not remotely human.

Sophie jabbed him in the shoulder, making his temples throb.

"What the fuck, Soph?" he yelled. There were too many women here. They were going to drive him crazy.

"Damn, Shane, how much did you drink last night?" Sophie asked, ignoring his surly behavior. "I haven't seen you this hungover since the Blackhawks won the Stanley Cup."

"Why are you screaming?" he asked, her voice like nails on a chalkboard.

Maddie came back in and handed him three pills. Right behind her, Penelope placed a glass of water on the table. "Take them, and I'll make you some toast."

The three of them clucked around him like mother hens and Shane said to Mitch, "Just fucking shoot me."

Mitch raised his coffee cup in a toast. "Cheers."

Five minutes later, when he didn't think he could take another second of their yammering, Penelope put two pieces of toast in front of him. "Eat. And hurry, we've got the call with the mayor's office in five."

Shane groaned. "Can't we reschedule?"

Penelope shook her head. "No."

Shane glared at her. "Who's the boss here?"

Penelope smiled sweetly. "Do you really want me to answer that?"

He ate his toast and thought about all the different ways he'd torture her, before letting her drag him away for an hour of hell with the mayor's office.

Cecilia cautiously knocked on Gracie's door, looking over her shoulder to irrationally check if anyone had seen her sneak out of the house.

Yes, she'd taken the coward's way out.

That hadn't been her intention. She'd been about to go into the kitchen and confront this thing with Shane head-on, but then she'd overheard them. Shane had been an absolute bear. He'd grumbled and barked and generally made himself impossible, but they'd all clustered around him.

They loved him. Respected him. Cared enough to make sure he'd eaten breakfast.

The loneliness crushed her.

Surrounded by people, she was alone. The people in her life didn't care if she was okay. Nobody inquired after her well-being. Hell, she'd relented and checked her voice mails this morning, but no one had even asked how she was. No, they all just wanted something from her. The advisers wanted her to check out a rumor floating around the Internet. Paul, from the communications team, wanted her advice on how to handle a tricky PR situation. The senator wanted her to talk sense into her mom. Miles wanted her to pose for some corporate thing on the thirtieth.

She didn't blame them. It was her fault. After all, she was cold. She didn't invite connection, so why should it disappoint her?

But it did.

So she'd slunk over to Gracie's in hopes of a refuge she didn't deserve. Through the glass, she saw her childhood friend walking down the hallway and Cecilia smoothed down her T-shirt.

The younger woman opened the door and smiled, her blue eyes warm with welcome.

Cecilia's throat tightened unexpectedly and she cleared it, but when she spoke her voice quavered. "Can I help you again today?"

She needed to be wrapped up in Gracie's cozy, lemon-cream-pie kitchen.

She braced herself for the no, half expecting Gracie to slam the door in her face.

Instead, her lips curved down and she stood back, hand on the door handle to let her in. "That bad, huh?"

And to Cecilia's shock, she burst into tears, right there on Gracie's doorstep in broad daylight.

Gracie, God bless her, didn't bat an eye. She wrapped an arm around Cecilia's shoulder and ushered her inside, murmuring, "There, there."

Cecilia wiped frantically at her eyes, more embarrassed than she'd ever been in her whole life. She sniffed. "I'm so sorry. This is humiliating."

"Don't be ridiculous." Gracie pushed her toward the kitchen and plopped her down on one of the chairs at her large farmhouse table.

More tears slid down her cheeks. "I haven't cried since I was fifteen."

"Well, that's just crazy." Gracie moved around her kitchen, making all sorts of noises. "Why ever not?"

"I don't know why," Cecilia said, although that wasn't true.

Never show weakness. Never break.

But damned if she wasn't broken now.

The thought made the hysterics start anew and Cecilia covered her face with her hands and wept in earnest. Now that she'd started, she couldn't seem to stop and she crossed her arms and buried her head and just let the tears fall.

Gracie smoothed a hand over her hair, making all sorts of nurturing noises that salved Cecilia's aching heart.

When she finally got herself under control, Gracie put a plate with one pink glittery cupcake in front of her. "Have a cupcake."

"I don't want to interrupt. I just want to help, okay?" Cecilia said, her voice pleading.

"Hey." Gracie sat down next to her. "Of course you can help, but first we talk. You're working on a cry eighteen years in the making, so make it a good one."

Watery-eyed, Cecilia looked at the other woman, more grateful than Gracie could ever possibly know. "You're a good woman, Gracie Roberts. You're just like your mama."

Gracie squeezed her hand. "I'm not even half as awesome as she was."

That wasn't true. "Do you have her chocolate chip cookie recipe?"

"Of course!" Gracie smiled and patted her clenched fists. "You wanna make them?"

Cecilia could still taste the melted gooey chocolate on

her tongue, even though it had been far too many years to count. "I'd love to."

Gracie pointed to the cupcake. "First eat and tell me what's wrong."

Cecilia picked up the cupcake and took a bite. Sugar, vanilla, and something she couldn't discern, but was unbelievably delicious, exploded in her mouth. When she swallowed she looked at Gracie, amazed. "I was wrong. You're better than your mom."

Gracie laughed. "You think that because you've given up eating and forgot how good things taste."

"I eat," Cecilia said properly before taking a very improper bite.

"I bet you eat salads with grilled chicken and nonfat dressing."

Cecilia wrinkled her nose and stuck out her tongue, her chest lightening considerably.

"You do!"

Yeah, she did. Every day for lunch. The. Exact. Same. Salad. She frowned. How depressing.

She sniffed and put the cupcake down. "Everybody hates me."

"I don't think that's true," Gracie said. "They don't know you. And I've got to be honest, you don't scream 'approachable.'"

"I know. I just feel . . . alone." The tears filled her eyes again. "It doesn't make any sense. I never minded being alone before."

Gracie tapped on her plate as though reminding Cecilia to eat and she dutifully complied. "You're not a happy bride."

The pastry turned to lead in her mouth and she had to force the bite down. "It's complicated."

She wanted to confide but didn't. Couldn't.

In her many years in politics she'd learned a very valuable lesson—always withhold information, even from those you trust. People talk and, sometimes innocently, give up valuable information without meaning to.

Gracie nodded. "But you're not going to tell me why?"

"I'm sorry, I can't." That statement alone was telling enough to be dangerous and Cecilia couldn't understand why she wasn't being more guarded.

Maybe for the same reason she'd cried.

"All right," Gracie said, holding up her hands. "I won't pry."

"Thank you." Cecilia finished the rest of the treat and wished for another.

Gracie read her mind. She got up and went to the counter, returning with the whole plate. "So, if you don't want to talk about your wedding, do you want to talk about Shane instead?"

Her cheeks warmed and she grabbed another cupcake, throwing caution to the wind. "Does everyone know?"

Gracie grinned. "Duh! Of course they do. It's the hottest topic of conversation since Maddie showed up at the bar in her wedding dress. The speculation is killing everyone. Well, not quite everyone. Professor Tight-Ass is as close-mouthed as ever."

That wasn't a surprise—James had no reason to speculate; he'd seen the evidence in detail. Cecilia nodded slowly. "Professor Tight-Ass, huh? He kind of reminds me of Indiana Jones."

Gracie stared at her for a full thirty seconds before shaking her head. "Back to Shane."

All Cecilia's amusement deflated like a hot air balloon.

"There's nothing to speculate about. Nothing is going on between Shane and me."

Not anymore.

He'd only touched her a few times. How could she miss it? An involuntary shiver raced through her as she remembered how he'd talked. She'd never hear such dirty things again. She swallowed.

Gracie's lips broke out into a huge grin and she leaned over conspiratorially. "Come on now, fess up. How is he?"

Temptation ate away at Cecilia's reserve. She wanted so badly to confess. "I didn't have sex with him."

"You did something. It's written all over you. Now tell me," Gracie said slyly. "I must know, because I'm sorry, that man is so hot he must fuck like the devil."

Cecilia coughed, choking on the frosting she'd licked off her finger. Then surprised laughter bubbled out. "I'm sorry to disappoint you, but I don't know." Curiosity got the better of her, and before she could stop the words she blurted, "You should have found out yourself."

Gracie waved a hand. "It's not like that with us. He's gorgeous and sexy and he's fun to flirt with, but we have no heat."

Cecilia picked up a napkin and dabbed at the corners of her mouth. "I don't know about that. You seem completely compatible to me." Three days ago she'd never have probed, but now she couldn't stop. Gracie had always made her forget about being polite.

"We are," Gracie said, her smile turning sly. "But you know that tension you have whenever you're in the same room with him? That pull?"

Cecilia kept her eyes wide-open, hoping to pass for innocent.

Gracie shook her head. "It's so obvious, Ce-ce."

"It is?"

"It about smacked me in the face that day you first showed up. Come on, admit it."

"All right," Cecilia said, trying to sound breezy. "I'm familiar with the tension to which you are referring."

Gracie chuckled. "Well, aren't you a blabbermouth?"

A smile quivered at Cecilia's lips.

Gracie gave a big sigh and continued. "Shane and I, in the same room, are easy and comfortable. If I slept with him it'd be Charlie all over again."

"You were with Charlie?" Cecilia slipped another cupcake onto her plate then helped herself to a glass of milk.

Charlie Radcliff had been her brother's best friend since he'd moved in with his aunt across the street when they were teenagers. Cecilia hadn't seen him in ages. Back in high school he'd been tall, dark, and very mysterious, and had driven all the girls crazy. "He was the quintessential bad boy when we were growing up. I didn't know you were together."

"Yeah, we were, kind of." Gracie ran a hand through her wayward mess of blond curls. "It's a long story."

"Tell me," Cecilia said, anxious to think about something other than her own problems.

"I wasn't in the market for a relationship. I was getting my business off the ground and barely had time to think. Men were the furthest thing from my mind. But then Charlie showed up." She grinned, tucking a lock of hair behind her ear. "And you've seen him?"

Not for a long time, but Cecilia got the gist. "Indeed."

"We kind of just fell into it. He liked sex. I liked sex. He didn't want commitment. I didn't want commitment. It was a match made in friends-with-benefits heaven. And it worked, for a very long time. Until one day I realized I'd stopped looking for anything else and he'd become a habit.

I started to feel . . ." Gracie trailed off, her brow furrowing as she seemed to search for the right word.

"Stuck," Cecilia finished for her.

"Yeah, stuck. And after Mitch and Maddie got together . . . Well, I'm ecstatic for them and she's the best thing that ever happened to your brother, but the way they are together—" She shrugged. "Well, you know."

A longing she kept trying to ignore whispered through her. "I know."

"I started to wonder if maybe there wasn't more to life than cupcakes and good sex." She leaned forward and glanced around the kitchen as though someone might be eavesdropping. "I want someone to look at me that way."

"I understand," Cecilia said, her voice soft. Was that what she wanted too? Was that why she was so restless and out of sorts?

She didn't know anymore. Before she'd come back to Revival her life had been perfectly clear and mapped out. She'd known exactly where she was going and what she needed to do to get there. She'd never questioned what she wanted. She'd had the same end goal—to run for office—since she was six.

Now, nothing was clear. And every time she started to examine that life map, she tucked it away instead and ignored it.

"And you know the really sad thing," Gracie said, picking up a cupcake and peeling the paper off. "Ending it was no big deal. We slipped right back into friendship as though we'd never given each other orgasms at all."

Cecilia's brow furrowed. "That's a bad thing?"

"Well, yeah, it is when you spent two years with the person. Shouldn't there be even a little drama? A sense of loss?"

"Good point. I hadn't thought of it that way."

"I love him, he's one of my best friends, but I wish I hadn't spent so much time just settling."

"But you made the change, and that's what's important."

Gracie tilted her head to the side. "You know, you're good to talk to."

Cecilia blinked at the compliment, completely taken aback. "I am?"

"I didn't even know that stuff was weighing me down." Gracie narrowed those clear sky-blue eyes of hers. "But don't think I didn't notice we need to talk about you and Shane."

Her stomach dropped like a lead weight. "There is no Shane and me."

"So that's why he was so angry he drank half a bottle of scotch and passed out cold?" Gracie shrugged. "Makes perfect sense."

Cecilia weighed the consequences, deciding confessions about Shane weren't the same thing as revealing her true relationship with Miles. Unable to resist, she peered over her shoulder to make sure nobody was listening. When she was sure the coast was clear, she leaned closer to Gracie and whispered, "He kissed me a few times."

Gracie scowled. "That's it?"

"Well, maybe a little more." But not enough to satisfy her.

"How was it?" Gracie's eyes danced. "He looks good."

Cecilia flushed just thinking about all the heat between them, simmering like a pot about to boil. "It was awesome. I don't even know what came over me."

Gracie slapped her hand on the table. "I knew it! Just how dirty is he?"

Cecilia laughed. This was so inappropriate, so unlike her, but Gracie had caught her up in the excitement and now she couldn't stop. "He's quite a . . ." She searched for the right word and finally settled on, "Talker."

Gracie sighed, a deep, long sound. "God, I miss dirty sex."

"Do you?" Cecilia straightened and took a sip of milk. "I'm not sure I've ever had dirty sex."

"Well, Ce-ce, let me tell you, it's a must, especially with a man like Shane Donovan. Trust me on this."

Cecilia frowned, all the cupcakes she'd eaten turning to a lump of coal in her belly.

She'd never get the chance now.

Chapter Eleven

The day had turned to shit.

Shane's eyes were gritty from lack of sleep. Everything that could go wrong had. Instead of passed out in bed, he'd been on the phone constantly. As his mom always said, there was no rest for the wicked, and damned if that wasn't the truth.

The newly appointed head of city planning was making this deal as difficult as possible. He didn't like Shane after some mishap Shane couldn't even remember.

The guy was a prick. And today he didn't have the patience.

Shane shook his head and said to Penelope, "Why did George have to have a heart attack?" He'd been doing contracts with the former planner for years without any problems, but this new guy had a real hard-on to screw him over.

Penelope, who'd been by his side, laptop at the ready, pushed her glasses up her nose. "Too much bacon?"

Frustration, mixed with the alcohol he'd consumed last night, was like battery acid in his gut. "Do you think he's going to pull the deal?"

A slice of panic, old and familiar, cut through him. If the guy pulled the contract, Shane would be forced to do layoffs. The city was 30 percent of his revenue. He wouldn't be able to reallocate the staff with that kind of loss.

Those people depended on him to feed their families.

Penny pressed her lips together. "I think he's going to try. But your relationship with the mayor is strong. We're honest. We deliver on budget and on schedule. Every time. He'll need a good excuse and won't be able to find one."

"Let's schedule time with the mayor to cover our bases."

Penelope nodded, jotting a note into her computer.

The phone trilled, causing the dull ache in his head to throb like a drum against his skull. Thankfully it was the house phone, and not his cell signaling another disaster, and he relaxed fractionally.

Penny patted him on the shoulder. "Let me get you more Advil."

"Thanks, Pen," Shane said, appreciating her fiercely. As always, she made his life better with her ruthless efficiency.

Thank God he'd had the good sense to listen the day shortly after Penelope had graduated from college, when she'd ambushed him in his office and convinced him he couldn't live without her. As Maddie's best friend, he'd grown up with her and been resistant as hell, but she'd talked him into it and he'd never once regretted it.

Today, with one problem after another, and him dull-witted from his hangover, she'd been on top of everything, pulling up e-mails, spreadsheets, and fact documents like a quick draw the second he needed them.

Bleary-eyed, he looked at her. "Remind me to give you a raise."

She laughed. "I'm going to take you up on that before your hangover recedes and you're back to telling me I'm a pain in your ass."

Just as Penelope turned to leave, Maddie entered the office. He raised a brow. "What's up?"

THE WINNER TAKES IT ALL 135

"Are you going to let her go for the rest of the afternoon?"

"Be nice, he's had a rough day," Penelope called as she went off in search of his much-needed pain relief.

Maddie pointed to the desk phone. "It's for you."

Shane frowned. "Who is it?"

"Gracie." Maddie propped herself on the door frame, making it clear she planned to listen.

He put his hand on the receiver and jutted his chin toward the hall. "Would you get the hell out of here?"

"Jeez, you're in a bad mood." Her tone irritating in that way only little sisters had. With a swish she waltzed out of the room, leaving him blissfully alone.

He picked up the phone. "Hey, Gracie, what's up?"

"I'm going to be nosy," Gracie said with no preamble. "I know it's none of my business, but I don't care. I'm butting in."

Any last remnants of Advil wore off in a whoosh. *For fuck's sake, now what?* He dragged a hand through his hair. "What's wrong?"

He didn't need any more bad news right now. He could barely think, let alone clean up any messes.

"It's Cecilia," Gracie said.

"What happened? Is she all right?" Jesus Christ, he couldn't handle it if something happened to her.

"No no, she's fine," she said in a rush before pausing for a few beats. "So it's true."

"Focus, Gracie." The words like bullets.

"You've actually got it bad for her, don't you?"

No. Sure, he lusted after her, but he'd lusted after women before, and would again. Yes, he was furious and doubted his ability to be in the same room with her without ringing her neck or fucking her into oblivion, but that was because he felt like a fool. She'd made him believe she wasn't an ice queen, that she burned hot just for him.

But he didn't have it bad for her.

He'd get over this strange fixation and things would go back to the way they'd been before he'd been forced to live in the same house with her. He clenched his hands into fists.

Except, she'd have a husband with her.

The thought was like an uppercut to the jaw, sending off another round of pounding in his head. "Gracie, would you get to the point?"

There was a long silence over the line. "Okay, but you have to promise me you won't ask me any questions."

"Fine."

"I shouldn't be telling you this."

"I said okay." She was working on his last nerve.

There was shuffling over the phone. "Because Cecilia opened up to me, you know, like back when we were kids."

"What. Happened?" Slow, measured, I'm-at-the-edge-of-my-patience words.

"Do you promise not to say anything?"

"Jesus. What do you want me to do? Pinky swear? Cross my heart and hope to die?"

"You don't have to get snippy about it," Gracie said, indignation ripe in her tone. "I'm doing you a favor."

God save him from this bunch of crazy women.

He took a deep breath and exhaled slowly, regaining control of a perilously frayed temper. "I'm sorry. I promise I won't say anything. Now, will you please tell me?"

"Okay," she said, her voice dropping down to a whisper. "Cecilia cried."

His chest gave a hard squeeze. "What do you mean, she cried?"

"She said she hadn't cried since she was a teenager, but she sat in my kitchen, crying her heart out. Over you."

That helpless feeling washed over him in a cold sweat. What was he supposed to say? Or do? "How do you know it was over me? Did she say that?" He couldn't imagine her making that kind of confession.

"Not exactly, but believe me, she was upset about you."

Shane wanted to punch something. Why did he feel bad about this? She was the one who failed to mention she was marrying another guy. Never once did she bring it up when he'd had his hands and mouth all over her. He shouldn't care that she was upset.

But he did.

He pushed out, through gritted teeth, "You're assuming. It probably has nothing to do with me."

"Don't be an idiot. It was because of you."

He forced the words out, despite the voice in his head insisting they were a lie. "Cecilia is not my concern."

"I see." Gracie cleared her throat. "I thought you should know."

"You thought wrong." His tone so sharp it could cut steel.

"There's something wrong here, Shane."

He tightened his grip on the phone receiver, so tight he was surprised it didn't shatter. "Her fiancé will have to fix it. She's not my problem."

"That's such bullshit. Don't pussy out."

He growled, a low, warning grumble. "I do *not* pussy out. Ever." And he had the track record to prove it. He pounded his fist on the desk because he needed something physical to relieve some of the aggression building like a storm. "What don't you people understand here?" His voice raised several decibels too loud. "*She's getting married!*"

"She doesn't love that guy," Gracie said, her tone stubborn.

"You don't know that."

"Of course I do. She didn't even mention him. Your name, however, was brought up quite often."

He refused to ask. "That doesn't change the fact that she's getting married."

She let out a short little scream. "You're being stupid."

No. He was being smart. He wasn't getting any more involved than he already was. "Good-bye, Gracie."

He hung up before she could say anything else that might convince him otherwise.

Penelope walked back into the room holding a glass of water and two rust-colored pills. "Here you go."

"Thanks." He drank them down and pointed to the door. "Go play with Maddie for the rest of the day."

"Are you sure?"

He nodded. "The meeting with the teamsters isn't until tomorrow morning, and we're at a standstill until then. So go."

Maddie walked into the room, carrying her cell phone. She plopped down on the chair. "Mom called."

"Is she having a good time?" Shane asked. After much prodding, they'd finally talked their mother into going to Ireland, a lifelong dream of hers. She was having a great time but called them daily for one reason or another.

"She said she tried to get ahold of you, but you haven't answered her messages."

Penelope patted his back. "It's been crazy."

Maddie frowned, her brow creasing. "Is everything okay?"

"Fine." He snapped the word, not sounding fine at all. "What did she need?"

The frown deepened. "She said you're going to the Children's Hospital benefit on Friday night back in Chicago."

He nodded. "I'll be back on Saturday."

"When you go home, she asked if you'd check on Aunt Cathy. She's worried she's lonely and doesn't have enough company."

Their eccentric, elderly great-aunt had no children, despite multiple marriages, and at eighty-eight was once again a widow. Shane sighed and put it on the mental list running in his head. "No problem, tell Mom I'll take care of it and head over there Saturday morning."

"Are you sure?" Maddie swiped her hair out of her face. "Maybe James and I can take a day trip?"

"It's fine. I've got it covered." He gave Penelope that look, the one that said *Get her out of here*.

Penelope smiled and gestured toward the entryway. "Come on, let's go before he changes his mind and I'm stuck here for the rest of the day."

Maddie jumped up and thirty seconds later they were gone and he was finally alone. He silenced his phone and rubbed his temples, his thoughts immediately going back to Cecilia and his phone call with Gracie.

Why had she been crying? And what exactly was going on with this engagement of hers?

Nothing about it made sense. Despite her flaws, he didn't see her as a cheater. And hell, even if she didn't have a moral compass, she cared so much about her image she'd never take the risk.

Besides, nothing about her seemed taken. Not once had she seemed conflicted when he'd kissed her. Wouldn't a newly engaged woman have resisted at least a little? And now that he'd touched her, he could no longer convince himself she'd be that cold.

The whole situation didn't add up.

He glanced at his computer. The Internet called to him like a siren's song and he didn't resist. He clicked the icon and thirty seconds later he'd located the article.

Senator Nathaniel & Mrs. Charlotte Riley announce the engagement of their daughter . . .

Shane skimmed the announcement, which said nothing of significance. It was a puff piece that gave him no clues. He studied the photo of Cecilia and Miles Fletcher. It was one of those posed engagement pictures, both of them staring off into space looking polished, rich, and barely human.

The Cecilia in the photo looked nothing like the woman he'd held in his arms. There was beauty but no warmth. No joy. It was just flat. She had her hands folded in front of her and on her left finger was at least a two-carat diamond engagement ring.

Where was her ring? What woman gets engaged and slips the ring off the next day? It's unheard of, especially with a rock like that.

He was pretty sure someone would have to pry Maddie's ring off her cold, dead finger.

So why wasn't Cecilia wearing hers? Why hadn't she mentioned the engagement to anyone? Sam was right. What girl did that?

And did he want to find out?

Cecilia walked toward the farmhouse, exhausted and drained, ready to lie down after her horrible night's sleep. But at the last second she veered off, and instead of going into the house she made her way to the backyard.

She didn't have to look for it. It was still there, to the left of the biggest willow tree. The path that would lead her to the river where she'd spent so many hours as a child. She didn't know why she was compelled to go there, and she supposed it didn't matter. The veil of leaves blocked out the sun as she walked through the wooded area. She took a deep breath, sucking in the scent of grass and oak and dirt. All reminders of the best times in her childhood.

Tears welled in her eyes when the trees cleared and the river appeared, glittering in the late afternoon sun.

It looked exactly the same.

Every morning she and Mitch would race through breakfast to meet Gracie and Sam. They'd spread out big white sheets, held down by their boom box, a big jug of lemonade, and the *Teen Beat* magazines Gracie had introduced her to.

They'd spent hours splashing in the river. Slathered with baby oil, lying out in the sun as Salt-n-Pepa, Sheryl Crow, and Ace of Base played on one of Gracie's endless mix tapes.

And she'd been just a girl.

The longer she stayed here, the more kinship she felt with that girl. The more she missed her. The more she wanted to be her.

Was that why she was sabotaging herself? Because she could no longer pretend that wasn't the case. Since she was six years old she'd been set on running for office. But now, with everything in motion, she couldn't work up the slightest bit of interest. And she couldn't understand why.

All she knew was that every time she thought about settling down to work, a knot balled up in her stomach and wouldn't ease until she did something else.

Shielding her eyes, she glanced up to see the big, overgrown tree branch hanging over the water. The urge welled inside her, fast and unexpected, but exactly right. She wanted to jump.

No. Needed to jump.

She didn't question the desire and kicked off her sandals as she stripped out of her pants and shirt, leaving on her bra and panties. She walked over to the tree and planted her hands on the trunk, surveying the branches to remember the path she used to take. The bark scraped her hands and feet but she didn't care; it felt familiar, like a home she didn't even know she had.

And she began to climb.

It was like riding a bike. She scaled the branches until she sat perched on the oldest and thickest one hanging over the river. When she reached the jump spot, she peered down into the water, a gray blue that glittered like gemstones in the sun.

It was higher than she'd remembered. Scarier. Her rational, adult brain clicked through all the risks associated with jumping into unknown water.

She shook her head. No. She was doing this.

She didn't know why it was important, but it was.

Heart pounding, she stopped thinking, and jumped.

The water was ice-cold as she plunged into the depths and came up screaming and gasping for air. She shivered, her whole body breaking out into goose bumps.

"What in the hell are you doing?" Shane's voice had her whipping around.

Arms crossed over his broad chest, he stood there looking like a thundercloud meant to rain on her parade.

She treaded water and stated the obvious. "I jumped."

"No shit," he said, and pointed at the tree. "Do you know how dangerous that is? What if you broke your neck?"

"It's fine." Her skin numbed to the cold. "I did it all the time as a kid."

"Twenty years ago!" he yelled. "Get out of that water, your lips are turning blue."

"Don't tell me what to do." Tone refined, despite the kick of temper in her belly. "Go away."

"No."

They stared at each other for a long, long time and even when her teeth started to chatter she didn't back down.

Finally, he dragged a hand through his hair. "Are you going to tell me the truth about this engagement of yours?"

She bit her lower lip and looked away. "No."

"See, Cecilia, that's the wrong answer."

She frowned and risked a glance at him, her legs still churning in the water.

He shook his head. "A woman in love answers differently."

Only then did she recognize how telling it was.

"Of course, most women in love don't go to bed with other men on their engagement weekend."

"We didn't go to bed." But the words rang false. A technicality.

Shane crossed his arms and stared at her with that green, piercing gaze, silent and waiting.

She wanted him to know. Wanted to tell him the truth.

It frightened her. It meant he mattered.

"You and I both know if they'd walked in five minutes later I'd already have been inside you."

She flushed hot, despite the icy water.

He crooked his finger. "Get out of the water. You're freezing."

She shook her head. "I'm not dressed."

"I watched you strip out of your clothes, and what I haven't seen, I've sure as hell touched."

"You pervert." She swam to the river's edge and took his warm hand as he helped pull her out of the water. "I see you didn't bother yelling until I was almost naked."

Skin like ice despite the sun on her back, she shivered.

His eyes darkened as his gaze slid over her body before he stripped off his T-shirt and pulled it over her head. "I didn't expect you to jump."

"You were wrong." The cotton, warm from his body, slid deliciously over her skin before falling to midthigh. It smelled like him. Like soap and sex and man. She shivered again for an entirely different reason than cold.

"I always am when it comes to you." He put his big palms on her arms and rubbed briskly. His movements were functional. Economical.

They shouldn't be sexy.

Or erotic.

But her brain processed them as sex and her breath caught in her throat.

His hands slowed, became a sensual stroke. "You look right in my shirt."

She blinked and peered up at him. Licked her dry lips.

His fingers curled around her jaw. "You're going to tell me what's going on, Cecilia."

The desire to give in and tell him everything was so strong she needed all her years of willpower to resist. "You can't save me, Shane."

Again, it was the wrong thing to say.

Those green eyes flashed, and she recognized the challenge gleaming bright. "We'll just see about that, won't we?"

Chapter Twelve

Cecilia didn't know how to handle dinner, but she didn't have a good excuse to skip out and she wasn't going to let Shane intimidate her.

He was just a man.

A man who confused her and made her question everything she knew about herself.

She stared in the mirror. She wore jeans, wanting to blend in with the rest of them. Her white V-neck top was simple enough. Her hair was pulled back into a low ponytail and her makeup was light.

But something was wrong.

She'd fussed and fussed with her hair and makeup, dressed carefully, but there was something different about her. As hard as she tried, she couldn't seem to capture the remoteness that had been so easy a few days before.

She smoothed the cotton over her stomach—all the cupcakes, cookies, and cakes she'd eaten were taking their toll and her stomach was no longer concave. So-called experts said sugar and flour weren't good for you, but they couldn't prove it by her. Cheeks no longer gaunt, she looked healthier than she had in eons.

Unfortunately, it seemed to be affecting her ability to perform her ice queen act.

She sighed, blowing out a hard breath. If she procrastinated any longer she'd be the last to arrive, and that would require her to make an entrance she certainly didn't want.

She put down her brush, swiped a pale pink lip balm over her lips, and went downstairs.

She was too late.

Everyone turned to look at her, including Shane.

Their eyes locked.

She froze on the threshold and the whole world stilled.

Green eyes flashed with some unnamed emotion, then shuttered closed. He turned back to his plate and the world sped up again.

With her customary dignity, Cecilia greeted everyone and slid gracefully into the chair, appreciating all those years she'd spent studying ballet to work on her poise.

Maddie was the first to speak, smiling broadly. "Gracie tells me you've been a godsend."

Cecilia thought about all the voice mails and e-mails she'd accumulated while she had ignored her life and helped Gracie in her lemon cupcake kitchen. "It's been a pleasure."

"She tells me you have a real knack for making pound cake," Maddie continued, looking at her with interest.

Cecilia laughed and across the table Shane's expression darkened, but she ignored it. "She's being kind. I think that's the only thing safe to give me. Although we did make chocolate chip cookies today."

Mitch cocked his head to the side. "You two used to be inseparable when we were growing up."

Next to her, James passed her a plate with hamburgers the size of her head. Daunted, she stared at them for a moment, then put one on her plate. She was on vacation. "It's been wonderful reconnecting with her."

"I hear congratulations are in order," Mitch said, his tone as though he addressed a witness on the stand.

While Shane glowered at her, Charlotte frowned, looking as though she might cry.

She shrugged. Wedding plans were the last thing on earth she wanted to discuss.

Mitch studied her, and for the first time Cecilia felt like he was really looking at her. It made her uncomfortable. Made her want to fidget, but she resisted.

"You look better than when you first got here," Mitch said.

All eyes turned to her.

With as much elegance as she could muster, she picked up a napkin and put it on her lap. "I'd been low on sleep."

"Have you been working too much?" Mitch asked.

Why did she feel like he was probing, searching for something? Her back straightened. "Not particularly."

"Have you talked to our father?"

"Mitchell," Charlotte said, her hands clenching tight. "Don't."

"What?" Mitch's voice turned hard. "I can't ask her simple questions?"

Awkwardness rolled over the table like a thick layer of fog.

Cecilia bit the inside of her cheek. Across the table, she sensed Shane's attention, heavy on her. It was a compulsion, the desire to look at him, and she didn't ignore it for long.

Expression guarded, he watched her far too intently to convey indifference.

Heat shot through her and her thighs clenched.

His gaze dropped to her mouth, lingered, then rose.

She tilted her chin and didn't look away. "As a matter of fact, no, I haven't talked to him."

"Why's that?" Mitch asked.

She broke the hypnotic contact and turned her attention to her brother. She was tired of playing it cool and gave up the ghost. "Because I'm ignoring his calls."

Mitch's expression widened in surprise, then he broke out into a grin. "I see. Welcome to the club."

Some of the heavy weight she'd been carrying around lifted from her chest. She raised a glass to her brother. "Cheers."

"I don't think this is a joking matter," Charlotte said, her tone stern.

"Mom," Cecilia said quickly, "we weren't joking. He asked, and I told him the truth."

"You didn't tell me you weren't talking to your father," her mother said, sounding hurt.

Cecilia waved her hand, thought briefly about the folly of discussing family business, then discarded it. "It's nothing official like with you and Mitch. I'm merely ignoring him."

Next to her, James chuckled but covered it up with a cough when Maddie shot him a glare. Cecilia smiled at him appreciatively and to her shock, he winked at her.

Mitch swallowed a bite of hamburger, then slanted a glance at Charlotte. "I'd think you'd be happy Cecilia and I are bonding."

Was that what they were doing? Bonding?

Charlotte frowned. "Over your father."

"Well, something good should come from all his fuck-ups," she said without thinking.

"Cecilia! Language!" her mother admonished.

Spine straight as an arrow, Cecilia sat primly. "I'm sorry, but how would you like me to say it? There's no spin I can put on it to make us family of the year."

Mitch laughed, shaking his head. "I might like you after all."

Maddie patted Charlotte's hand and nodded. "Don't worry, I'm sure this is healthy."

"It's unnecessary to be so caustic," Charlotte said, but the tension in her face relaxed, and Cecilia tried to ignore the stab of envy. It wasn't Maddie's fault she was such a lovely person.

With his knife, Mitch pointed back and forth between Cecilia and him. "Have you met us?"

Look at that, finally something in common with her brother.

Maddie cleared her throat and shifted in her chair. "Let's talk about something else."

An impulse took hold of Cecilia, surprising her. She wanted to know her future sister-in-law better. Wanted to see who she really was instead of the perky, cute-girl role Cecilia had placed her in. "Maddie, do you need any help with your wedding plans?"

Maddie's whole face lit up, transforming her from pretty to breathtakingly radiant. "I'd love that."

"Great," Cecilia said, picking up a bowl of corn on the table and scooping a heap onto her plate. "My only commitment is Friday. I have to go back to Chicago to go to a benefit, but I'll be back Saturday."

Maddie blinked. "The Children's Hospital benefit?"

"Yes," Cecilia said, her good mood evaporating. While she donated to the hospital every year and helped organize several of their events, this wasn't something she looked forward to. She'd committed to attend with Miles as part of her engagement duties.

It's all for the campaign, she reminded herself.

She frowned. A campaign she hadn't even thought about.

She remembered her mother's question on the day she arrived. Why *did* she want to run for office? She was on vacation. She was simply taking some much needed relaxation before she started the heavy lifting of the upcoming months.

At least that's the spin she sold herself today.

"Shane," Maddie said, ripping Cecilia away from her pondering. "Isn't that the benefit you're going to?"

Her attention snapped to him in time to see a muscle jump in his jaw. "Yes."

An entirely inappropriate jolt of excitement shot through her. Which was very wrong. Horrible. She was going with Miles. She put on her calmest expression. "Why are you going?"

His eyes narrowed. "I'm giving a speech."

How had she missed this? "I see."

"Why are *you* going?"

She couldn't very well blurt out the real reason, so she gave an answer that was 75 percent truth. "I've done work for the board. I go almost every year."

Maddie beamed, shifting back and forth in her chair like she had ants in her pants. "How convenient. You guys can drive together."

Cecilia had to stop herself from gasping. "Oh no, I'm sure that's not necessary."

Shane said nothing. Just watched her with those jungle-green eyes of his.

"Don't be silly," Maddie said. "Why should you take two cars when you're going to the same place and plan to be back at the same time?"

Because she didn't think she could be alone with him without wanting to jump him. But, of course, she couldn't say that.

Shane remained silent.

Cecilia's brows furrowed and she thought frantically,

finally hitting on a good reason. "I need my car to get around the city."

Maddie waved her hand. "Take your car; Shane has extras."

Mitch grinned, wearing that amused, fond expression he reserved for his soon-to-be wife.

Cecilia glared at Shane. Why was he so silent? He'd barely said two words. She narrowed her eyes and tilted her head toward Maddie, hoping he'd get the hint and help her out.

Instead, he shrugged. "Makes sense to me."

Maddie looked like she was about to burst with some unknown delight Cecilia couldn't understand. "It's settled then. You'll drive together."

Damn it. There was that excitement again.

She looked at him with his perfect face, that blond disheveled hair and killer body. A regular female fantasy come to life. She couldn't be alone with him. Trapped in a car for three hours.

She'd talk him out of it. Later.

The phone rang and Maddie jumped up. "I'll get it."

James smiled innocently. "It's kind of you to take one for the team. It saves gas and the environment."

"Go green," Cecilia said drily. This middle Donovan brother was quite an enigma, with his reserve and dry comments.

Maddie came back into the room.

"Who was that?" Mitch asked.

She slid into the chair. "Gracie. You guys will have to entertain yourselves tonight. Cecilia and I are going out."

"We are?" Cecilia straightened in her chair.

"Yep. She said, and I quote, 'Cecilia promised we'd go to Big Red's and get our drink on.'"

Cecilia's lips quirked. "Does that sound remotely like me?"

Maddie laughed. "Nope, but eat up. We leave in thirty."

Three hours later, Shane, James, and Mitch sat nursing their beers and watching a baseball game on the big-screen TV. Shane pretended to watch, but his mind was preoccupied with Cecilia.

It was just like Sam said. Every day she spent in Revival she got a little less reserved, a little less pinched. She'd looked absolutely gorgeous at dinner, even with her hair pulled back in that tight ponytail.

He'd about broken into a sweat every time he'd looked at her.

That T-shirt she wore. He shook his head. Unless it was wet, a white T-shirt should be boring, but hers stretched and clung to every curve. Plunged to expose the swell of her breasts.

He'd been so distracted by her cleavage and her surprisingly real behavior he'd barely been able to concentrate. His brain only cleared once to take the gift Maddie plopped into his lap. He'd snatched at the chance to drive with her.

Even though logically he knew it was a mistake.

But then again, he'd never been much of a logic guy. Instinct had never steered him wrong and he wasn't about to start ignoring it now—despite all the evidence to the contrary.

There was something between him and Cecilia. He didn't know what, but it was more than lust. As hard as he tried to talk himself out of her, it hadn't stuck.

Instead of focusing on her lies and her engagement, all through dinner he'd only been able to think about the way she kissed him. The sound of her throaty laugh. The way she felt under his hands.

And how she'd looked as she jumped from that tree branch.

Complete and utter abandon.

It had been his undoing.

He didn't think she was in any better shape. Not with the way her gaze kept drifting to his, her blue-gray eyes filled with longing.

The chemistry between them had been so hot, so palpable, it had felt alive. By the end of the meal, her nipples had been hard and the way she'd squirmed in her chair made his cock ache and strain against his zipper.

He'd had to force himself not to lunge for her right there at the table.

He'd been plotting a way to corner her, but then Gracie had shown up and his opportunity had passed.

Cecilia had come bouncing down the stairs, her hair a loose, wild mess around her shoulders. A fierce, primal possessiveness had shaken him to the core and he had to clench his fists so he didn't order her to stay home like some Neanderthal.

Those porn-star lips had curled into a sassy smile that his primitive brain took as a challenge, and then she'd been out the door.

She confused the hell out of him.

It's like she was transforming before his eyes.

The crowd cheered from the TV speakers, jarring Shane from his thoughts. He shook his head as though he'd been in a trance. "What happened?"

Mitch chuckled. "The Cubs hit a homer."

"Oh," Shane said dumbly, straightening from his slumped position on the couch.

Mitch assessed him with that lawyer's gaze.

"What?" Then wanted to kick himself for the telling defensiveness.

"Are you going to tell me what's going on between you and Cecilia?" Mitch asked.

In the recliner, James sat reading a book. He raised his head, expression alight with amusement.

Shane squinted at the TV. "What makes you think there's something going on? She's getting married."

Mitch scoffed. "And you're pissed as hell about it."

"I'm not. I just think it's strange she never said anything."

"Do I look like an idiot to you?"

James put his book on his stomach and folded his hands. "This conversation seems familiar."

"Would you stay the hell out of it?" Shane barked. He didn't need a sledgehammer over the head to recognize this was the same conversation he'd had with Mitch about Maddie not too long ago.

Mitch grinned before taking a long pull from his beer bottle. "Well, I know you're not sleeping with her."

"Why do you say that?" Shane asked, answering entirely the wrong way. The correct answer was silence.

Mitch shrugged. "You wouldn't be this on edge if you were."

"You're making it hard to relax," James said.

"I'm sitting here minding my own business."

"Grinding your teeth," James said helpfully.

A meanness rose inside Shane. Mitch was right, he was on edge and damn aggressive about it. "Gracie looked pretty damn hot tonight, don't you think?"

"I don't know what you mean." James's tone was far too indifferent for a heterosexual male. Then he grinned and shifted his attention to Mitch. "The only reason they're not screwing is because I interrupted them before he could seal the deal."

Shane growled, sitting up. "I warned you."

James shrugged, unconcerned.

Shane narrowed his eyes. "At least I'm not exhausting myself running to deal with my sexual frustration."

"I'm training for a marathon," James said drily.

They were brothers, and in Shane's mind James had broken code, so he had to pay. That's justice. "Sure, that's why you needed to run again after Gracie came in here like a walking wet dream. Tell me, how do you think that top even stays on? I bet there are plenty of guys desperate to find out right now."

"She can do what she wants. She's not my type." James spoke each word slow and distinct, but his knuckles were white on the chair.

Shane snorted. "I believe that. I've seen your type. And that's what kills you, doesn't it? That you can't control it, even though you want to."

James's gaze turned to pure menace and he said to Mitch, "When I walked in, Shane had her on the kitchen counter practically undressed. So now we've both seen your sister naked."

"I don't want to hear this," Mitch said.

Shane saw red and yelled, "That's a lie! I haven't seen her naked. And James sure as hell hasn't." Shane had only touched her and seen glimpses of various parts. Something that it now seemed imperative he rectify immediately.

"All right, calm the fuck down." Mitch shook his head. "Jesus, you two are pathetic."

Shane and James engaged in a minute-long staring contest reminiscent of grade school recess, while they weighed the consequences of making it physical. But in the end, they remembered they were adults in their thirties and shrugged it off, turning their attention back to the game nobody was really watching.

Fifteen minutes passed in complete silence before Mitch punched him in the arm.

"Hey," Shane said, rubbing the spot. "What's that for?"

"For messing around with my sister."

"I'd say I was sorry but turnabout is fair play, and you're not in a position to talk, considering you violate my sister nightly."

"True." Mitch rubbed the stubble on his jaw. "How long are we going to sit here without going to see what they're up to?"

Shane stood, not even pretending to play it cool. "Let's roll."

They turned to James, who looked back at them, his jaw a hard line. "Count me out."

Shane jerked his thumb toward the front door. "Come on, everybody knows you want her. It's no big deal."

Mitch shoved his hand into his pocket, bringing out a set of keys. "Well, not everyone. Gracie doesn't have a clue."

"I don't want her," James said, but stood anyway.

"Yeah, yeah," Shane said and clapped his brother on the back, sympathizing.

Uncooperative lust was a real bitch.

Chapter Thirteen

A cotton cloud.

That's what Cecilia felt like. A wonderful, fluffy, white cloud where nothing could hurt her. With the help of something called a Jägerbomb she forgot about her future, her lack of motivation, and her campaign. Forgot her father's betrayal and her engagement to a man she didn't love.

Blissful relief.

Nothing mattered except the country music pounding through her head, these women who'd taken her into their fold, and Jägerbombs.

Fabulous Jägerbombs.

When they'd arrived, she'd ordered her normal white wine, but Maddie and Gracie insisted this was better. Cecilia had to agree. The drink's contents were a mystery, but she felt divine. Alert and alive. Ready for anything.

She swung her arms around Maddie and Gracie, hugging them close. "Thank you so much. I never get to have any fun."

Gracie laughed. "There she is, the Ce-ce I know and love."

Maddie raised her glass. "Damn, I'm having a good time."

Sophie whooped, some of her margarita slopping over the sides as she took another gulp.

Penelope shook her head, pressing a finger to her temple as though she was getting a headache. Since she'd volunteered to be designated driver she was dead sober while the rest of them were on the drunk side of buzzed.

A song blared over the loudspeakers, the bass vibrating through her body as a country song came on. The dance floor shifted, the patrons moved into lines as they began an organized dance. Cecilia narrowed her eyes, watching the steps. "What's this song called?"

"'Save a Horse (Ride a Cowboy),'" Gracie said.

"I like it," Cecilia said.

Sophie grabbed her hand. "Let's go dance!"

She was so cute and small, Cecilia couldn't help grinning and patting her on the head.

Sophie scowled, batting her away. "I'm not a puppy!"

"But you're soooo cute," Cecilia said in a voice that sounded nothing at all like her.

Penelope grimaced. "Yikes, don't say that."

Little Sophie balled her hands into fists. "I am not cute. I'm fierce."

Maddie gave her a smacking kiss on the cheek. "You are." She winked at Cecilia. "She used to get me into so much trouble."

Cecilia was about to answer, but the dancers on the floor turned and clapped, then walked forward two steps before kicking out their heels, distracting her. How long had it been since she danced? Years of lessons perfected her technique as she'd worked relentlessly to obtain an acceptable level of poise. She'd danced at functions all the time, a nice waltz, gliding effortlessly around the room with some random partner, subtly leading when her companion didn't know what he was doing.

But had she ever just cut loose? Danced for the fun of it?

The dancers took another turn, repeating the steps from before.

The speakers blared the country song.

She studied the dancer's feet. She could do that. It was easy. Cecilia downed the rest of her drink, slamming the glass on the bar. "Let's go."

Sophie, Gracie, and Cecilia made their way to the floor, leaving Maddie behind with Penelope to keep her company.

Freedom sang in Cecilia's heart in time with the music and alcohol streaming through her blood. For tonight, she had no responsibility. Nobody to approve or disapprove of her. Nobody to please.

Tonight she could be whoever she wanted.

People parted, making room for them as they fell into line. Cecilia studied the dancer's feet stomping on the wood floor. It took four beats to figure out the pattern and two more to catch the beat of the song, and then she was off.

All the years of practice paid off, because she took to the dance like she'd been born to it. Next to her, Gracie and Sophie stumbled, laughing as they missed steps. Sophie yelled over the song, clutching her hand. "Damn girl, how do you do that?"

Cecilia laughed. "Twelve years of ballet and five years of ballroom dancing."

She spun, her head going deliciously dizzy, before she clapped.

One song turned into another and the steps modified, but she'd always been a quick study and caught right up. The music washed over her, filled her up with the kind of happiness she hadn't felt in so long she almost didn't recognize it.

She let go. Sweated. Laughed.

And in that moment she was free.

The song changed, slowing down in tempo, but before

she could be too disappointed, a tall guy in a black Stetson grabbed hold of her waist and swung her into his arms.

He fell into a quick tempo waltz that Cecilia glided into as though they'd been dance partners for years.

Under the rim of his hat, he was quite good-looking with his tanned skin, high cheekbones, and full, masculine mouth. He didn't make her heart beat fast like Shane, but his brown eyes were warm instead of cold, looking at her with interest instead of distrust. Big hands pressed into the small of her back. Lazy in his charm, he smiled at her. "Name's Levi."

She thought about protesting. But why should she? It was just a dance. She relaxed into his embrace. "Cecilia."

He leaned down. Close enough the brim of his hat touched her forehead. "It's a pleasure to meet you. You're not from around here, are you?"

She shook her head. "I'm from Chicago."

His hand slid tighter around her waist. "Well, Cecilia, you sure don't move like a city girl."

It might be the best compliment she'd ever received in her life and she beamed at him. "Why, thank you."

"Hands. Off," a deep, unmistakable voice said from behind her. "Now."

Heart lurching into a frantic beat, she craned her neck. It wasn't the drinks making her delusional. Shane was really there. Big and mean, as though he was ready to pound the first person that crossed him.

She shivered. "What are you doing here?"

"Yeah," Levi said, pulling her closer. "Back off, buddy."

Shane crossed his arms, his biceps rippling, pumping up before her very eyes to strain the fabric of his black T-shirt. "I'm going to give you to the count of three before I break every one of your fucking fingers."

She tried her best to work up some proper indignation over his behavior but couldn't make it stick. Not with that twisted sense of female satisfaction warming her, going straight to her head and making her dizzy. He was jealous.

Like, super jealous. Dangerously jealous.

A giggle bubbled in her throat and she repressed it. That was wrong. Very wrong. The correct response was outrage, but damned if her body cared about that. Deep down, in that secret part of her, she was thrilled. Nobody had ever been jealous over her before.

She looked at the guy, what was his name again? She searched her memory and finally remembered. "Levi, can you excuse us?"

Levi let her go. "Is he your boyfriend?"

She started to say no but Shane grabbed her arm. "Yes, don't touch her again. Got it, *buddy*?"

In surrender, Levi held up his hands. "Sorry, dude, we were just dancing. Maybe she shouldn't move like that i. you don't want people to get the wrong idea."

Move like what?

Shane grunted, gripping her arm tighter. "I'll take it under advisement."

Cecilia blinked, finally coming back from her ego-drunk daze enough to allow feminism to take its hold. "Hey!"

"Don't test me, Cecilia," Shane said, his voice hard. And then he had her on the move, practically dragging her toward the door.

"Shane!" she yelled over the loud music, but he didn't seem to hear her. He bulldozed past anyone in his way, striding with single-minded focus toward the exit.

He pushed through the heavy barn doors and dragged her outside. Mild spring air hit her cheeks and the Jägerbombs rushed in her head. Danger and lust spiked the air as he stalked through the parking lot and around the corner to the side of the building.

A couple was already there, locked in a hot embrace. He

cursed, veered around them, and walked straight into the woods that lined the property.

"Shane, what's wrong with you? What are you doing?" Branches crunched under her feet as he pounded through the forest.

When he came to a large oak, he pushed her against it, his expression thunderous. "What am I doing? What are you doing, Cecilia?"

His gaze was predatory, exciting and scaring her at the same time. A strange and delicious cocktail of emotions that made her pulse beat fast and wild. "I was dancing!"

"No shit," Shane said, his stance aggressive. "Quite a show you were putting on there."

"I wasn't putting on a show."

"The hell you weren't." He raked his hand through his hair. "Fuck, Cecilia, half the men in the place stopped what they were doing to watch you."

She waved a hand. "Don't be absurd. You're just jealous."

He stalked toward her, crowding her against the tree. "You're damn right I'm jealous."

She blinked. "You admit it."

Big hands gripped her hips, holding her still. "It's pretty obvious, isn't it?"

Her breath quickened. He was so close. Closer than she'd ever thought he'd be again and she couldn't resist the temptation of him. She ran her hands up his arms, bowing her back in offering. "Yes."

"Jesus." His thumb pressed on the pulse pounding in her throat. "How much have you had to drink?"

She bit her lip. "A lot."

The anger seemed to roll off of him as his eyelids hooded. He groaned and brushed the shell of her ear with his lips. "So I can't fuck you against this tree."

Body clenching at his words, her head thumped on the trunk. "Do you always talk this dirty?"

He bit her earlobe, pulling on the sensitive flesh with his teeth. "You bring out the worst in me."

"Lucky me." She twined her fingers through his hair.

"Do you have any idea how much I want you right now?" Voice low and thick with sex, the question stirred the fine hairs at the nape of her neck.

She shook her head.

"Enough that I don't trust myself to stop."

She arched, rubbing against his erection. Thrilled when his breath caught on a hiss. "Who says I want you to stop?"

A muscle jumped in his jaw. "Do you have to pick now to be a temptress?"

"What's wrong with now?" She actually puffed out her bottom lip in a pout—something she'd often bemoaned about other women and here she was, pulling the same trick.

And she didn't have any conflict about it.

Not when his eyes turned that particular shade of green.

"I will not take you against a tree while you're drunk."

How disappointing. Of course, she should have counted on that. The man clearly had a hero complex. "Are you done being mad at me?"

"For what?"

She frowned. The list was quite lengthy at the moment. Best to focus on the minor stuff for the time being. "For dancing?"

"No." The word sounded flat, but she detected the barest hint of amusement. Although that might be the alcohol making her hopeful.

"All right." She'd had fantasies that played out like this. Tying Shane Donovan up in jealous knots, driving him crazy. It was so unlike her. So different from who she was normally, but she was drunk enough to play it out. She stood on tiptoes and stretched into him like a cat. "What can I do to make it up to you?"

"Never dance again. I don't think I can take it." He pressed his erection against her stomach.

She wrapped herself around him and his arms twined around her waist. She nuzzled his neck, licking over his rapid pulse.

He growled, low in his throat like an animal, and it excited some deep-rooted, female part of her. "Cecilia," he said, his voice a rasp against her skin. "You're playing with fire. I'm feeling dangerous."

She nipped his jaw.

In a flash, he shoved her against the tree, his big body trapping hers.

Oh yes, this was what she wanted. What she needed.

He gripped her chin and forced her eyes to meet his. "Cecilia, pay attention. Once I start, I'm not going to be able to stop. You're going to get screwed, out in the woods, against a tree. Tomorrow, you'll wake up with scrapes on your back. I'll mark you. Bite your neck. Bruise your wrists. Take you so hard, your pussy will be swollen and sore. So this stops now. Understood?"

Cecilia understood he was trying to talk sense into her, but his little speech had the opposite effect. She about melted into a puddle at his feet.

And she wanted it all. Was wet with desire. The temptress was in full force, unwilling to be dissuaded. She wanted him crazy. So she said the one thing she thought would make him throw caution to the wind. "You know the other night? That first night?"

His head snapped back and his brow furrowed. "Yeah."

She met his eyes. "I came."

"Ah, fuck." And then he was on her.

His mouth claimed hers in a hard, brutal rush.

It was an onslaught.

A possession.

And she gave in. Surrendering as she'd never surrendered to anything in her whole life.

His tongue stroked hers, demanding. She moaned, licking into him as she climbed up him, needing closer. Harder. Needing to feel like his.

She hooked her leg over his hip. Adjusted her body until his cock nudged the sweet spot between her legs. On a low, animal-sounding growl, he thrust violently against her, slamming her into the tree and scraping her back, just as he promised.

He stilled.

Desperate, she rocked back, moaning. "Please, yes. Shane."

"Goddamn it," he said against her mouth. Kissing her with the type of primal brutality she'd never dreamed of but now knew she couldn't live without. He lifted his head. "You're going to make this up to me."

Drugged with passion, she lifted her heavy lids. "Whatever you want."

He manacled her wrists, lifting them above her head. "That is a dangerous thing to promise."

"Can't you tell?" She bit his bottom lip. "I'm a woman on the edge."

"Christ, Cecilia." Then his mouth covered hers and he kissed her until she gasped for breath.

He moved down her throat, biting her neck, then licked and sucked until she practically purred. She twisted, her breath a fast rise and fall that matched the frantic beat of her heart. "Please, Shane, I want to touch you."

In answer, his grip on her wrists tightened, while his other hand slid under her shirt to cup her breast. He unclasped the bra with one deft hand and peeled back the cups. He rubbed a thumb over her exposed nipple, circling it over and over again until she bowed from the excruciating pleasure.

He didn't let up.

Didn't stop.

He rolled the hard bud, pulled and twisted until her belly coiled tight.

"Shane," she whispered, gasping when he squeezed hard enough to bring tears to her eyes. A sharp ache speared through her core and her inner muscles clenched and throbbed. "Oh God, Shane." A broken plea.

Deep in her belly, need coiled tight.

So. Damn. Tight.

She cried out. Afraid she was going to break in two. On the precipice of some sort of cliff she was too afraid to throw herself off.

He let go of her wrists. She clutched at his shoulders, digging her nails deep into the cotton of his shirt. The bark of the tree scraped her skin as he yanked her top over her breasts and cupped them both in his strong hands.

It was exquisite torture.

She keened, her back arching. It was too much. He was only touching her breasts, but he was doing so much more. He was shattering something inside her. Pushing her to a place unknown.

Fear, desire, and need coalesced, making her feel desperate and out of control, thrown headlong out of her comfort zone and into panic. "Shane, please . . ."

His teeth scraped against the skin of her neck. He moved lower, pushing her breasts closer together. He played and toyed with her nipples the way nobody else had ever come close to doing, before sucking first one, then the other, into his mouth.

He licked, sucked, rolled his tongue over her hypersensitive flesh. He nudged his cock right up against her clit and rocked at the same moment he bit the tip of one nipple while squeezing the other one.

A desperate, needy moan from deep in her throat.

His fingers slipped inside the waistband of her jeans, dipping lower and lower, the stretch fabric of the denim allowing him access. She splayed her legs wide.

Lifting his head, he groaned, sliding inside her with first one, then two fingers. "Do you know how wet you are?"

She shook her head.

He withdrew his hand, and painted her lower lip with her own juices, shocking her. Her eyes went wide and he smiled before leaning in and tasting her lips. It was the most erotic thing anyone had ever done to her.

Her knees buckled and he caught her, making sure she was steady while he worked down her zipper. "I'm going to take you hard and fast. That's what I need."

"Yes," she said against his mouth.

Strong fingers slid inside her panties, rubbing her clit until her head fell back and she gasped with the pleasure. Thumb still circling the bundle of nerves, he dipped inside, hooking his finger and rubbing a spot that made her jolt with sensation. "Oh God!"

He laughed. "There's what I'm looking for."

She grabbed his wrist, but he gently pushed her hand away.

It was so intense. So . . . Jesus . . . she didn't know. It was like being ripped apart by pleasure. "Shane. Fuck. Shane."

He hit something and she couldn't help it, she screamed.

He kissed her, rubbing that spot, over and over again, until she thought she might go mad.

She started to fight it. It was too damn much.

A soft whisper in her ear, "Let go, Cecilia."

And she did.

The orgasm rushed over her like a railroad train, barreling through her defenses and battering into her with a shock that bordered on violent.

She started to cry. She didn't know where the tears came from but once they started to fall she couldn't stop them. The spasms still wracking her body, she buried her face in his neck.

"Shhh, you're okay." Voice unbearably soft as he stroked her hair.

Despite the orgasm and the tears, she didn't want to stop. She needed him inside her. To fill her. Here, tonight, she needed to belong to him. She lifted her head and met his gaze. "Take me."

He brushed away her tears as his fingers slipped from her body. "What am I going to do with you?"

"I don't know." The words a mere whisper.

"Cecilia," he said, voice so thick it was almost unrecognizable. "Why are you getting married?"

All that heat and desire cooled in an instant as reality dropped like a bucket of ice over her head. She blinked back the swell of tears. "Please don't ask me."

Green eyes darkened, flashed, then shuddered closed. He ran a hand through his hair and blew out a hard breath. "Tell me."

Why? Why was he doing this now with the orgasm still trembling in her body and her need for him so desperate? She pressed her lips together.

He sighed, pulled down her T-shirt and stepped away. "I can't do this. Won't do it."

Anger she wasn't entitled to boiled hot inside her. "I thought you said you wouldn't be able to stop."

He looked away, off into the trees to some distant spot

behind her. "I thought I couldn't, but then I remembered you're getting married and won't tell me why."

He was right. Of course, he was right. She nodded. "I understand."

"Do you?"

"Yes," she said, tugging down her top over the V of her jeans, still open and exposed to him. He was so close. And she needed him. Selfishly needed him. Something inside her couldn't tell him the truth.

He shook his head. "All you need to do is tell me the truth. Because I know damn well you're not marrying for love."

"Why does it matter?" She pulled up her zipper with a hard yank. The alcohol coursing through her bloodstream betrayed her, sending her emotions spiraling downward at warp speed.

"Marriage matters, Cecilia," he said, his voice so soft it sent a shiver down her spine. He gripped her chin and forced her gaze to meet his. "I want the truth. It's that simple."

She pulled away and stepped around him, crossing her arms over her chest and walking at a brisk pace toward the bar.

In her experience that wasn't how the truth worked. If she told him her plans and reasons, he'd just try to talk her out of it.

She wasn't ready for that conversation. Wasn't strong enough. If she talked now he'd learn the truth: she didn't know who she was anymore.

And the truth scared her more than she could ever admit.

Chapter Fourteen

Shane watched Cecilia walk through the bar, her spine rigid as a ruler. He dragged a hand through his hair and cursed himself for the hundredth time.

What had he been thinking? Stopping like that?

He could be inside her right now, but no, he had to go and prove a point. He'd been half crazy with lust, desperate to take her, but then she'd looked at him with those huge, watery, storm-filled eyes and the words had popped out.

And he wanted the truth. *Needed* her to tell him the truth. Which bothered him on some visceral level.

Three steps ahead, her fine ass swayed in too-tight jeans as she stalked through the bar like she owned the place.

He'd never thought it would be like that with her. Yes, they'd had chemistry, but hell, how could he have guessed? With all those severe business suits she wore, he'd thought she'd need coaxing. That he'd have to work to make her mindless and crazy.

But it hadn't been anything like that. She'd been as crazy and wild as he was.

He shuddered, remembering the way she'd orgasmed almost violently.

The way she came, it would haunt him forever.

She tossed her hair over her shoulder and every guy in the room took notice. Who could blame them? Despite her anger, everything about her had loosened. From the wild tumble of waves swinging around her shoulders, to her swollen mouth and rich-girl walk. It transformed her from classically beautiful to drop-dead gorgeous.

Their hungry gazes ate her up and Shane wanted to tattoo something across her forehead so they'd stop staring.

The unfamiliar possessiveness beat at his chest, worrying him. He'd never been jealous before. It must be the case of the blue balls riding him hard. That his predicament was entirely of his own making wasn't lost on him.

A guy wearing a trucker's hat leered at her breasts and the need to stake his claim on her overwhelmed him. He caught up to her and wrapped an arm around her waist, tugging her close. "Don't think this is over, Cecilia."

A sharp intake of breath. "I'm mad at you."

"I'm mad at you too." He scraped his teeth over her neck and she shivered. "But it doesn't change a damn thing."

She swung around. Those storm-blue eyes flashed, and she planted her hands on her hips. "We need to stop this."

She was right, and he didn't care. He gave her his most cocky grin. "Have you ever screamed when you came before?"

She narrowed her gaze. "You're twisted."

He curled his hand around her neck, wanting to make sure every guy in the place knew she was his. "You're just figuring that out now?"

She shook her head, as though he was too exasperating for words, before pointing to the right corner of the bar. "I spotted everyone over in the back booth." Then she turned on her heel and walked away.

Although still hard as a rock, his mood improved marginally and he followed at a much slower pace. The crowd parted to reveal the group from the house, with the addition of Charlie, who must have gotten off work. Cecilia strode through the people with her head held high, her back straight. Like if she walked regally enough no one would question where they'd been for the last thirty minutes or why she was marked by him in all ways but the one that really mattered.

Everyone at the table watched them with some sort of shit-eating grin on their face.

Chin still tilted high, Cecilia stopped in front of the table. Shane crowded behind her, close enough to feel the warmth of her skin.

"Charlie," she said, her voice sounding like smoke. "I haven't seen you in forever."

Charlie raised a brow at him then gave Cecilia a slow, long appraisal. "You're looking . . . well."

"Thank you." She gestured, her hand flying in a circle in Charlie's vicinity. "You're all grown up."

"So are you," Charlie said, giving her a wicked smile. "Although you were considerably neater the last time I saw you."

Cecilia shrugged. "We got lost in the woods."

"Is that what we're calling it these days?" Charlie asked.

"All right, that's enough." Shane's brain heard Charlie's tone as flirting, even though the rational part of him hovering in the background said he was overreacting.

Cecilia glanced over her shoulder and frowned before beaming at the table. "Can we scoot in?"

The girls only stared at Cecilia in wide-eyed shock.

"Pretty please," Cecilia said.

Shane frowned then remembered all the drinks she'd consumed.

There was a sudden flurry of movement and everyone squeezed in tighter.

Cecilia slid into the booth next to Charlie.

Mitch shook his head. "Now can I give you shit?"

Shane crossed his arms over his chest. "For what?"

Mitch cocked a brow before slipping his arm around Maddie.

Shane eyed the microscopic spot next to Cecilia, far too small for even Sophie to fit in, then pulled over a chair from another table and sat down.

Everyone looked at him. Except Cecilia, who paid elaborate attention to the drink menu.

He raised a brow. "What?"

"Oh, nothing," Penelope said, always one to smooth over an awkward situation.

James got that sly tilt to his mouth. "So, Cecilia, are you going to dance again?"

"No," Shane said, practically growling the word.

All heads swiveled toward him.

Of course, he had no control over what she did, but Cecilia's dancing had already given him a heart attack, and he didn't think he could take any more.

Cecilia glowered and threw her hands up in the air. "For the love of God, what do you have against dancing?"

Feeling uncomfortably irrational, Shane narrowed his eyes. "I've got nothing against it, except when you do it."

"What's wrong with the way I do it?"

Nothing at all. Not a single damn thing. She danced like sin and sex. He'd about lost his mind when he'd spotted her on the dance floor. Those hips an erotic sway, breasts bouncing, her cheeks flushed and healthy. And then that guy dared to touch her, and all common sense had fled.

Shit. He dragged his hand through his hair. He had to get this jealousy under control. Later. He gave her his most menacing glare. "I left my bat at home."

"You're not any fun at all." She puffed out her lower lip in a pout that made him want to bite her.

Instead he turned to his sister and her friends. "All right, what in the hell did you give her?"

Maddie pressed her lips together and Sophie looked away.

Gracie smiled innocently. "Jägerbombs."

"Jägerbombs!" Well, that explained the perkiness.

"Yeah, so?" Gracie shrugged. "She'd never had them before."

James frowned, looking stern and disapproving, causing Gracie to huff, "Don't look at me like that!"

Charlie winked at Cecilia. "So, Jägerbombs, huh?"

"They were super good," Cecilia said.

"I can see that." His lips quirked, and he ran a finger down the red spot Shane left on her throat. "You've got a hickey on your neck."

She waved him away. "Oh that. Forget that and tell me what you've been up to."

Shane resisted the urge to growl at the other man for daring to touch her and said drily, "Is it time to go home yet?"

Fifteen minutes later everyone was piled into various cars and Shane slid into the backseat next to a fading Cecilia. She curled up like a kitten, resting her head against the car door. The parking lot lights streamed in through the glass, highlighting her patrician bone structure. Long lashes drifted closed as she yawned.

Mitch pulled out of the parking spot and the car was silent for a good five minutes before Maddie peered back at him from the front seat. "Is she asleep?"

He reached over and jostled her but she didn't stir. "Yeah."

He gritted his teeth. She belonged nestled next to him,

not leaning away from him. The distance was just another reminder that she belonged to some other guy.

"So," Maddie said in a slow, deliberate tone.

"Maddie, I'm not in the fucking mood." The night was catching up to him, making him cranky.

Mitch studied him through the rearview mirror of his BMW. Not a cheap car among those Rileys. Although, in fairness, he wasn't exactly driving around in a beater anymore. "What's your plan?"

"Plan?" The back of Shane's skull started to ache and he rubbed the back of his neck. "I have no plan."

Maddie glanced back, her gaze on Cecilia. "She's different around you."

"I think you're confusing me with the Jägerbombs." Last he'd had her alone she'd been furious. A heaviness settled into his gut.

Maddie shook her head. "You're wrong."

He sighed. "It doesn't matter. When she goes back to Chicago she'll be the Cecilia we're used to, just like she always did. This is summer Cecilia."

Mitch's brow furrowed. "Who told you that?"

"Sam," Shane said. "And Gracie."

The car fell quiet and he stared out the window, watching rows of cornfields zip by. It was dark and fatigue had him questioning.

What exactly was he doing?

It wasn't like him to ignore the truth. And the truth was Cecilia was marrying another guy. She might not talk about him. Might not wear his ring. But he was out there, and at the end of the day she belonged with him.

His fingers tightened into fists as he looked at her in the darkened vehicle.

Why did she have to be this way? To think he used to tell himself he'd have a million things to pick her apart over if he really knew her. She wasn't anything like the woman he'd built up in his head.

And he was more tied up in her than ever.

They pulled into the driveway and he attempted to rouse her, but she lay limp, her breathing heavy.

"She's out." He opened the door and slid from the vehicle, jutting his chin toward the front door. "I'll carry her."

Maddie ran up the stairs, the keys jangling from her fingers interrupting the still quiet of the night.

He hauled Cecilia into his arms and she promptly burrowed close. Those long, tapered fingers of hers twining around his neck as she laid her head against his chest. In silence, they walked into the foyer and up the stairs. A minute later he laid her on the bed. She moaned in protest and tried to pull him down with her, but he untangled himself and straightened.

Mitch and Maddie stood in the doorway watching him, and he glanced pointedly at the door. "I'll take it from here."

Maddie opened her mouth as if to speak, but Mitch put his hand on the back of her neck and she nodded. A second later the door was closed and they were alone.

Against the innocence of the white and lavender quilt, Cecilia looked somehow wanton, her hair spread out on the pillow in a tangled heap, her cleavage spilling from her top. He pulled off her shoes before rolling her onto her back and unzipping her jeans. He nudged her, gripping her waistband. "Lift up, baby."

In the darkened room she lifted her hips and he slipped her pants down her long, long legs. He skimmed his hands up her smooth thighs. He wanted to lick every part of her.

Possess every part of her.

"Shane," she said, her voice a sleepy whisper.

"Let me get you out of this shirt. Can you sit?"

She let him pull her up but remained rag-doll limp as he stripped the cotton T-shirt from her body. When he laid her back down on the mattress, he ran a hand over her flat belly.

"Did you call me baby?"

"Yeah, I did," he said, waiting for some sort of sassy rebuke.

"I like it," she murmured, surprising him. "You call the other girls honey." She rolled to her side, folding her hands under her cheek.

He pulled down the comforter, working it under her hips so he could cover her. When she was tucked in, he stared at her face, soft in the moonlight. He ran a finger over her silky skin.

She wasn't his.

She burrowed under the covers and let out a soft sigh.

He stood and left her untouched to sleep alone in his cold, empty bed.

Chapter Fifteen

Cecilia woke with a start. Skin clammy, her stomach rolled. Sweat beaded at her temples as a hard wave of nausea crashed through her.

The Jägerbombs had betrayed her.

She jolted straight up. Another wave swelled, threatening to overwhelm her.

Oh no.

A shiver.

She was going to be sick. She bounded out of bed only to realize she wore only a bra and panties. A vague memory of Shane helping her out of her clothes, his hands on her hips and a brush of a finger over her cheek.

Desperate, she stumbled around the room, looking for a shirt to cover her.

Another violent clench of her stomach.

There was no more time.

She bounded from the room and ran down the hall to the bathroom, slamming the door and falling to her knees just in time to empty her stomach.

Her belly gave a savage heave just as the door opened and someone walked into the small room.

"You're sick," Shane said, stating the obvious.

She retched into the toilet, waving frantically and yelling into the porcelain bowl, "Go away!"

A wrenching surge left her gasping.

"Poor thing," he said, his tone way too amused. He closed the door, leaving her blessedly alone to wallow in her sickness.

Only he returned a minute later and covered her with a cotton robe, helping her into the sleeves.

The fabric slid over her skin and she was equally grateful and horrified. She started to say thank you, but another wave crashed over her and she once again had her head buried. The expression *praying to the porcelain gods* finally made perfect sense.

Off to her left the water turned on, and ten seconds later Shane was sitting on the edge of the tub.

She wanted to die of humiliation. She was a sweaty mess, hovered over a toilet making disgusting noises. "Privacy!"

Of course, he ignored her. Instead of leaving, he gathered her hair, banding it between his fingers, while her stomach lurched again.

A cool towel fell across her neck and he pressed a palm over the washcloth to hold it close.

God, it felt so good. She shivered. It was pure heaven on her hot, sweaty skin.

Heaven turned into hell as another wave hit her.

It went on for what seemed an eternity, but was probably mere minutes. An endless, embarrassing cycle of sickness. Shane stayed by her side the whole time, refreshing the washcloth with cold water from the tub, that strong steady hand on her neck.

She dry-heaved, wanting to kill herself.

His broad palm rubbed down her back, so warm and strong. "That's a good sign."

Eyes a watery mess, she rested her head on the rim of the seat. "Good sign?"

"Everything's gone, you're through the roughest part." Fingers trailed up and down her spine.

She heaved again, her stomach not getting the message that it was empty. "This is humiliating."

He chuckled. "You'll get over it."

"I hate Jägerbombs," she said pitifully.

"Most people do after a night with them."

Stomach finally seeming to settle, she sat on her haunches. He flushed the toilet. "Feel better?"

She stared at him. He sat on the edge of the tub, his chest bare and a pair of sweat shorts clinging to his powerful thighs, looking completely unfazed. Why was he here? Helping her?

Didn't most men hide away when a woman was at their worst? And she was clearly a mess. Her makeup had to be everywhere. Her eyes were watery, her nose runny, the taste in her mouth foul.

But he didn't seem apt to leave.

He released her hair, slid the washcloth from her neck and rewet it before washing her face off. He was so tender, so considerate, her chest squeezed.

Why did he have to be like this? Why couldn't he stay in the box she'd put him in? She gazed into his green eyes, filled with concern, and admitted the truth.

She was falling for him. Falling hard. Like diving off a skyscraper where there was nothing below but concrete to catch her. She swallowed the sudden tightness in her raw throat that had nothing to do with being sick. "Why are you doing this?"

He smoothed the washcloth over her brow and along her hairline. "Doing what?"

"Taking care of me." The urge to cry, so foreign to her last week, now a familiar companion, welled. Nobody ever took care of her. Not since she was a little girl.

His lips pressed together as though containing a frown. "Why wouldn't I?"

She brushed her hair back, her stomach finally calm. "I'm a disgusting mess."

Not even close to perfect. Nowhere near composed.

He smiled, trailing a finger down her cheek. "Yeah, you are."

Exhaustion stole over her and without thinking she put her head on his knee. He stilled for a fraction of a second, and then stroked her hair, soft and gentle.

It was so like him. On the surface he was all gruff blunt force, but his heart was pure. Sure and steady and strong. For years she'd conditioned herself to be the best, to never show any weakness, and never give a man the upper hand when she could keep it for herself. But right now she wanted to stay here, sitting at Shane's feet, her head resting on his thigh and his hand brushing her hair, forever.

Eyelids growing heavy, she closed her eyes but murmured, "I need to brush my teeth."

"Shhh, just rest," he said quietly. He gathered her in his arms, picking her off the floor.

"My teeth," she protested but had no more strength left.

He didn't answer, just held her as he walked down the hall and kicked open her cracked-open door before placing her down on the bed.

The soft sheets were heaven against her clammy skin and she sank into the mattress. He padded away only to return with a glass of water. He held it out to her. "Drink this."

With considerable effort she propped up on her elbow

and gulped, the cool water a salve on her dry, sore throat. "Thank you."

Their gazes met and held, and the world tilted, shifting under her feet before settling again.

"Lie down and get some sleep," Shane said, his voice low.

"Don't leave me." She slipped under the covers and put her head on the pillow. She couldn't bear for him to go. "Please."

Several moments ticked by in the quiet room before he gave her a small nod. "I won't," he said, slipping into the bed behind her and tucking her close.

Ah, yes. She relaxed into him. His arms enveloped her. Had anything ever felt this good? Sleepiness crawled through her like a drug, but she managed to say, "Shane."

He kissed her temple. "What, baby?"

She couldn't go to sleep unless he knew he was important. Until he understood. "I want to run for congress."

There was a long pause before he said, "Okay."

"That's why I'm getting married." Her lids drooped.

He stiffened behind her but didn't make any move to back away.

She yawned, snuggling into him. Had anything ever felt as good as his arms? "I've never even gone on a real date with Miles Fletcher. He's never laid a finger on me."

She'd deal with the consequences of her admission tomorrow, but tonight she needed him to know.

"And he never will." His voice a low promise in her ear.

She shivered, and laced her fingers with his. "I'm not a cheater."

He pulled her closer. "We'll talk tomorrow."

She nodded, drifting off to sleep, feeling cared for, for the first time in as long as she could remember.

* * *

Cecilia felt remarkably good when she woke up, with hardly even a headache. Once she'd taken a shower and scrubbed away the last remnants of sickness from the night before, she'd felt almost normal.

She eyed her phone, abandoned on the secretary's desk overlooking the window. She walked over to it, skimming the missed calls and voice mails. She flicked on the screen and looked at the e-mail icon.

She had a hundred e-mails.

She chewed the inside of her cheek, staring at the life waiting for her.

Just the thought of it sat like a weight on her chest. She had to stop procrastinating. It wasn't like her. She'd always dealt with the truth, no matter how bad, head-on. So what was she doing?

And why?

She wanted to believe it was the arrangement with Miles and her impending nuptials that had her avoiding everyone back home, but now she wasn't so sure. She couldn't work up the energy to care. There were a thousand details to work out, but strategizing for her campaign held no appeal. Dealing with her father and his latest list of political problems didn't call to her the way it normally did.

She was tired. Tired of him. Tired of the game.

But she didn't know the reason.

She threw the phone back on the desk and walked out of the room without a backward glance.

Right now, all she wanted was to talk to Shane.

She'd figure out the rest. She always did.

She found him in the downstairs office on the phone, his brow furrowed in concentration as he listened to the caller. She propped herself on the wood frame and watched him.

Everything about him was powerful, from the authoritative way he spoke to the way he moved. She'd grown up around powerful men, but there was something different about Shane. It was like his leadership was innate. He didn't have to force it. Or cultivate it. It was part of who he was.

Listening to him talk, it was clear he was involved in some sort of disagreement, but he was entirely calm. His voice level. Every statement he made rang with confidence and certainty.

She'd worked with enough politicians to know true leadership skills were a rare commodity. Most had to work on it. It had to be studied and learned. It took conscious effort.

But she'd bet Shane had never practiced a day in his life.

He wore power like a second skin.

He glanced up from his computer, catching her standing there. The hard, drawn lines of his face relaxed, his gaze lit up, and his lips curved into a smile that made her heart speed.

Cecilia blinked. Shocked. He was happy to see her.

The knowledge made her warm all over. She could become addicted to making Shane happy.

He waved her in and she sat on the couch to wait for him to be done.

Their gazes locked.

All that heat, all that chemistry sparked to life. Images of what they'd done last night filled her mind. The way his hands had been so hot on her. The sure way he touched her body. The way he'd made her come.

She shivered. Wishing with everything in her that he hadn't stopped. Soberness changed none of the wildness she'd felt last night.

His eyes darkened. He told the caller he had an emergency and he'd call them back, hanging up without waiting for an answer.

She crossed her legs, sliding her hand along the couch arm. "I didn't mean to interrupt."

"We were starting to go in circles, always a sign they need a break." He got up from the desk and walked over to the entryway, closing the glass French doors and sealing them alone in the office.

"Is everything okay?"

He frowned. "We're trying to iron out some issues on this city contract."

"Is it serious?" She pointed to the now-closed doors. "I can leave and let you get back to work."

"It is serious. But I don't want you to leave. We're at a stalemate." He walked over to her with a lethal grace.

"Do you want to talk about it?"

"Later," he said, joining her on the small love seat.

"You're very good at that," she said, loving the way his firm thigh pressed against hers.

"Good at what?"

She shifted, ever so subtly, wanting to be close to him. Wanting to feel that protected, intimate feeling from last night. "Leadership. I can see why you're so successful."

He shrugged, throwing one arm along the sofa's back. "I never really thought about it."

"Good leaders don't have to," she said. She wanted to cuddle in his arms. The desire was so unlike her, she didn't know what to make of it.

"I'm not so sure I'm all that good, I just do what I have to."

"Like I said before, that's bullshit." He looked away, and she knew she'd touched a nerve, but it didn't stop her. "You didn't accomplish what you have by chance. It doesn't just happen to you. Why aren't you proud of it?"

"Who says I'm not?" His voice turned hard, but to her surprise he put his hand on her knee.

"I do. You minimize it. And when anyone says anything about it, you act like you're embarrassed."

He stared out the window and Cecilia didn't think he was going to answer, but then he sighed and squeezed her leg.

"I'm not embarrassed. It just doesn't feel like an accomplishment. Before my dad died I didn't have any plans beyond having a good time. I wasn't a bad kid, just a slacker. I never thought beyond the next weekend and how much money I needed in my pocket." He frowned, shaking his head. "When he died, everything was so desperate. I was in pure panic mode. Something just took over. I put my head down and bulldozed through every obstacle that came in my path. The first couple of years, I had three jobs, one of which was for my uncle Grady."

He met her gaze, his green eyes flat. "He works for me now. Some bullshit family job pushing paper, because I owe him."

She swung her leg. "Do you feel guilty?"

"Not guilty . . . Just . . . I don't know." He looked away again. "Responsible. His was the first company I bought out. I made it clear if he didn't sell he'd end up going out of business because there was no way he could compete with me." He smiled scornfully. "I was nice about it, but the gist was there."

"Why couldn't he compete?"

He shrugged. "I was better, more competent, more competitive, and more desperate than he could ever be. We lived and worked in the same neighborhood and he started losing guys to me, and bids. I didn't mean to put him out of business, but my family wasn't even close to being financially secure. Once I started I couldn't stop. Even now, I see the numbers in my bank accounts, but I always feel like I'm one step away from disaster."

She wanted so badly to reach out and touch him but stopped herself. Instead, she said in a soft voice, "But you did it. You saved them. They're all successful adults. You did a good job."

"I don't know. It still doesn't feel like enough."

"I think that's habit. To everyone else, you're a hero."

He laughed. "I'm sure they'd disagree."

She was absolutely sure they wouldn't but didn't say that. Nor did she push anymore, her instinct telling her to back off.

He rubbed his palm over her thigh, sending a shiver of awareness tingling over her skin. "How do you feel?"

"Shockingly good." She surprised herself by covering his hand with hers.

Their fingers twined. So natural and right, she could only stare at his long, tan fingers entwined with her small, paler ones.

"That's the advantage of throwing it all up."

She flushed, covering her face with her free hand. "I'm so humiliated. I wish you wouldn't have seen that."

"Why?"

"Because." She shook her head. "I was messy and gross, and that's not how I want you to see me."

"I kind of liked it."

Her head jerked up. "Are you crazy?"

"It makes you real, Cecilia. Human." He tugged her hand, and she scooted forward. "I'm not sure I've ever seen you look so beautiful."

The air heavy with things unsaid, she frowned. "I'm not sure thank you is the appropriate thing to say here."

"I don't care about you being appropriate."

She tilted her head to the side. "You don't, do you?"

"Not even a little bit." He tugged again, sending her

practically into his lap. His lips covered hers before she could protest.

And just like that he sucked her in.

She kissed him back. Her tongue stroking his, bold and demanding.

Wanting him. Needing him. He deepened the kiss, and she moaned against him. Wanting to crawl into him.

He pulled away, his lips hovering over hers. "It's time to tell me about this stupid fucking idea of yours."

Cecilia shifted away, stood abruptly, and began to pace around the room. She wore skinny jeans and a sleeveless flowy top, and ballet flats. The suits hadn't made an appearance since her first day here.

She took three laps around the room before she finally said, "I idolized my dad growing up. All I ever wanted was for him to be proud of me." She gave Shane a wry smile. "Mitch was the opposite. He couldn't care less, so of course everything came easy to him. But I wasn't that lucky; I had to work. While Mitch didn't even have to crack a book to get an A, I had to study for hours."

Cecilia and Mitch barely had a passing acquaintance with each other. It was hard for Shane to picture them young and in the throes of sibling rivalry. He narrowed his eyes as she lapped around the room again. "Go on."

"There was only one area where I had Mitch beat. I loved politics while he hated them. For as long as I can remember, a career in public service is all I ever wanted." She sat down on the chair farthest from him and folded her hands in her lap. "Did you know I went to law school too?"

He nodded. It had been a footnote in her file.

Another small smile. "Most people don't, because I

wasn't close to being a superstar like Mitch. And I didn't do it to practice. I did it to understand the system. I didn't even bother taking the bar exam. The day after I graduated, I started working for my father. Most people don't realize my dad is a self-made man. He's brilliant in the same way Mitch is. When he met my mom he was a poor scholarship kid."

Shane didn't think marrying into old money qualified as "self-made," but he wasn't about to debate the semantics. That's how Cecilia saw him, and that's what mattered.

She sliced a hand through the air. "Anyway, I might have been his daughter, but he didn't believe in free rides. I worked my way through the ranks, starting as the coffee girl. And I did it all. Worked my ass off to make sure I was the best at every single task until nobody could dispute my dedication or my brains. I sucked up every single bit of knowledge I could with one motivation." She held up an index finger. "I wanted to run for office. And every time I'd get discouraged, or upset, this one goal got me through it. Helped me focus."

Her expression lined with distress, she took a deep breath.

Shane crooked a finger. "Come here, Ce-ce."

She sucked her bottom lip through her teeth, looking at the seat she'd vacated next to him.

She got up and walked toward him. Just as she was about to sit down she veered off, pacing once again around the room.

On her next lap around he caught her wrist and held her still. "What are you afraid of?"

Her eyes clouded, turning more gray than blue. "I don't want you to hate me."

It was an honest, vulnerable answer. So unlike the woman he'd believed her to be, that his chest squeezed. And then it hit him. Under the balls-to-the-walls, take-no-shit career woman—Cecilia Riley craved approval. He stroked a thumb over the soft skin on the underside of her wrist. "That's not going to happen."

The fine bones in her hand flexed. "You don't know that."

"I do." He tugged on her wrist. "Now, come sit."

Skittish as a rabbit, she sat down next to him.

He entwined their fingers and spoke in a calm tone he knew would sooth her. "Go on."

The muscles in her throat worked as she swallowed hard. "After his scandal, it occurred to me that everything I'd ever achieved was for him. I'd done nothing for myself. Everything I did, my life, my career, my contacts, were all because of him. Every time he skirts responsibility for a mistake it makes him more arrogant. More sloppy. Eventually he'll screw up and when he goes down, I'll go down with him. I'd forgotten."

When she didn't continue, he nudged. "Forgotten?"

"That I'm weak."

He scoffed. "That's not a word I'd ever use to describe you."

She stared at the floor for a very long time, so closely, as though she studied the grains of wood under her feet. "Nobody knows this, and I'm trusting you."

"Hey," he said, taking her chin and turning her face toward him. "You can tell me anything."

Her brow furrowed, creasing in concentration. "I'm starting to believe that."

"That's because it's true."

She glanced away, turning her head. He let her go, understanding she needed the illusion of privacy to speak what was on her mind. "I made inquiries, after the scandal. In Washington, I looked . . ." She lowered her voice. "For another job."

He pressed his lips together to keep from smiling. "I see."

"I don't even think I was serious. I did it for reassurance. To gain a sense of security about my future. Only everyone assumes I'm my father's lackey. He keeps me behind the scenes, so nobody really knows the things I've accomplished on his behalf."

Expression turning hard, she shook her head. "You know how he skated through that whole blackmail fiasco virtually unscathed?"

"Yeah, it was pretty miraculous."

She pointed to her chest. "That was me. I orchestrated the whole thing. And that's not all I've done. You'd be shocked at the things I've handled without anyone being the wiser."

The senator's media campaign had been impeccable after the scandal. Anything that could have gone his way did. Within a month everyone had forgiven him, brushing over any indiscretion with the careless ease of a twenty-four-hour news cycle.

It was impressive, but Shane wasn't sure what it had to do with Cecilia's running for office.

She exhaled a long, hard breath. "I came back home and spent the weekend holed up in my town house and came face-to-face with the truth: in that world, I'm nothing without my dad."

"Cecilia," he said, his voice taking on a sharp edge. "To quote you, 'that's bullshit.'"

Her head jerked back as though he'd slapped her. "But it's not. It's honest. It forced me to take action. To stop living my life for him. I need to do this. For me. It's what I've always wanted and I'm not going to fail. I refuse."

He could see the determined tilt of her chin, that spark of defiance in her storm-blue eyes. Arguing the point now would be a fruitless endeavor. He sighed. "And I suppose this is how Miles Fletcher comes in?"

She nodded, squeezing his fingers. "Please don't think I'm awful."

How had he missed this? This desire to please and be approved of? "Just tell me what's happening and we'll figure out a way to fix it."

Her expression flashed with gratitude before dimming. "There's no other way. It doesn't assure a victory, but it helps. Without marrying him, I'm virtually guaranteed to lose."

"You don't know that," he insisted, having an impossible time understanding how she could even consider it. "This isn't the eighteen hundreds, Cecilia. For fuck's sake, there are gays in both the senate and the house."

"But you know what they're not?"

Even though he already knew, he shook his head.

She blew out a breath. "Single."

"I can't see how an entire campaign could rest on your marital status. That's ridiculous."

"It's not, but the other factors aren't things I can control. I'm too young, a woman, and I've had a hard time garnering support from the party."

"Why?"

She shrugged, tugged her hand away and studied her nails. "You didn't think you're the only person who thinks I'm an ice queen, did you?"

He winced. How many times had he thrown that barb at her—casually, almost cruelly, over the last nine months? In the handful of times he'd seen her, more than a couple.

"But I know," she said, her voice taking on a plea. "I know I can change their minds, I just need practice. I've always been behind the scenes, and that's where being cool under pressure is what works. In time, given the right opportunity, I'll gain my footing."

What a complicated mess. It didn't make sense to him. But he was sure about one thing: Cecilia believed whole-heartedly she needed to marry Miles Fletcher. In her mind, this guy was the path to fulfilling her lifelong dreams.

Shane thought it was crap, but he was smart enough to know now wasn't the time to talk her out of it. "How does Miles help? Besides being a warm body?"

She stood up and started pacing again and Shane didn't even attempt to stop her.

She ran a hand through her hair. "He's very well respected within the party. He also has deep pockets and relationships with some key lobbyists."

Shane narrowed his eyes. "What's in it for him?"

She stopped on a dime. "Excuse me?"

"You said there was nothing physical between you, so what does he gain out of this?"

Her brow furrowed. "What does that matter?"

Shane sat forward, putting his elbows on his knees. Something wasn't adding up here and it wasn't like Cecilia to gloss over details. "You don't even know, do you?"

She bit her lower lip. "I didn't ask."

He tilted his head to the side. "Let me get this straight. You have a file on me that includes almost every single detail of my life, but it didn't occur to you to ask a basic question about the guy you're supposed to marry?"

Her whole body grew rigid, and while she was dressed casually, she may as well have just slipped into one of her severely tailored business suits. "It doesn't matter. I didn't care."

"Why?" The word held more bark than he'd intended.

"Because I didn't think about it!" She threw up her hands

and flopped down into an armchair across from him. "I was busy coming to terms with the fact that everything I believed was a lie. I'm not special. My father doesn't care about me, Shane. He thought nothing about marrying me off because Miles would be a good ally. I am a pawn."

She was hurt, deeply. But he couldn't help asking the question. "Then why are you playing by his rules?"

She looked at him, her expression hollow, her eyes distant and remote. "Just because he's a shitty father doesn't mean he's not right. Now I've got something to prove and I'm not giving up, so don't even ask me."

Chapter Sixteen

Cecilia put on a bright face and stepped into the kitchen, where Maddie, her two friends, and Charlotte sat around the kitchen table. "Good morning."

Four heads swiveled in her direction. Sophie grinned. "Well, well, well, and how do you feel today?"

"Great, actually." Cecilia pushed her hair from her cheeks, realizing she'd forgotten to clip it back.

"Lucky you," Sophie said. "Sore?"

Cecilia's cheeks heated at least fifteen degrees.

Penelope slapped Sophie's arm, shushing her.

"Ewww!" Maddie said, but grinned right along with her friend.

Her mom's gaze narrowed as she took a sip from one of her grandma's teacups decorated with little roses and gold trim. "What happened last night?"

"Nothing," Cecilia said quickly. "Nothing at all." She cleared her throat. "So what's on the agenda today? And how can I help?"

Maddie straightened the piles of papers in front of her and flipped over a page in a spiral notebook. "Well, let's see . . ."

Penelope sighed and picked up her coffee. "On that note, I've got to run to a conference call."

Maddie frowned. "Why?"

"We're having some issues with the city contract deal, and I'm sorry, but they don't wait for anyone, not even your wedding."

That must be the deal Shane mentioned. Cecilia made a mental note to ask him about it. She knew people, including the mayor, so maybe she could help. Not that it was any of her business, but still, it couldn't hurt.

"You're supposed to be on vacation," Maddie said, huffing.

Penelope patted her friend on the shoulder. "I love you like a sister, but being ordered about by you and your never-ending list is not a vacation."

Maddie's lower lip puffed out in a pout. "I know, I'm terrible, aren't I?"

Sophie threw her head back and laughed. "The worst! I almost miss the old days, when anything wedding-related was a four-letter word."

"I know," Maddie said, worrying her hands. "I'm so nervous this time. I want everything to be perfect."

"It will be, dear," Charlotte said, the affection so clear in her voice Cecilia's heart gave a little lurch.

She wanted her mom to sound like that when they talked. She picked up a napkin from the table and wiped at an imaginary spot.

Penelope glanced at the clock, squinting behind her glasses. "I'll be done in a couple of hours."

"Can't Shane do without you?" Maddie asked.

Penelope waved her hand around the room. "You've got three people ready to help you. Shane's only got me."

A stab of jealousy knifed through Cecilia from out of nowhere and she had to fight an urge to stand and yell *No, you're wrong. He has me!* She took a deep breath to quell the desire and let logic prevail. Penelope meant work.

There was nothing between them.

Cecilia peered more closely at the other woman.

Her hair was a lush, mink brown, so thick and shiny she could be in a shampoo commercial. Behind those thick, black frames her eyes were a startling blue. Crystal clear and direct. And her face was pretty. Like really pretty. With the no-nonsense, capable demeanor she wore like a second skin, Cecilia hadn't realized. Did Shane?

Where was this coming from?

Penelope must have sensed her heavy gaze because she frowned. "What? Do I have jelly on my chin?"

"No, nothing like that. You're quite pretty," Cecilia blurted. Clearly the Jägerbombs hadn't left her system yet.

The other woman twitched, as though the statement surprised her. "Oh. Um, thank you."

Sophie pressed her finger to her lips. "Shhh, don't say anything nice. Penelope hates to be complimented."

Cecilia's chest gave another squeeze.

How wonderful would it be to have friends like this? Friends who understood your idiosyncrasies and patterns? Your strengths and weaknesses? She couldn't even imagine. Was that bad? To be removed from life? From connections? The song lyrics from that old Simon and Garfunkel song filled her mind. She was an island.

Was that going to be her? What had Shane called her last night when she'd been drifting in and out of consciousness? Summer Cecilia? That when she returned to Chicago she'd go back to being the woman she'd always been?

Was that true? Could she be summer Cecilia back home?

She didn't think so. Not in the world she lived in, where one had to keep one's friends close and enemies closer. Not where one wrong move could be her undoing.

* * *

Sitting in the kitchen, Shane pinched the bridge of his nose and popped another two Advil, thankful for the five minutes of quiet in a house that was bursting with people. Miraculously, everyone was gone and he was finally alone, and his fucking cell phone was quiet. He'd given up on e-mail, asking Penelope to go through the hundreds of messages, answer what she could, and mark the ones he needed to deal with. Not a task he asked of her often, but with this current shit storm with the mayor's office, he had to delegate something so he could focus.

The deal was starting to unravel and he only hoped he could recover when he met with the mayor. Politics was a fine line, and the city planner seemed intent on sabotage, which infuriated Shane. The guy didn't have to like him, but he was fucking with people's lives. If the guy found a way to kill the deal, Shane would be forced to cut staff. Those people depended on him and construction was still a recovering business.

Where would they find jobs? His skull throbbed.

The back door opened and he had to stop himself from slamming his fist on the table and growling at the person to get the hell out. He glanced up to see Mitch walk through the door. He gritted his teeth to keep from snapping. He'd heard it was impolite to kick someone out of their own house.

Mitch threw his computer case on the bench of the built-in hall tree next to the back door. "Hey, where is everyone?"

"Out." The word more terse than it should be.

Mitch raised a brow. "Tough day?"

Shane shrugged. "I've had better. This negotiation with the city is in the crapper."

"Can't say I miss Chicago politics." Mitch tossed his keys into the bowl on the counter and strolled to the fridge, opening the door. He held up a beer. "Want one?"

Recovered from his love affair with the bottle of scotch from a couple of nights ago, he nodded.

Mitch pulled another bottle from the refrigerator and slammed the door shut. He slid a bottle across the table, and it landed in front of Shane. Mitch took a seat. "Want to talk about it?"

"Terms and conditions stuff. I have a great relationship with the mayor, but this new guy in charge of city planning is an asshole. He's angling to pull the contract and fighting me on every single point. On shit that I would have hammered out over a steak dinner and drinks with the old guy without even breaking a sweat." And he was trying not to worry about the ramifications if the negotiations failed. He'd fight tooth and nail for his people, but if David Jackson got his way, Shane wouldn't have a lot of options.

Mitch scoffed. "One of those, huh?"

"Yeah, and I'm not his favorite person. We had a run-in about five years ago. He lost. Now he's got it in his head to make my life a living hell." Shane shook his head.

Mitch took a drag off his bottle. "When will it be done?"

"Don't know." The worry sat heavy in his stomach. "We meet again the Monday after the wedding."

Mitch grinned. "At least you'll be back home instead of this madhouse."

Shane raised his gaze to the ceiling and said, "God, deliver me from all these women."

Mitch chuckled. "I'll be happy when this is over and I'm not banging into someone every time I turn a corner."

Happy to be distracted from his current trouble, Shane asked, "What kind of a guy has a household full of people invading his space before he gets married? You should be off in Vegas."

Mitch sighed. "The kind of guy that wants to make your sister happy."

Shane drained the rest of his beer, standing to grab another one. He tilted the bottle in Mitch's direction. He nodded.

Shane grabbed two more from the fridge. "Did you ever think you'd be this whipped?"

Mitch laughed, the sound good-natured. "Nope, not in a million years." Then he shrugged, almost chagrined. "But she's worth it. This is important to her and I'm smart enough to know it's temporary. Soon everyone will leave and it will just be the two of us again."

As he sat back down at the table, Shane experienced a squeeze of envy that surprised him.

As much as it annoyed him to be surrounded by a bunch of people all the time, there was a comfort in it too. He found he didn't relish the idea of going back to his empty house. Decorated by some professional, it was nice, but not lived-in. A house but not a home.

Not at all how he grew up. Their three-bedroom brick bungalow had been messy, run-down, overcrowded, and full of family.

Mitch stretched back, resting the bottle with a loose grip on his stomach. "So do I have to bring it up?"

Shane scrubbed a hand over his jaw, instantly wary. "What do you want to know? Not that it's any of your business."

"True," Mitch said, nodding slowly. "While I'm surprised at your involvement with my sister, it's not what I'm curious about."

Shane's gaze narrowed. "Then what is it?"

"Do you know what's going on that's got everyone all upset? I've been thinking it through and I'm positive it has something to do with this farce of an engagement, but I haven't been able to piece through all the details."

"What makes you think the engagement's not real?" Shane asked, diverting the question back to him.

"Please, my sister might not be perfect, but she's pretty much walked the straight and narrow her whole life. There's no way she'd hook up with you if that marriage was the real deal."

Shane shrugged, not about to divulge Cecilia's secrets. It would be her choice, not his. "Have you tried asking her?"

"Yeah, you were there that first day and she stone-walled me."

"You cross-examined her in front of a bunch of strangers." Sometimes he wondered how these Rileys could be so smart in some ways and so stupid in others. "What did you expect? For her to spill her guts right then and there?"

Two lines formed over his brow, and the corners of Mitch's mouth dipped. "I hadn't thought of that."

"Because you're a dumb-ass."

Mitch raised a brow. "So you know but aren't going to tell me."

"You're just proving my point here."

Mitch nodded and took a slug of beer. "Interesting."

Shane gave him a level-eyed look and kept his mouth shut.

"So where are the girls?"

"I think they went over to Gracie's."

Mitch grinned. "Wanna call Sam and Charlie for a game of pickup?"

Off and on, Shane had thought about what to do about Cecilia and her insistence that she only had one option. Something was off about the whole thing, but he couldn't figure it out and it was making him twitchy. A game was just what he needed. "Make the call."

* * *

After the day Cecilia had spent with the girls, she felt like a whole new woman. All these years she'd underestimated the importance of belonging, of having women to talk to. She thought about her "friends" back in Chicago. All those polite lunches where nobody laughed; they smirked. The last thing she'd do was tell them her secrets. Even the women she'd known almost all her life. She didn't trust any of them. But she trusted the women she'd spent the afternoon with.

Even if she couldn't reveal her secrets.

She liked them. Liked their easy affection with each other. Liked their not-so-gentle prying into what was going on between her and Shane. It made her feel . . . accepted.

Not something she was used to.

She refilled her glass of iced tea from the pitcher on Gracie's counter and turned just as Maddie entered the room.

Over the course of the afternoon, she'd helped Maddie organize and prioritize the rest of her wedding list. Then she'd divided the list of responsibilities among the women by what she perceived as their areas of strength. Gracie took care of the caterer and related food items, Sophie got decorating, she gave her mom vendor confirmations, Maddie took actions that couldn't be delegated, and she took the leftovers. They'd been done in no time flat.

She'd had fun doing it. It was such a relief. Her mind had turned off and she hadn't thought about her engagement, her family, or her campaign.

The sense of accomplishment warmed her all over, reminding her why she'd always loved working in the first place. An idea niggled in her mind, something important but elusive that hovered in the corners of her subconscious.

Maddie beamed, and the thought evaporated into thin air. "I'm officially in love with you. Thank you so much."

"It was my pleasure," Cecilia said, feeling a swell of pride that she'd actually managed to connect with her soon-to-be sister-in-law.

"I'm ahead of schedule now." Maddie glanced around the kitchen then lowered her voice. "Don't tell Penelope, but I think you could give her a run for her money."

Cecilia laughed. "Your secret is safe with me."

Maddie tucked a lock of hair behind her ear and did another paranoid visual sweep. "I know this is none of my business, and this is a bit forward, but I need you to do me a favor."

Shoulders stiffening, Cecilia was instantly alert. Knowing better than to make a promise without knowing the terms, she said cautiously, "I'll try."

"Please don't hurt my brother." Maddie nibbled on her lower lip, gaze darting around the kitchen as though afraid someone would pop out from the cabinets. "See, the thing is, he'll do anything for the people he cares about. And I do mean *anything*."

Cecilia nodded. "He sacrificed a lot for your family after your dad died."

"He did," Maddie said, her voice impassioned. "Once he gets something in his head, he'll move heaven and earth to make it happen. The cost, especially to himself, is irrelevant. That's the way he is."

"I know," Cecilia said softly, a trickle of unease skittering through her.

"I understand your situation is . . . complicated, and believe me, I relate, but please, be careful with him. Because he's falling for you. Hard."

Some long-repressed, girlish part of Cecilia wanted to

ask what he'd said about her. An impulse she ignored, but she did want to ease Maddie's mind as best she could. "I can't explain anything right now. I know it looks bad. But I do care. I'm not sure he's really falling for me. I think it's just, well"—she waved a hand in the air looking for the appropriate words to say to Shane's sister—"You know how he is once he decides he wants something."

"True, but I see the way he looks at you. And with your marital status up in the air, he'd never get involved unless he couldn't help himself. It's not just attraction like when you two first met. Something's changed."

Cecilia frowned. She'd been so careful back then. Not like now, where everyone, save her mother, knew something was going on between them. "You knew?"

Maddie smiled. "Of course."

"But how?"

She outright laughed now. "Let's just say when you've been struck by instant lust you tend to recognize the signs."

Cecilia nibbled her bottom lip. "I'm doing my best here, Maddie. This wasn't something I expected, and I'm still navigating my way."

The time for avoidance was coming to a close. Her actions didn't just affect her anymore, they were affecting the people around her. If she wasn't careful she'd hurt Shane and lose the developing relationship with this group of people who no longer seemed like strangers. The more time she spent with them, the more she started to feel like she belonged.

"I understand," Maddie said, picking up her glass. "All I'm asking is you remember that once he takes that final plunge, there's nothing my brother won't do for you. So if you're going to marry another guy, please end it before he dives in the rest of the way."

"I will," Cecilia said, that unease growing into a full-blown bad feeling.

Maddie smiled, but her green eyes, the same shade as her brother's, were still clouded with worry. "Just remember this about Shane: He never asks for anything in return. No matter what he's laid on the line."

A band squeezed around Cecilia's ribs. "Do you think I'm an awful person?"

"No," Maddie said, then came over and locked Cecilia in a hug.

Cecilia froze for a second, once again uncomfortable with the display of affection, but then hugged her sister-in-law back, and something relaxed in her.

She wanted to be part of them. To fit together the way they all did.

When Maddie pulled away, she smiled. "I know better than most people that appearances are deceiving. Don't forget, I ran out on my wedding and hooked up with your brother my first night on the lam." She chuckled, seeming to recollect some private memory. "Not exactly my shining moment, but sometimes these things can't be helped."

Cecilia cleared her throat, wanting to express her gratitude and realizing how infrequently she offered anyone any genuine emotion. She forced the words out because she felt them and was sick of being uncomfortable. "Thank you. I know I'm not the warmest person, but I appreciate how you've included me in all the family stuff."

Maddie's brow furrowed, her auburn brows forming a deep V. "That's because you *are* family. And I don't believe for one second you're cold. You're slow to warm up, just like your mom and brother. But once you get going you're totally awesome. I hope, with time, you'll start to think of me as a friend and not just as the girl who's marrying your brother."

"I'd like that too," Cecilia said, meaning it.

Sam wandered into the kitchen wearing a pair of gym shorts so low-slung they showed the cut of his lean hip. Cecilia could only stare at him, this man she still mentally viewed as the boy she'd grown up with. His skin was lightly tanned, his lean muscles ripped across an impressive chest and six-pack abs, and his blond hair was a disheveled mess.

She blinked, and then blinked again. Damn, he had quite a body on him.

"Sorry, girls," he said in a slow drawl. "Just passing through."

Maddie cocked a brow. "Show-off."

He stopped on a dime and gave Maddie a slow, leisurely glance. "There's one thing I've learned in life: when you're about to play basketball with a bunch of overly aggressive, possessive guys, it's best to have any advantage you can."

Cecilia lost her focus on what he was saying. Where had scrawny little Sam gone?

Maddie's lips tilted down and she crossed her arms. "What the hell does that mean?"

He grinned, all cocky and full of mischief. He chucked Maddie under the chin. "It means telling Shane and Mitch you girls were checking out the goods is sure to throw them off their game."

Wait, Shane was playing basketball?

Cecilia lifted her chin and said in her haughtiest voice, "Excuse me, I never check men out. It's not in my nature."

His lazy gaze turned on her. "Then Shane won't believe me, now will he?"

Why did she feel as though she'd been caught in a lie?

She put on her most impassive expression. "I have no control over him."

Sam shrugged, unconcerned. "We'll have to see about that, now won't we?"

Maddie planted her hands on her hips. "Don't even try that on us. We're on to you."

"I'll see you ladies outside." He grinned and sauntered away.

Cecilia turned to Maddie. "Why do I feel like we've been issued some sort of challenge?"

"Oh, because we have."

"What do we do now?"

Maddie laughed. "We fall for it, of course."

Shane stood talking to Mitch as Sam and Charlie huddled under the basketball hoop at the end of the long driveway planning some sort of strategy.

"What the fuck are you two doing?" Mitch yelled. "Trading makeup tips?"

Sam waved him away. "Shut up and get your own game plan."

Mitch rolled his eyes and cocked a brow at Shane. "You know the plan?"

Shane gave a sharp nod. "Kick their asses."

They pounded fists.

"Done," Mitch called out.

Charlie and Sam ignored them.

Shane shook his head. "This isn't the NBA. Get a move on."

Charlie shot him the finger and went back to talking to Sam.

Three minutes later, all the girls filed out of Gracie's house.

Sam smiled. "Now we're ready."

Before they could start, Maddie ran over and threw herself on Mitch, pulling him down and kissing him like she hadn't seen him in ten years.

Shane made a disgusted sound. "Would you knock it the hell off?"

Out of the corner of his eye, he saw Cecilia press a finger to those porn-star lips to keep from laughing. She'd changed into a black tank top and white shorts. Her breasts swelled over the scooped neckline and her legs were endless. He yanked his gaze away.

Mitch pulled away from his sister and patted her ass. "Miss me, princess?"

"Always," Maddie said, mooning at him.

Shane sighed, a long, heavy sound.

Charlie held out his hands. "I thought you were ready?"

"Geez, chill," Maddie said, then sashayed off the driveway and plopped down on a lawn chair between Penelope and Sophie.

Charlie shook his head. "That girl needs a spanking if I ever met one."

Shane punched him in the arm. "That's my sister."

"I didn't say I'd do it," Charlie said, a hint of his Southern roots laced through his drawl. "Just that she needed one. She's getting sassy."

From behind him Cecilia laughed, a full-bodied smoky laugh that shot straight to Shane's balls and made him shiver with lust. He whipped around, giving her a cocky smile. "What are you laughing at?"

She pressed her lips together. "Oh, nothing." She sat forward, resting her elbows on her knees and his gaze slipped to her cleavage.

Charlie gave him a sly grin. "Maybe she needs one too."

Shane shifted his attention back to Cecilia, assessing. An image of her round ass over his knee made him contemplate ditching the game and finishing what they'd started last night.

Cecilia shook her head, her whiskey hair swaying around her shoulders. When had it gone from razor straight to wavy? "Don't even think about it."

He scrubbed his hand over his jaw, thinking about it anyway.

She cocked a brow at him. "Try it and you'll be sorry."

Charlie jabbed him with an elbow. "Well, shit, now she's outright challenging you."

Mitch punched him in the arm. "Hey, that's *my* sister."

Cecilia's eyes widened, her gaze jerking toward her brother. Her whole face lit up, as though she couldn't believe anyone would stand up for her. Shane's heart gave a hard little *thunk* against his ribs.

From the sidelines, Gracie raised a hand. "Um, I'll take a spanking."

Everyone laughed except for Sam, who scowled. "For fuck's sake, you're my sister!"

She rolled her eyes. "Well, I didn't mean you, dummy."

Charlie grinned and winked at her. "Just name the time and place, honey."

"Still my sister!" Sam yelled.

Gracie ignored him and took a sip of her drink. "You know we're not doing that anymore."

Charlie laughed and turned back to the court.

Shane looked at Cecilia, who looked right back at him with that eagle-eyed, level stare of hers. The one that said she wasn't scared of anything, least of all him. His whole body heated with lust, because he read the challenge there too. That I-dare-you tilt of her lips. He walked over, and not once did she glance away.

When he stood in front of her, she raised her head, and the sunlight kissed her skin and turned her hair to spun gold. "Can I help you?"

Oh, that smooth, prim voice—as though she was deliberately trying to entice him.

He ran a finger over the line of her jaw, not caring who watched. Satisfaction swelled as she shuddered ever so slightly. "Challenge accepted."

She smirked. "I don't know to what you're referring."

He laughed, catching her game and liking it. "Then you're going to be in for quite a surprise, now aren't you?"

Sophie whistled, long and low. "Girl, you are in trouble."

Cecilia shrugged, sitting back in her chair and crossing her legs. "I'm not afraid of him."

She wasn't. It was one of the things he liked best about her. One of the things he wasn't sure if he could live without.

Chapter Seventeen

Cecilia shot a nervous glance over at Shane, all lazy and relaxed, as they made their way back to Chicago. Despite her protests, he drove. They'd argued about it, a fun, good-natured argument that had her fighting not to laugh, but in the end she'd relented. With Shane she'd learned to pick her battles, and this one didn't seem worth it.

But now, an hour into the drive and nothing to occupy her but endless cornfields, the conversation she'd been dreading sat like a lump of coal in her belly.

The last couple of days had been odd. They'd talked. He'd held her hand as they sat on the couch and watched movies with the rest of the crew. He'd given her mad, passionate kisses that left her breathless, but he'd made no move to get into her bed.

It was like having a nineteen fifties courtship.

And now she had to go and ruin it.

She twisted her hands, fidgeting in her seat, worried.

The reason for her worry frightened her. About ten minutes into her fretting she realized she was scared to death that once she told him about attending the benefit with

Miles, he'd leave. Then she'd be shut out, and she'd grown far too used to his warmth.

She cared. A lot. This was no longer some chemical attraction. This was real.

And that was wrong.

She frowned, shifting in her seat. As soon as she told him the truth about tonight, he'd go back to hating her.

"All right," he said, his gruff voice startling her from her troubled thoughts. "Spit it out."

She nibbled her lower lip and diverted. "How do you know something is wrong?"

He gave her a sidelong glance before turning his attention back to the rural road. "Because I know you."

Was that right? Did he? "You do?"

He shook his head. "Don't try to distract me, just say what's on your mind so you can relax."

She blew out an exasperated breath. He made it sound so easy! "I can't!"

"Why's that?" He sounded so warm and casual. How would he sound after he found out?

"Because," she said, clenching her hands. Suddenly it was too hot and she punched the air conditioner down. "I'm afraid."

He raised a brow. "That's a new one."

"You don't think I get afraid?"

He shrugged. "Not often. And if you do, it doesn't seem to slow you down. You're more a take-the-bull-by-the-horns type."

She crossed her arms and decided to take offense. "What does that mean?"

"Exactly what you think it means." He reached over and squeezed her knee. "Now stop distracting me, woman."

It wasn't going to work. He wasn't going to let her lure him into an argument. The jerk.

A green mile marker flew by, reminding her of her drive into Revival. It seemed like a lifetime ago. She hadn't been happy, per se, but her life had been clear. Her path set. Now, nothing made sense.

She took a deep breath and exhaled loudly. "Okay, you know how I'm . . ." She cleared her throat and waved her hand in the air, unable to come right out and say it. "You know . . ."

"You know?"

She punched the air down to sixty. "Engaged."

His shoulders tensed fractionally, but he nodded.

"Well, this benefit, my plans were made a long time before you and I . . . became . . . well, whatever this is."

"Not willing to put a name on it, huh?" The question sounded far too amused for the subject matter. He had to know where she was going, but seemed unperturbed by the whole thing.

"What would you call it?" she shot back.

He chuckled. "Nice try, Ce-ce."

She wrinkled her nose. How could he make being a jerk so appealing? "Anyway, with my plans in place . . ." The words stuck in her throat as though they were glued there.

"You're going with him." It wasn't a question.

Miserable, she nodded and braced herself for his wrath. She waited.

Waited.

But it didn't come.

Instead, he shrugged and punched the air back up to sixty-five. "I figured as much."

"You did?" An irrational thread of annoyance snaked its way down her spine. He didn't even sound upset.

"It's a high-profile benefit, and I know you're looking to be visible. I did the math."

"You're not upset?" Here she'd been expecting him to

hate her again, or at least raise his voice. Something. But he acted like she'd told him the sky was blue.

"I'm not happy, but it is what it is." He gave her an innocent smile that raised the hairs on the back of her neck and put her on instant alert. "Besides, you're not the only one with prior commitments."

Her spine snapped ruler straight. "I see. You have a date?"

"I do, although I'm not sure you know her." Again, his expression was angelic. "Harper Holt."

"Oh." While the name sounded vaguely familiar, Cecilia couldn't place it. It didn't matter who the woman was, Cecilia instantly hated her. "Well, great. It all works out then."

"Yep," he said, so casually she wanted to gouge his eyes out.

She turned and stared out the window. How could he? It was completely unfair of her, but she didn't care. She hated him. He was the most despicable man alive. Harper Holt. She sounded obnoxious.

And just like that, the name clicked. Rushing into her mind like a runaway train. The name was from the file she had on him.

Hot with anger, her cheeks flamed. She whipped around and jabbed a finger at Shane. "Harper Holt, the CEO of Innovate?"

"So you do know her." The corners of his mouth quivered. Was he trying not to laugh?

"Your *ex-girlfriend*!" she yelled, surprising herself. She wasn't a yeller.

He shrugged, as if this was no big deal. "She's a friend and doing me a favor."

Jealousy, unlike anything she'd ever experienced in her life, made her lose her normal grasp on rational behavior. Fists clenched tight, her nails digging into her palms, she said, "How could you?!"

"How could I what?" His casual tone grated over her last

nerve. "Do I really need to remind you that you're going with your fiancé?"

She sputtered. "That's different!"

"How?"

"It just is."

"Because you don't like it," he stated matter-of-factly.

She contemplated ways to torture him, including shoving bamboo shoots under his fingernails. "I've never had sex with Miles. I've never even kissed him."

He frowned at her. "I'm not having sex with Harper."

"But you did." She desperately wanted to stop talking to give herself a chance to calm down, but she couldn't seem to get her mouth under control.

"I dated her for a year."

She let out a scream. "This isn't the same thing."

"I know. I'm not the one getting married."

"That doesn't mean anything!"

He jerked the car to the side of the road, coming to a screeching halt, then gave her a hard-eyed look. "Then why the *fuck* are you doing it?"

She gulped, and wished she'd kept her mouth shut.

It was underhanded. Shane knew that and didn't care. One of the things he'd learned about Cecilia was that she was stubborn as hell.

He raised a brow, putting his hand on the back of her seat. "Well? Why?"

Her expression flashed with emotion: anger, jealousy, fear. "You know I have to."

"Why do you have to?" He hadn't pushed before but intended to now.

"Stop trying to change the subject," she yelled, her voice going squeaky.

"This is the subject, Cecilia."

"I don't want you to go with her." She sniffed, her chin tilting with that telltale defiance.

"Well, I don't want you to go with him, but what we want and what's happening isn't the same thing."

Her lashes lifted and her eyes were more gray than blue. "Are you doing this on purpose? To make me jealous?"

One of the things he liked best about Cecilia was he didn't have to pull any punches, and he didn't soften the blow. "Of course."

She blinked. "Why would you do that?"

He trailed a finger down her smooth cheek. "I could have canceled, but I didn't intend to be the only jealous party here."

"You don't even seem like you care."

"I care," he said, his voice softening considerably. "More than I should. More than I can help. But I know I can't talk you out of it. Even though I think it's the stupidest hare-brained scheme I've ever heard."

"You don't understand how it is."

God, she was stubborn. He asked the one question she'd yet to answer regardless of how many times he'd prompted. "Why do you want to run for congress?"

"Because it's what I've always wanted." Parroting the same line of crap she kept giving him.

"Don't you see, Cecilia," he said, stroking down her neck, "that's not a good enough reason."

Twin lines formed over her brows. "What are you trying to say?"

He sighed. "Once I had lunch with a candidate for alder-man and I asked her that same question. She talked about changes she wanted to make in the schools, greenhouse gasses, bringing government back to the people, getting her community involved. She was so passionate. She couldn't stop talking about all the things she wanted to accomplish. I didn't say more than five words the whole meal."

Cecilia's shoulders had gone stiff. That remote expression slid over her face, keeping everything hidden. "You don't think I can do that?"

He looked her dead in the eyes, hoping she understood his distinction. "I absolutely believe you can do that. Hell, Cecilia, you've won the respect and loyalty of every single person in that overcrowded farmhouse in less than a week. If you can do that, you can sway voters."

Her chin shot up another notch. "Not my mother. She's barely talking to me."

"That's your own fault."

"How can you say that?"

"She's your mom; she knows you're making a mistake. It's killing her."

She opened her mouth but he held up a hand. "Let me make my point before we start talking about your family, which, let's be honest, will take the rest of the drive."

She huffed, crossing her arms. "What's your point?"

"I'm not saying you *can't*, I'm saying you don't want to."

She pressed her body against the window. "You're wrong."

He shook his head. "I'm not. I've never seen anybody less excited about fulfilling their lifelong dream."

"That's not true," she said, shaking her head. "I'm just taking a break. To rejuvenate."

Stubborn. He'd planted the seed, now he just had to see if it grew, or if she threw it out with the rest of the weeds. "Whatever you say, Cecilia."

He straightened in his seat, checked his side-view mirror, and when the coast was clear pulled out onto the highway. The car was silent, save the purr of the engine and blast of the air conditioner Cecilia seemed to keep at arctic levels.

Five minutes passed before she huffed, "What kind of a name is Harper Holt?"

He laughed, shaking his head. "I'm sure if you get to know her, you'll like her."

"Not in a million years," Cecilia said, her tone wry. She sniffed. "But I suppose you made your point."

He took her hand and brought her fingers to his lips. "If it makes you feel better, like you, I really did have these plans in place before we . . ." He winked at her. "You know, whatever this is."

She stared at him wide-eyed. "How is that supposed to make me feel better?"

"It wasn't completely out of spite."

She started fidgeting in the bucket seat again, all that nervous energy twisting away inside. "Why did the two of you break up?"

"We were better as friends. We both grew up in working-class families on the South Side. Because of that we tend to find the same things insufferable, so when we don't have dates we help each other out."

"And that's it?"

He knew what she was really asking but was too proud to admit, and he put her out of her misery. "I'm not going to lay a finger on her if that's what you're worried about."

"You're not?"

"Nope." He shot her a menacing glance. "Just like Miles isn't going to lay a finger on you."

She looked at him like he'd suggested she jump off the George Washington Bridge. "Of course not."

He shook his head. Didn't she see how wrong it was to marry someone she couldn't even stand the thought of touching? Frustration gnawed inside him. He wanted to pound some sense into her, but he couldn't. She had to figure this out on her own. He wasn't going to be the one to talk her out of it. "Then we understand each other."

She nodded.

He squeezed her fingers. "I want you to do something for me."

"What?"

"Saturday, I have to visit my aunt and I want you to come with me."

"You want me to go with you?"

"Yes, I do."

She scooted over and put her head on his shoulder. "Okay."

He kissed the top of her head. "Good girl."

She elbowed him in the ribs but she laughed. "You're impossible."

They fell into a comfortable silence that passed for five miles before she sighed.

"What's wrong?" he asked.

"You know, I do realize how fucked up this is."

He squeezed her thigh. "Just as long as you know."

Shane had dropped her at home, leaving her alone to stew in her own restlessness before that evening's benefit. He'd had errands to do, a meeting with the mayor, and things to catch up on now that he was back in town. After a mind-blowing kiss that'd had her plastered against the wall and breathless, he'd turned on his heels and left. Now she wandered around the house, which seemed empty and cold, and didn't have the slightest idea what to do with herself.

Shane's words kept playing in her brain over and over, like a broken record.

He was right.

Ever since she was six, all she'd had was the single-minded goal of running for office. It was the one driving pursuit that had kept her fed and moving forward when things got tough.

When she got lonely.

But all this time she'd never stopped to ask the real question: Why? She'd studied great politicians her whole life and they had passion and conviction in common. Where was hers?

What did she want to accomplish besides checking it off her lifelong to-do list? Her mind was blank.

She blew out a frustrated breath. She'd like to blame the trip to Revival and Shane, but that wasn't the truth.

Why hadn't she asked about Miles's motivation? What was in it for him?

Well, there was only one way to find out. She picked up the phone and scrolled through one of the many missed calls until she found Miles's number.

It rang three times before he answered with his customary clipped hello.

She wanted to throw up at the sound of his voice but made sure her tone was modulated and controlled. "Hello, Miles."

"Cecilia, darling, so glad you called." There wasn't even a trace of agitation that she'd been avoiding him.

"How are you, Miles?" she asked, all of her defense mechanisms kicking into high gear. And she could feel it, her old, regular self slipping over her.

"Very well, dear."

She tried to picture him. His dark hair was touched with gray. His brown eyes were sharp with intelligence and his face handsome enough. But she had no sense of *him*. She was supposed to marry this man. They were supposed to live in the same house and share a life and she didn't even know his birthday or his favorite color. She frowned. They were strangers.

And he seemed as content as she to keep it that way.

"Have you gotten my messages?" he inquired, his tone all business.

"I'm sorry I haven't returned your calls. With the wedding, things have been hectic."

"I understand."

Who was this man? And what did he want from her? Because men like him always wanted something. She propped her hip against the counter, putting her palm on the cool, untouched marble surface. "Miles, why are you marrying me?"

There was a pause over the line before he answered. "We all know you'll do better in your campaign if you're married."

Her bullshit radar pinged, loud and clear. She narrowed her eyes. "No, why are *you* marrying *me*?"

"A relationship with your family will prove valuable for my business." It was smooth. One of those practiced evasions they were all so good at.

"How so?"

More silence. She watched the digital clock tick by.

Finally, he sighed. "Your father is on various energy committees that will potentially impact my business. It's in my best interest to keep him as an ally."

"And you have to marry me to do that?" It sounded good but didn't quite add up.

He laughed, one of those polite business laughs, nothing like the boisterous sounds Shane made. It barely touched Miles's lips, let alone his belly. "I have no interest in regular women. My first love will always be my company. Now, if we can move on to the business of this evening, I do have a meeting I'm running late to."

How was she not a "regular" woman? she wanted to ask, but was smart enough to know the conversation was over. At least for Miles. She, on the other hand, intended to do more digging. A tiny thrill shot through her, the way it always did when she had a puzzle in front of her that needed to be unraveled. It was one of her favorite parts of her job. "Yes, this evening."

"I'll come fetch you at seven."

What, was she a dog? "Very well," she said, her voice calm and collected. "I'll see you then."

"Make sure you look your best, darling. People are watching."

She wondered what he'd say if she gave him a nice little "fuck you," but instead forced a smile on her lips. "I am my father's daughter."

"Yes, you are." Tone way too pleased, he disconnected.

Cecilia didn't like it one bit. They were up to something and, boy, hadn't she made it easy for them?

As soon as she hung up she called her father.

He answered on the second ring and said in a hushed, angry voice, "Where have you been?"

"In Revival," she said, her tone holding a distinct chill. "Where you sent me."

"One second." All background noise ceased and she knew he'd put her on mute. She waited a full minute before he came back on the line. "What exactly has gotten into you? Do you know how many times we've called you?"

She ignored the question. "What is Miles Fletcher getting out of marrying me?"

"What?" His voice rose and she envisioned the florid flush on his face. "We are in crisis here. Your mother is threatening to file for divorce. We need you here to help deal with the fallout before it hits the paper."

She straightened, steeling her spine and squaring her shoulders. "No. Answer my question."

"What the hell does it matter? He's going to get the job done and help you on your little campaign. Be thankful and focus on the real issue here."

She wrenched back as though he'd slapped her. The truth hit her in the face and stung. He was humoring her.

She narrowed her gaze. "I suppose the real question is, what are you getting out of this?"

"Cecilia," he said, his voice tinged with the edge of panic, "listen to me. Your mother wants to divorce me. How are you going to help fix this?"

Incredulous, she shook her head. "Fix it yourself."

She hung up.

She turned to stare out the window, ignoring the ringing phone. What exactly were they up to? Oh, she believed Nathaniel was in a panic and needed her aid. After all, getting him out of scrapes was what she did best. But that didn't negate the fact that she was right. Miles and the senator were getting something out of their unholy union that had nothing to do with her bid for congress. That was just a happy coincidence.

Now it was only a matter of finding out the truth.

Chapter Eighteen

Shane kept his eyes glued to the long, red carpet laid at the entryway of the Field Museum, waiting for his first glimpse of Cecilia, and virtually ignored his date.

Harper elbowed him in the ribs. "All right, what gives?"

He jerked his gaze away. "Huh?"

"You've been acting strange since we got here. What's going on?" Harper looked as stunning as ever in a floor-length, strapless dress that hugged her curves in all the right places. Her blond hair was piled on top of her head, high-lighting the slim curve of her neck and high cheekbones. She looked lovely, and normally he enjoyed her company, but all he could think about was Cecilia.

Where was she? Would he be able to contain himself when she got here?

He took a sip of his watered-down drink. "Nothing."

She smiled, her red lips curving. "Who is she?"

His mind flashed with images of Cecilia. Her hair a wild mess after he'd run his hands through the whiskey strands. Storm-blue eyes glassy with passion after he'd kissed her.

And that mouth. That goddamn mouth that would be the death of him.

His cock stirred and he shook it off, reminding himself summer Cecilia wouldn't be here tonight. The ice queen would be in attendance. He'd like to believe it would make the night easier, but that was a lie. He knew her secrets now. Knew who she was under the mask.

The last couple of days at the farmhouse had been hell as he kept his physical distance. He increasingly ached for her and he'd be claiming her tonight.

He shrugged. "No one."

"Sure," she said, then smoothed her dress. "Good thing we're no longer dating so I don't have to be jealous."

Time to change the subject. He tilted his head to the side. "How's work?"

She laughed, but the sound didn't shoot through him like Cecilia's did.

Fuck. It was official. He had it bad.

"It's like that, is it?" Harper waved a hand. "It's fine. Just landed a huge client that promises to be some pretty cutting-edge technology."

"Tell me about it." His mind drifted to all the things he planned to do to Cecilia the second he got her alone. Truly alone in a way they hadn't been for way too long.

There wasn't one person to interrupt him.

Harper fingered a sparkly necklace around her neck. "You're already not listening."

"Sure I am," he said, his gaze stealing to the clock. Cecilia should be here by now.

"You're officially the worst date ever," Harper said, her tone good-natured. Thankfully they'd been friends longer than they'd tried dating and she wasn't perturbed by his lack of attention. There hadn't been anything but comfort between them for a long time.

He shifted back to the entryway. Streams of well-dressed,

overly coiffed couples filed in, dressed in black. Impatience roiled through him. He wanted her here. Now.

Then she was.

And it knocked the breath right out of him.

He broke into a sweat.

Jesus. Fucking. Christ.

He was going to kill her.

He'd been wrong. The ice queen was nowhere to be seen. Summer Cecilia was here and she looked absolutely drop-you-to-your-knees gorgeous.

Her dress was a pale, shimmery color that looked like she'd been dipped in white-blue ice crystals. It glided over her body, plunging down to her navel before skimming over her lean but now healthy frame. Gone was the pale, tired-looking Cecilia, and in her place stood this goddesslike creature.

A violent possessiveness coursed hot in his blood, mixing with his insatiable desire, throwing him off balance. The urge to throw his jacket over her beat an irrational rhythm in his chest.

"There she is," Harper said, startling him from his thoughts.

"What?" he asked, still unable to take his eyes off Cecilia. Her hair was down, tossed in waves that made her look sexy as hell. He wanted to run his hands through it. Fist it tight and force her into admitting she was his. And only his.

Harper said something, but it was too distant to pay attention to with the blood rushing in his ears.

The only thing marring Cecilia's perfect image was the man on her arm.

Miles Fletcher was all wrong for her. He looked like her damn father. Watching them walk down that carpet, smiling and stopping to talk to people, violated the laws of nature.

That should be him. Them. All vows he'd made to play it cool tonight diminished in an instant.

He was fighting for her.

He wouldn't cause a scene, but goddamn it, she belonged with him.

And nobody was taking her away.

Cecilia spotted Shane the instant she walked in the room, staring at her with that look in his eyes. The one that said he wanted her. That he was coming for her.

The dress had been worth it. She'd taken one look at the dress she'd originally planned to wear and discarded it, picked up her keys, and gone shopping. The second she'd spotted the dress, she'd known.

The expression on his face confirmed everything she'd thought when she'd tried it on.

Even from across the room, she could feel the heat rolling off him in waves, feel his predatory nature stalking to the surface.

She shivered, and Miles frowned down at her. "Didn't I say you'd be cold in that dress, dear?"

She ignored the comment. As she'd ignored all the comments he'd made since he'd picked her up. A society-rag photographer stopped her, and she plastered a smile on her face as he took a picture of Miles and her.

She got it. He didn't like the dress.

Well, she wasn't dressing for him.

She'd dressed for Shane.

She'd waited anxiously as they made their way around the room with false cheer and a plastic smile. Kissing cheeks, doling out compliments, and making small talk with endless groups of people. The act was so second nature she could do it in her sleep.

You look lovely.

How are your children?

I heard about your (insert accomplishment). How wonderful.

On. And on. And on.

But something had changed; she could barely remember why this was important. Why any of this mattered.

The more she thought about it, the more convinced she became that she didn't want to go back. Oh, she loved politics, that was true, but she wasn't sure she loved being the main event.

She'd think about it later. Right now she had to make her way through this crowd to get to the only man that mattered to her at the moment.

Finally, after what seemed an eternity, she stood in front of Shane and his date. The woman was a stunner in black. Together, with their golden blond hair and strong features, they made a striking couple. Jealousy reared up then died a quick death when Shane narrowed his gaze on her. All threat and heat and promise. He nodded. "Cecilia."

"Shane." Was that husky voice hers?

Their gazes locked, and held, far too long to be polite.

Miles jostled her elbow, breaking the hypnotic stare. She plastered on her biggest smile before turning to Shane's date. "You must be Harper. Shane's told me about you. I'm Cecilia Riley."

The woman's eyes widened, her lips curving into a knowing grin. "It's a pleasure to meet you. How do you know Shane?"

Cecilia met his gaze. "My brother is marrying his sister. We're going to be family soon."

One brow rose up Shane's forehead as his expression turned smug. "I suppose that's true. Interesting."

Miles shifted at her side, his cold fingers tightening on her elbow, a signal he expected an introduction. She cleared her throat. "This is Miles Fletcher."

"Cecilia's fiancé," he said, holding out his hand.

She cringed at the word and Shane's shoulders stiffened. Harper's expression widened. "Is that so?"

"Yes." Miles put a hand on her lower back and his fingers pressed against her bare skin. She had to stop herself from recoiling. He turned to Shane. "Are you taking care of my girl in Revival?"

Heat climbed up Cecilia's chest.

Shane drained the rest of his drink before smirking. "Oh, I'm taking care of her, all right."

It was wrong. Very wrong. But the laughter bubbled inside her. She stared down at the floor and recited the Gettysburg Address in her head to keep from giggling.

Harper cleared her throat. "When's Maddie's wedding?"

"Next week."

"I'm happy for her," Harper said politely.

Shane was like a compulsion and Cecilia couldn't help raising her gaze to meet his eyes.

So hot. So intent. She shivered. She wanted to be alone with him. Needed him away from Miles and Harper.

The silence turned awkward, but still she couldn't look away.

Harper jingled her drink glass, snapping Cecilia from the spell. Expression wry, Harper shook her head at Shane and Cecilia before turning to Miles. "I could use a refill." She smiled pointedly. "Can I accompany you to the bar?"

Cecilia wanted to kiss her in gratitude.

Miles was old-school polite and wasn't in a position to

say no without looking rude. He peered down at Cecilia.
"What can I get you, dear?"

Cecilia said, "Champagne would be lovely, thank you."

Miles narrowed his gaze on Shane. "Donovan?"

He flicked a glance at Harper. "She knows what I'm
drinking."

"Very well." Mouth pursed in a firm line, he touched Cecilia's elbow. "Are you sure you won't accompany us?"

Wild horses couldn't drag her from this spot. "No, I'm
fine, thank you."

Harper took Miles's arm and tugged him away. Miles
gave Cecilia a stern look of disapproval before leaving her
alone with Shane.

Cecilia's smile was polite, while inside desire churned
hot. "You're right, I do like her."

Shane's eyes narrowed and he took a step toward her,
crowding her space. "Where's the rest of your dress?"

Cecilia smoothed a hand over her abdomen. "Don't you
like it?"

"Turn around." His tone was hard and commanding.

She pivoted in a slow circle.

"It has no back."

And barely a front. "I was feeling daring."

He took another step toward her, his green eyes piercing.

They were too close. Anyone observing them would see
the intimacy between them. She should step back, but
couldn't. Wouldn't.

His gaze locked on hers, dipping to her mouth for a
moment, then down her body like a caress. "With the way
I'm feeling, you're lucky I don't take ahold of you right now
and show every single person in this room I know exactly
how to take care of you."

The possession in his tone thrilled her to the very tips of
her toes. "Does that mean you like it?"

"That depends."

"On what?" Her breath came fast, and the rational part of her brain told her to put a stop to this, but her senses had taken leave. She found she liked rousing Shane's primitive instincts.

"Did you wear it for me?"

"Yes," she said, her voice dropping down to an intimate whisper.

"Meet me in the bird exhibit in ten minutes." His fingers flexed as he named the ancient, least exciting, farthest exhibit away from the main action. "That's bound to be deserted."

She nodded. All her senses heightened to hyperaware as she anticipated being alone with him. Somewhere secluded. And free.

"I'm in a dangerous mood, Cecilia. Be prepared." His head dipped and his voice lowered. "You're not going to look the same when you come out."

By the time Cecilia showed, Shane felt like a caged lion. He grabbed her, pushed her into the first alcove he found and then his mouth was on hers.

His hands were everywhere. Sliding over silk and skin.

She tangled her fingers in his hair, moaning against his lips as his tongue plunged into her.

It was a mean kiss. A kiss filled with all sorts of dirty promises.

It enflamed him until he was like a feral beast, ready to drag her to the floor and claim her in the most primal way possible.

He cupped her breast and squeezed her nipple until she jerked against him.

It was too much. Too fast. Too dangerous. But he could not get enough. He shoved her hard against the wall, reaching under the slit of her dress and palming her silk-covered mound. He ground the heel of his hand against her clit until she rocked beneath him.

He tore his mouth away and gripped her throat as he rotated his hand. "This is mine. Nobody touches you but me."

Her head fell back against the wall as her hips moved. "Yes, yes."

It was like he was caught in some sort of primal, lust-filled fever. "Say my name."

"Shane," she moaned, and he slipped his fingers under her panties to find her wet and ready for him.

"Do you want my cock?"

She reached for him, her palm stroking over his erection. "Yes. It's all I can think about."

He plunged inside her hot, tight center, first one finger, then two, catching her cries with his lips, then skimming down her throat to suck the sensitive skin on her neck.

Marking her.

Her fingers worked his zipper, slipping inside to grip him in a tight hold. He groaned, pumping his fingers in and out of her swollen core, loving when her body quickened and her muscles clamped down.

"Shane. Jesus." She pulled him down, demanding, and his mouth claimed hers.

Their breath rose and fell in a harsh wave as he devoured her with a kiss so raw, so dirty he may as well have been pounding into her right then and there. With a low growl, he pulled away, working her clit with his thumb until she was on the very brink of orgasm. "I am going to fuck the hell out of you later. Nothing and no one is going to stop me. You're going to be sore for a week. You're not going to be able to walk without thinking of my cock inside you."

She came. Just like he knew she would.

Her body clamped down on his fingers in hard, rhythmic

waves of release. He kissed her, capturing her cries until he wrung the last contraction out of her and she went limp.

She blinked up at him, her eyes dazed, her cheeks flushed. He pumped one more time, and then left the warm haven of her body, the primal fury still beating in his blood. His fingers glistened and he met her gaze, then, very slowly, painted her lips.

She gasped, her pupils dilating as he rubbed her lower lip before raising his hand and sucking his fingers clean. The taste of her clinging to him was pure torture, but damned worth it. He lowered his head. "You smell and look like sex. And for the rest of the night that's all you're going to be able to think about."

She let out a long breath. Eyes still glassy, she gripped his shaft in a tight squeeze. "I want to suck your cock."

Shocked, he jerked. She'd never said anything so overt.

She rose to her tiptoes and whispered in his ear, "That's what I'm going to be thinking about. Because I am going to drop to my knees for you."

He closed his eyes, picturing her on her knees before him. He took a deep breath, fighting to control the ache in his body that demanded *right now*. "Baby, whatever you want, it's yours."

"All I want"—she gave him a long stroke that nearly sent him over the edge—"is you."

Dinner was a dreadful ordeal. Cecilia couldn't wait to be done with the whole thing.

The quick, powerful orgasm in that private alcove with Shane had left her shaken, her worldview altered, and she hadn't recovered since.

The climax had done nothing to take the edge off.

She was more aroused than ever. Every nerve ending

seemed on fire, agitated and needy. Her skin was hot, tight to the touch. Nipples painfully hard, rubbing against the silk of her dress and reminding her of Shane's tongue dragging across her flesh that night in the woods. Between her thighs, she ached, so swollen and wet every shift of her legs made her have to bite the inside of her cheek to keep from moaning. With every breath she caught the faint scent of sex and Shane, and it worked her into a near fevered pitch.

Unable to help herself, her gaze drifted to where he sat several tables over. She clenched her hands under the table, her nails digging into her skin. Tux jacket unbuttoned, shoulders impossibly wide, he leaned back in his chair.

Gooseflesh broke over her skin. He was just so gorgeous.

Like they'd developed a type of sixth sense, he lifted his head, his gaze locking on hers.

Mine, mine, mine. The words pulsing like a heartbeat between them.

And she felt it, deep down in her belly. His possession. His utter hold on her. Shane captured her so completely she didn't know how she'd ever let him go.

His arm rested on the table, and very slowly he rubbed his thumb and two fingers together in a slow, rhythmic circle that held her transfixed. She flushed. Nipples puckered even tighter as she shivered. Her breath came in short quick bursts. She couldn't stop watching, remembering how he'd thrust his fingers hard and fast inside her, almost forcing her to orgasm.

"Cecilia." The sharp jab of her name on Miles's lips ripped her attention away.

"I'm sorry," she said, her dinner companions coming into focus.

Miles gave her a slight frown. "Mrs. Winston asked you if we'd set the date yet."

She plastered a smile on her face, rubbing her ring finger where Miles's engagement ring sat heavy and wrong on her hand. A reminder she'd chosen the wrong path and now had to figure out how to fix it. "No, not yet, but we're thinking next spring." It sounded good.

"You make a lovely couple," Mrs. Charles Winston the third said before her gaze dipped to Cecilia's plunging neckline, her wrinkled lips pursed in disapproval.

"Why, thank you," she said in her sweetest, most serene voice.

Across from her, Buffy Thompson, a regular on the social circuit, smirked. "What an interesting dress."

Like most of them, she'd married for money and status over love. At least twenty-five years her senior, her husband sat next to her. His gaze drifted to Cecilia's cleavage and Buffy frowned. Her sly, shifty gaze raked over Cecilia with a scorn she was unable to express through her Botoxed, frozen face and implanted cheeks.

Cecilia had a sudden urge to say, *You know, all that plastic surgery makes you look all sorts of fucked up.*

Yep, Shane was wearing off on her.

They'd be stunned. Gape at her with their mouths open like fish out of water. The devious thought brought a smile to her lips, and she wished she sat here with Shane, who'd understand how ridiculous these people were.

Instead, she said politely, "It's from a little boutique on State. I went shopping this afternoon and fell in love with it."

The dress was nothing like her. She stuck to the basics for these events, black and gray with severe lines and classic cuts. Nothing too revealing. Nothing too sexy. Nothing too eye-catching, so she'd blend into the crowd.

But she hadn't been able to resist when she'd seen it. It flowed over her body in the most daring and provocative way. All she could think of was the look on Shane's face when he'd seen her.

Her attention drifted back to him. Their gazes locked before she looked away.

The dress had been worth it.

Even though every other person in the room hated it.

Buffy shifted in her seat, shoving up her own inflated cleavage in the process. "I've never been there."

"You should go," Cecilia said, resisting the urge of Shane. "The owner is quite lovely. She designed the dress herself."

Buffy's nose wrinkled. "I stick to only the top house designers myself."

Cecilia flashed her most polite smile. "They look darling on you."

This had to be the most boring conversation she'd ever had while someone was trying to insult her in that subtle, oh so sophisticated way they had.

Her brow furrowed. Was she any better? She'd never been one to trade insults unless provoked, but she hadn't stopped them either. How many women had she quietly dismissed because they didn't look proper enough? Or stuck out in a crowd? How many times had she rolled her eyes at abandoned displays of affection?

Was this the kind of woman she wanted to be? How she wanted to live her life? Full of thinly veiled barbs and insults disguised as wit, breaking people down instead of building them up?

Maddie and her friends weren't like that. Sure, they teased and joked around, but their affection and loyalty were clear. They loved and supported each other. They liked each other. They were real.

Wasn't that better? More desirable?

Before she could think any more about it, the chairwoman of the evening went to the podium and started speaking, thanking everyone for their generous donations and making the night a success.

She beamed and held out her hands like a car show spokesmodel. "And please welcome Mr. Shane Donovan, who not only personally donated a hundred thousand dollars, he also generously matched all his employees' contributions. Without his continued support for the underprivileged in this community, there would be a lot more needy kids out there."

Polite applause filled the room and Cecilia had to resist the urge to stand up and cheer him on. He buttoned his jacket then made his way to the podium. She was filled with a pride she had no right to but couldn't contain.

The room quieted and Cecilia experienced an irrational stirring of nerves. Other than his sister's engagement party, she'd never seen him speak. She clenched her hands in her lap.

His gaze sought her out in the room and his lips lifted in a small, secret smile when he spotted her and her stomach eased.

"Thank you," he said, his low rumble filling the speakers and making her shiver.

"As most of you know, I didn't grow up with money. Like a lot of working-class families in Chicago, we lived paycheck to paycheck. But I didn't know what poor was until my dad died in a car accident that left my sister in a coma. We had no health insurance. Hospital bills quickly became overwhelming, and I remember the frustration I felt because I couldn't get her the best care. I didn't have access to the top doctors in brain injuries, or hospitals with state-of-the-art equipment. We were lucky—my sister got better, but many families aren't so blessed."

He smiled, completely charming, and her heart swelled. "For a lot of families, the difference between excellent care and mediocre care is the difference between life and death."

Behind him, a picture of a little African-American boy filled the screen. He was bald, and his huge, melting-chocolate eyes were haunting. The mere sight of him had Cecilia itching to go to her checkbook and write an additional donation. "This is Tyler, who was diagnosed with a rare form of leukemia. The free clinic doctor told his parents he had less than a year to live and there was nothing to be done."

He was beyond articulate, his speech well modulated and polished. Compassion and warmth rang in his tone as he continued to talk. "But thanks to the programs made possible by people like you, Tyler had the best care money could buy and is now in remission."

He talked for ten more minutes. With every minute that passed, her heart swelled and she fell for him just a little bit more.

Chapter Nineteen

Shane drove to Harper's house, forcing himself to maintain a reasonable speed. His mind was so preoccupied with getting to Cecilia, he hadn't said more than five words.

Next to him, Harper sighed. "She's getting married, you know."

Over his dead body. He debated arguing the point but abandoned the idea. "I don't know what you're talking about."

She laughed. "You don't think that's fooling anyone, do you? Miles Fletcher would have to be deaf, blind, and dumb to miss that there's something going on between you and Cecilia Riley."

Satisfaction settled in his gut. Good, because Miles couldn't have her. She was his. He'd decided, and when he put his mind to something there was nothing that would stop him, no obstacle he wouldn't overcome. But Harper didn't need to know that. "We're living in the same house; any familiarity you're picking up on is because of proximity."

"Whatever," Harper said, tone filled with disbelief. "I never thought you'd go for someone like her."

Shane jerked his head, narrowing his eyes. "What do you mean, like her?"

"She's a socialite. Although she's quite beautiful, I always thought you'd pick a woman with substance."

Anger rose to a quick boil. He clenched the steering wheel. "You don't know the first thing about her."

"I know enough. Enough to know she's not like us."

The light turned red and when the car came to a stop he turned toward her. "What do you mean?"

Harper's red lips parted in the glow of the streetlights, closed, then opened again. "It's hard for people like us. We don't really fit in anywhere. The people we grew up with, still working their trade jobs, resent us. The people we socialize with now look down on us because we didn't grow up with money. We're nomads."

The light changed to green and he sped up, wanting her out of the car. There was truth to her statement, but he'd never cared much about acceptance. He had the respect of the people who mattered, and that was good enough. "I don't give a shit about belonging."

He pulled over to the side of her building and didn't bother throwing the car into park, making it clear he wasn't staying. Harper twisted in her seat, a frown on her lips. "I'm only saying this because I care about you and don't want you to get hurt."

"I'm fine, Harper." He glanced pointedly toward the door.

Expression creased with concern, she pushed open the door. She started to get out but then turned and looked over her shoulder. "Don't kid yourself, Shane. You might not care what people think, but women like Cecilia Riley sure as hell do. Don't ever forget that."

By the time Shane reached Cecilia's house he'd blocked out his conversation with Harper. He didn't care what Harper believed. She didn't know Cecilia.

His stubborn brain rebelled. She *was* marrying someone she didn't even like, for her image. Of course she cared what people thought.

But he didn't want to think about that now. He just needed to get to her. Mark her and make her his.

Shane pulled into a parking garage a half block from Cecilia's house, swung into a spot, then made a mad dash out of the car, walking at a clip that may as well have been a run. He bounded up the steps of her townhome two at a time. He rang the bell, trying to catch his breath.

When the door opened, he lost it again.

She'd changed.

Lungs burning with lack of air, he could only gape at her.

She put her hands on black-lace-covered hips. "I've been waiting for you." The smoke in her voice finally matched the lushness of her mouth.

Still unable to speak, he stepped inside, afraid to even touch her for fear he'd lose all control. She wore black garters, sheer stockings that exposed the smooth expanse of her thighs, and a black corset that made her waist impossibly small and her cleavage spill over.

She looked at the door behind him. "You forgot to close the door."

While he'd been struck mute, she seemed calm and collected. He managed to grope for the handle and push the door shut.

The second the latch clicked, she sank to her knees.

Jesus. Fucking. Christ.

He was going to have a heart attack and die right there.

Slim fingers worked at his belt, her movements smooth and graceful as she slipped his zipper down.

This wasn't how he'd imagined this moment. Wasn't what he'd planned. But damned if he had the power to stop her.

He leaned against the door, threading his hand through her hair, playing with the silky strands.

Thick lashes rose as she looked at him, her eyes dark and filled with heat. His thumb found her pulse, beating rapidly in her neck. She smiled, wicked and sure, sliding a finger into the waistband of his boxer briefs, a slow tease that made him weak in the knees and his cock so hard he thought he might burst.

He fought the desire to take control. It would be much more comfortable for him, but he didn't want to ruin this for her. He stroked a thumb down her neck. "You are so gorgeous."

She trailed her nails lightly over his balls and he sucked in a hard breath.

This was torture.

"I think you just like me on my knees."

He had to taste her. Bending, he twisted her hair in his fist, tilted her head, and gripped her jaw, holding her still for a hard, demanding kiss. A moan vibrated against his palm, setting off an indescribable feeling of power as he ate at her mouth.

Her kiss was a surrender, and he took full advantage, slanting his head to deepen the angle and claiming her until they were both breathless. When he lifted his head, he whispered against her lips, "I love you on your knees."

Her fingers squeezed his aching shaft. "I've been thinking about this all night."

"Thinking about what?" Arrogantly wanting her to say it.

"Sucking your cock. Driving you crazy. Licking you all over."

His fingers tightened in her hair. "That's what you were thinking about through dinner?"

"Yes. And how I'll finally get to be with you." She licked his erection, swirling her mouth around the tip, making him dizzy with lust. Never breaking eye contact, she pulled him into her mouth, then slowly, with a suction that made his eyes roll into the back of his head, she sucked before releasing him. "I was so wet."

"Cecilia," he said, his voice ragged and broken.

Her pink tongue slid up and down the length of him, pressing on the vein, lingering on the sensitive spot at the base. His head *thunk*ed against the glass pane of her door as her hot mouth enveloped him.

"Fuck." He gripped her hair and let her set the pace instead of thrusting the way he wanted. How many times had he fantasized about this? Those full lips wrapped around his cock?

And now here she was, and it was about killing him.

She sucked, pulling hard before freeing him with an audible pop. She sat back on her heels and looked at him. "I think you're confused."

Having no idea what she was talking about, he blinked down at her.

She ran her hands up his thighs, the tux pants hanging loosely from his hips. "I can feel you holding back. I want to see you lose it."

He stroked her cheek, his lust straining at the seams of civility. "You don't know what you're asking."

"Yes, I do." She licked the head of his cock again, circling over the tip like she ate ice cream. "Give it to me, Shane." Her storm-blue eyes flirted up at him. "Please."

She watched from her position on the floor. Watched the struggle and uncertainty pass over his face. Not trusting her to know what she was asking for, even though she knew perfectly well. He might understand how she was wired, but she understood him too.

She wanted him to lose it. Wanted to see that arrogant, controlled man who ripped orgasms from her body, gain his own pleasure.

"Please," she said again, her voice pleading.

Again, his expression flickered, almost pained, his skin taut over the hard slash of his cheekbones.

She squeezed his shaft, hard under her hands. Stone covered with hot silk. "Shane, use me."

She witnessed the exact moment recognition sank in. His mouth twisted into a sensually cruel smile. Eyes darkening to the deepest of emerald, his already tight grip on her hair twisted. He yanked her head back, the sting of pain making her gasp.

Then he took her mouth. Claimed it. A hard, demanding, brutal kiss that left her shaken and throbbing. She wrapped her hand around his neck and arched to meet him.

It was a kiss meant for his pleasure. It was predatory, domineering, and mean.

And she loved it.

Her whole body thrummed, every nerve ending on fire, overloaded from sensation.

He ripped away, straightened, and guided her lips to his cock, where he thrust into her mouth. It wasn't gentle. It wasn't restrained.

He took what he wanted.

And she let him because it's what she wanted too. He needed this. She didn't know how or why she knew, but she did. She relaxed her throat and jaw, submitting to his pleasure.

Like an animal, he growled low in his throat. His expression turned feral as he fucked her mouth. She grasped his shaft with her hand to increase the pressure but he pushed her wrist away as he shook his head. "Just your mouth, baby."

She complied, resting her hands on his hips to keep

steady while he thrust in and out, his lids half hooded, his breath hard.

It was the oddest, strangest feeling. As she sat on her knees and let him have his way with no reservations, she should have felt less, but she didn't. She'd never been so aroused. Had never felt so powerful. So alive.

She moaned. As her throat vibrated, his head fell back, his tempo increasing. His shaft swelled between her lips. Filling her. Completing her. She groaned again, long and loud, her nails digging into his skin as she increased the pressure.

On a roar, he thrust once again and bathed the back of her throat.

Over and over he jetted into her mouth, and she gulped down every drop as she watched through lifted lashes. His expression broke apart, his lips parted and gasping for air, completely abandoned as he lost himself to her.

He released his grip on her hair. Her neck tingled as the blood rushed back and he slipped from her mouth. He shook his head, rubbing his thumb over her swollen lips. "What are you doing to me?"

Emotions she couldn't name threatened to overwhelm her. "The same thing you're doing to me."

He grabbed her hand and pulled her from the floor. He wrapped her in his arms and kissed her long and slow, almost drugging her it was so intoxicating. When he raised his head, he said, "Upstairs."

She nodded, turned, and led the way.

When they entered her bedroom, she stopped at the edge of the bed. Behind her, his palms rested on her shoulders and slid down her bare arms. She shivered.

He trailed his mouth over her neck. "Cold?"

Hardly. She was burning up. "Since the day we met, anytime you touch me, I shiver."

His fingers trailed over her shoulder blades, rubbing along the edge of the corset she'd worked herself into before his arrival. "Me too."

She craned her neck, looking back at him. "Really?"

"I've wanted you from the second I saw you. Even hidden under all that ice." He kissed her. "You look incredible in this."

"I bought it for you." She'd known it would be tonight.

"Sit on that chair." He pointed to the antique lounging chaise at the end of her bed, covered in dove-gray velvet.

Suddenly nervous, she did as he asked. She sat on the edge, looking at him as he thoughtfully assessed her. With his big hands, he parted her legs, palms hot and strong against her skin. He slid a finger up and down her lace panties, damp from her arousal. "You're wet."

She gulped, nodded. Not understanding what was happening between them but knowing it was significant.

He traced the edge of her panties then slipped his fingers inside to circle her swollen clit. She shuddered. The pleasure was as sharp as a blade.

His jaw hardened. "You're always wet for me."

"Yes." She answered simply because it was the truth.

He grasped both sides of her panties. "I'll buy you another pair." Then he shredded them and tossed them onto the floor.

Heady from desire, she gasped, remembering that first night in the kitchen. *Let's not pretend, if a woman ever needed her panties ripped off, it's you.* That was the thing about Shane, he always got what he wanted.

He draped her against the arm of the chair, lifting one leg onto the chaise while the other stayed on the floor. She was open and exposed to him. He pressed her knee, opening her wider. More obscenely.

She would have been embarrassed if it wasn't for the heat in his eyes and the trickle of wetness on her thighs.

He practically purred in satisfaction, as he rubbed her clit in slow circles, sending lightning bolts of sensation through her body. "If you were sitting next to me during dinner I would have played with your pussy through every course."

Her head fell back on the chair as her hips rose to meet him. Yes, this was all she needed. Shane's talented fingers and wicked tongue.

"Would you have liked that?"

"Yes," she said, on a breathless moan. She ground her teeth as a frustrating, relentless need coiled tight but refused to break. His touch was enough to drive her crazy but too light to make her come. And she needed to, urgently. Had never been so desperate for it. Impatient, she grabbed his wrist and attempted to force his hand to a firmer pressure.

He laughed and batted her away. "I'm not done with you."

He stopped.

And she wanted to kill him.

He yanked down the top of her corset, lifting her breasts so they spilled free. He sat on the edge of the chair and dragged his thumbs over her nipples.

Pleasure radiating down to her core, she arched.

He licked at her lips, slowly trailing a path down her neck, pausing to scrape his teeth over her pounding pulse before continuing on. He pressed his mouth against the hollow of her throat, skimmed over her collarbones before licking one hard nipple. He laved it with his tongue before moving to the other.

Back and forth he went.

Sucking, licking.

It was exquisite torture.

A tease meant to drive her mad. His teeth scraped along

sensitive flesh until her hips rocked. She cried out, "Shane, please, Shane."

She chanted her plea over and over again, mindless.

But he was relentless. Exacting in his pursuit to drive her insane.

When her nipples were swollen and red, gleaming with wetness, he pulled back and stood.

She blinked at him.

He pulled out his phone and her eyes tracked his movements.

Dazed, drugged with the steady thrum of desire rushing in her veins, she frowned in confusion.

"I want to take your picture. Looking desperate and wanton and gorgeous. I want you to do this for me. And only for me."

A million scandals filled her mind, of men and women brought down by pictures they'd taken. How many times had she lamented their stupidity? Shaken her head at their naïveté? Everyone knew in today's digital world nothing was truly safe.

It was the hardest thing he could have asked her to do.

Shane watched her. Phone in hand, his eyes narrowed.

Of course, this wasn't about the picture. It was about trusting him. And in his expression she saw he expected her to say no. To refuse.

Logic dictated she be prudent. But she wasn't going to do that, because she trusted him.

Slowly, she nodded. Stupidity be damned, she could give him this.

Something primal flared in his eyes and he jutted his chin toward the back of the chair. "Lean your head back."

She did. He walked over and spread her hair out like a fan before his lips claimed hers.

When she was breathless, almost light-headed with anticipation, he released her mouth then sucked on her nipples until they were once again plump and wet. Then he pushed her legs wider apart.

And she let him.

He stood back, admiring his work before shaking his head. "Damn, that's perfect." Then he raised his phone, his thumb sliding over the screen. "If only I had my good camera here, but this will have to do."

Then he snapped the picture, the flash going off. "Put your hands over your head."

She complied. He growled his satisfaction. Then the pictures began, one right after the other, the light flaring then burning out over and over while something miraculous happened.

With every click of the shutter, her inhibitions slipped away, leaving her so aroused, she almost vibrated with it. She arched her back, her lips parting as he played with her nipples and clit. Almost pushing her over the edge only to pull back and start all over again.

Her eyes closed and she surrendered. Lost herself completely to Shane and his hands moving incessantly over her body. It was the sluttiest, most erotic thing she'd ever done and she was so wet it started to trickle down the crease of her thighs.

At long last, he was finally satisfied, and the clicking flash stopped.

Drugged with passion, she opened her eyes in time to see him toss the phone to the table. He stood, shucking off his clothes, then he grabbed her and pushed her to the bed.

"Jesus, Cecilia," he said, his voice hoarse. He splayed her thighs and fisted his hard cock, kneeling over her. "That was the hottest fucking thing I've ever seen."

She couldn't speak, just arched her hips in invitation. He ripped open the condom with his teeth before tossing the wrapper aside and rolling it over his erection. His movements frantic and hurried.

She couldn't stand it. Couldn't wait.

With a smooth hard thrust, he entered her. And she cried out in relief. Finally. At long last, he was a part of her, and she was home.

She gasped as her tight, swollen flesh stretched around him. Her nails dug into his back. "Shane, I need you so bad."

"I'm here, baby." He kissed her, his hips circling in time with his tongue.

The rhythm driving her mad, she gripped his hips, feeling the flex of muscles as he moved inside her.

Harder. She needed harder. She dug her nails deeper into his skin, and he took it as the sign it was, moving faster inside her.

The pressure coiled tight.

She couldn't breathe.

Their mouths parted and she groaned as he started to pound into her.

It was like something broke between them.

All traces of civility gone, she clawed at his back as he thrust over and over.

Deeper and deeper.

The sound of their flesh filled the room. The headboard banged against the wall and they made animalistic noises in the back of their throats.

The room became hot. Sticky. Damp with their sweat. The scent of sex, of them, infused the air.

She was poised to come. Desperate for it. But she held back, not wanting this wild, crazy recklessness to end.

His cock surged into her.

Her hips rocked, furiously.

The pleasure spiraled out of control.

Spinning tighter and tighter as their movements grew more and more frantic.

And then, it happened.

The orgasm ripped through her like it would tear her apart, and she screamed, forgetting everything but this man inside her, the beat of her heart, and the waves and waves of pleasure storming through her body.

He followed her, shouting her name as he came, triggering another ripple of climax until they both lay exhausted and panting for breath.

He rolled off her, pulling her with him so she lay with her head on his chest, nestled in the crook of his arm. His heart hammered under her ear, matching the rapid beat of her own and she closed her eyes, waiting for the rhythm to slow.

"Holy Mother of God." His voice a hoarse rasp.

Boneless with satisfaction, she wanted to agree but couldn't get her mouth to work.

Fingers trailed a path down her back, pausing when he got to the laces. "Sit up and I'll get you out of this."

"Too tired," she said, her eyes already heavy.

"You can't sleep in this, it's too tight." He shifted, pulling her up.

She hugged her arms around her knees, resting her heavy head on her folded arms.

He worked at the laces, pulling the fabric free. "How'd you get yourself into this?"

"YouTube videos." Her voice thickened with sleep.

He laughed then licked down her spine.

She shivered.

He moved behind her and then his breath was hot on the shell of her ear. "You have an exhibitionist streak in you."

She shook her head. "That's all you."

"Do you want to see the pictures?"

Despite her exhaustion, her body stirred to life. "I don't know, are they embarrassing?"

The last of the laces fell away and then she was naked, and he lowered her back to the bed. Her skin a decadent, delicious slide against her cotton sheets.

He traced a path over her bare breasts and around her nipples, which beaded and puckered under his touch. "I'm sure you'll think so."

The bed bounced as he reached over for his phone and all traces of sleepiness disappeared.

He opened the picture application and handed it to her.

She put the phone facedown on her stomach, not sure she wanted to look.

"Come on, don't be chicken. We both know you loved taking them." He chuckled, his voice low and wicked. "Believe me, the evidence is there to prove it."

She flushed, jabbing him in the ribs. "You're impossible."

"Trust me, Cecilia. They'll embarrass you, but deep down I know you'll like them."

"How do you know that?"

He dipped his fingers under the sheets and ran his fingers over her swollen flesh. "Because you're already wet thinking about them."

She frowned. He was right. Curses. As much as she didn't want to look, the curiosity was there. She opened one eye and glanced quickly before putting the phone down again.

He laughed but didn't prod further. And finally she worked up her courage and looked again.

They did embarrass her.

And arouse her.

An odd cocktail that had heat rushing between her legs. Was that even her? How could that be her? There were no traces of the severe woman who had walked into that Revival kitchen. There wasn't a person alive that would look at these pictures and call her an ice queen. Picture after picture with her legs splayed obscenely, breasts plump and exposed, expression wicked.

Shane leisurely circled her clit, slicked with desire. "It's so damn good, Cecilia."

She stopped on an image of her head thrown back, legs spread, his fingers mimicking his movements, and her breath caught. "The best."

"You like them," he whispered low in her ear. "You're already burning up. Wet and slick and ready."

Her expression on the screen mirroring her desire, she could only stare transfixed as Shane's talented fingers continued to torment her.

"Tell me you like them." One finger slid into her swollen core.

She looked like a sex object. "I like them."

His thumb found her clit and she jolted with pleasure. He nipped at her ear, his cock hard now against her thigh. "Those pictures are better than any porn man ever created."

"You're biased," she said on a pant, arching her back as he touched her exactly the way she liked.

He gripped her chin and forced her eyes to his. "Since I'm the only one who's ever going to see them, my opinion is the only one that matters."

She twined her hands around his neck, pulling him close. "You're right. You are the only one that matters."

Chapter Twenty

The next morning Shane sat in Cecilia's kitchen, watching her lick powdered sugar from her fingers. She'd already devoured two of the doughnuts he'd run out and bought this morning.

There was no denying the truth any longer. He was a goner.

He didn't know how or why it had happened. She wasn't the woman he'd envisioned for himself, but damned if that mattered. Every second he spent with her, he fell a bit more.

Those pictures sealed the deal. He hadn't expected her to trust him. Had expected her to say no and had been prepared to accept it. It would have put a wedge between them, but she hadn't let that happen, and now he was more bound to her than ever.

One whiskey-colored brow rose. "What are you looking at? Do I have powdered sugar on my face?"

He smiled and reached across the trendy but impractical copper table and wiped at her cheek. He sucked the sugar off his thumb. "You weren't even eating a week ago."

She swallowed then took a sip of black coffee. "I know, it's like my appetite turned on and I can't turn it off." She took another bite of doughnut and shook her head, talking around the bite. "These are so good. Like, the best ever."

He chuckled. "They're Hostess. I got them from the Walgreens at the corner."

"I don't care. I'm never going to be without them again."

He propped his elbows on the table. "There's a doughnut house in my old neighborhood that will give you orgasms, they're that good."

Her eyes lit up. "Orgasms, huh?"

"Yep."

"I guess it's a good thing we're going there then. I do need orgasms. I've been running a little short."

He laughed and pinched her.

She leaned back in her chair and rubbed her stomach. "Miles mentioned that I've gained weight. I don't think it was a compliment."

"I'll kill him." Shane growled, fighting back a possessive jealousy that was calmed only by the knowledge she'd spent last night with him.

She shrugged. "My jeans are a little tight."

"Cecilia, there's no arguing you're a gorgeous woman, so I know you'll understand when I say this. But when you showed up in Revival you looked like shit."

She grinned ear to ear. "Gee, Shane, tell me what you really think."

He grabbed the edge of her seat and scooted her closer, pulling her off her chair onto his lap. He slid a hand up her smooth, bare thigh, squeezing the curve of her hip. "At least you know you can depend on me to always tell you the truth."

"Good point." She shifted, moved and straddled him, the fabric of his dress shirt parting to reveal her naked body. "And what's your current assessment?"

He palmed her ass. "You're extremely fuckable."

She slapped his shoulder. "That's not a compliment!"

"Sure it is."

She straightened, a proper expression sliding over her features that signaled he was about to get a talking-to, most likely about something feminist. "Men aren't at all discerning. It's common knowledge they'll sleep with anything, given the opportunity."

"Not true," he said, hugging her close and burrowing his nose in the side of her neck. She smelled like sex and him, like he'd marked her so completely she carried his scent. "I've never slept around just because I could. I leave the man whoring to Evan."

She narrowed those storm-blue eyes of hers. "Really?"

"Really." He shrugged, running his hand up and down her thigh. "Empty sex isn't at all satisfying."

She ran a finger down his jaw, and smiled. "It's cliché, but I never knew what I was missing until you."

Satisfaction pumped fast in his veins. "Oh yeah?"

She licked his lower lip, then nipped, her white teeth scraping over his flesh. "You're very dirty."

He shifted her so she nudged the hard ridge of his cock. "I can get much dirtier."

Her eyes lit up and her lips tilted. "Hmmm . . . I find that hard to believe."

He rocked her into his erection. "Challenge accepted."

Her gaze turned a bit dazed, her eyes glassy, but before she got too comfortable he slapped her ass, hard.

She sucked in a breath, jerking as her pupils dilated. "Hey! That hurt."

It should have; his palm stung. "That's the idea."

She glared, but squirmed on his lap, rubbing against his hard cock. He gave her a knowing grin. "Gave you a little jolt too, didn't it?"

Her chin tilted. "Certainly not."

He smirked. "Fine, then I won't do it again."

She opened her mouth. Shut it. Opened it again. Then closed. Her brow wrinkled as something akin to confusion passed over her face. She blew out an exasperated breath. "You're impossible."

He squeezed the flesh, heated from where he'd slapped her, and her gaze dimmed. He kissed her, a quick brush on the lips before setting her back. "Come on, it's time to get ready, we've got a lot of things to do today before we work our way back to Revival."

She puffed out her bottom lip, surprising him with a pout. "What about accepting the challenge?"

He lifted her off his lap and set her on her feet. "You'll just have to wait and see what I come up with, now won't you?"

Cecilia waited on the front steps for Shane to pick her up. The late spring air brushed over her skin and she closed her eyes, lifting her head to the sun. The sounds of the city filled her ears as the leaves blew with a gust of wind that swept hair across her cheek.

Had she ever felt this good? This alive?

A loud roar ruined her serenity and her lids snapped open in time to see a motorcycle barreling down the street. A huge, loud bike of black and silver chrome vibrated through the streets and down her spine.

She waited for it to pass so she'd once again be plunged into peace. Only that didn't happen. The motorcycle pulled up in front of her house. Her heart gave a lurch. The driver flicked the engine off and removed his helmet.

It was Shane. Smile devastating and dangerous, he gave her a long, thorough glance before nodding. He looked every inch the quintessential bad boy in jeans, worn shit-kicker biker boots, and a black T-shirt. Like every good girl's fantasy and every father's nightmare. Utterly gorgeous and delicious.

Cecilia vacillated between wanting to jump him and being terrified! She walked down the steps to the sidewalk, pointing to the beast of a machine. "What's this?"

He grabbed her wrist and tugged her close, brushing his mouth over hers and making her shiver. "It's a Harley."

She shook her head. "You don't actually expect me to get on that thing, do you?"

"Yeah, I do." He flashed a devious grin. "Are you scared?"

"Motorcycles are dangerous." She scowled at the bike before squinting at the design on the tank. "Is that your company logo?"

"It's a custom build. A friend of mine makes them."

She held up the skirt of her sundress, a pale tan number with white trimmed stitching around the edges and a white sash for a belt. "Look at what I'm wearing."

"You look like a rich girl."

She huffed, crossed her arms, and tapped her matching low-heeled sling-backs. "I *am* a rich girl."

His chin jutted toward the leather seat behind him. "Get on."

Fear and temptation pulled at her in equal measure. "Shane Donovan, you know perfectly well I'm not dressed for riding a motorcycle."

Like a total guy, he shrugged. "I'll grant you pants would be better. But we're not going too far and I won't take you on the expressway. Tuck your skirt between your legs and me and you'll be fine."

"That doesn't make me feel better."

"Get on, Cecilia."

She wrinkled her nose, hemmed and hawed, then finally

plopped on the back, adjusting her skirt around her legs and wedging the fabric between them so she didn't flash everyone. A flair of heat shot through her as her thighs straddled Shane's hips.

She ignored it.

He twisted around and handed her a helmet.

She puffed out her bottom lip in a pout that kept making an appearance. "This is going to ruin my hair."

"Don't be such a girl."

"I am a girl."

He gripped her chin and nipped her bottom lip. "A gorgeous girl."

"Don't try and flatter me," she said, disgruntled. "I'm not going to like this."

He grinned. "I'll make you a deal. Do this for me and, if after, I haven't converted you, I'll never make you ride again."

"Deal," she said, putting the helmet on.

He followed suit before turning over the engine. It roared to life, echoing in her ears.

The vibration raced up her spine and traveled like lightning over her skin. A rush of exhilaration raced through her veins like wildfire.

He twisted the handle, revving the engine.

She felt it everywhere. Pulsing and shuddering between her legs. He gunned the motor again and she jolted, letting out a startled, "Oh!"

Gripping him tighter, she bit her lip as her clit throbbed. "Jesus!"

He laughed, the sound filled with wickedness. "Hang on."

He pulled out onto the street and she clutched at him for dear life. Muscles trembling, her heart beat furiously against her ribs as adrenaline raced through her blood.

It was terrifying.

Exhilarating and arousing.

As the city flew by, the wind whipping over her skin, she was free.

Twenty minutes later they were in front of a brick bungalow and Cecilia's whole body vibrated with tension and the rush of danger. A powerful aphrodisiac that had her knees wobbling as Shane helped her off the bike.

He grinned down at her. "See, that wasn't so bad, now was it?"

"You're a jerk!" Oh God, she was on fire. She was never going to forgive him.

He curled his hand around the nape of her neck. "Admit it, you loved it."

"I didn't," she whispered, all her feigned indignation melting away as she rose to her tiptoes and kissed him.

The kiss was slow and deep.

His arm wrapped around her waist, pulling her close as his tongue tangled with hers like a dance. Desperate to get closer, she threaded her fingers through his hair.

Their mouths slid together. Parted. Shifted. Then merged again.

His fingers tightened around her neck. At her waist.

She arched, stretching her body to mold against him in that special place where only he fit.

Her fingers traced his jaw as his lips branded her.

Her breath came fast, an urgent rise and fall that matched his.

He growled, a low, deep sound that vibrated through her with a power that matched his beast of a motorcycle. He pulled away, licking her bottom lip. "We have to stop. Now."

She nodded, her vision hazy. "Yes."

His teeth scraped over her swollen lip. "On the way home, I want you to take off your panties."

At the thought, she shuddered. He made her crazy. Depraved. "Oh no."

"Oh yes. I like the thought of you looking so prim and proper, while your slick pussy rubs against the seat and my back."

Her knees turned to jelly.

He chuckled and patted her ass. "Let's go."

Cecilia sat in the high-back chair as Shane's great-aunt Cathy looked her over from head to toe. In her late eighties, her hair was snow white, her skin wrinkled, but her blue eyes were razor sharp. She wore a T-shirt that proclaimed her *Team Jacob* and Cecilia could not contain her grin.

The older woman shifted her attention back and forth between her nephew and Cecilia. "I don't appreciate you neckin' in the middle of my front yard, boy."

A flush crawled up Cecilia's neck and splashed on her cheeks, but she managed to keep her chin held high.

Shane stretched out his long legs and hooked one ankle over the other. "Sorry about that, Aunt Cathy." Not sounding sorry at all.

"What would your momma say?" Aunt Cathy asked, her expression sly.

Cecilia pressed her lips together.

Shane laced his fingers over his stomach. "I suppose you could call her and find out."

His aunt reached between the cushions of her antique brocade couch and pulled out a pack of cigarettes.

Shane shot off the chair, stalked over to her and held out his open palm. "Hand them over. You're not supposed to be smoking."

She waved him away. "I'm eighty-eight, boy. If I want to smoke, I'll smoke."

"It's not good for you." He tried to snatch them, but she yanked her hand back. "Auntie," he said in a warning tone.

In response, she lit a long, slim cigarette and took a long drag.

Shane sighed and returned to his seat.

Cecilia grinned. It was adorable.

"And what about you, girl?" The older woman looked at Cecilia with her sharp gaze. "Didn't your momma ever tell you no one will buy the cow if you give the milk away for free?"

Shane shot her a smirk, one brow raised.

With the poise gained through years of practice, she picked up her cup of tea. "I must have missed that lesson somewhere along the way."

Shane chuckled.

Aunt Cathy took a long drag of her cigarette and blew out a billow of smoke. "I made all five of my husbands wait until the wedding night. But I'm old-fashioned that way."

"I see," Cecilia said primly.

After another long puff, his aunt tilted the lit cigarette toward Shane. "Your mom said you'd change my oil."

Shane sighed. "Why don't you let the mechanic I sent over here do it?"

Her painted-on brows slammed together. "I don't want some stranger handling my car. It's a classic."

"It's a Buick."

"Exactly." She pointed toward the kitchen. "My back stairs need some fixing too."

"And I suppose I have to fix them?" Shane said, his tone wry and amused.

"It's the least you can do for your old auntie."

Ten minutes later, Cecilia sat on the little wooden deck as Shane banged away at the second-to-the-bottom step. Just watching his muscles bunch and flex as he worked the hammer had her feeling all melty and shivery inside. She tilted her face to the sun, wishing it were ten degrees hotter so he'd take his shirt off.

"Hand me that screwdriver, baby." He held out his hand, reminding her of that day when she'd found him under the kitchen sink.

It seemed like a lifetime ago. His voice, once so cold when he'd talked to her, now burned hot in that special way reserved only for her.

She handed it to him. "You're amazing."

He stilled, his head lifting from his task to look at her.

"Is there anything you can't do?" Unable to resist, she trailed a finger over his jaw. "You take care of everyone."

Green eyes darkening, he shook his head. "I'm not doing anything that anyone else wouldn't do."

"Liar." She brushed a kiss over his mouth.

"Careful, or Aunt Cathy's going to have more than making out to complain about."

She grinned and he went back to fixing the steps.

She wasn't wrong. He took care of everyone. If anyone in his family had a problem he was there, handling it so they didn't have to.

But who took care of him?

I could. The thought whispered through her mind, startling her. She wasn't a caregiver. Not like he was. Shane deserved a woman who'd make him a home. A woman who'd fuss over him. Cook him dinner and harp on him about eating. He deserved someone who'd nurture him for a change.

She wasn't that kind of woman.

But still, she couldn't stop the fantasy that she could be that person. Not the homemaker, per se, but the person Shane needed. Deserved. It was bright and crystal clear in her mind. Alive and vivid, fitting like a missing puzzle piece inside her.

She wanted it. Wanted that life she could sense with Shane. And today, she felt brave enough to reach out and touch it. To believe in the possibility that it could be real.

Chapter Twenty-One

Later that Saturday afternoon, Cecilia looked out the window of their car as they drove down the interstate, watching the dense outer suburbs, with their overdeveloped strip malls and super centers, give way to flat farmland.

In silence, Shane drove beside her, both of them content not to speak. It was nice. Perfect, like nothing she'd ever had before in a relationship and it unraveled the tension inside her.

She'd been thinking all afternoon, coming to grips with the truth. All this time, all these years, she'd been lying to herself. Holding on to the dreams she'd created as a child with such single-minded focus, she'd never realized she'd outgrown them along the way.

She may as well have been saying she wanted to be a fairy princess.

The weight, sitting heavy on her chest, lifted and she knew what she had to do.

She was going to put an end to her fake engagement. All she needed to do was figure out how. And she thought she finally had a real idea of what she might do with her life. She'd been thinking about what she was good at, what she actually enjoyed about her job. Some might call her crazy, but she loved cleaning up the messes; it gave her a perverse thrill to take something that seemed unfixable and spin it into salvageable.

How many times had she done that for her father? For his colleagues? Why couldn't she make her living doing that? Hell, there was a plentiful market for damage control; she had tons of connections, and the thought actually excited her instead of filling her with dread.

As soon as she worked out all the pieces, she'd tell Shane and see what happened. Because she didn't know what their future held. All she knew was he filled an empty space inside her, and the more time that passed the more she didn't want to be without him.

Did he feel the same way? She thought he might, but they'd spent so much time carefully avoiding any talk about their future, their feelings, and what was happening between them, she wasn't sure.

Out of the corner of her eye, she scoped him out, blond, relaxed, and gorgeous behind the wheel. He wore a navy T-shirt that strained around his biceps, and she followed the lines of his arm, the tanned skin and veins running the length of his forearm. The light dusting of golden hair, his strong wrists and the talented fingers that made her feel protected. Would he want someone like her?

He glanced over at her. "I can feel you thinking."

She bit her lower lip. He always did that. So carefully in tune with her—her likes and dislikes, her wants and desires, her moods. She'd never had that before. It made her feel . . . cared for. Like she mattered. She twisted in her seat, resting her back against the door so she could look at him more directly. She'd intended to say something light, unwilling to risk a topic she wasn't ready to talk about yet, so the question that popped out of her mouth surprised her. "Why do you feel guilty about your success?"

"I don't." The answer quick and sharp, like a right jab.

"Yes, you do. It's like you think you've got to apologize for it."

"I don't. I just don't see the point in making a big deal about it. It wasn't a thought-out plan."

She shook her head in disbelief. "Of course it was. You plan and take care of everything. That's your nature."

His knuckles tightened on the steering wheel, turning white. "That's not nature, it's necessity. If my dad hadn't died, I'd be a slacker, probably working some odd job, living paycheck to paycheck."

"I don't believe that for a second."

"Well, you don't know what you're talking about."

She touched his thigh and spoke softly. "You don't have anything to feel guilty about, Shane. What you've done is remarkable."

The muscles under her palm tensed. "Doesn't change the fact that I would have been a thug if I had the choice."

"I doubt that, but even if it's true, so what? That's not what happened."

He frowned. "I hate knowing he had to die in order for me to become a good man."

Ah. There was the crux of the problem.

She shifted in the bucket seat. "You're right, if your dad hadn't died, you would have been a different person. Maybe you'd be poor. Or a slacker. Or maybe you'd be an accountant."

He gave her a sharp look of disapproval and she laughed before putting her head on his shoulder. "What I do know is that regardless of what you would have become, you would have been a good man."

"You don't know that," he said, tone stubborn and absolute.

"The other night, when the girls were over at Gracie's house, Maddie kept telling stories about you." Her future sister-in-law had tried to be subtle, but Cecilia recognized the hard sell when she saw it. Not that it had been necessary. She was already hooked on his virtues, as well as his more devious qualities. "Maddie told a story about some party she went to in high school where she got a little rowdy and picked a fight with the wrong guy. Do you remember that?"

The muscles under his shoulder flexed and rippled before settling again. "Yeah, I got a call from James that she was in trouble, which at the time was pretty much par for the course."

"She said you rescued her, then knocked the guy out cold."

He chuckled, clearly a fond memory. "He didn't make that mistake again."

"She also said you climbed up a tree and rescued her cat, Fluffy. Kicked a bunch of guys' asses for messing with James. Stole evidence from Sister Margaret's office so Maddie wouldn't get in trouble for some graffiti she'd drawn. And took the rap for Evan when he pulled the fire alarm so he wouldn't get thrown off the football team." She glanced at him. "Is that all true?"

He scowled. "Maddie talks too much."

Cecilia smiled, shifting to rest against his shoulder again. "But you're smart enough to get my point."

He sighed, the long, heavy sound of a man who knows he lost an argument. "Only because you used a sledgehammer to make it."

She laughed. "I use the tools necessary to get the job done."

* * *

Later that night, back at the farmhouse, everyone sat around the poker table while Shane shuffled the deck of cards. Money exchanged, chips in a neat stack, he nodded at Cecilia sitting across from him. "Do you know how to play?"

She shot him a scornful look. "Of course."

His lips quivered. "How the hell should I know? You don't look like a card player."

Cecilia rolled her eyes and grabbed a cherry Tootsie Roll Pop from the pile next to Sophie and unwrapped it with a nonchalant shrug of her bare shoulder. "I'm okay."

Ha. He knew right then she was a shark. He narrowed his gaze, appreciating the swell of her breasts in her red tank top. The way her hair brushed her shoulders in loose waves. "Hmmm."

"Just deal, for fuck's sake," Mitch said.

Shane ignored him and continued to watch Cecilia.

She smiled back sweetly before licking the red candy with the tip of her pink tongue.

He lost his train of thought, his hands stilling on the playing cards.

"We can't possibly be this annoying," Mitch said to Maddie.

Maddie shook her head. "No way."

Sophie clucked her tongue. "Yes, way."

Penelope poked him in the arm. "You need to shuffle."

Gaze glued to the woman across the table, he split the deck into two piles.

Cecilia sucked the red lollipop between those porn-star lips of hers, distracting him as she twirled it in her mouth, reminding him of the way she sucked cock.

He fumbled the cards and they flew in a haphazard heap on the green felt table in front of him.

She pulled the candy like a slow tease from her mouth,

swirling her now-bright-red tongue, and raising a brow. "Problem?"

Little temptress. How exactly was he going to get her back? "Nope."

She glanced pointedly at the cards. "Are you going to deal? Or just sit there?"

Oh, wasn't she just asking for it? Of course, to deliver he needed blood back in his brain, which was proving quite difficult.

Since the second they got back, they'd been surrounded by people, and he hadn't been able to touch her all day. He frowned. Did he really have it *that* bad? Surely he could go ten hours without having her.

Her tongue slid lazily over the round, red tip and his cock hardened to the point of pain.

Well, shit. That's exactly how it was.

Penelope lost patience and sighed, gathering up the cards for him.

The sucker slipped between Cecilia's lips. Jesus.

He dragged a hand through his hair and took the deck back from Penelope. "I can do it."

"Can you?" Penelope asked, the sarcasm clear in her tone.

Sure he could. Cecilia puckered her lips, placed the rounded tip of the lollipop between her pursed lips and twirled it in a slow circle.

He snapped. "Would you stop that?"

She removed the sucker and held it elegantly between her thumb and forefinger. Lips stained an obscene pink that made his breath catch, she asked, "Stop what?"

"Mouth-fucking the sucker. It's distracting."

Maddie, Sophie, and Penelope all gasped. "Shane!"

Gracie, Charlie, and Sam laughed.

Mitch groaned.

Cecilia, however, remained perfectly composed, not even having the decency to blush. "I have no idea what you're talking about. But if you're distracted, that's your problem."

She twirled the lollipop again, gently pushing it between her lips and then retreating. "I'm here to play cards."

Charlie gave Cecilia a long, slow once-over that had possession thumping through Shane's chest. "I've got to side with Shane here, it's pretty damn distracting."

Shane narrowed his gaze. "Don't look at her mouth."

Charlie shrugged. "Sorry, man, she's got a hot mouth."

Smile pure sin, Cecilia tilted her head. "That's very sweet of you, Charlie."

Sweet? It wasn't sweet. Shane growled. "Eat it normal."

"I am." She licked. "You just have a dirty mind."

Of course he did, as she well knew. But hell, even if he didn't, he'd have to be a dead man to not have illicit thoughts.

He started to speak but Mitch cut him off. "Deal the fucking cards."

Shane cocked a brow at her.

She smiled back.

He dealt while she ate her lollipop as though she was auditioning for Lolita.

Thirty minutes later, he was twenty dollars poorer and Cecilia, with her red-stained lips, had a big pile of chips stacked in front of her.

Gracie pointed at her. "You're no fun to play with."

Cecilia clucked. "Don't be a sore loser."

Gracie stuck her tongue out.

Cecilia laughed.

Sophie lifted one of the suckers sitting on the table. "What's in these things? Magic?"

"I'll be right back." Cecilia met Shane's eyes, smiled,

then rose to her feet with the grace that bespoke of her years of dance training.

Shane's gaze raked over her. The jean skirt she wore was so short it barely hit the curve of her thighs. Where had that outfit even come from? Because there's no way the Cecilia that showed up that day in the kitchen owned that outfit. "Where are you going?"

"Bathroom," she tossed over her shoulder while she sashayed down the hall.

Everyone looked at him expectantly and when he said nothing, Gracie asked, "All right, what did you do to her?"

"I didn't do anything," Shane said, grinning despite himself. Little vixen. They were right; he was responsible. Obsessed with exploring how far he could take her, he'd grown increasingly depraved.

"Yes, you did," Gracie said, shaking her head. "She ate three cupcakes and didn't even ask how many calories are in them."

Cecilia was becoming a sugar fiend, and it put a nice curve to her body. And he wanted to eat her up constantly. "Yeah, so?"

Sophie jumped in helpfully. "Then there was the lollipop."

Sam rubbed a hand over his jaw. "It was like watching porn."

Yeah, it was. Excellent porn. And suddenly he couldn't wait a second longer. "I'll be right back."

To a myriad of groans, he stood, racing out of the room to find his wayward temptress.

Cecilia put her ear to the bathroom door and listened, waiting for the heavy fall of Shane's footsteps.

She'd given quite a performance, practically daring him

outright. He wouldn't be able to resist the challenge and he was bound to follow her.

Her nipples hardened and her clit throbbed.

Jesus, she wanted him.

He'd been driving her crazy all day. Hot, smoldering glances. The stroke of his finger down her bare arm. A squeeze on her hip. Lingering looks at her mouth.

She was on fire. And she couldn't wait any longer.

Boots treaded down the hall, and she flicked off the faucet she'd left running, opening the door with perfect timing to smack right into him.

He growled. Hands on her hips, he backed her into the bathroom and kicked the door shut with a hard slam that sent a jolt of excitement racing through her.

"Shane," she said, her voice too breathless to be innocent.

He answered by pulling her tight against his body, fisting her hair and slamming his mouth onto hers.

She melted in an instant.

Lips demanding, he claimed her in an intense rush of lust that left her dizzy.

She rubbed her breasts against his chest, meeting his seeking tongue with her own.

Instantly hot.

Instantly wet.

Instantly throbbing with insatiable need.

She clung to his mouth, digging her nails into his shoulders as he kissed her so raw and dirty he may as well have been inside her.

He pulled away, cupping her breast and stroking his thumb over the nipple. "Having fun, Lolita?"

Breathless, she panted, "Yes, take me."

His green eyes flashed, and he wrapped his fingers

around her throat. He nipped at her bottom lip. "You have everyone fooled, don't you? You're not proper at all."

Desperate, she reached for the button on his jeans. "Not since I met you."

He consumed her with another heart-stopping kiss, his thumb pressing into her wildly pounding pulse.

She lowered his zipper, worked her way past the elastic band of his boxer briefs to wrap her fingers around his shaft.

He groaned against her mouth. "Cecilia. Fuck. So damn good."

It was powerful, the knowledge that this man wanted her. Was as crazy for her as she was for him.

She stroked, her grip tight and sure. Not at all gentle. The way she knew he liked best.

He circled her nipples through the thin fabric, raising them to a near painful peak.

She squeezed his cock. "I need you, now."

The statement was like striking a match. He groaned, turned her around until she faced the mirror. Their eyes met, and he yanked her skirt over her hips, tearing her panties. They fell to a heap on the floor. He put a palm on her back, pushing her forward until her clit was pressed up against the porcelain sink.

In the vanity mirror, their gazes locked.

"I want to come inside you." The tone of his voice rough, fissioning through her nerve endings.

They'd used condoms. Always. But suddenly she needed it. Needed him. "Yes."

"Are you protected?"

With a sharp nod, she lifted her hips in invitation.

His gaze turned utterly feral. He bent, covering her back with his big body, and grasped her throat. The image in the mirror hypnotic, so arousing, she jerked. Her clit rubbed against the now-slick porcelain. His lips brushed the shell of her ear, while his eyes stayed hot on hers. "Good. It'd be hell to stop and I need it, Cecilia. Need to feel your hot, wet pussy on my cock."

Her inner muscles contracted at his words, wanting to be filled. As always, he read her mind and guided himself in.

Swollen from all the sex they'd had last night, the angle made her impossibly tight. Stretched. She spread her legs, rising to her tiptoes, dropping her head until he was fully seated.

He gathered her hair in his fist and pulled. "Watch."

Her eyes flicked open as her muscles rippled around him.

Expression flashing with primal male satisfaction, he bit down on the curve of her neck, sending a shock wave through her body. "I knew you'd like that."

He pushed into her. So slow, when she wanted him to go fast. She threw her hips back, trying to control the tempo.

But he was having none of that.

He shook his head. "No, my way." His lids hooded as he placed one big hand on her hip, slowing her down.

He thrust back in, demonstrating complete mastery in even strokes. His shaft dragged across engorged tissue, enflaming every nerve she had, lighting her on fire. Building a tension so deep in her core she thought she might die with the sheer torture.

Her fingers clenched on the edge of the sink, her gaze glued to the hard lines of his face. "Shane, please, harder."

The tension grew. And grew. But refused to release.

"No." Another smooth thrust. "I've been dreaming about this all day. You feel like fucking heaven and it's going to last."

Her muscles clenched, his words heating her.

"Besides"—another nip on her throat—"this is payback."

And it had never been sweeter. Hotter. More erotic. Her nipples grew impossibly hard, rubbing against the fabric of her bra. She angled her hips, opening her legs wider to get more pressure on her clit.

He yanked her back, angling her hips away from the sink. The friction she desperately needed, gone. He slapped her ass, hard. "No coming yet."

A jolt of electricity shot through her. She liked this. Too much for comfort, which increased her arousal by a hundred times. She bit her lip. The tension built to a fevered pitch.

He slid his arm around her waist, bent low close to her ear. "That's right, baby, you can't hide from me, I know *exactly* what you like." His fingers tightened around her throat. "Who you are."

He did. It was like, with him, she was the woman she was always meant to be. She circled her hips, arching into him, making them both moan with pleasure.

"Again," he said, and she complied. He pushed forward to meet her, their bodies grinding together.

It was so slow. So excruciatingly slow.

And each time he filled her he became more a part of her.

Sweat beaded along her spine as her pleasure keened into tight focus, where all thoughts ceased to exist.

They moved together, almost languid, but hot, thick desperation filled the air. Like they couldn't get close enough.

"Shane." His name a gasped, breathless plea. Sensation built inside her, taking her higher and higher but never cresting.

He slammed powerfully into her wet, swollen, aching core.

"Oh God." Her voice almost unrecognizable, her fingers clenched on the sink.

He cupped her breasts, pulling down the fabric of her

tank top so they swelled over the top before unhooking her bra. Then his fingers were on her nipples, playing with the hard buds in time with his strokes.

"Watch." That gruff, low voice.

She shuddered, looked into the mirror again, catching his gaze.

So hot on hers, so possessive and primal, her inner walls clamped down on his cock.

He growled, pinched her nipples, sending another bolt of fire racing along her nerves.

He shook his head. "No, not me, you."

Her gaze clung to him for a moment, then she faced herself in the mirror. Who was that woman looking back at her? Hair a wild mess around her face, cheeks flushed, her lips swollen. She looked undone, worked up, crazy in lust. Like she'd do anything.

Her gaze fell to his big tan hands playing over her breasts, strong and powerful against her pale skin.

She throbbed. Everywhere. Energy pulsed through her as he took her higher and higher, until she thought she might break.

He covered her back with his chest. "So hot. And wet. And tight. Only for me."

One hand slid down her stomach, his fingers played over her clit. Mindless, she groaned. "Yes, only you, Shane."

"You ready, baby?"

She nodded.

His pace increased, his thrusts impossibly deeper.

She cried out. Threw her hips back to meet him.

The small powder room filled with the sound of their harsh breath. Their bodies slapping together as the air grew humid with desire and sex.

Need, deep inside her, threatened to break her in two.

He pounded into her.

She wound tighter.

Tighter.

Tighter.

The orgasm crashed over her, consuming her. She cried out and his hand clamped over her mouth as she screamed, climaxing uncontrollably.

He buried his face into her neck, low growls vibrating against her throat as he thrust into her. His teeth scraped over the sensitive skin at her throat as he came, spilling inside her, filling her up, setting off another wave as they shuddered together.

He kept moving, thrusting, drawing out the pleasure until they were nothing but a helpless, limp heap of sweaty bodies.

She looked into the mirror. Gaze intense, he watched her. Out of nowhere she blushed.

Everything about the sex had been raw. Desperate and unbearably intimate. She felt exposed. Vulnerable.

He put his palm on her back, the weight of his hand strong and steady. "It will be okay, Cecilia."

She blinked. The realization swept through her like a tornado.

She loved him. Hopelessly.

It terrified her.

He pulled out, turned her around, and gathered her in his arms.

She buried her head in the curve of his neck, sucking in the spicy male scent of him. And she felt safe. Home. Emotions welled inside her, her throat closing over as she fought to push it all back down.

She needed him.

He stroked her hair. "It will be okay. I promise."

Of course he promised, because there was nothing Shane couldn't do if he put his mind to it.

She nodded against his neck. "I'm okay."

His thumbs pressed under her chin until she looked at him.

She met his gaze.

"I'm not going to be able to let you go, Cecilia. I just can't."

Relief filled her, and the tightness in her muscles relaxed. "Okay."

He kissed her. "We'll figure it out."

She nodded. "Yes."

It was simple and not simple at all.

He rubbed a thumb over her cheek. "I'll give you whatever you want, you know that, right? And if that means running for congress"—he shuddered, but his green eyes were light with amusement—"for the wrong party, we'll figure it out."

She wanted to tell him that she didn't think she wanted to run, but then she looked into his eyes and saw it—what Maddie had talked about that day.

Shane Donovan would do anything for her. Anything. If it was in his power to give it to her, he would. No matter the cost. It gleamed there, bright and true. He'd move heaven and earth for her.

And for the first time she felt accepted. Cared for.

Neither of them had spoken the word, but it hung there between them. A silent promise, still too soon to say out loud.

She reached up and ran a finger over his jaw. "Who takes care of you, Shane?"

He blinked, confusion clouding his gaze. "I don't know what you mean."

"You take care of everyone else, but who takes care of you?"

He opened his mouth, closed it, frowned.

Before he could collect his thoughts, she stood on tiptoes and brushed her mouth over his. And made a promise of her own. "I will."

Chapter Twenty-Two

Cecilia practically danced on air the following morning as she slathered lavender body lotion over her legs and mooned over Shane.

Last night had been the best night of her life. He'd lavished her body with attention, making love to her over and over again, their joining all the sweeter for the time in between. Long, wet kisses. Soft exploration. And talking. Low, intimate conversations until he was wrapped tightly around her heart. Interwoven into the fabric of her skin.

Her phone beeped but she ignored it. The only people calling were the people she didn't wish to talk to at the moment.

But she wouldn't ignore them for long. She was telling her father she wouldn't marry Miles.

As for her future plans? She liked the idea of starting something of her own. Something she was responsible for and that allowed her to have control over her destiny. She'd even opened her laptop and done some research. Started making a list of people to talk to.

She smoothed lotion over her legs. She'd figure out the details. What mattered now was she felt excited and alive.

She intended to cling to that crystal clear vision of her future from yesterday.

Her phone beeped again.

And again.

And then again.

She frowned and walked over to the desk where her cell lay abandoned, to see fifteen missed calls from her father and five text messages. Since he wasn't a man who resorted to texting, curiosity got the better of her and she opened her messaging app.

We need to talk. It's urgent.

Cecilia, it's imperative we speak.

Two more messages of equal urgency and then the last one raised the fine hairs on the back of her neck.

We need to talk about Shane Donovan and your future.

Her heart started to pound. She took a deep breath and blew it out. Her time was up. She'd have to tell her father the truth and call off her faux engagement.

She pressed his contact number. It rang once before he picked up.

"I see I finally have your attention." He used the cold, stern tone that had always turned her into a mess when she was younger.

But it didn't work. Not this time. "What do you want, Father?"

"We have a problem on our hands. I flew into Chicago yesterday to deal with it and now it's time to clean up your mess. I need you back in the city in five hours for a meeting with Miles."

Dread crawled up her throat. She'd lived in fear of his disapproval for so long, it was a hard habit to break. But she ripped the Band-Aid off because Shane deserved it, and she intended to keep the promises she'd made to him last night. "Dad, that's not going to happen. I know we need to talk, but I can't marry Miles. I'm not marrying him."

"Based on your behavior at the benefit I assumed you'd say that, so I suggest you read my last e-mail. Go ahead, I'll wait."

Panic beat wildly in her chest. Something was wrong. She could feel it in her bones. She clicked the e-mail icon and opened the last message from her father.

Subject: We're prepared to release this at five o'clock today.

She opened the PDF document. Everything inside her stilled, became cold and dead, like she'd been frozen into a statue. She quickly skimmed the article, a detailed account that claimed Shane was contributing to slush funds in order to obtain city contracts.

Bile churned like battery acid in her stomach. A wave of nausea swept through her and threatened to bring her to her knees. Her voice shook when she put the phone back up to her ear. "But this isn't true."

"It doesn't matter if it's true," he said, his voice ruthless. "I happen to know the new city planner isn't too fond of Donovan and is looking for any excuse to pull the plug."

She felt sick. She knew about the troubles Shane had been having with the planner. His worries about his staff if the contract was pulled. "You're blackmailing me?"

A long pause. "Think of it as motivation."

"Why are you doing this?" She shook her head. "Why do you even care if I run for congress?"

He laughed, and she hated him. "Do you really think this is about you?"

Tears pricked in her eyes and she sat on the bed. All her happiness evaporated into thin air like a desert mirage. Of course, she'd forgotten, it never had anything to do with her. "I'm your daughter. Doesn't that matter to you?"

"I'm doing this for your own good. What? You're going to blow your whole future for an affair with a construction worker?"

She didn't bother arguing that Shane was so much more. "Yeah, that was the plan."

"You're smarter than that. I trust I'll see you in five hours."

More than anything in the world she wanted to throw his threats in his face, but she couldn't. She could not let Shane suffer because of her.

She wanted to run to him and tell him everything. But she couldn't. He could never find out. She knew him now, knew the lengths he'd go to for the people he cared about. She'd seen it in his eyes. In every move he'd made the night before.

If he found out, he'd refuse to be intimidated. He'd sacrifice that contract for her.

Last night she'd promised to take care of him, and that's what she needed to do. Even though he'd hate her for it. She closed her eyes. "I'll be there."

Shane went to find Cecilia when she hadn't shown up for breakfast. When he'd left she'd been about to take a shower, but it had been over an hour and he still hadn't seen her.

At breakfast on the patio, the conversation had swirled around him, but he hadn't paid any attention because all he could think about was her. After last night he could no longer ignore the truth. He loved her. And he was pretty sure she loved him too.

In the darkness, they'd told each other in a million silent ways.

It was too fast. Too quick. But it knocked him over the second she put her hand on his cheek and said she wanted to take care of him. He'd never believed he'd needed that, or even wanted it. Taking care of his family, that was his job and he'd done it willingly. But Cecilia was a woman who could shoulder the weight with him.

It wouldn't crush her.

She was too strong for that. Too stubborn. Just like him.

He knocked on the door then pushed it open. The room was empty, the bed neatly made, lace curtains blowing in the springtime breeze.

But she wasn't there.

He frowned, a trickle of unease sliding irrationally down his spine. A paper rustled on the desk, under the old-fashioned telephone. He walked over and picked it up.

Shane, I had to run into the city for an emergency meeting, but I'll be back tonight. C.

The note didn't make him feel better.

Why wouldn't she have talked to him? Called him? Hell, texted him?

She left a note?

What the fuck did that mean?

He ran down the stairs and flew out onto the front porch, but her car was already gone.

She'd slunk off to Chicago? Without one word?

From his pocket, he fished out his cell. There were no

messages. He dialed Cecilia's number and it went straight to voice mail.

Something had happened; he was sure of it.

With the note clutched in his fist, he walked back inside, down the hallway, through the kitchen door and straight out to the back, zeroing in on Charlotte Riley. "She's gone."

Charlotte's fork paused midway to her mouth before she lowered it slowly back to her plate with hardly a clang. "Pardon?"

Anger and panic churned inside him, seeping out of his pores as aggression. "Cecilia. Your daughter. She's gone."

The older woman's golden eyes darkened. "She left?"

Shane threw the crumpled note on the table. "She said she had an emergency meeting and would be back tonight."

Her expression cleared and the rest of the table seemed to let out a collective sigh.

Charlotte picked up her fork again. "Oh well, she'll be back."

Shane shook his head. "Something is wrong."

Maddie's mouth turned down. "Shane, she had a meeting."

"Bullshit." It was all bullshit. They didn't know her like he did. Every instinct he had was on rapid-fire alert and he was never wrong.

Mitch put his hand on the back of Maddie's chair. "I'm sure everything is fine. My father probably had a problem she needed to fix."

Shane's hands clenched into fists. "She's not even speaking to your father."

"But she still has a job to do," Mitch said rationally, making Shane want to punch him.

"She would have said something to me; she wouldn't just leave."

Mitch glanced pointedly at the paper on the table. "She left a note."

"You don't know shit."

James cleared his throat. "She'll be back tonight and you can talk to her then."

Charlotte's expression turned distressed, and she fiddled with her napkin in her lap. "I have to agree with Mitchell. Cecilia's always been single-minded when it comes to work."

Shane pinched the bridge of his nose, trying to get them to see reason. "She currently has about twenty voice mails and a hundred e-mails she hasn't looked at in days. Her laptop is still sitting in her bedroom in the case. She couldn't give a fuck about work."

"Shane!" Maddie jerked her head toward Charlotte and scowled.

"It's okay, dear." The older woman patted his sister's hand.

James pursed his lips. "What do you want us to do?"

Shane looked at them, sitting there relaxed at the table. They all thought he was being irrational. Acting crazy. Even though he knew he was right.

But what could he do? Chicago was a big city, she wasn't answering her phone, and she'd be back tonight. He shook his head. "Nothing. Forget it." He swiveled on his heel and walked back into the kitchen to collect himself.

A minute later the back door opened and he turned around to find Cecilia's mother standing there, her hands wringing. Her gaze shifted uneasily around the room, then it settled back on him. "I—" She cleared her throat. "I didn't realize you were so involved with Cecilia."

His jaw hardened and he nodded sharply. Damned if he was going to deny it. She was his.

Charlotte looked past him. "I knew there was some tension between you, but I didn't know it moved past attraction."

What was he supposed to say? He wasn't about to admit

they were sleeping together. Although clearly she was the last to know, since they hadn't exactly been discreet. He shrugged and said noncommittally, "I care about Cecilia."

"That's clear," she said, a small smile lifting her lips. "But that's what worries me."

"Don't be." Shane didn't quite get where Charlotte was going, but he was 100 percent certain he didn't want to know. "Everything's fine."

"Do you know? About her plans?"

"Yes."

They stared at each other, neither inclined to provide the details of said plans. Finally, Charlotte nodded. "When Cecilia was four years old, she put on a musical talent show for me and her father."

The subject change was abrupt and Shane frowned. That sense of foreboding knotted in his gut, but he said nothing.

The older woman took a deep breath then slowly exhaled. "She banged away on our grand piano and her father laughed and made an offhanded comment that we didn't have to worry about her being a great concert pianist."

If Shane needed any further incentive to dislike Nathaniel Riley, his wife had just handed it to him. "He sounds like a real stand-up dad."

Charlotte's expression darkened. "I know how it looks, and you can judge another time, but that's not the point."

Shane was instantly contrite. "I apologize. My mom raised me better than that, I'm just . . ." He trailed off, not knowing what to say.

"Concerned," she said.

He nodded. An understatement, but it would do.

Charlotte continued, "The next day she came to me and said she wanted piano lessons. She pestered me for a week until I relented. She took lessons until she was eighteen, practicing sometimes hours a day until she was given all the best solos."

"That doesn't surprise me," Shane said. "She's very tenacious."

Charlotte twisted a strand of pearls around her slim neck. "But here's what most people don't know."

He raised a brow.

"Cecilia hates piano. Hates it."

The point now crystal clear, his stomach dropped.

Charlotte frowned, twisting the necklace tighter. "All those years, all that practice on something she didn't even like, just so she could prove she could do it. So she could hear him say he was proud of her. That's the only reason."

His throat felt like dirt. "And you think this is one of those times?"

She nodded. "I do."

The doubt crept in, and he hated Charlotte for it. He shrugged, as though unconcerned. "I'll consider myself warned."

Then he turned and walked away.

Chapter Twenty-Three

Cecilia walked into her father's reception area, her head held high, her heart breaking. She smoothed down her hair, stretched too tight in a severe ponytail that matched the severe cut of her black business suit. She'd had fifteen minutes to go home and change. By the time she'd left her place, summer Cecilia was nowhere in sight.

She'd had to leave her behind to deal with what was to come.

It was the only way.

She strode briskly across the carpeted floor and into his office without knocking. As she expected, they already waited for her, their heads bent low over the papers spread out on the conference table.

In her smooth, polished voice she said, "I'm here, reporting for duty."

They looked up and, for a second, she paused dead in her tracks. She'd never noticed how similar they were. In their politician's suits, neatly trimmed hair, and jaws gone slack from too many dinners out. In another fifteen years Miles Fletcher would be her father.

She walked over to the table, put down her briefcase, sat down, and folded her hands on the table, taking control of the situation. She might be their victim, but she refused to act as such. She nodded. "Well, lay your cards on the table, gentlemen."

Her father smiled, the lines around his mouth softening. "There's my girl."

Her chin tilted. "I'm not anyone's girl." Except Shane's.

Miles leaned forward, mimicking her posture, his expression smooth. "Cecilia, we're sorry it had to come to this, but I can assure you, we're on your side."

Cecilia met his gaze, unwavering. "Do not patronize me. Now let's get your sordid little blackmail scheme on the table so we can get down to terms."

Miles sighed. "None of this would have happened if you'd chosen to be more discreet in your affair with Shane Donovan."

"And," her father said, his tone now ice, "if you would have returned our calls."

She shrugged. "I was busy."

Miles covered her hand with his. "I understand this isn't a love match, and I expect there will be occasions where one of us will need to scratch a particular itch. Over time, we'll learn to appreciate each other, but I'm not unreasonable. You can have your liaisons but, for obvious reasons, we can't have you flaunting them in front of everyone." He lowered his voice as though the room was full of hidden microphones. "You brought him home with you."

How did they know that? She shook her head. It didn't matter.

She glanced at her father. He looked tired. Hope and some misguided sense of loyalty had her wanting to give him a chance at redemption. "Are you really okay with this? Listening to your daughter and her fiancé casually discuss extramarital affairs?"

Nathaniel steepled his fingers, narrowing his eyes. "You agreed to this arrangement."

The hope died a slow, painful death.

"You're right, I did." There was no point in not taking responsibility. This mess was entirely her own doing. "My relationship with Shane Donovan isn't really the point, is it?"

"No," her father said flatly. "And if you insist, you can keep him as long as you practice the utmost discretion."

She laughed, the sound full of scorn and bitterness. "He's not a puppy. So, give me the terms. What do I have to agree to so you don't hurt Shane?"

"Simple," Miles said, his voice almost cheerful. "Our agreement hasn't changed. We'll continue to support your campaign efforts as long as you continue to be a good, dutiful wife."

A sudden weariness overtook her, seeping into her bones. How many times had she sat in meetings like this? Normally they weren't about her, but the tone never changed. The endless negotiations, the backroom deals, the exchange of information for profit or silence.

It. Never. Fucking. Ended.

And she'd had enough. She was just plain tired of it. She didn't want this life anymore. Maybe she never had. She'd been content to be in the background, moving chess pieces around until the strategy fell into place.

She didn't want to be her father or Miles.

Very carefully, she said, "And if I no longer want to run?"

Her father's gaze narrowed, then he shifted his attention to Miles, who nodded. "That would be fine."

And the lightbulb finally flipped on. "That was just a bargaining chip to get me to agree to the plan, wasn't it?"

Miles folded his hands, regal and polished. "Of course we supported your endeavor, but it was a lofty goal."

They'd never believed in her for a second. Two weeks ago this would have cut like a knife, and while the hurt still stung, it didn't devastate her. How could it, when she hadn't really believed in her either?

But Shane believed. And she couldn't fail him.

"And the real goal?"

"As you know, between my family's money and business endeavors, I have the capacity to generate the funding necessary to ensure a successful campaign. I've spent years positioning myself in the party and with the lobbyists, but your father's connections will cement my position. With our marriage, and your father's support, I will run for governor in the next election." Miles smiled, as though she should be pleased to learn of his plans.

Her father's expression lit with an excitement she hadn't seen in a long time. "He can do it, Cecilia. And it doesn't end there. We're planning on the Oval Office."

The ultimate dream he'd never been able to realize.

Miles puffed up, his chest actually expanding as he leaned back in his chair.

Cecilia looked back and forth between them. "So, at the end of the day, all this is about power. That's it?"

"It's the White House," Nathaniel said.

Cecilia snorted, and both men frowned. "Based on the history of Illinois governors, you have a better shot ending up in jail than you do the White House."

Miles flushed. "I don't need money."

No, he just needed power. A headache started at the base of her skull. "I don't understand why you need me."

Nathaniel leaned forward. "You know everything about politics. You understand the life, the demands, the deals. You're going to make an excellent first lady. This is what you've been raised for. What you were made for."

She shook her head. "To be somebody's wife?"

"My wife." Miles smiled as though waiting for a thank-you. "And you have certain talents that aren't easy to come by."

And there was the truth. The real truth. She sat back in her chair. "I'm good at finding out secrets."

"Not only that," her father said. "At spinning them to our advantage. Your skills can be used to our benefit."

It sickened her. Made her lose hope in humanity for a fraction of a second until she remembered that this wasn't how most people lived. Most people were good. Shane was good. "And as long as I stick to the plan, you'll leave Shane alone?"

"Yes," Miles said. "He's not a threat to us. We have no interest in him outside of your involvement."

"Fine, but I want assurances. Guarantees."

The two men glanced at each other then back at her.

"What?"

"I want you to call the mayor tomorrow and get that contract pushed through. I want it signed. Yesterday." The demand was a long shot, but she gave it her all.

Nathaniel's expression turned regretful. "That pushes the leverage in your favor, dear. And I'm afraid I can't have that."

"You don't trust me?"

"No, not in this case."

This man she'd hero-worshipped her whole life thought of her as nothing more than another obstacle he had to maneuver.

Although in this case, it was for good reason. She'd absolutely have used the shift in power to her favor.

"All right then," she said, standing. "We'll play out our hands. I'm leaving. I'll be in touch."

The two men rose to their feet, and her father smiled his cold politician's smile at her. "One day, when you're first lady, you'll know this was for the best."

She turned and when she got to the door, she looked over her shoulder. That need for approval snuck in, despite her best efforts, and she said softly, "You know, all I ever wanted was for you to believe in me."

The senator nodded. "I do. That's why we need you on our team."

It was the saddest thing he'd ever said to her.

Defeated, she left, the tears clogging her throat.

Some tiny part of her had hoped inspiration would hit and she'd think of a way out of this. But nothing had come to her.

She had to break things off with Shane.

She couldn't allow him to be hurt. Not because of her.

Those silent promises she'd made didn't mean anything. Not now.

Thank God she'd kept her plans a secret; as far as Shane knew, she was still going through with the wedding. She didn't know how she'd manage to convince him that ending their relationship was for the best, but she had no other choice at the moment. Not with that contract at stake. He'd never allow Miles and her father to intimidate him, and he would lose everything. She couldn't let that happen. This time, he needed someone to take care of him.

There was no other way.

Shane's mood was as dark as the night sky. He'd drunk beer after beer, sitting in the swing on the front porch waiting for Cecilia.

All day, he'd called. Texted. She hadn't responded.

The woman in his bed last night, desperate and pleading for his touch, would not have done this. It had only been a short time, but she kept in contact with him in a thousand ways.

Unless she had a damn good reason, she didn't just cut off communication.

And his gut told him to be on guard. That things weren't going to end well.

So here he sat, waiting for the other shoe to drop.

The front door opened and James stepped out on the porch, closing the door softly behind him. He barely made any sound, moving like a jungle cat in the darkness. That's the way his brother was, all stealth.

Shane took another sip of beer. "I don't want company."

Almost every person in the house had visited him over the past couple hours and it was starting to drive him batty.

James slid onto the porch rail, balancing himself on the edge. "Yeah, I know."

"So you can leave."

James shook his head. "Nope, I'm not going to do that."

The swing swayed under his heavy weight. "Suit yourself."

James had a calm steadiness about him, and after a few minutes the knot of tension in Shane's gut eased. He took another sip of beer and scoffed. "I really fucked up this time, Jimmy."

"You don't know anything's wrong." Tone calm and reasonable. Irritating as hell.

"I know," he said, the words flat.

James craned his neck and searched the yard as though looking for something. "You're probably right. But I think you should trust her."

"I do."

James shook his head. "No, you don't. You want to, but you don't. Because you know she can crush you. And you've grown dependent on being invincible."

The tension reared back up like a bucking bronco. It was so much easier to argue the semantics instead of focusing on his overwhelming feelings for Cecilia. "Where the hell do you come up with this crap?"

"I read a lot," James said, his voice wry. "You like being the superhero. Saving the day. That's your deal."

"That's not my deal."

"But Cecilia doesn't need you to rescue her. Her situation, it appeals to you because it puts her in the role of damsel in distress, but she won't quite fit your mold, will she?"

Defensiveness raced through his blood. "What are you saying, I like weak women?"

"No, but you like to have the upper hand, and Cecilia doesn't give you that. She doesn't need anything from you."

"That's not true," he said. A chill passed through him. For the first time since his dad died, he needed someone. It wasn't possible she didn't need him back.

James shrugged. "What do I know?"

They fell silent.

James wasn't the type to belabor a point. He'd said his piece and Shane could either take it or leave it.

And he was leaving it.

He didn't want to rescue Cecilia.

He frowned. Or did he? Was that what he waited for? Why he hadn't pushed? Was he entertaining a fantasy of swooping in and saving her from her evil father and his henchman?

No. It couldn't be.

He swallowed hard. He'd never been good at lying to himself, and the truth hit him like a smack in the face. That's exactly what he was doing. And he was pissed as hell because she'd gone off and left him powerless.

Hell, she hadn't even invited him to the battle.

He shook his head. "You're an asshole."

James laughed. "So I've been told."

Weary, Cecilia climbed the front steps of the farmhouse, a feat that seemed more difficult than climbing Mount Everest. When she hit the top step Shane spoke, startling her.

"Where the fuck have you been?" His voice low and filled with anger.

She was exhausted. Beaten and beleaguered. But she shrugged into her ice-queen persona because it was the only way she knew to protect herself. In a cool tone, she said, "I left you a note."

She walked over to stand in front of him, wanting to sit on the swing and cuddle into his warm embrace, or at least sag against the wall, but she couldn't let herself do that.

Never show weakness. Never break.

She smoothed the wrinkles of the black business suit she still wore.

A bitter, scornful sound that vaguely resembled a laugh shook his shoulders. "All right, Cecilia, lay it on me."

She blinked. She'd wanted to put this off until tomorrow, but somehow he already knew. How?

As though disgusted, he shook his head. "Don't you get it? I know you. Not the bullshit you tell other people. But *you*. You don't even realize it, do you?"

The tears threatened and she bit her lip. "Realize what?"

"You and I have been in near constant contact since you got here. Hell, Cecilia, you tell me when you're going to the bathroom. So when you disappear with a one-line note and turn off your cell phone, it's a tell, Ce-ce. You should know that."

She frowned. She did know. Only she hadn't realized she'd kept in such close contact. It had been so natural, she hadn't noticed. How silly of her. She blew out a breath and gathered the last little shreds of her tattered reserves.

She was doing this for him. To protect him. He'd hate her and never forgive her, but she was doing this because she loved him. Unable to face the expression on his face, she stared at the ground.

"Just get it over with." His voice was as defeated as she felt.

The words stuck in her throat, but she forced them out. "We need to end this." Nausea rolled through her.

"Why? So you can marry some guy you don't even like, to run for a seat you don't even want?"

"I want it. It's all I ever wanted." She parroted the words she'd been saying for months. Hollow, empty words. She might as well be saying she wanted to fly to Mars, that's how little meaning they had. She soldiered on. "I have to see this through."

He stood from the swing and walked over to her as the chains rattled, breaking through the silence of the night. When he came to a stop, he gripped her chin and forced her to look up at him.

Tears pricked at her eyes and she pushed them back down. She could not cry. Not yet. When she was alone, but not in front of him.

He looked deep into her eyes, searching her gaze for what felt like an eternity. His jaw hardened. "I don't believe you."

She swallowed. "You don't have to."

"Do you love me?"

The question came from nowhere, almost knocking her to her knees with their power. Unable to stop them, the tears swelled and spilled onto her cheeks and she whispered the biggest lie of her life. "No."

"Liar."

He kissed her. His mouth hard and desperate on hers.

She tried to order herself to stop, to not kiss him back, but she couldn't.

Instead, her lips clung.

He slanted his head, deepening the connection.

Their tongues stroked.

His mouth like heaven, her body warmed as tears tracked down her cheeks, melding with the heat of their lips.

His arm wrapped around her waist, pulling her close, feasting off her like she was the most decadent meal. Until she was breathless, arching against him.

Needing him.

Wanting him.

He gripped her hair in his fist and tore her away. "Don't lie to me, Cecilia. Tell me the truth."

It was like a bucket of ice water. She stepped away and he released her, his arms sliding away and taking all his warmth with them. His expression darkened as his mouth firmed. She met his gaze, hiding everything she felt deep inside, letting her ice-queen mask slide into place.

She didn't have to lie. "I am going to marry Miles Fletcher." She braced herself, waiting for his wrath, but it didn't come.

Instead, he stepped away, his features transforming back into that cold disdain he'd always shown her. "Fine. I'm not going to stop you."

It broke her heart, because she knew what it meant. She'd severed the bond between them. Crossed a line and there was no going back. She nodded. "Good."

He nodded back, as though they'd just come to terms on a business agreement. "Let's agree to stay away from each other for the rest of the trip."

Her tears dried as her spine straightened. It was happening. This was the end. "Agreed."

His lips curved into a sardonic twist. "After the wedding,

we'll only have to see each other on holidays. Before long it will be like this never happened."

It was done. She needed to be alone so she could cry. "Good night, Shane."

She left him. Turned away from her heart and that future she'd clutched to her last night. Calling on all her years of training, she walked through the door, straight down the hall, into the kitchen and out the back door.

She started to make her way to the river, but took a sudden detour, walking to Gracie's before she could even process why she was doing it. Her chin quivered as she pounded on the back door.

Sam opened it, took one look at her, and dragged her inside. "I'll get Gracie."

She didn't ask how he knew, but he did.

Thirty seconds later Gracie came into the kitchen.

Cecilia took one look at her and burst into tears.

Chapter Twenty-Four

Shane needed something a hell of a lot harder than beer. He needed numb. Complete obliteration. His hands gripped the rail of the porch. Why was she doing this?

She loved him. He felt it in his bones. So why?

He didn't know. And he supposed it didn't matter.

He'd seen the determination in her eyes. She meant it.

The door opened, and his chest welled with hope that she'd come back, only to be dashed when Mitch came outside.

He handed Shane a bottle of scotch then sat on the swing. Shane opened the bottle, flung the cap into the bushes, and took a long swallow. The alcohol burned going down, coating his throat and stomach like acid. He rested his body against a pillar and looked out onto the moonlit yard.

It reminded him of his sister. The flowers and trees artistically arranged in a way only she could accomplish.

At least she was getting a happy ending.

He could be grateful to the Rileys for that.

Mitch sighed and pushed the swing with his foot. "The more things change, the more they stay the same."

Shane took another drink. "What the hell are you talking about?"

Mitch grinned. "Last year at this time we were drinking scotch, but the situation was reversed."

Shane scoffed, thinking back to that conversation about his sister and Mitch, a lifetime ago. "I think I liked the last one better."

Mitch shrugged. "Speak for yourself. I've gotta admit, I never saw this one coming."

Shane's only answer was another long pull on the bottle. The alcohol seeped through his blood and made his head fuzzy. "Yeah, well, me either."

"What are you going to do about it?"

He shook his head. "Nothing I can do. She's insisting she's going to marry Miles Fletcher. What the fuck am I supposed to do?"

Mitch scratched his chin, brow furrowed. "She's always been stubborn like that. But it doesn't make a whole lot of sense to me. I didn't think she was capable of it, but she's got it bad for you." He grimaced. "It's painfully obvious. And believe me, I've tried hard as hell not to look."

"Now you know how I feel." Shane dragged a hand over his hair. "But it doesn't matter. It's over."

"You think?" Mitch held out his hand and Shane passed him the bottle.

"Yeah." The word left a metallic taste in his mouth.

"I don't know, I think I'm going to be stuck with you," Mitch said, repeating the words Shane had spoken to him last year.

Shane shook his head. He didn't have any hope. Not with

that look in her eye that had told him everything. "Only because you're marrying my sister."

Mitch took a long drink and passed the bottle back. "Only because I didn't let her go."

"Miles Fletcher is going to be your brother-in-law, so you'd best get used to the idea." Shane looked out on the yard, his brain finally going numb. "And word to the wise, he cheats at golf, so watch his strokes."

Mitch laughed. "Never trust a guy who cheats at golf."

Exactly.

But that was Cecilia's problem now. It had nothing to do with him.

At Gracie's house, Cecilia had cried herself hoarse. When no more tears were left, she'd fallen into an exhausted, restless sleep. In the light of day, she'd sat up, disoriented, the comforter Gracie had placed over her pooling at her waist.

Her head hurt, her throat was scratchy, and her eyes were swollen and puffy to the touch. She'd never cried that hard in her life. She'd sobbed. A hysterical blubbering mess, and Gracie had witnessed the entire thing.

The whole, humiliating breakdown.

A couple of weeks ago she would have been horrified, but now all she felt was grateful she'd had someone to turn to.

She got up and padded on bare feet to the kitchen, where Gracie was baking.

Bowl in hand, she turned, a smile on her face that died when she saw Cecilia. "Wow, you look horrible."

"Thank you," Cecilia said, stumbling for the coffeepot.

"Here, let me." Gracie ushered her to a seat and poured a cup of coffee, then grabbed a plate of muffins, setting them in front of Cecilia. "They're banana nut muffins. I figured you'd need the potassium after all that crying."

Cecilia's eyes filled with tears and she grabbed the other woman's hand. "Thank you, Gracie. I don't know what I would have done without you."

"Of course, Ce-ce. That's what friends are for."

She swallowed. She had friends now. Or at least, *a* friend. A friend she'd lose after the wedding when she went back to Chicago and slipped back into her old life.

Unless she managed to miraculously change her destiny.

Gracie moved back to the counter and started measuring with her big, industrial-size scale. "Maddie's already called to gossip. I didn't know what to tell her, so I just said you were fine."

"Thanks," Cecilia said.

Gracie started cracking eggs into a separate bowl. "She said Shane and Mitch got rip-roaring drunk and they're sleeping it off."

Shane. How could she ever face him again?

In went a pound of butter, and Gracie turned to look at her. "Why are you doing this?"

"It's complicated."

Gracie frowned, but before she said anything, Charlotte knocked on the back door.

"I'll get it." Cecilia got up from her chair and opened the door.

Her mom's expression widened. She reached out and put a hand on Cecilia's arm. "Are you okay?"

"I'm fine," she said, closing the back door to step out into the yard so Gracie wouldn't be disturbed.

Charlotte's golden eyes were troubled. "Yesterday, I thought . . . well, it doesn't matter. I was wrong. Cecilia, is it true? Do you love Shane?"

"Who said that?" She desperately wanted to confide in her mother, but she just couldn't. Things were already horrible between her parents. If her mom found out what Nathaniel was up to, there was no telling what Charlotte would do. Or who she might tell.

She couldn't risk Shane.

"Nobody had to," Charlotte said, pointing a finger at her face. "It's there in your eyes."

Cecilia evaded the question. "The plan is still in place. I'm marrying Miles."

To her shock, her mom's eyes filled with tears and she pressed a finger to her lips. "Cecilia, no! Please don't do this."

"I have to." Nobody would ever understand, and she'd have to live with that. Everyone would go back to thinking she was just a cold fish, and that was okay.

Unless she could come up with a plan to save him. But right now, her options were limited; there were too many variables, too many facts she didn't know.

Charlotte gripped her hands, her fingers cold against Cecilia's skin. "You've always fought so hard for your father's approval. You never quit. You can do anything if you put your mind to it. So I'm begging you to think about this. For once, fight for yourself. Not him."

All the air was sucked from Cecilia's lungs as her worldview spun like a top and finally settled back into place with a new perspective.

Isn't this exactly why her father and Miles wanted her on their side? Because she had skills, valuable skills she'd used countless times to her father's advantage. Wasn't this what she'd been thinking about doing? Creating a small firm to deal with these types of precarious, damaging situations?

It was what she was best at and it was time to use that to *her* advantage instead of everyone else's.

She had power. And maybe, if she was lucky, she could fix this mess instead of falling victim to it. She squeezed her mother's fingers. "I will, Mom, I promise."

And she would, just as soon as she figured out what to do.

Two days later, Cecilia sat in her brother's small office in her customary power suit. While Mitch was still in a meeting, she looked around the cluttered space.

It was small, littered with law books that ran the length of one wall. The desk was worn and lived-in, the exact opposite of his office back in Chicago, which had been spacious, slick, and understated with the opulence one required from a lawyer who billed over four hundred dollars an hour.

She used to wonder how he'd borne it. How he could stand being shoved away in this tiny, nowhere town, but it made sense to her. He'd changed. He wasn't part of that glossy world any longer. She used to feel sorry for him, but now she saw him as he really was. Happy. Lucky. He'd found his place in the world.

Would she ever find her place? A place she could sink into?

Shane could be that place for her—she knew that—but she was invisible to him now. She'd moved into Gracie's spare bedroom and only seen him once. One terrible, tense moment when he looked right past her. She would have believed he didn't care at all, but she knew him, saw the pain lurking in the depths of his green eyes.

A look she desperately wanted to fix.

The door opened and she blinked back tears she hadn't known were there. Wiping under her lashes, she turned to face her brother. Over the past couple of weeks she'd gotten to know him, but he was still a stranger.

He nodded, filling the room with that larger-than-life presence he wore like a second skin. So innate to his nature, he didn't even have to try. His office might be small, but his suit was custom tailored and expensive, reminding her of the man he'd been before.

She narrowed her gaze, studying him. How had he managed to blend the two? Or did Donovan blood have some sort of special ingredient that made a person whole?

One brow rose up his forehead. "Why are you looking at me like that?"

She blinked again, waving a hand. "Sorry, I was just thinking about how you were before and how much you've changed."

His mouth lifted at the corners. "Deep thoughts for an afternoon visit."

"Probably." Awkwardness seeped between them, filling up the space like sludge. She wished it wasn't like this. She needed a family now. Something to anchor her, but neither one of them was demonstrative, and she didn't know how to bridge the gap.

"What brings you here?" he asked, moving around his desk to sit down on a chair that squeaked under his weight.

She started to get down to business, but instead tilted her head to the side. "Do you ever miss it?"

His expression widened before turning to speculation. "Chicago?"

She nodded. "Your old life?"

He picked up a pen from the cluttered desk and gestured her to the chair. "Not anymore, but at first I did."

She sat on the chair he'd indicated, crossing her hands neatly in her lap. "Because of Maddie?"

"She's a big part of it, yes. I offered to go back for her, and I would have. But ironically, I would have missed this place. Revival is home now. My life in Chicago is the past."

Her throat tightened and she huffed out a breath. Now that her emotions had broken free she couldn't get them back under control. They'd taken on a life of their own. She cleared her throat and tried again. "I'm happy for you. You did it. You have a real life and I admire what you've done."

"Thank you," he said, sounding surprised.

She should move on but couldn't, not before she gave him the apology he deserved. "I'm sorry, for all the things that went down. I wish I'd done things differently."

He shrugged. "It doesn't matter now. It all turned out for the best. And it wasn't your fault, it was mine."

She blew out a breath. "I didn't know about the deal between our father and Thomas until after the fact. But if we'd been close enough for you to tell me what was going on, I could have stopped you from destroying that evidence. Maybe together we could have figured out another way." She wanted to believe back then she would have done the right thing and helped her brother.

"It wouldn't have made any difference."

"I guess we'll never know now." That was the thing about the past; it couldn't be changed.

He twirled the pen in his fingers. "I appreciate the sentiment. But, for the record, I don't blame you."

She bit her lip, words she'd never told him welling in her throat. She had to pretend with Shane, but in this, with her brother, she could be real. "I used to be so jealous of you. Did you know that?"

He blinked before slowly shaking his head. "No, I didn't. Although I can't see why."

The corners of her mouth lifted. "Simple. You were everything I wanted to be, and you didn't even have to try."

He sat back in his chair and laced his fingers over his stomach. "That's funny, I always thought you were the perfect one."

"I only pretended to be. It's always been work." She took a deep breath and continued, "Our father says I have the brains but lack the passion and killer instinct you have."

"Shit, Cecilia, I'm sorry." His jaw firmed into a hard line. "It's not true, you know."

Tears spilled down her cheeks, but she didn't try to hide them. Not anymore. "For life in politics, yes, it is. I'm learning to accept it. I know he never told you, but he used to sing your praises to me all the time. Always comparing, and no matter how much I worked, how hard I tried, I always came up short."

He reached into a drawer and pulled out a tissue, getting up and walking around the desk to hand it to her. "He's an asshole, Ce-ce."

"I know."

Unnamed emotions tightened his mouth before he held out his hand. "Come here, you look like you could use a hug."

She stared at his outstretched palm for several seconds before taking it and allowing him to pull her into a big, brotherly bear hug. She began to cry in earnest and he rubbed a large circle over her back. "You've really got it bad for Shane, don't you?"

She nodded against his chest.

"So what's the problem?"

She took a deep breath and stepped away. "That's why I'm here."

His gaze narrowed.

She clutched the damp tissue in her fist. "I need your help. I can't trust all my normal contacts. They're all too close and I can't risk him finding out. I know I don't deserve it, but you have to help me figure out a way to blackmail our father."

Surprise flashed over his expression, then his jaw hardened. "All right, what the fuck has he done now?"

Chapter Twenty-Five

Shane walked into the kitchen to find Mitch, Maddie, and Cecilia huddled together at the table.

The conversation cut off abruptly and Maddie's gaze slid guiltily away.

All his instincts went on high alert.

"What's going on?" he barked.

He couldn't even look at Cecilia. Every time he did, desire for her knotted in his gut like a fist squeezed too tight. He was permanently pissed off that no matter how much he tried to talk himself out of it, he still wanted her.

Mitch shook his head. "Nothing."

His sister chewed on her bottom lip and Cecilia frowned at her before saying, "We were going over wedding plans."

Unable to avoid looking directly at her, he drank her in. She looked terrible. Back to tired, hollow eyes. In a white blouse and severe knee-length skirt, summer Cecilia was gone. He scowled. "You look like shit."

She cringed and Maddie yelled, "Shane! What the hell?"

"Well, she does." He refused to say he was sorry.

Cecilia's face twisted before smoothing over, and she touched Maddie's arm. "It's okay."

Fury roiled inside him. "Don't fucking apologize for me, Cecilia."

Her storm-blue eyes snapped. "I wasn't. I was merely telling Maddie not to defend me."

The sane, rational part of his brain took a backseat as the anger he'd been carefully containing came to a scalding boil. "I'll say whatever I damn well please."

"Nobody's stopping you," she said, her tone ice-cold.

God he was sick of it. Sick of her sleeping at Gracie's. Sick of her slinking away whenever they were in the same room. Sick of that vacant expression she tried to pass off as calm.

Mitch stood, holding out his hands as though in surrender. "Let's all calm down."

"Why don't you fuck off?" Shane shot back before shifting his gaze to Cecilia. "I'm not going to apologize. You look like hell. If you're so goddamn happy, why do you look like that?"

Cecilia's expression flashed and she crossed her arms.

Satisfaction pinged through him. Yes, now he was getting somewhere. He jutted out his chin, fully aware he sounded like an arrogant ass but unable to stop himself.

He needed a reaction. Needed to prove the woman he loved was still there, fighting to break free.

"Stop it," Cecilia hissed. "You don't look so hot yourself."

Maddie stepped between them. "Hey, come on, please. We only have a couple days before the wedding. Can't we just keep it together until then?"

He looked at Mitch and Maddie and said in a deadly voice, "Leave."

Maddie shook her head, casting a worried gaze at Cecilia. "That's not a good idea."

Cecilia gave him a look that would have shriveled his

balls if he didn't know her so well. "It's fine, Maddie. I can handle him."

Maddie opened her mouth but Mitch took her arm. "Come on, princess."

"But—"

Mitch ushered her out of the room before she could continue, leaving Shane alone with Cecilia for the first time in three days.

All logic, all rational behavior fled with the closing of the swinging kitchen door. He had only one thought.

One driving need.

He stalked over, grabbed her by the arms, pushed her against the refrigerator and slammed his mouth over hers.

It was like all hell breaking loose.

He hadn't touched her in days and he devoured her. Feasted on her like a glutton. So desperate for the taste of her, he kissed her hard enough to bruise.

And she was just as hungry.

A low, mewling sound left her throat, and she plastered herself against him.

Their mouths melded together. Full of tongue and teeth, and gnawing lust.

He gripped the sides of her blouse, ripped it apart, sending the buttons flying.

On a moan, she rose onto tiptoes. Her hands curled around his neck to bring him closer.

He palmed her breasts, flicking open the front clasp of her bra and peeling away the cups to free her. He stroked her nipples with his thumbs and she purred deep in the back of her throat.

He couldn't stop kissing her. It was like a maddening itch he couldn't scratch and his mouth became more demanding.

More arrogant.

Rougher.

Faster.

Harder.

Deeper.

He pushed her skirt up her thighs and she hooked her leg on his hip.

His cock ached and he rocked against her. She cried out, the sound vibrating against his mouth as she met his strokes. He was so damn hard. So damn crazy. He gripped her hips and ground his erection between her legs.

And then they were moving together, fully clothed, dry fucking like a couple of desperate teenagers. His fingers clasped her thigh. The muscles moved and flexed under her smooth skin as she rocked her hips.

He growled low in his throat.

He fumbled between their bodies, unzipping his jeans and fisting his cock, which throbbed in his hand. He pulled the fabric of her panties aside and slammed inside her wet, waiting pussy.

God yes.

He tore his mouth away and thrust deep.

"Shane, please, yes." Her words half wail, half moan.

It was like coming home.

He gripped her thigh and thrust again.

And again.

Faster and harder.

He set a dirty, angry rhythm.

She worked her hands under his shirt, her nails digging into his lower back.

He fisted her hair, jerked her head. "Look at me."

Her lashes fluttered and lifted, her storm-blue eyes glassy with lust.

He twisted her hair around his palm. "Mine."

She came, her orgasm rippling down his shaft, tearing his own climax from him.

The roar welled in his throat and he kissed her, swallowing her cries, and his, as they shook and came together in a mad, frantic rush of heat and lust and sheer fucking madness.

He pressed his forehead against hers, panting for breath. Shaken, emotion flooded through him, making his chest ache and his skin grow tight.

"Shane." His name a drawn-out, whispery plea, she tangled her fingers in his hair.

He jerked back. A strange rush of panic he hadn't felt since his father died made his heart beat too fast. He stepped away, shoving his cock back in his pants.

She looked completely undone. Her white blouse gaping open, her full breasts a rapid rise and fall, her skin flushed pink, mouth swollen.

He'd done that to her. Any man looking at her would know what she'd been doing. That she'd been thoroughly taken.

But no matter how hard he took her, no matter how frantically he tried to claim her, he couldn't.

She stayed stubbornly right outside his grasp.

"Shane," she said again, stepping toward him.

He stiffened, shaking his head. "I'm sorry. I don't know what came over me."

She blinked, her eyes going bright, turning an electric blue. "I . . ." She trailed off, looking as lost as he felt.

"I won't touch you again."

Cecilia felt sick. Since this afternoon, when they'd been so reckless, a bad feeling had settled into the pit of her stomach. Maddie wasn't making it any easier as they stood in the empty kitchen where Shane had made such ruthless love to her.

Everyone was outside. Maddie had lit the yard with twinkle lights, which glittered like fairies, transforming the backyard into a wonderland. But instead of enjoying it, she fretted over Cecilia.

Cecilia hugged herself. "I'm fine. Trust me, go out and enjoy yourself. You're getting married. Please, focus on that."

Maddie twisted her engagement ring, her grandmother's ring, on her finger. "I will, it's just I don't feel right keeping this from Shane."

When Mitch and Cecilia had concocted their plan, he had one condition. It wasn't even a condition, more a requirement. He absolutely refused to keep what they were doing from Maddie.

Cecilia had protested, but on this he wouldn't relent.

And since he held the contacts and information she needed, she'd had no choice but to agree.

The Donovans were a loyal bunch, and that made Maddie a wild card.

Cecilia pressed a finger to her temple. "We talked about this. I cannot tell him. If he finds out, you know what he'll do."

"But he's so unhappy," Maddie said, glancing out the window.

Frustrated, Cecilia gritted her teeth. "Please, give me time. I can do this. I know I can. There's something there. And Mitch's friend will find it."

"Actually, Logan is Shane's friend. He's the one that helped break your father's blackmail scandal."

The knot of tension curled into a tight ball. "Great. How do we know he won't tell him?"

Maddie waved a hand. "Mitch took care of it. Logan's a professional. He wouldn't break under torture."

It didn't ease Cecilia's mind. There were too many balls in the air, and she had no control over the situation.

Penelope walked in, closing the back door quietly behind her. She looked back and forth between Cecilia and Maddie, her blue eyes sharp behind her glasses. "All right, what's going on?"

Maddie shook her head. "Nothing. Everything's great."

Penelope's lips thinned into a firm line. "Don't give me that, I've known you since kindergarten. Something is wrong."

Cecilia's phone beeped. She pulled it out of her pocket as Maddie and Penelope argued about something that happened on the playground when they were in third grade, which lost Cecilia completely.

It was a text from Logan. Still nothing on Fletcher, but we're good on Jackson.

She took a deep breath. At least they were getting somewhere. She typed out, Thanks, keep me posted.

Finally, something was going her way. It wasn't Miles, but right now she'd take anything, and the city planner would have to do. For now.

She tucked her cell back into her pocket.

"You're not doing anything rash, are you?" Penelope asked, crossing her arms.

"No!" Maddie said.

Before they could go any further, Cecilia stepped in. She knew the mayor personally but didn't have any contact with the planning office, and she didn't want to raise suspicions. The last thing she needed was the mayor calling her father to figure out the political reason for her visit. That left the woman in front of her. "Penelope? Since you're Maddie's best friend, can I ask you a favor? A favor I'd need you to keep from Shane."

Penelope's back stiffened and one perfectly arched brow rose.

Maddie pressed her hands together as if in prayer. "Please, Pen, I'm evoking the girlfriend code."

Penelope frowned. "From third grade?"

Maddie nodded solemnly.

Penelope sighed and turned her attention to Cecilia. "What do you need?"

Cecilia didn't hesitate. "A meeting with the city planner tomorrow morning."

Penelope instantly bristled, gaze narrowing. "Why?"

"Because I need to speak with him urgently."

"What about?" Penelope crossed her arms. "Clearly there's something going on here. I'm not letting you near Shane's project without knowing."

Cecilia understood the mistrust, but it still stung. "I can't tell you now, but I will as soon as I can."

Maddie put a hand on her friend's arm. "Pen, it's okay."

Penelope's jaw turned into a stubborn line. "Listen, I don't know what's going on, but I do know whatever fling you and Shane had is over. And it sure as hell didn't end well. Do you honestly think I'm going to set up a meeting with the guy holding up a multimillion-dollar contract and a hard-on to screw over Shane, without knowing why?"

Well, when she put it like that, she had a point. Cecilia sighed. "There are people out there right now who are willing to crush the deal and damage Shane's reputation. But when I walk out of that office tomorrow, you will get an e-mail saying Jackson agrees to the terms. I promise you."

"How?"

"I prefer not to say. But I have Shane's best interest at heart."

Maddie nodded. "She's telling the truth, Pen. I'm vouching for her."

Penelope crossed her arms. "Why?"

Maddie looked at Cecilia and smiled. "Because she's family."

Chapter Twenty-Six

At eleven thirty sharp, Cecilia strode into David Jackson's office.

The head of city planning was an older gentleman, in his midfifties, with salt-and-pepper hair and blue eyes. He was a nice-looking, distinguished man, but there was a hardness to his face. A meanness in his eyes. He nodded, not getting up from his desk to greet her.

"Mr. Jackson," she said, her voice cool and professional. She gestured to a seat. "May I?"

Another nod. He leaned back in his leather chair, steepling his fingers. "How may I help you, Ms. Riley? Or should I say, how can I help your father?"

Keeping her expression impassive, she smiled. "Actually, this isn't about him."

"Then what is it about?"

Cecilia had had a lot of unpleasant conversations in her day, and she always thought it best to get straight to the point. "Your contract with The Donovan Corporation."

"What does that have to do with your father?"

Nothing. But he didn't need to know that. She tilted her head to the side. "Why don't you let me worry about that? I understand you've had some contractual disagreements."

His lips formed a thin, stubborn line. "I'm not at liberty to discuss them with you."

"We'll have to see about that." She pulled out a manila envelope. Since he was caught in the crosshairs between her and her father, she should feel bad, but his actions were so despicable she couldn't work up a lick of sympathy. She tossed the envelope on his desk. "Maybe this will change your mind."

She thought she detected a hint of a tremble in his fingers as he reached for the package, but couldn't be sure. He opened the sealed envelope, looked at the contents, then put the package back on the desk.

She smiled sweetly. "I never understood why, in this day and age, people are still taking pictures."

She thought of the pictures Shane had taken of her. Pictures she never should have allowed, considering her background, but had allowed to be taken with abandon. Of course, she'd done that with the man she loved, not a barely legal prostitute wearing nothing but white stockings, pigtails, and Mary Janes.

He folded his hands on his desk. "What do you want?"

She leaned forward. "Only what's right. Those contracts signed. I trust Shane and his legal team will receive an e-mail agreeing to the terms within the next hour?"

Before he could speak there was a knock on the door and it swung open.

The mayor of Chicago stood in the entry.

Well, she couldn't have timed his entrance better herself. Cecilia stood, beaming at him, and opened her arms. "Teddy, it's lovely to see you."

"I heard you were in the building." Theodore Lombardi looked like a cross between Tony Soprano and Santa Claus as he walked over and hugged her.

When she stood back, she said, "How's Marion? Is she feeling better?"

"Yes, much," he said, rubbing her arms. "Your mother's visit cheered her considerably." He looked past Cecilia to a pale-faced David. "I trust everything is okay here."

She looked pointedly at the city planner. "Yes, I was just making some rounds. It's been awhile since I visited."

The mayor winked at her. "Getting ready for your wedding?"

"Something like that," she said, noncommittal.

He smiled at Jackson. "I trust you're taking good care of my girl."

David swallowed hard. "Yes, sir."

Teddy gave her a kiss on the cheek, patting her arm with affection. "Stop by after you're done and we'll catch up."

"Of course, I wouldn't leave without saying good-bye." She picked up the envelope from David's desk and smoothed her finger over the edge.

"Wonderful," Teddy said, closing the door behind him.

With her best smile, Cecilia turned back to David. "I trust you have no further objections to the terms."

He shook his head. "And all this will go away."

"The handshake deal will certainly put you in my good graces, but nothing goes away until those contracts are signed. So I suggest you hurry."

"How do I know you won't renege on the deal?"

"You don't." She picked up her briefcase. "I'll give you the pictures and the flash drive, but you and I know digital lasts forever. Rest assured, I have no interest in you or your extramarital activities. I just want those contracts signed and the deal put to bed. Understood?"

He nodded and she left.

Other than putting her one step closer to ensuring

Shane's safety, she wasn't pleased with herself. She didn't relish blackmail the way her father did.

Besides, there was still work to be done.

Shane sat in the farmhouse's office staring blankly at his computer screen, while Penelope rattled off a list of pending action items he needed to take care of but couldn't work up the energy for.

Cecilia was gone, again.

Where, he hadn't a clue, but she'd left by herself in the wee hours of the morning and hadn't been seen since.

"Are you even listening?" Penelope asked, startling him from his thoughts.

"Yeah," he said, playing with the mouse sitting next to his laptop. "The Kramer project."

Penelope put down her tablet and sighed. "That was five minutes ago."

He shook his head, straightening in his chair. "Oh."

She looked at him, her blue eyes steady and assessing. "You've really got it bad for her."

He pointed to her iPad. "Your list."

Someone knocked at the front door. It swung open and his brother Evan sauntered into the foyer like he owned the place.

Shane called to him, "Hey, in here."

All six-foot-five-inch of gridiron badass, Evan glanced over at them. A cocky grin slid over his face, and he plopped his bag in the middle of the floor before strolling over to lean against the door frame.

"What's up?" He glanced at Penelope. "Hey, little Penny, still working for the man?"

Penelope's mouth curved into a disapproving frown.

"Pen-el-oh-pee." She drew out her name very slowly, like Evan might be too dense to understand.

Another shit-eating grin. "Where's my baby sister?"

Shane sat back in his chair and laced his fingers behind his head. "She's out. Where's Mom and Aunt Cathy?"

Evan tilted his chin toward the front door. "They stopped to talk to Soph."

Penelope shifted in her chair and pointed to the bag. "Are you going to take care of that? There's no maid here."

Before Evan could answer, James walked in and clapped their youngest brother on the shoulder. "I thought I heard you. You finally made it. How was surfing off the Australian coast?"

Evan's eyes hooded, taking on a lazy, droll expression. "Twelve-foot swells and hot girls. It was a good time."

Penelope snorted, and Shane smiled. His brother was one of those guys who'd never really grown up. Not that he had to; as far as Shane could tell, the NFL was nothing but an extended frat party to Evan. Yeah, he worked his ass off for the game, but off the field he played equally hard.

Evan held out his hands. "What do you have against hot girls, Pen?"

"Nothing at all." Her expression closed. "It's just hard to believe you're thirty-one."

Shane raised a brow. "I trust you left the Playboy bunny at home this time."

Evan rolled his eyes. "Dude, that was like, months ago."

The last woman his little brother brought around sat on his uncle's lap and posed for pictures with him in a minuscule dress that barely covered her ass. His aunt Marie had thrown a fit. One thing led to another, and Shane had spent an hour calming everyone the hell down. He didn't have the stamina for that. He nodded. "Just checking. I don't want Maddie's day ruined."

Evan's gaze hardened and the laziness rolled off him. "I'm not going to ruin her day."

"Just keep yourself in line."

"I'm in line, *dad*." The last word delivered with a healthy amount of sarcasm.

A muscle under Shane's eye started to twitch.

James frowned and patted their youngest brother on the shoulder. "Let me show you where we're staying."

"We're not at the house?"

"It's a little crowded, so the Robertses are letting us crash in the apartment over their garage."

Evan straightened. "Hmmm . . . Gracie Roberts. Now there's a woman that I wouldn't mind getting my hands on."

James's expression hardened, flashing with anger, his hands clenching into fists. In typical fashion, Evan was already heading into the foyer and didn't notice. James's face twisted before settling into his normal calm expression.

Then he slowly walked out of the room.

Shane turned to Penelope, who wore her own pinched expression. He raised a brow. "There's going to be trouble."

Penelope raised her eyes to the heavens. "With Evan, isn't there always?"

"You've got a point." He didn't have the energy to deal with it right now. Not with Cecilia gone and out of his grasp. He woke his computer from sleep mode, scrolling through his e-mails. The top one was from the city planner, and he opened it with a sigh, steeling himself for whatever new obstacle the guy threw at him today.

When he read the e-mail, Shane frowned. "Huh, that's interesting."

"What?" Penelope asked.

"Jackson, from the mayor's office. He agreed to the terms with no further changes." Thank God something was going his way. Relief stole through him, making his shoulders slump. Only now did he allow himself to admit how terribly worried he'd been.

"I can't believe she did it," Penelope said.

Shane's head shot up. "You can't believe *who* did *what*?"

Behind her dark frames, Penelope blinked, straightening in her chair. "Huh? Nothing. That's great. I'll notify legal."

His eyes narrowed. "What aren't you telling me?"

"Nothing." She was a horrible liar. He was her boss, but they were also friends.

"Penelope," he said in a warning tone.

She shifted in her chair, crossing her legs and uncrossing them. "Honestly, I don't know anything."

"This has something do with Cecilia, doesn't it?"

"Why would you say that?" she countered, giving him the confirmation he needed.

He should push her and find out what she knew. Her first loyalty was to him. He could break her, but didn't. If he did, he wouldn't have an excuse to talk to Cecilia.

Cecilia left the building, got into a cab, and twenty minutes later sat in Logan Buchanan's office. She shifted in her chair. The man was intimidating.

He looked like the ex-military man he was, dangerous and lethal, even in a custom-tailored navy suit. His eyes were a piercing ice blue that looked straight into her. She swallowed, nervous despite herself.

"How did it go?" His voice was low and deep, like maple syrup trickling down a tree.

"I showed him the pictures, and he agreed. Now we wait for confirmation."

He smiled, and it was pure sin. "Can't imagine he'd refuse with those pictures. His wife is a good Christian woman, real pillar-of-the-community type. He'll do what needs to be done."

She nodded. "I've been in politics a long time; people will do almost anything to cover their ass."

"Amen to that," he said, amused.

"And Miles, do you have anything on him yet?"

Expression inscrutable, he shook his head. "Nope, nothing."

Dread pooled in her stomach. "What does that mean?"

He shrugged. "It's only been a few days, but usually there's a thread of something. When you know where to look, people aren't very good at hiding. If I had to guess, he's probably clean."

She bit the inside of her cheek. She'd been so sure. So positive. She clutched her briefcase. "Everyone has something to hide."

He raised a brow. "What are you hiding?"

She lowered her gaze and pressed her lips together. The only things that could be used against her were the things she'd been doing with Shane. But she'd been preparing for a public life since she was old enough to talk. Even as a teenager she'd never done anything that could come back and bite her.

"Some people are just clean," he said, his voice soft.

"And you think this is one of those times?" It was what she'd feared. While she believed she'd secured Shane's contract, she had no guarantees Miles and the senator wouldn't publish the article anyway. They could still do considerable damage to Shane's reputation. She couldn't allow that. Which left her with only one option.

"I'll keep looking, but yes. So far, there's nothing."

"Okay, thank you." She stood.

He got to his feet and held out his hand. "I'll see you at the wedding."

She snatched back her hand mid-shake, as though she'd been burned. "You're going to be at the wedding?"

His lips quirked. "Shane's a good friend. I've known Maddie for years. Of course I'll be at the wedding."

She blinked. "But our . . . arrangement . . . it's private. Confidential?"

His gaze narrowed. "You don't want Shane to know." It wasn't a question.

She shook her head. "He *can't* know."

He crossed his arms over his broad chest, looking like an immovable object. "Can I ask why?"

"It's a long story, but it's for his own good."

"We have a signed contract, and I wouldn't be in business for long if I didn't abide by the confidentiality clause in the agreement."

A tiny easing of relief. "Then I have your word?"

"You do."

She turned to leave, but stopped when he said, "Cecilia."

She looked over her shoulder, asking the silent question.

"You know when he finds out he's not going to be too happy about this."

"I know."

"Then I trust you have a good reason."

The very best reason. "I do. I understand Shane is your friend, and I promise if I pull this off, he won't stay angry for long."

"Good," he said with a sharp nod.

Down in the lobby, she sat on a bench and called Mitch. He picked up on the second ring. "What's up?"

"He didn't find anything on Miles."

A pause over the line. "It's still early."

"I know, but he said he thinks Miles is clean. He's almost certain."

Mitch sighed. "Then you don't really have a choice, do you?"

"No, I don't." She hung up.

She'd been dreading this moment. The reckoning. She'd hoped to deal with the situation through Miles, but in her heart she'd known it wouldn't be that simple.

If she wanted to save herself, she'd have to turn on her father. She'd known it was coming, had been committed to the choice that day she'd talked with her mother in Gracie's backyard. But now that it was here, the finality gave her pause. Once she did this there'd be no going back. Her relationship with him would be ruined. She'd have no career to fall back on. At thirty-three she'd start her life over from scratch.

She'd be starting her business without a safety net.

Her chest tightened. As much as she hated him, she'd still spent a lifetime adoring him. Working to make him proud. To prove she was worthy. It wasn't simple like in the books or movies. One epiphany didn't wipe out all those years of wanting him to love her.

All her life she'd chosen him.

And now, it was time to choose herself.

Chapter Twenty-Seven

Decision made, Cecilia didn't waste any time calling Julie, her father's admin.

"Where have you been?" Julie asked as soon as she picked up the phone.

Cecilia ignored the question. "I need on his schedule. Today. Now, if possible."

In the background, her e-mail dinged and her heart leapt in her throat. Right on time.

"He's got Paul in there."

"Good. I'll be right over." She hung up, strode from the lobby and out onto the Chicago streets.

Fifteen minutes later, she walked into his office without knocking. Paul was still there. The two of them sat at the war table where Cecilia had spent years of her life.

The senator's head lifted. "Cecilia."

"Dad," she said, and turned to Paul. "Please excuse us. I need to speak to my father alone."

He looked at Nathaniel for confirmation.

He nodded, and Paul gathered his things and left.

"To what do I owe the pleasure of your company?" He looked old and tired, the skin under his eyes bagging. "Your mother already told me I'm not invited to the wedding, if that's what this is about."

"No, it's not." She sat down at the table. "I'm done being the liaison between the two of you."

His skin turned pink, but she was pretty sure it was out of anger instead of embarrassment. "Fine. Is this about your campaign?"

"No, I'm not running for office." Just saying the words brought a huge sense of relief. Like a thousand-pound weight lifted off her chest. "Oh, and by the way, I quit."

The words brought her freedom. Like chains falling one by one from her body, leaving her naked and vulnerable, but alive.

He blinked, looking stunned, but then his face cleared. "I assume that makes sense, considering you'll need to devote your time and energy to Miles and your life together."

On a roll now, she scoffed. With every word she spoke, she grew stronger. Determined. Powerful. "I'm not going to be doing that either."

"Then what?" he asked, his tone careful and controlled.

She tilted her head to the side. "I'm going to start a little PR firm that specializes in damage control. You're the one who always said that's my strength. You're right. I like it and I'm good at it."

Just saying the words out loud made them real, and she experienced a bolt of excitement. She could do this. She had contacts and connections. She could build it from scratch and it would be something to call her own.

His brows furrowed. "I'm not sure how Miles will feel about that. You'll have to discuss it with him."

She shook her head. "I don't see why, since I won't be marrying him. You two will have to make it to the White House without me."

His expression turned to fury. "You may be my daughter, but I suggest you don't force my hand."

She folded her hands on the table. A stillness came over her, filling her with a calm sort of peace. He, not she, had drawn this line in the sand. "Is that what you're calling it these days? Call it what it is: blackmail."

"Incentive."

She smiled and waved a hand. "Whatever." She picked up her phone and pressed the e-mail app. The message from Mitch sat in her in-box and she pressed the icon to begin the download. "I went to the mayor's office today." She clucked her tongue. "It turns out the city planner has a schoolgirl fetish, so he's going to be signing those contracts, regardless of any press releases."

Nathaniel gaped at her.

She held up a finger. "One problem down, but what to do about you and Miles? I don't trust you to not hurt Shane and, see, I'm not going to let that happen."

His complexion turned florid with rage. "Cecilia, what have you done?"

"Incentive. Just remember, *Dad*," she said, the word full of scorn, "you started this. I'm the woman you created. I fix messes, and I'm fixing this one."

"I only want what's best for you," he said. "You can't give this up to start a silly little consulting firm."

It wasn't going to work this time. She swiped through the first part of the download to find what she wanted. "I'm sure it's hard to believe this right now, but I do love you. I believe there was a time you were a good man. I tried to find something on Miles. That's proving difficult. Unfortunately, that leaves you."

He held up a hand. "Are you doing this because of Shane Donovan?"

"You brought him into this, not me. I suggest you don't say another word about him."

He blew a hard, irritated breath.

"Now where was I? Ah yes, incentive." She trembled a bit from anger and loss. The loss was there, and she let herself feel it, because it was true and honest. That was the woman she wanted to be now. Real. "I have the pictures. I don't want to use them, but if I have to, I will."

"What pictures?"

"Of you and the intern."

His expression cleared and she could see the relief wash through him. "Everyone knows I was drugged. There were prescriptions to prove it. Their scheme was exposed, Cecilia. It poses no more threat to me."

This was it. Once she did this, she'd be free. She swallowed and dove into the deep end. "No. I have the *other* pictures."

A flicker crossed his face, but then it was gone. "I don't know what you mean."

Filled with disgust and sadness, she slid her phone across the table. "I must say, I've seen far too many dirty photos today."

He looked at her phone, complexion paling to an ashy gray. The photos the blackmailer had sent to her father last year had been a warning. But Cecilia now had the real ones, the ones he'd been really worried about. Pictures that showed her father and the intern locked together in an embrace, his eyes open, his hands participating. Pictures her mother would never forgive.

Weariness settled into Cecilia's bones. She shook her head. "I didn't want to believe it. I wanted to trust you. Believe in you. Even though I'd seen you together and knew you slept with her."

"Cecilia," he said, his voice a croak. "Have you shown these to your mother?"

"No. Mitch and I agreed we wouldn't show her unless we had no choice." She wouldn't ever hurt her mom like that. There was no need.

"Your brother?"

She nodded. "He's had them all along. I think, like me, he hoped you'd do the right thing and redeem yourself."

His fingers tightened on the phone, his knuckles going white. "How could you do this to me? Your own father?"

"I learned it from you. Never show weakness. Never break. Isn't that what you always taught me?"

He dropped the phone and it clattered on the wood table, the sound seeming to echo in the silence of the room. "What do you want?"

"Nothing much, certainly nothing that means anything to you," she said, feeling sad. "Just my freedom."

She took her phone, closed the offending pictures, and tucked the cell into her purse. "I trust you'll take care of Miles and any fallout from the engagement being called off?"

He nodded, then looked at her. He'd aged twenty years in the last few minutes. "I didn't sleep with her."

Even now he lied. Because with him, it was never about what was right, but about protecting his ass. Chest heavy, she gathered her things. "It doesn't matter much, does it? As you're fond of telling me, perception is reality."

The bar where Mitch and Maddie met had been transformed for the rehearsal dinner and Shane barely recognized the dive. Sophie, Penelope, and Gracie had strung lights all over the place, casting the room in a golden glow. They'd pushed together several tables to form one big square, covered in white linens, filled with flowers and sparkling candles. The girls had gone over the top with decorations and the place looked incredible. A party befitting his baby sister.

As they milled around the bar, Maddie was radiant in a yellow sundress with her soon-to-be husband at her side.

At least he wouldn't have to worry about her anymore.

Shane was happy for her. Everyone was having a great time.

Except for him.

Cecilia was still gone. Disappeared without a trace.

He'd wanted to ask where she'd run to, but had kept his mouth shut. These next couple of days were about Maddie and Mitch, so he'd put on a happy face and act as normal as possible. Because that's what his sister deserved.

Sunday he'd be back home, and he'd go about forgetting Cecilia. In time, the memory of these two weeks would fade. When he saw her again, summer Cecilia would be gone, and she'd be back to being someone he might want, but could resist.

At least that's the story he sold himself.

He couldn't believe she hadn't shown up. Nobody had even asked about her. It was like she'd vanished, only existing in his own mind.

Gracie let out a loud, abandoned laugh, startling him from his thoughts in time to watch Evan pull a tipsy Gracie into his lap. She tried to pull away, but Evan held her tight. She laughed, pushing at his arms. James shot them a dark, thunderous look before he got up from the table and walked away, disappearing down the hallway.

Shane shifted his attention back to Gracie, who smiled that dazzling smile at Evan, but her gaze lingered on where James had gone.

Shane sighed. Something would need to be done about that soon.

His mom, happy, her cheeks pink with pleasure, sat

down next to him. She patted his hand, her eyes going bright. "You're a good boy."

He smiled, his throat feeling a touch tight. "Thanks, Mom."

"Did I thank you for sending me to Ireland?" she asked, her tone almost girlish from all the champagne she'd drunk.

He grinned at her. "Only about a million times."

"Your daddy would be so proud of you." She leaned in conspiratorially. "He always said you were the right combination of smart and brave. That once you set your mind to it, you could do anything. And he was right. Look at you. Look at what you've become."

His chest squeezed. "I didn't know he said that. He always yelled at me for being a fuck-up."

His mom slapped his arm. "Language! Well, sure he yelled at you for not applying yourself, but in private . . ." A smile ghosted her lips as if she was remembering something fond and wistful. "But in private he used to say, 'Shannon, I know I should worry about that boy, but I don't. He's gonna be just fine.'"

Shane had never known that. Maybe Cecilia was right after all. Maybe he'd always had it in him. Maybe he didn't need to feel guilty about only making something of himself on the back of his father's death. "You don't think I became like this because he died?"

Her brow furrowed, her expression turning puzzled. "Now why would you think a silly thing like that?"

He shrugged. "Because I was a fuck-up."

She narrowed her gaze as though contemplating correcting him again, but then she grinned, a loopy, buzzed grin that shaved fifteen years from her face. "You were always as stubborn as a mule. Maybe it would have taken awhile longer for you to find your way, but once you latched on to something, you never let it go. That's just the way you were made."

He was going to have to let Cecilia go.

More than anything he wanted to go at her like a bull-dozer, knocking some sense into her until she had no more fight in her and she was forced to agree with him. But he couldn't do that, not this time. He needed her to be the one thing he didn't have to beat into submission.

And that wasn't going to happen.

He gave his mom's hand a quick squeeze. "Dad taught me everything I know."

She scoffed, waving a hand. "Except for money. Neither one of us was ever any good at that. I have no idea where you got your money sense."

"You gave us a strong family. That's better than money."

"I guess we did that right." She took a sip of whiskey, served in honor of the bride, and pointed at her daughter. "She won't run this time."

"Nope, not a chance."

Shannon tilted her head, studying Mitch. "He's a good man."

Shane looked at his brother-in-law. He was family now.

It was odd. Maddie's first fiancé had been around for years, but he never belonged the way Mitch did. "Yeah, he is."

She patted his hand again. "And if he ever hurts her, I know you'll take care of it."

He laughed for the first time in what felt like a year. "I will, but he won't." The guy would move heaven and earth to make his sister happy.

As if he heard Shane, Mitch put a palm at the base of Maddie's spine and leaned in, whispering something in her ear. Her face turned up to him and she stood on tiptoes, sliding her hand around his neck and bringing him close for a kiss.

Shane shook his head. They really were disgusting to watch.

His mom waved her drink, toasting the couple in her own private way. "One down, three to go."

He chuckled, shaking his head. "Don't get ahead of yourself."

She huffed. "A woman can dream. Here I am, all of my kids in their thirties and still no grandchildren. I'm the only one of all my friends without a little one."

In feigned sympathy, he clucked his tongue. "Poor thing, how can you go on?"

She laughed.

The door opened and Cecilia walked in, knocking all the air out of his lungs in one fell swoop.

She looked un-fucking-believable.

She wore a gray-blue sleeveless dress that matched her eyes, skimmed over her body, and ended at indecent length on her thighs. Her legs were endless, long and lean, and she wore sky-high sandals. Hair piled haphazardly on top her head, loose tendrils spilled out, framing her high cheekbones.

She was glowing. Radiant.

He wanted to storm over there and demand to know why the hell she looked so good when he felt like utter crap. He tightened his fingers around his glass.

"I don't remember Cecilia being so pretty," his mom said next to him, but her voice was like a fog. "She's very beautiful. Like a movie star."

His mom had no idea she twisted a knife in his gut. He managed to mumble, "Yeah, she is."

Cecilia's gaze searched the room, finally coming to rest on him.

He'd thought it was the blood rushing in his ears that silenced the room, but then he realized everyone had stilled, looking at them.

Her expression flickered when she saw him and then she began walking toward him.

He could do nothing but stare, eating her up with his gaze. It didn't matter how much he told himself she wasn't his, when he looked at her, in his heart, she was.

He could barely pull air into his lungs by the time she stood in front of him. He had to curl his hands into fists to keep from reaching for her. To keep from running his hands up those smooth thighs. He knew just what they felt like under his fingers. How she shuddered when he touched her.

He met her gaze, direct on his. Her porn-star lips were glossy and pink and he tried not to think about how his cock looked between them and failed. He nodded. "Cecilia."

"Shane," she said, then turned to his mother, smiling. "Mrs. Donovan. It's lovely to see you."

"You too, dear," Shannon said, glancing quizzically at Shane.

"Did you have a nice trip?" Cecilia inquired, confusing him. What was she talking about?

His mom nodded. "It was lovely."

Shane shook his head to get blood back in his brain. Was she making polite chitchat?

"Wonderful," Cecilia said before turning to Shane. "Did you get an e-mail today from the city planner?"

Confounded by the direction of the conversation, he nodded. "Yes."

Her throat worked as she swallowed, as if she was nervous, even though her expression conveyed nothing but confidence. "And? Did he stop giving you a hard time?"

He narrowed his eyes. "What the hell is going on, Cecilia?"

She straightened. "Did he agree to the terms of the contract?"

"Yes, but—"

She cut him off. "Did the contract get sent to your legal department?"

Why did he have a bad feeling about this? He glanced around and found everyone watching them with avid interest. He frowned.

From across the room, Penelope called out, "He put a rush on it. The contract will be signed next week."

"Thank you," Cecilia said, smiling at Penelope. Cecilia reached into her small purse and pulled out her cell phone, flipping through the screens before handing it to him.

He read a text message from her father.

It's done. You're free.

A thousand questions pouring through his mind, he looked at her. "What have you done?"

"Only what I promised." She trailed a finger down his cheek, her touch sending a shudder through him. "You asked me a question the other day and I lied. Will you ask me again?"

He'd didn't need any clarification. He knew the one. "Do you love me, Cecilia?"

She smiled, leaned down, twining her hand around his neck. "Yes, I do."

Relief, swift and powerful, swept through him. The world spun crazy for a fraction of a second before righting itself. All the missing pieces clicked into place and *finally* she felt like his. He ran his hands up her thighs, not caring that everyone watched them or that his mother sat right next to him, staring with her mouth agape.

"Tell me." He needed to hear the words.

Her hands tightened, as though afraid to let him go. "I love you, Shane Donovan."

"I love you too." And then he kissed her.

Forgetting everyone and everything except for this woman who completed him. She was his equal in every way. The one who would walk through fire for him, and, from what he pieced together, had.

In the distance he heard clapping and whistles, and he pulled away to whisper against her lips. "We need to get out of here."

"Yes, we certainly do."

Chapter Twenty-Eight

Cecilia posed for another picture with her new sister-in-law as Shane watched her from a table, surrounded by his family. He laughed, but as always, his gaze sought her out anytime she was out of his reach.

She beamed, winking at him.

She'd done it. She'd saved him. Saved them. Not that he was thankful. When she'd told him the whole story, she'd thought he'd burst a blood vessel. He'd yelled and ranted for fifteen minutes until she'd gotten bored and finally calmed him down by, well, going down. She giggled. He'd been pretty sedate after that.

Maddie elbowed her. "What are you laughing about?"

"Oh, nothing." Between smiles she said, "Are you sure you don't mind the DJ changing the song?"

"Nope." Maddie forgot the pose and grinned at her. "Right now I'd do anything for you for making my brother so happy."

"The pleasure is all mine." She shivered, remembering last night. They'd gone to a motel instead of back to the house. A seedy, roadside pit that was the crassest place she'd ever stepped foot in. But it had a bed. A big bed they'd put to good use, where they got to be as loud as they wanted.

And they'd been loud. Like, embarrassingly loud.

She'd loved it.

The director came out of the reception hall and nodded to Maddie. She squeezed Cecilia's elbow. "It's time."

She grabbed the bouquet of flowers and walked over to Shane, smoothing down her pale green bridesmaid's dress. "That's our cue."

Over the speakers the DJ announced, "And now a dance with the lucky couple who caught the garter and bouquet."

Shane and Cecilia took a spot on the dance floor. He wrapped his arms around her.

The song came on. "Ho Hey" by The Lumineers. He stepped in perfect time, taking the lead. She let him, because that's how it was with them. Sometimes he took the lead, and sometimes she did. They balanced each other out.

Lashes fluttering, she flirted up at him. "I picked this song for you."

"Did you now?" His hands skimmed over her skin, making her shiver.

He smiled, leaning down to nuzzle her neck.

"I think they planned this," she whispered, melting into him.

He laughed. "What was your first clue? When they threw it right to us? Or when they all stepped back?"

She grinned. "They were very subtle."

The chorus came on and she sang along with it.

He cupped her chin, running a thumb over her cheek. "Of course, she sings."

"Only for you," she said, her voice thick with emotion.

He brushed his mouth over hers. "You're mine now."

"I always was."

"I've been thinking," he said, his green eyes gleaming.

"The other day when I was running with Jimmy I spotted a FOR SALE sign a couple houses down."

She pulled back to see if he was serious. "You want to buy a house here?"

"Yeah, I do. A second home where we could relax and be with family. The house is a wreck, a total teardown, but I like the thought of building something for us from scratch. What do you think?"

Her throat closed over. Between crying, laughing, and smiling, the muscles in her neck ached, but it was so worth it. He was worth it. "Do I get to help?"

"I don't know. Are you going to argue with me?"

She slipped into that ice-queen mask for old times' sake, and said in her haughtiest tone, "Of course."

"Brat." He pinched her.

"I love the idea."

"Good, because I definitely like summer Cecilia."

She laughed, kissing him. "Oh, she's here to stay."

His teeth scraped the side of her neck. "Is it time to leave yet?"

"No," she said, her body heating.

"Please," he whispered, his breath hot in her ear. "I haven't been inside you for a whole six hours. It's been torture."

"I saw a supply closet where we could rectify that."

A rumble of appreciation.

She bit his ear lobe. "I'm not wearing any panties."

He jerked up. "Song's over, come on."

She laughed as he hustled her off the dance floor, the last notes of the song playing in the background.

Like the song said, she finally belonged. To him. To her. To them.

She stopped, tugged his arm, and when he turned around,

she flung herself at him in a fierce kiss. Surrendering to him and falling open-armed into the future.

When they broke apart she whispered, "I love you."

"I love you too, baby." He walked backward, tugging her hand, smiling.

With him, there was never a price. He came for free.

And he was hers.

Craving Something New?

Keep reading for an excerpt from

THE NAME OF THE GAME,

the next novel in

Jennifer Dawson's fantastic series.

Available in Fall, 2015.

"How can you drink that stuff?" Gracie Roberts wrinkled her nose at the offending protein shake in James Donovan's hand. Of course, his drink of choice wasn't her business, but whenever she was around the stuffy professor for more than five seconds she couldn't resist the urge to antagonize him. In her defense, as a baker, his obsession with health food went against her nature.

How could you trust a man who didn't eat sugar?

One brown brow rose as he stared at her, not speaking. Behind black, wire-rimmed frames, his cool evergreen eyes studied her in a way that she could only describe as dismissive. A look he'd given her since the first day they'd met. At thirty-three, she'd rarely met a person she didn't like. Since she'd been a little girl she loved people and people loved her right back.

That was, until she'd met one Professor Donovan.

Living hundreds of miles away meant she should be able to avoid him, but he came with her best friends and was therefore impossible to escape. And since Gracie loved her friends, she was stuck with James. Now she was spending one of her few weekends off helping Cecilia move and enduring the presence of her nemesis.

She sighed. The things she suffered for friendship.

She crossed her arms over her chest and glared at him. "What are you looking at?"

A flickering glance. "Not a thing."

She tried her best not to engage in battle, but everything about him this morning irritated her, and she couldn't help it. Normally, whenever she had the misfortune of being in his company, he wore some shade of tan slacks and a polo shirt that made him look like a customer service rep for Geico. The geekwear, as she dubbed it, minimized all those hard, lean muscles he worked so hard to hone.

His boring apparel was one of the few things she appreciated about him.

But today, he wore jeans and a vintage-inspired, faded blue, *Empire Strikes Back* T-shirt. In theory, the shirt should be classified as geekwear, but he wore it far too well. The color made his green eyes pop and called attention to his sharp, high cheekbones. The cotton stretched over his broad chest and flat abs. Abs she'd had the misfortune of seeing whenever he ran along the river in back of her house, and abs that certainly didn't belong on a professor of forensic anthropology.

To her annoyance he looked kind of hot. That was, for a complete nerd.

Aggravated at the very thought, she planted her hands on her hips and glared at the offending drink. "Why don't you drink chalk? I'm sure it tastes better."

"This drink contains the perfect blend of protein, carbohydrates, and vitamins." James eyed the powdered-sugar doughnut resting on a paper plate at her fingertips. "Which is more than I can say for that fried, sugary monstrosity you're calling a breakfast."

Ha! How dare he? Doughnuts were universally loved.

Only sickos and crazies didn't like them. Gracie opened her mouth to blast him, but before she could, his older brother came to his rescue.

Shane held out his hands in the big, expansive kitchen like a referee breaking up a couple of prizefighters. "Let's not start another round of the food wars. It never ends well and it's going to be a long day."

Next to him, Cecilia nodded. "We appreciate the help this weekend, but it's only been an hour and you've bickered nonstop."

Disgruntled, Gracie pointed at him. "He started it."

James gave her a disapproving scowl he reserved specifically for her. "*You* started it. I was standing here minding my own business."

"You insulted my doughnut!" A stray blond curl flopped into her eye and she pushed it back behind her ear even though it never stayed put.

"After you turned your nose up at my shake." He crossed his arms over his chest and his biceps rippled.

For a second, the corded muscles running the length of his arms distracted her, but she quickly shook the image away and snorted. "Shake! That's an insult to shakes. Real shakes are made with actual ice cream. And I'm not talking low fat frozen yogurt either. I'm talking—"

A loud, piercing whistle filled the air and Gracie covered her ears.

Cecilia's four-carat diamond ring flashed, nearly blinding Gracie as she sliced a hand through the air. "Please. You two are already giving me a headache."

Shane slid a big hand around Cecilia's waist, pulling her close. "And I'm the only one allowed to upset her." He leaned down and kissed his future wife's neck.

Between Shane and Cecilia getting married, and newlyweds Mitch and Maddie, the constant lovefest grated on

Gracie's last nerve. She was ecstatic for her friends, over-joyed for their happiness. But Shane and Mitch weren't ex-actly shy about their desires, and Gracie had to witness or hear their public displays of affection all too often. Last night she'd had to put a pillow over her head, Shane and Ce-cilia had been so loud. Gracie could only hope they had soundproofing in their new place or their mothers would have strokes the next time they stayed overnight.

And . . . Gracie was big enough to admit she was a tiny bit jealous. She loved herself a little PDA, only she had no one to PDA with. The year anniversary of her unintentional celibacy had come and gone and she was starting to get a bit twitchy. Abstinence hadn't been the plan; she'd dated plenty, only no one had flipped her switch enough to get her into bed.

She shot a sidelong glance at the professor. He probably thought kissing in public was as disgusting as doughnuts. Hell, he probably only had sex in the missionary position with the lights off. Anyone that uptight would be a complete dud in the sack.

When Shane's tongue flicked over Cecilia's skin, Gracie wrinkled her nose. "Hey, stop that." She jerked a thumb at the professor. "You're going to give him nightmares."

Shane sucked on Cecilia's neck, his teeth scraping over the soft skin. Gracie couldn't blame her friend one bit when Cecilia's eyes practically rolled into the back of her head.

Unlike his brother, Shane Donovan was not the kind of man who fucked with the lights off.

James sighed, a deep, heavy sound of the resigned. "Once again, you've managed to lose me."

Shane lifted his head and grinned at his younger brother. "She thinks you're a prude, Jimmy."

James scowled for several seconds and then shook his head as though Gracie was just too silly for words. With-out a word to defend himself, he picked up the box labeled "kitchen" off the counter and started toward the door. "You make a gazillion dollars, so why aren't you paying for movers?"

That was actually a good point. "Hey! He's right."

"Holy fuck, you agreed with him." Shane craned his neck and called after his brother. "Did you hear that, Jimmy? She agreed with you."

"I'll mark it down in my calendar and drop dead of a heart attack," James said wryly, and out the door he went, thus concluding round 513 of their ongoing battle.

"That's it? That's all I had to do?" Gracie grinned at Cecilia. "Think of all the time I've wasted."

Shane narrowed his green eyes. At first, Gracie had thought all the Donovans shared the exact same eye color, but James's were different. A cool, crisp evergreen amongst the rest of the clan's warmth.

"Do you have to antagonize him?" Shane asked.

Indignant, Gracie placed a hand over her expansive cleavage. "Me? What did I do?"

"Don't play innocent. You bait him. You've been baiting him since the day you met." Shane slid a hand onto the counter behind Cecilia and when her friend shivered a little, Gracie suspected he'd worked his fingers under Cecilia's black top. Again.

Gracie sighed.

Cecilia nodded. "I'm afraid he's right."

Gracie rolled her eyes. "Ugh. I miss the days when you guys didn't constantly agree with each other."

Cecilia grinned at Shane, her sleek ponytail perfectly in place even though they were doing manual labor. "I'm trying, but I can't seem to work up a good mad."

Shane tugged her mane of caramel-colored hair. "I'm sure you'll think of something soon."

"How about the fact that you don't have movers?" Gracie

asked. She wasn't sure how much longer she could stomach their ooey-gooey love. Between them and the stuffy professor, her body couldn't decide if it was stuck in bad porn or *The Sound of Music*.

Shane's hand settled on Cecilia's neck. "The movers will be here in thirty. Ce-ce wanted to take care of the important stuff herself."

"Oh, all right." Gracie smiled at the happy couple. "It's hard to believe six months ago Cecilia cried on my couch over you and now you're moving in together."

Cecilia's expression held nothing but complete adoration as she gazed up at her fiancé. "Pretty crazy, huh?"

Shane brushed her lips with his, his mouth soft on hers, and Gracie looked away.

In six months Cecilia had changed her entire life around. She'd gone from a shut-off, work-obsessed career woman stuck in a job and life she hadn't wanted, to the vibrant woman she was now. In six short months, she'd quit her job, fired her father, made amends with her brother and mom, started a new business, and fallen in love with Shane. Now she'd moved into a brand-new house and was getting married.

And Gracie hadn't even managed to get herself laid. She shook her shoulders. Enough of that. She had a great life. She had everything a woman could want: a thriving business, great friends, and a beautiful home she shared with her brother.

If she lacked a bit of reckless craziness, she had no one to blame but herself.

James strolled back into the room, moving with an easy grace that irritated her. Irrational and unfair, but true nonetheless.

She'd be hard-pressed to pinpoint why she'd taken a dislike to him. Other than his addiction to health food and exercise, there wasn't anything the least bit objectionable about him. Unlike his testosterone-laden alpha brothers, he was quietly handsome in a bookish sort of way. At six-two, he was the shortest of the three Donovan brothers, and there wasn't any-thing threatening about him. He was an ordinary guy. Noth-ing at all exceptional. She should go out of her way to flirt and flatter him, like she did with most men she met, but she didn't. She couldn't even muster a smile for him.

"What?" James asked, startling her out of her thoughts.

Her stomach did an unwelcome little jump, as it some-times did when he gave her that hard glare and his jaw got all stern. She waved a hand. "Oh, nothing."

He shook his head as though she exasperated him. "Are you going to get to work, or stand there?"

Gracie huffed. "Um, I was here an hour before you."

A quirked brow. "But did you do anything?"

"You are such an ass." Gracie shook her head at the ceil-ing. How would she survive this day? Let alone the whole weekend?

"You're getting repetitive." James cocked his lean hip against the island countertop and took another drink of his disgusting shake. "You've already told me that twice today."

Gracie searched her mind for a proper comeback, only to find herself flummoxed. Another reason he irritated her. While she'd never admit it in a million years, she often got tongued-tied around him. She hated it!

Ignoring him, she whirled around to Cecilia. "Do you see what I have to put up with?"

Cecilia pressed her lips to suppress a laugh.

Shane, however, did not have the same problem. "You did kind of start it."

Cecilia elbowed him in the ribs and shushed him before crooking her finger at Gracie. "Come on, let's go start on the bedroom."

Shane grabbed Cecilia's wrist and tugged her back, bending down to whisper something in her ear that made color splash onto her cheeks before letting her go. Cecilia wobbled, then righted herself, a secret smile on her lips and a quirked brow. "We'll just have to see about that, now won't we?"

Shane gave her a long, slow once-over. "Yeah, we will."

Gracie rolled her eyes. God help her.

Cecilia spun on her heel, head held high. "Come on, Gracie." As she passed, Shane smacked her on the ass and she yelped. "Hey!"

Shane laughed and Cecilia glowered, although the huge grin on her lips gave her away. Gracie sighed, a bit wistful, as she followed her friend up the back staircase.

Nobody had smacked her ass in, like, *forever*.

The bedroom was in complete disarray. Clothes were piled up everywhere; shoes and purses littered the floor. Cecilia eyed the bed wearily. "Remind me never to move again."

Gracie scoffed. "With the house you bought, why would you need to?"

"It is pretty spectacular."

"I guess that's the kind of house you get when you land one of Chicago's richest businessmen." Gracie pointed to Cecilia's engagement ring. "That and a huge rock. Let me see it again."

Without the slightest hesitation, Cecilia flashed her hand. "I told Shane it was too much, but you know how he is."

Gracie cupped her friend's hand as the huge emerald-cut diamond flashed. Shane Donovan was a go-big-or-go-home type of guy. The ring sparkled in the bright early fall sun filtering in from the window, hypnotizing her. "I will never understand how the professor was hatched from the same parents."

Cecilia sighed. "Please, please, please be nice to him."

Gracie dropped her hand. "I'm nice."

"You're horrible to him. Why can't you be sweet like you are to everyone else?"

That was the million-dollar question. Without a good answer, Gracie shrugged. "Isn't hating cupcakes enough?"

Cecilia's brow creased as if she was giving the question serious thought. "He's a little obsessive on the health food, I'll grant you, but still, he's a good guy."

"He's condescending."

"No, he's not. He has a dry sense of humor."

"You know perfectly well he doesn't have any sense of humor."

"He does," Cecilia insisted. "Just not where you're concerned."

"See, we're even." One of those unwelcome moments of truth hitched in her belly. Even though she didn't like him, it irritated her he didn't like her back. What did that say about her? Did she really need everyone to love her?

Cecilia pressed her lips together before sighing. "You're going to be together all day and most of the weekend. Do you think, for me, you could try to get along? At least until the engagement party is over? After this weekend you won't have to see him until Thanksgiving."

Gracie wrinkled her nose and then hugged her friend. "All right, I'll be nice, but only because you asked me to."

"Thank you." The taller woman hugged her back. "And thank you for helping me. I owe you big-time."

Gracie stepped back and eyed the mountain of clothes on the bed. "That you do. Now let's get to work."

She could be nice to James for forty-eight hours.

Maybe.

* * *

James Donovan watched Gracie climb the back stairs, her fantasy-inducing ass encased in a pair of tight jeans that clung to her showgirl legs, in annoyed awe. The sentiment pretty much summed up his yearlong, animosity-filled acquaintance with her. The tight red T-shirt she wore displayed her hourglass figure in all its lush glory, and he'd about broken into a cold sweat as soon as he saw her.

If it was just her body it would be one thing, but her face was equally compelling with those dancing cornflower-blue eyes and wild mess of blond curls that refused to stay tamed no matter how many times she tucked them behind her ears. She was an odd mix of heart-stoppingly cute and wickedly sexy.

His jaw clenched. The kick of lust he felt bothered him. James's mind and body had been under control for a long time, and his attraction to the blond sex goddess was a reminder of parts of him better left behind. He wished for the thousandth time she'd meet someone.

When she'd stopped seeing the Revival sheriff she'd been involved with when he'd first met her, James had been sure she'd hook up with one of his brothers. Women like Gracie *always* went for guys like his brothers. At first he'd assumed Shane, because they'd hit it off so well, but that hope had been dashed as soon as Cecilia had shown up.

At his sister Maddie's wedding his youngest brother, Evan, had been all over Gracie, but to James's surprise she'd rebuffed all his advances with that good-natured charm she turned on everyone but him. James still didn't understand why. His brother was a six-five, star NFL wide receiver. Evan hadn't heard the word no since he was fourteen. Instead of an affair, they seemed to have settled into a flirtatious friendship and Gracie remained stubbornly unattached.

James supposed it was a good thing she hated him. Despite all his years of discipline—

"Are you going to do something about that?" His brother's voice interrupted his thoughts.

James jerked his attention away from the staircase Gracie disappeared up and rested his palms against the marble countertops. "I don't know what you mean."

Shane's green eyes narrowed. In that moment, with that particular expression on his face, he looked the spitting image of their father, and James experienced the dull ache of loss that never really went away, no matter how much time passed. "The tension between the two of you is becoming annoying."

"It's not tension," James said in a cool, well-modulated tone. "It's dislike. There's a difference."

"Bullshit. Stop beating around the bush and take care of it before you get a permanent case of blue balls."

"Charming as always." James kept his face relaxed and impassive. He'd made damn sure no one knew the extent of his lust for Gracie, but of course, he didn't fool his oldest brother. "In case you haven't noticed, she's not a fan."

"For a smart guy, you sure are stupid."

James raised a brow. "At bare minimum I require my partners to respect me."

Shane grinned. "Respect is overrated. Take her to bed and get it out of your system."

An image of tangled sheets and a naked Gracie filled his mind, but James shook it off. "Mind your own business."

"I don't understand you at all."

That was pretty much par for the course. James had never been like the rest of them and never would be. Their baby sister, Maddie, might be the tiny one in the family, but she was all fierce and spirited like his brothers. James accepted a long time ago he was the odd man out, and he'd given up wishing he could be like them the night his father died and his sister had lain in a coma.

His siblings were impulsive. They saw what they wanted and went after it. James was reasonable; methodical. They didn't get it and he didn't blame them. It was hard to explain to a bunch of people who thrived on risk that he liked his life orderly. Neat. Discipline and structure had helped him survive and become the man he was today. It had saved him and he had no desire to go back. He liked his life boring and predictable, even if nobody understood it.

Yes, he'd like to go to bed with Gracie and lose himself in her body and all that heat. But he'd examined the situation from all angles and saw no practical reason to satiate his desire. If, on the off chance she agreed—a highly unlikely scenario as she'd made her disdain crystal clear—it would be a disaster. Their personalities were at complete odds.

She was all wild chaos and he was a man who appreciated control.

There was nowhere for them to go but down a rabbit's hole. And it would end with her hating him more than she already did.

Sex was the only upside.

While it was a considerable upside, in the end it would do more harm than good. Instinct told him that not knowing how she'd feel under his hands and mouth was a good thing. The last thing he needed was the memory of what it felt like to slide inside her. Or how it would feel when she came.

He shook his head to clear the illicit thoughts. In the end, they were oil and water. Incompatible in every way that mattered to him.

"Stop thinking and just do it already." Shane's exasperated tone matched the expression on his face.

James didn't bother to explain what his brother would never understand. "Don't we have boxes to move?"

"Chicken shit," Shane said.

"Smart," James corrected.

"Well, if you won't do anything about the situation, at least stop rising to the bait. She wants a reaction."

"I'm fairly certain she doesn't want anything from me." James turned around and picked up a box, thinking through Shane's statement.

Why did he fight with her? He didn't fight with anyone else. Was arguing a way to engage her? To hold her attention since he couldn't sleep with her?

He couldn't dismiss the idea entirely. Not when he thought about how her sharp tongue made him hard. She might lay down the kindling, but he added the flame.

He must have some motive. A motive he'd have to analyze at a later date when she wasn't around to distract him.

But to Shane's point, not rising to her bait was a concrete action he could take. He'd be around her the whole weekend. More than enough time to see the cause and effect of being cordial. He could try being nice for forty-eight hours. He turned the idea over in his mind and couldn't see the harm.

He'd ignore Gracie's barbs and be pleasant to her. He managed civility with colleagues and students at the university every day; surely he could apply the same strategies here.

It was only a weekend. How hard could it be?